Praise for

# IMMORTAL GIFTS

"Probably one of the weirdest books I've read this year but also one I'll think about for a while."

-Nikki on Goodreads

"Fresh and insightful"

-the famous agent who rejected it

# Also By Katherine Villyard

**Immortal Vampires Series**
Immortal Gifts

**Standalone**
Love Stories

# IMMORTAL
# GIFTS

# IMMORTAL GIFTS

Book 1 of the Immortal Vampires Series

## KATHERINE VILLYARD

Flower Feather Press

Atlanta, Georgia, USA

This is a work of fiction. Names, characters, businesses, places, events, locales, and incidents are either the products of the author's imagination or used in a fictitious manner. Any resemblance to actual persons, living or dead, or actual events is purely coincidental.

Published in the United States by Flower Feather Press, Atlanta, Georgia, USA
ISBN 979-8-9868330-7-1

Published 2025
https://www.katherinevillyard.com

I dedicate this book to:

Dora, 2004-2021.
Miles, 2016-2020
Persephone, 1991-2006
Devorah, 2022-2022

I love you forever, from this world to the world to come,
between the worlds, in all the worlds. May your memory be
a blessing.

And to:

# Timothy R. O'Neill 1943-2023
Author, camoufleur, Jungian, friend. His critiques made
this novel a better book. I'll miss you, Tim, and will hope
to see you in the world to come. Baruch dayan ha'emet.
May his memory be a blessing.

# Table of Contents

NORTH

ATLANTIC OCEAN

LONDON

N
W E
S

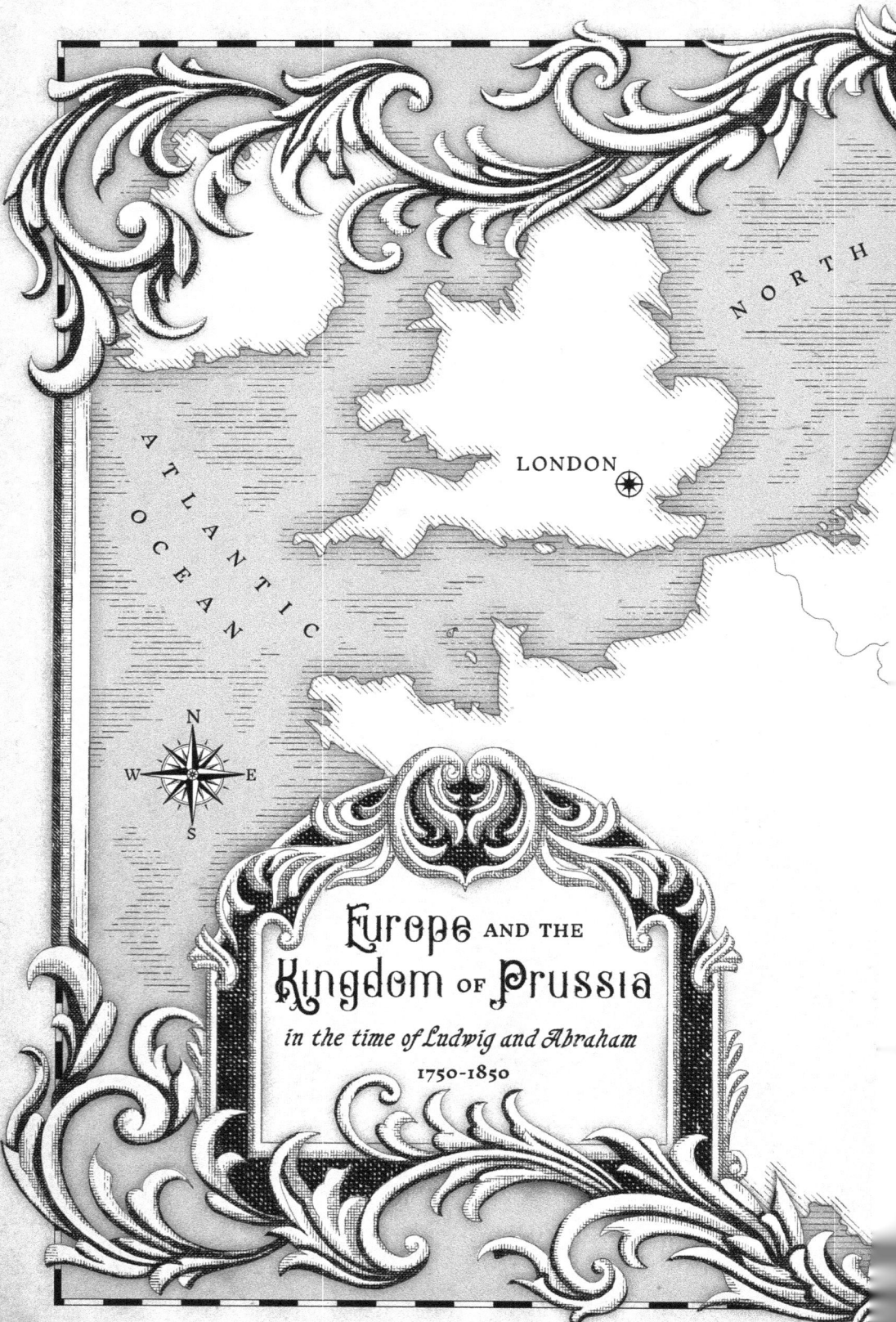

## Europe AND THE Kingdom OF Prussia

*in the time of Ludwig and Abraham*

1750-1850

SEA

Kingdom of Prussia

BERLIN ◉

WRESCHEN ✦

ROSENHEIM ✦

The Berlin Music Academy

# The Thing About…

Abraham
December 16, 2018

The thing about Destiny is that she's a bleeding heart.

Oh, you thought I meant destiny, as in fate? No, Destiny is my wife. Blame her mothers for your confusion. Hippies. Well. What do you call a couple of turn-of-the-century lesbian Wiccans, if not hippies? Perhaps I'm not up on the latest terminology, but in my experience, everything old becomes new again.

As I was saying, Destiny is a bleeding heart. She's a veterinarian, and she's forever bringing home sickly kittens for me to bottle-feed. Me, because I don't sleep. Sometimes I nap in a coffin in the basement, but really, as long as I stay out of the sun, I'm fine.

It's what Destiny calls "my little problem." She's as sympathetic about it as she is about elder cats in kidney failure, or orphan kittens, or dogs with cancer or broken legs. We've had dogs, cats, birds, rabbits, rats, and an iguana, but it's usually cats. I don't drink any of them; they're pets, and Destiny is a vegetarian.

Not that rats and iguanas are tasty. Especially iguanas. Do not recommend. Well, I hear there's one species on Saint Barthélemy, but... no. No, right now I subsist on "donations" from my wife—who gets regular iron testing on the excuse of vegetarianism—expired blood bank stock, and what I can scrounge up on the internet. I've drunk more than my share of rats in my time; they used to be plentiful, like fast food on every corner. They still are in New York. Honestly, the pet ones are so cute that I have some regret about how many I've drunk. The aggressively overabundant ones in the city, not so much.

So, Destiny is a bleeding heart, and every adorable fluffy-wuffy animal that dies destroys her.

I can relate, because eternity is boring without company, and yet company is not, for the most part, immortal. Cats are delightful, but their lives are the blink of an eye. I've loved many women, and even a few men, but it always ends the same way: old age, failing health, and death—with a few notable exceptions.

You might think that my kind doesn't know death. No, death and I are old friends, old enemies, the familiarity that breeds contempt. Death comes for everyone I love. Destiny says that the cycle of life and death is holy. Perhaps, but it's also cruel. We value things for the effort we put into them, and paradoxically value both youth and experience. If you don't believe me, look at every job listing. So while you're becoming your best and wisest self, your body is slowly and inevitably betraying you to make room for the next generation. Yours is. Not mine. You might think that death becomes easier to cope with over time, but no. It's worse.

I've learned the hard way that I don't want the ones who clamor for immortality. No, no, the ones with sympathy for my "little problem" are more likely to be good and kind companions, and yet, all too soon, they're gone. I thought that perhaps things that are ephemeral are the things that are the most precious, but it's hard to be philosophical when I think about losing Destiny.

So I've offered, twice. She doesn't think it suits her vegetarian ideals. Too much being raised with "An it harm none do what thou wilt," the Wiccan creed.

What can I do? I love her. And so I continue our relationship as it is, knowing that it will devastate me in the end. I honestly don't know how I'll cope.

---

Destiny
December 16, 2018


THE THING ABOUT Abraham is that he has a little problem, and he thinks his little problem is a solution.

Well. That and he's *beautiful*. Like, girl-pretty. I don't

think he knows. I took one look into those huge dark eyes, and it was like I've known him forever.

Do you believe in reincarnation? I do. But I digress.

The cycle of death and life sucks balls, but it's also natural. Holy, even. The old have to die to make room for the new, no matter how much that hurts. Every foster kitten that I cry over adopting out is space for a new kitten. Abraham is adorable bottle-feeding kittens, by the way. Don't tell him I said so. But without death, there can be no room for new births.

Speaking of death and birth, I suppose, he wants to know if I want to be a vampire. I don't. It's not like I faint at the sight of blood or anything. I believe blood should stay in the body if possible, and that I should do my best to do no harm.

And there's Abraham, and the thought that he's guaranteed to outlive me is a selfish relief, to be honest.

I've asked Abraham how old he is. He says he doesn't remember. He plays violin like a God, though. Like someone who's practiced for a very long time.

A *very* long time.

# Till Death Do Us Part

Abraham
Atlantic Highlands, New Jersey
December 28, 2018

We were watching television together in our pajamas, curled up under a blanket on my red Victorian horsehair sofa. Destiny was wearing a satin bathrobe and was sitting with her head on my shoulder, smelling like soap and lavender shampoo, warm and soft. Ivan sat on my lap, purring. Victoria sat pressed up against my thigh, with her sleek black fur and bright gold eyes. Our cat Inanna was sleeping on her back in the leather chair. Our home could get drafty in the winter, but it wasn't frigid. Well. Perhaps I was the wrong person to ask.

Destiny channel-surfed, looking for something interesting on the television. She settled on the news. They announced that independent presidential candidate and Internet Personality Thomas Hopkins had been "deplatformed," and fortunately, they explained what that meant. Apparently, his web provider had decided that he was too offensive and refused to host his site any longer. There was some discourse about free speech and what content it covered.

They showed a blurred, censored version of his website—although I could still make out a swastika and a Confederate battle flag—with a voiceover of him. "Free speech must include discussion that I consider abhorrent, much like it must cover my speech. Otherwise, the term is meaningless." There was something familiar about his voice, but I couldn't place it...

...until they showed his photo. A serene olive-skinned face; high, dark eyebrows; and a balding pate, with a fringe of frizzy black hair. I knew him as Thomas—just Thomas; no one had told me a last name. I was reasonably certain due to the circumstances of the introduction that his surname wasn't "Hopkins." I froze, staring at the screen like the proverbial deer in the headlights modern Americans describe.

Ivan, agitated, jumped off my lap and left the room. I heartily agreed and resisted the urge to get up and pack my belongings. My hands were shaking, I realized, and I shoved them under the blanket to hide them. Victoria glanced up at me, looking worried.

"If you elect me president," Thomas said on the television, "I'll get rid of freedom of religion and the clause about 'cruel and unusual punishment.' Torture is good! Torture works! And if it saves innocent lives, it's completely justified. It's been almost two decades since the brave soldiers at Abu Ghraib were prosecuted, but I haven't forgotten them! God bless Guantánamo!"

Yes, Thomas *would* say that. I noted he wore what resembled red Inquisitor robes, which would surprise someone who'd never met him. Not me, though. I'd heard that he was an actual Inquisitor during the Spanish Inquisition, which might explain his pro-torture stance. Bastard.

The announcer pointed out that Thomas's prior day job was prison warden, and I was so horrified that I missed most of the rest of the feature. I registered they were discussing whether his forums incited violence; and whether freedom of speech covered hate speech.

"It's only a temporary setback," he said. "I've already found another web host and am simply waiting for something called 'DNS' to repoint." He smiled, beatific. "The internet has been such a blessing to my ministry."

His "ministry." Appalling.

I didn't like being in the same country as him. To be honest, I didn't enjoy being on the same planet. Thomas wasn't the reason I'd moved to America, but I'd previously moved to London because of him. Perhaps it was time to return. I asked Destiny, "What would you think of moving to London?"

Destiny pulled away and turned to stare at me. "What? That's random!"

No, it wasn't. It was fight or flight. "Seriously."

Her brow furrowed. "I'd need to get a vet license in England. We'd have to take health certificates for the pets. We'd be too far from my mothers." She gazed down at Inanna, who was now sitting at her feet, washing her paw. "No? I like my nice, normal life the way it is."

Those things weren't an issue. I had Dave for my trust fund—reliable Dave, who asked no questions—and I had an excellent source for fake identities. I'd never tried to find a connection for falsified vet credentials, but I supposed I hadn't had a need for them. Things were harder to falsify nowadays, and getting more difficult all the time, but we could manage and bring her mothers with us if necessary. It wasn't like Destiny needed to work at all, married to me, but she'd said she *wanted* a career.

I sighed. "I guess that goes for Germany, too." Although, on second thought, the current climate in Europe made me reconsider. "Canada?"

Destiny turned to face me, expression and voice concerned. "What's gotten into you?"

Honestly? Changing my name and moving was my standard response to legal problems or Thomas issues. Usually not as far as London, but... suffice it to say that I had a love/hate relationship with changing my name and moving. Sometimes metamorphosis was a refreshing change, and others it was an incredible nuisance. Preparation made all the difference.

I was *not* prepared. We had a wedding vow renewal scheduled in a couple of days!

Ludwig
Rosenheim, Bavaria
September 10, 1762

AFTER MASS, I PICKED UP the Bible and carried it into Father Thomas's office.

Father Thomas had a serene face and a deep speaking voice. He was balding, his hair forming a dark fringe around the sides of his head, and he had strong features and warm-toned skin that spoke of a southern climate. His sermon today had filled people with passion, although I suddenly realized I couldn't summarize it. So embarrassing! Clearly, I needed to be more attentive.

His prior sermons—the ones I could remember—scared me, but I suppose they *should* have frightened me: host desecration, deals with the devil to sicken entire cities... I had hoped I would enter a safe cloister and be alone with my lovely books, untouched by that sort of ugliness. Surely God was the creator of all that was beautiful, after all. Our church reflected that: all graceful, serene white and gold arches, bright and soaring, and the ceiling painted to depict heaven.

"Your piety is so beautiful and pure, Ludwig," Father Thomas said, as I set the Bible back on a shelf in his office, a place of honor. It was two hundred years old and was an object of art, each letter typeset by hand with the utmost care for beauty, with exquisite drawings in the margins and headers, beautifully bound. No one ever had to tell me to approach it with proper reverence, like they did with some of the younger boys who would come to serve immediately after engaging in giggly jests with one another.

Father Thomas continued, "And your family's donation was much appreciated. We need that money to protect the church from Jewish machinations. I've posted a guard on our well, of course, to keep them from giving us all the plague, so their donation will help make us all safer."

I'd never actually met a Jew, so I didn't know how to respond to this.

"Do you think you would have trouble with a vow of poverty, coming from a noble house as you do?"

I considered this. "I love beautiful things... but I suppose I needn't own them." To be honest, I was more dismayed at the idea of shaving my head in a tonsure, as I was vain about my blond hair, but I believed this to be a character flaw. Besides, my brother, Friedrich, would get the barony. I'd briefly wanted to be a musician, but my family had made it plain that they wouldn't stand for such nonsense. I needed to do something with my life, after all, and the Church was the usual lot for second sons.

Father Thomas smiled at me, warm and indulgent, and patted my shoulder with a massive, fatherly hand. "And chastity?"

"That," I said, surprising myself with the passion in my voice, "is not an issue." The very idea repulsed me. It was all too intimate! Invasive. I found some people more aesthetically pleasing than others, but this never translated into wanting to touch them in an improper way.

Father Thomas raised an eyebrow at me, but all he said was, "Very good." He walked out of the room, towards the confessionals, and left me in his office, staring out over the pews.

I realized later that he hadn't asked me about obedience.

———————— ∞ ————————

Destiny
Eatontown, New Jersey
December 31, 2018

I HADN'T SLEPT THAT WELL the night before the vow renewal. Nightmares. I'd spent the night at my moms', so maybe it was the unfamiliar bed? They'd gotten rid of the one I'd slept in when I left for college, and replaced it with one that I'd never gotten used to.

I didn't know where it came from, but I'd always been afraid of fire. Do most people know where their phobias come from? I didn't remember any traumatic experiences, but even when I was a little girl, I'd sometimes dream that the house was on fire and I needed to get our pets out. Maybe the fear of fire was from stories of witches burned at the stake, because we were all Wiccans. Maybe it was a metaphor for one's safest place—one's *home*—not being safe after all. Who knows?

I'd had that dream again the night before. I was in a burning house trying to escape with my cat Inanna—who was currently at home. But in the dream,

I was holding Inanna in my arms and looking for an exit that wasn't blocked by fire, and when I woke up, I was still too afraid to go back to sleep. When that happened at home, I'd get Abraham to tell me a story about his past. I don't think he was offended that I sometimes fell asleep during them.

We always had pets when I was little. Mama Morgan was a dog person, and Mommy Bridget was a cat person. We had big mellow tomcats and less patient lady cats who would let me dress them up in doll clothes, and small dogs and medium-sized dogs I would put party hats on and have tea parties with. I've always loved animals; I had mice, rats, hamsters, birds, rabbits... That's probably why I became a vet, and is definitely why I don't eat animals.

So I was tired, and my mothers took me to a spa, where I fell asleep during the massage. I couldn't believe that I'd agreed to a midnight New Year's Eve vow renewal. Of course, I'd been well-rested at the time.

I mean. I wanted one, too. We'd gotten one of those generic justice of the peace things, and we both wanted something more... spiritual.

After the spa, there was the cosmetologist whom we'd hired to do my hair and makeup for the vow renewal. We set up in the living room, with the lavender sofa and the Indian pillows and all the Wiccan-themed posters and crystals, and my moms' wedding broom. I fell asleep again while she was working on me, and when I woke up, I was delighted that I looked like a fairy princess and not a drooling, shambling zombie. Wanting to be beautiful on your wedding day is patriarchal and buying into the idea that a woman's worth is in her looks—but I still wanted to be beautiful at my vow renewal. That's societal pressures for you. I wore my red hair down to please my husband, but the cosmetologist curled it and put flowers in it.

I'd inherited my red hair, green eyes, upturned Celtic nose, and Scots/Irish pale skin color from my mother Morgan, who was my biological mother. I sometimes regretted that they hadn't chosen a donor who looked more like Bridget—chestnut-brown skin, thick curling hair, broad nose, full lips. Bridget had almost carried me, as there had been drama with Morgan's family—they disowned her. Morgan had left her parents' Catholic Church for Bridget's Wicca, and they'd raised me in the more queer-inclusive faith. Bridget's parents also reacted poorly, although there was now a somewhat chilly détente. They still weren't happy that Bridget was gay, but they made a big show out of not mentioning it.

I was proud to be a product of their love story. I'd always known there was someone out there for me as well—speaking of societal tropes, but whatever. I still knew. Abraham wasn't what I expected, but...

It was his eyes. Okay, no, we were a good match in that he loved classical music and cats as much as I did, and we both had kind of a philosophical bent? You know, common interests, similar goals—we both wanted kids and a quiet, normal life—all that. Sexually compatible. But... there was something about him. When I gazed into his eyes, it felt like we'd been friends all my life.

Okay, he also wanted me to turn into a vampire. I... no? I supposed I might change my mind over time, but it seemed unlikely. But he was willing to take no for an answer, so...

"Honey?" Bridget said, interrupting my reverie. "Do you need a cup of tea?"

"She needs *coffee*," Morgan said. It was an old joke and an old play argument.

"I need caffeine in some form," I admitted. "I'm not picky which."

"Did you have the dream again?" Bridget asked.

I nodded, and Morgan left the room. There was clattering, and the sound and smell of coffee brewing in the kitchen made me smile.

Bridget bit her lip, but all she did was take my hand and squeeze it.

I'd always suspected I had died by fire in a previous life. I thought Bridget suspected, too, but she'd never said so. She often looked like she wasn't saying something when we discussed it—biting her lip, pressing her lips together...

Morgan came back with the coffee, lots of cream and sugar—the way I liked it. I took a sip of the sweet, creamy, bitter goodness. The cosmetologist winced and pulled out the lipstick again.

───────⌇───────

Abraham
Atlantic Highlands, New Jersey
December 31, 2018

WE STOOD SIDE BY SIDE in our living room: Destiny in a long, sleek, strapless white dress, holding a bouquet of white roses and calla lilies, and me in a black silk tuxedo, my shoulder-length brown hair pulled back. She had a little crown of white roses in her beautiful long red hair and wore understated makeup. She also wore flat-heeled shoes because she was two inches taller than me. I didn't mind—I liked tall women—but she also said it was more comfortable. Perhaps this was elaborate for a vow renewal, but we both craved something more meaningful than our first ceremony.

We lived in an old Victorian farmhouse, with wooden floors and a beautifully carved mantel, and our living room was in tones of red and gray, with warm wood, brown and black and white. The room had decorative columns on either side of the curving staircase, with lovely scrolling spandrels between them. There was wood paneling, with a bit of gray wallpaper across the top. I had a faux-antique ceiling light, made to resemble a candle chandelier with crystals that probably weren't crystal. An antique Persian carpet and a grand piano made in 1911 tied the room together.

I'd pushed our red Victorian horsehair sofa back against the wall to make room for the party. A table in the corner held a television, neither huge nor tiny, showing the New Year's Eve ball-drop countdown; the guests had been told that the ceremony would happen right after the start of the new year. The rest of the room had an antique wooden bar; a long wooden table with a white tablecloth and vases of roses at each end; a table with a wedding cake that I couldn't eat, of course. It smelled divine, however—sweet and creamy. I also had some wooden chairs with red velvet cushions and some brown leather armchairs. We could have used more seating, to be honest. We rarely had a lot of company over.

We had set one corner of the room up as a photo area, with a backdrop depicting a snow scene and an immense quantity of flowers, with lights and a professional photographer. Destiny and I had already posed at length, but the photographer was planning on taking both still photos and video of the ceremony. At the moment, guests were posing, complete with silly faces and gestures.

Outside, it was all snow and distant ocean. I could pretend the world was dressed in white for the occasion. If we went upstairs, there were city lights across the water, but the party was downstairs.

I'd hired a bartender, and we had an open bar... but it was still a small party. Mostly Destiny's family, friends, coworkers... and my two guests: my lawyer and my accountant, Dave. To be honest, I was a bit of a recluse, or perhaps a crazy cat man. I've always been shy, and ever since... well. Let's say that I didn't like to attract a lot of attention. There was someone I didn't want to find me.

The guests were all wearing formal clothes. Dave appeared awkward, as he was much more comfortable with numbers than with people. He once told me he could see whole narratives, battles for power, etc., in numbers. I didn't ask him what he saw in mine; I was curious, but asking would raise more questions than I wanted to answer. He'd driven in from New York City, which struck me as a brave thing to do on New Year's Eve. Dave was about my height and had curly black hair, a tan skin similar to my own, thick glasses, and a hearing aid. He wore an expensive-looking suit that fit him poorly, as if he minded the time shopping more than the cost of the clothing.

"Louis!" Dave called across the room, and my attorney turned around. He was very blond, *very* handsome, and very flashy, and I'd known him for about a hundred and eighty years. His suit probably cost as much as some people's cars, and fit like it was tailored for him... which I suspect it was.

Ludwig—"Louis"—wandered over, a wineglass in his hand. "Is Abraham keeping you busy?"

Dave laughed. "He's very laid-back. Just looks to see that the numbers are going the right way from time to time."

Ludwig raised an eyebrow at me. I shrugged in response and went searching for my cats.

My darling black cat Victoria was hiding somewhere, as cats do, but friendly Ivan was trotting around the room with his tail in the air seeking pets, as cats usually don't. But Ivan had been a bottle baby with an eye infection and had seen so many vets that he was unfazed by people and considered them his devoted subjects and instant best friends. I'd considered making him the ring bearer but decided he was just as likely to make the rings hockey pucks as to bring them to us on cue. He was a cream tabby, very handsome. I'd dressed him in a little black bow tie for the occasion, and Victoria in a pink collar encrusted with rhinestones. Ivan twined around my ankles and gazed up at me with adoring bronze eyes, and I scooped him up and kissed him on his furry golden head. Destiny's tortoiseshell cat, Inanna, had immediately bolted into the kitchen cabinets and hissed at me when I checked on her, so I decided she could spend the party in her

Fortress of Solitude if she chose, and declined to dress her in party finery. After all, Inanna had a reputation for attacking landlords and repair people. I'd rather she not launch herself at our guests.

Victoria had been my primary source of emotional support when a previous relationship ended and my ex started referring to me online as *that Goth psycho who thinks he's a vampire*—no name, of course, but our mutual friends knew who she meant. Cats have always been my truest companions in times of isolation.

Lucy—Destiny's vet tech—walked over. She was wearing a violet gown that complemented her deep brown skin, and wore her hair in a series of braids. "Where's my favorite lady?" She meant Victoria.

I appreciated her asking. "Hiding. This is a lot of guests for her." Ivan fidgeted in my arms, so I put him down.

Lucy pouted and scooped up Ivan, who purred graciously at her. "Such a good boy! You should tell your sister to come out and see me. I'd hate to drive all this way and miss her." Ivan shifted his weight and tried to escape, so Lucy put him down. "Congratulations, by the way. I was delighted when you left your number for Destiny."

My cheeks warmed slightly, but I smiled. "Thank you."

The ball dropped on the television, and we all stood around and chanted the countdown. "Ten... Nine... Eight... Seven... Six... Five... Four... Three... Two... One... Happy New Year!" I leaned over and kissed Destiny, probably getting a light coating of lip gloss.

And then a couple of Destiny's coworkers—Alicia and Eric—started singing Wagner's *Lohengrin* wedding march—off-key, with the lyrics "Dun dun dun dun!"—but that wasn't the reason I winced. I held up both my hands and said, "Please. No Wagner, I beg of you." I tried to keep my tone light, but Wagner was a noted antisemite who wrote offensive essays about the Jews, and his work—if Alicia and Eric even realized it *was* his work—had no place in my home, let alone at my vow renewal. Fuck Wagner!

Alicia and Eric blinked at me and swayed drunkenly, mouths slightly slack, but Destiny's mother Bridget smiled at me and said, "I wouldn't want Wagner if I were you, either. No Wagner, please, everyone! No Wagner!" I appreciated her understanding and support.

Destiny's mother Morgan leaned over and murmured something to Bridget, and Bridget answered quietly, "I'll explain later," gesturing in a way that was probably meant to tell Morgan to drop it.

Bridget wore a long, flowing, hand-painted purple silk dress with elaborate glass beads sewn onto it, and a pretty beaded headdress. Morgan wore a tuxedo with her short red hair. Bridget was a cellist and I'm a violinist, so I felt a certain string player affinity for her.

As a preamble to the ceremony, I placed a hand-painted document on a table in front of Destiny's mothers. It was written in Aramaic with the letters forming a tree. "Will everyone please sign the ketubah?"

"It's pretty," Morgan said. "What is it?"

"Um..." My cheeks were warm. "I promise to provide your daughter with food, clothing, and, um, conjugal relations..."

Destiny's drunk coworkers hooted. Dave said, "Hey, it's a mitzvah!" If you don't know, a mitzvah is a commandment or good deed, and yes, it's also a euphemism for Sabbath marital relations.

"...and if we divorce, she gets a portion of my assets."

There was an awkward pause. Dave winced in my general direction. "Louis," on the other hand, appeared unruffled.

All right, so I've heard a ketubah described as the least romantic document imaginable—basically a prenuptial agreement, and intended to protect the woman rather than the man. I wanted one. They're usually beautiful, and I wanted to promise my wife those things. There wouldn't be much in this ceremony that was Jewish, and... I wanted one.

People gathered around signing it. Dave gave me a sidelong glance over the rims of his glasses before signing it. Well. He was my accountant, and also Jewish, so he understood what he was signing. It's traditional to have two adult male Jews sign it as witnesses. Dave was the only guest fitting that description, so I had everyone sign. It's not like it was legally binding, after all.

Bridget said, "All right, we're starting. Settle down, please. Please join hands in a circle."

Everyone gathered in a circle surrounding us, holding hands. Ludwig, Dave, Morgan, and Lucy—still glancing around occasionally for Victoria—each held a ribbon-wrapped pole with a corner of a prayer shawl tied to each pole as a chuppah, or wedding canopy. Other than those four, only Bridget, Destiny, and I were inside the circle. They put the poles into the waiting vases on the floor, but stood by to make sure they were stable.

"Dearly beloved," Bridget said. "We are gathered here today to witness the vows of Abraham Levy and Destiny

Andrews Levy. Brought together by pets, joined by love. We wish you joy. We wish you a long life together. We wish you children."

"Give me grandbabies!" Morgan interjected. There was laughter, but it was a bit awkward on my part, as my first wife, Flora, had told me vampires can't. Vampires are only made one way.

I picked up the ketubah and read it aloud. It was, as I said, in Aramaic, and had a melody. So it's perhaps more accurate to say that I sang it—*B'ezrat Hashem Yitbarech... B'shlishi bashabat esrim v'chamesh yom l'chodesh Tevet sh'nat chameshet alafim ush'va me'ot...*, etc., etc.—and then I placed it on the table. One usually has the rabbi, or another expert, read the ketubah, but it's hard to find a rabbi willing to do an interfaith ceremony. I didn't even ask around, assuming that the Wiccan elements would shock them. Reading the ketubah myself was, as the modern Americans would say, a flex—a very subtle flex, as Dave was the only person in the room who might understand the significance.

I continued by picking up the cup of wine and saying, *"Barukh atah, Adonai, Eloheinu Melekh ha'olam, borei p'ri hagafen."* Blessed are You, Lord our God, King of the universe, Who creates the fruit of the vine. I took a sip, then offered the cup to Destiny, who took a sip. I placed the ring on her finger, and said, "With this ring, you are consecrated to me according to the law of Moses and Israel."

Destiny picked up the ring and said, "Isis, Astarte, Diana, Hecate, Demeter, Kali, Inanna. With this ring I pledge myself to you, between the worlds, in all the worlds, so mote it be." She placed the ring on my finger.

I caught sight of Dave, who stared wide-eyed and open-mouthed, perhaps shocked by the idolatry of Destiny's Wiccan vows. I stifled a smile, although it felt a little uncomfortable to me as well. But I'd adjusted to the idea of an interfaith marriage. My previous wife was Christian, after all.

Bridget smiled. "Please clasp hands."

Destiny and I clasped left hands. Bridget took a silk cord and tied our wrists together—a Wiccan element for my wife. "This knot expresses your eternal bond of love. Within this knot, I bind all the wishes, hopes, love, and happiness wished here for you." Her lips twitched in a quirky grin. "By the power vested in me by an ad in the back of *Rolling Stone* magazine, I pronounce you husband and wife. Blessed be!" Technically, she didn't have to say this because we were already married, but she had insisted.

"Blessed be!" Destiny and Morgan repeated. Everyone else kind of mumbled. Count of Wiccans in the room: three.

We slipped our hands out of the knot, and I drank half the wine—tart and delicious, but I was after the glass—and handed it to Destiny. She drank the other half. I wrapped the glass in a cloth napkin, put it on the floor, and stepped on it as is Jewish tradition. There are a lot of reasons given: it commemorates the destruction of the Temple in Jerusalem, makes a loud noise to frighten away demons, symbolizes the fragility of human relationships, symbolizes sexual release, and is a symbol of breaking down barriers. There's also a belief that each couple was once a single soul that was shattered like the glass—an idea I find distressing, since my first wife is dead, so it implies that either she or Destiny is a second choice. The glass stomp is the mark of the end of the ceremony, which was much better than our previous wedding, but almost certainly not kosher. It would have to do.

*"Mazel Tov!"* Dave shouted, but he was the only one. Count of Jews in the room: two.

Jewish legend calls the person who once shared your soul your bashert, and says that before you were born, God chose you and your soul mate for each other. This person is your destiny, your fate. Was it possible to have more than one soul mate? Mainstream Judaism didn't do reincarnation, but some of the mystical sects, like the Kabbalists, did. But it felt like an idea that I needed to approach cautiously, to avoid dishonoring one of my wives by mistake.

I kissed the bride and walked over to the table to put the ketubah into a matted frame I had ready next to it, then hung it over the wooden mantle. Now I had exchanged vows in front of our friends, and was proudly displaying our ketubah. *Now* the ceremony felt complete. I felt a swelling of almost complete joy, along with a distant pang that *till death do us part* wasn't long enough.

Ludwig gathered up the four corners of the chuppah and carried it back to my guest room, presumably. He passed Lucy, who was trying to coax Victoria out from under a side table. Victoria allowed the petting, and even did her patented "sit up tall and look adoring," but drew the line at being picked up, so Lucy petted her again and let her be.

When I came back, Dave was telling Destiny, "Congratulations! Apparently, your husband's love language is paying off your student loans." He took a sip of his martini.

Destiny laughed and glanced over at me, smiling, her eyes gentle. "Yes, he's very thoughtful."

I kissed her on her soft, warm cheek. I know it's cliché to say that one is lucky in love, but Destiny is unique. She's what people like her mothers call "an old soul," wise beyond her years. In my way, I'm both old and young; in her way, so is she.

"*Kol haKavod* on the Aramaic," Dave said. "You speak it like a native."

I smiled. "Hardly."

Ludwig returned and stood on the sidelines, watching the discussion with a smile.

"Seriously," Dave said, leaning closer. "Did you study to be a rabbi or something?"

I shrugged. "I did a year of Talmud study at a yeshiva about a million years ago." I really did study for a year at a yeshiva in what is now Poland, back in 1839 or so. It was my mother's condition for my going to the Berlin Academy of Music the following year.

Dave raised an eyebrow at me. "Were your parents, like, super frum or something?" He was asking if my parents were very observant.

I didn't really want to get into it, so I shrugged and said, "You could say that. Long story." No offense, Dave, but that's above your pay grade.

Morgan did something with her phone and the speakers played the Dixie Cups' "Chapel of Love." Destiny sang along. Some of the other guests groaned, but, by all means, the Dixie Cups rather than Wagner. Not that I don't love classical music—classical music is my life—but... fuck Wagner.

I pulled Destiny close, stretched out one arm in front of us in a silly pseudo-tango. Her dress whirled, as did her hair, and she laughed. I got the impression that she didn't know the tango, so we made it up, wandering the room cheek to cheek, followed by spinning. Our guests giggled, and so did we. Bridget and Morgan watched us side by side, swaying gently together.

After the dance, Destiny said, "I think we need a sectional sofa and a big screen TV in here. Our TV sucks—no offense."

The idea mildly appalled me, but marriage involves compromise, so I was almost certainly replacing my beloved antique horsehair sofa with a sectional. Oh, the humanity! I took another sip of beer. In the corner, Bridget and Lucy were chatting quietly. It looked like Bridget was reading Lucy's palm.

"Where are you going on your honeymoon?" Alicia asked.

Destiny waggled her eyebrows and said, "The bedroom."

My cheeks were warm, but I'd already announced to the room that I'd promised my wife *conjugal relations*, after all. Dave spat out his martini. So much for its being a mitzvah? Everyone laughed, including Dave, who wiped the martini off his chin. Everyone but Ludwig, who raised a bemused eyebrow.

"I don't do well on airplanes," I said, patting Dave on the shoulder.

"You can get Xanax for that!" someone suggested, and burst out laughing. My dismay must have shown on my face. My problem was vertigo and nausea, not anxiety, and the idea of being drugged and nauseated...

Eric held out his hand. He was tall and blond and had a boyish face, currently flushed pink with too much alcohol. "Congratulations! I work with your wife, but I don't think Destiny has mentioned what you do…"

Ah, yes, the American obsession with *what one does*—also known as shorthand for being introduced by your class and income. The European in me was unamused.

I shook the proffered hand and told the truth. "I was born into a banking family and live off my investments." I also used to be a famous musician under another name, and earned a lot of money from that, but I didn't share that information. Basically, over a hundred years of compound interest. The tricky part was setting up a trust. You know. So people wouldn't notice that I wasn't dying. It used to be a lot easier to get a fake identity before computers, but one can still do it. That was part of what "Louis" was for.

The trust was what Dave was for. I could manage my own money. It's just that Dave was better at it, and enjoyed it so much more than I did. I preferred to devote my life to the violin.

Eric blinked at me. "Ah. Um. You have a lovely home."

"Thank you."

"You're not going to, I don't know, go to college or whatever? What are you, twenty? Twenty-one?"

"Old enough to drink," I said. In fact, Eric was driving me to drink, so I asked Dave if he wanted another martini and headed to the bar for a pastry stout. I should really have been more patient with Eric.

I returned and handed Dave his martini and took another sip of beer.

"What do *you* do?" Ludwig asked, eyeing Eric over a glass of wine.

"Oh, um, I'm a vet, you know," Eric said. "What about you?"

"I'm a partner at Cooper, Richmond, and Strauss, but I prefer to think of myself as a patron of the arts."

"Ah," Eric said. "Um. Cool? You must be one of their youngest partners. Did you go to law school in your teens, or do you have a portrait in your attic?"

Ludwig just smiled.

"He's older than he looks. He just has a baby face," I said.

Ludwig gave me a withering glare, but Eric appeared satisfied.

Eventually, we had to kick all our guests out into the snow. We stood together, waving and repeating "Good night, good night," until we finally had the house to ourselves... although I called Dave a cab. He was singing "Chapel of Love" off-key, and dancing like he was in a sixties girl band while he did it. I hoped he wouldn't be too embarrassed in the morning.

I pulled Destiny into my arms. I kissed her and said, "Have you given any thought to...?"

Destiny shook her head. "No, I'm still a vegetarian."

I tried not to wince. It was, to my mind, a romantic offer! Let's make *till death do us part* meaningless and replace it with *forever*. Forever, and forever, and not a measly half-century or so of watching her body betray her, slowly and inevitably. Having been in this position before, I can assure you of the horror of arthritis and broken hips, of heart attacks and strokes. And yet I continue to do this to myself. Life without connection is meaningless.

She squeezed my arm; it must have shown on my face. "I don't want to celebrate our vow renewal by becoming a vampire, Abraham. I want to have some nuptial TMI and then go to bed."

I burst out laughing. Was she protecting the cats' innocent ears? "I bought you a nicer bed... all the better to TMI you in..."

"Thank you." She kissed me on the cheek. "You're not going to carry me over the threshold?"

"You already live here."

It was Destiny's turn to laugh. "Fair enough. It just seemed like a kitschy 1950s movie thing, and sometimes you're a little old-fashioned."

"It's... not our custom," I said. Honestly, I thought it was Italian, I could have been mistaken. "So, about that TMI..."

She giggled, and I picked her up and carried her into the bedroom—white, with cream wallpaper and a new four-poster bed with a lacy white canopy—replacing the antique bed, which I'd sold. I had to help her undress. Women's fashions of the day are much better in that regard than they were in the past, but wedding dresses are still... a thing.

I unzipped the back of the dress, and she let out a long sigh. "I can breathe! I can breathe again!" I helped her out of it and hung it up. She had elaborate "shaping" undergarments that she had to escape. The shaping garments were unnecessary; her shape was *perfect*. My clothing was much easier to remove. When I was finished, she looked lovely, yet exhausted. "Are you too tired?"

"Oh, shut up," she said, and fell over backwards, pulling me onto the bed with her.

I *love* modern women. Tall, smart, spirited, sexually liberated... Sorry. I'm permanently nineteen. I also love women with really long hair, but that's the fashion of my youth speaking. Destiny had gorgeous waist-length red hair.

She'd also made her wishes known. In that case, I had a delightful duty that I had publicly promised to perform.

———————⌒⌒⌒———————

Ludwig
Rosenheim, Bavaria
October 13, 1762

"LUDWIG," FATHER THOMAS SAID as I was preparing to change and leave. "Please come with me to my office and close the door. I have an important matter to discuss with you."

Oh dear. I followed him, chewing on my lower lip, and closed the door behind me. I wondered if I had done something wrong, and if I was in trouble. I sat on a plain chair in front of his carved wooden desk.

"I've had my eye on you for some time." He leaned forward, lowered his voice. "You must hold what I'm about to say in the strictest confidence."

"Of course!"

"I'm a member of a secret order and think you would be a suitable candidate." He smiled. "We're defenders of holiness, and we fight to protect the true faith."

I was astonished and flattered. "Me? Do I have to take my vows first?"

"You would make your vows directly to me."

I blinked. This sounded... unorthodox. "These would be my novitiate vows? To you?"

"The order is not strictly monastic. We must be mobile to face threats at their source."

I considered this. It was sounding like this might not be what I'd wanted. "You said 'fight.' Do you mean literally?"

"Yes."

I was no sturdy farmhand, nor was I even an adequate fighter. I was, in fact, the despair of my instructor at arms. Despite being right-handed, I insisted on fencing with my left to protect my calligraphy hand from possible injury. Given any choice in the matter, I limited my exertion to lifting large, heavy books, or musical instruments. I bit my lip and stared at the plain brown carpet.

"It's all right," Father Thomas said. "The initiation process will make you strong, physically as well as spiritually."

I continued staring at the floor. I'd really had my heart set on a nice, quiet monastery, not nasty, brutish physical fights. "I... I'm very flattered, but I..."

Father Thomas smiled at me. "Let me tell you more. You will receive a gift, a special magical ability unique to you." He continued to speak, and as he did, I realized that I very much wanted to join his order. Unfortunately, I didn't recall what he had said to convince me. It was almost as if I had dozed off and awakened with a new opinion. "Will you accept?"

"It would be my honor and my privilege," I said, and I meant it with all my heart.

"Wonderful. Please kneel."

I went to my knees on that plain brown carpet, being very careful to keep my cassock and surplice from getting dirty.

Father Thomas came and stood over me, imposing in his black and white vestments. "Repeat after me: I, Ludwig of Gravenreuth..."

"I, Ludwig of Gravenreuth..."

"Do of my own free will and accord, free of any coercion..."

There was something that sounded off in those words, but I said them anyway.

"Solemnly swear to protect the Catholic faith..."

This I repeated with more enthusiasm.

"And to obey Father Thomas in all things."

I didn't understand my trepidation, so I said the words.

"Close your eyes."

I dutifully closed my eyes.

There was a pause, then he pressed a cup to my lips. I drank, even though it tasted wrong. My eyes fluttered open.

"You know how, through the miracle of transubstantiation, wine becomes the blood of our Savior?"

I nodded and gazed at the cup thoughtfully.

"You're about to become closer to that miracle than you expected." Father Thomas smiled, a not-very-comforting smile. "This is my blood, shed for you."

I stared into the cup. It really resembled blood.

"There may be a little pain." He held out a hand. I took it, and he helped me to my feet.

I was still staring at him, uncertain, when he suddenly lunged at me, faster than the eye could see, and bit me on the neck, a sharp pain. We sailed backwards into a stone wall, hard enough for me to see stars. My head throbbed. I whimpered and tried to escape, but he grabbed me by the hair and pulled hard, tilting my head to one side, presumably for better biting. My scalp stung.

"You're hurting me!"

Father Thomas responded with a groan and yanked my hair more violently, clamping his other hand on my shoulder hard enough that I would have bruises. Surely, I only imagined an erect member under his vestments. Either way, I felt violated.

Tears sprang to my eyes, and my vision was swimming. "Please," I whispered. "Stop."

He was making loud slurping noises on my neck now. I tried to bat him off me, but I was feeling so weak, so very weak... The room spun slowly, and my vision blurred.

He pulled away and groaned again. "You're delicious." His teeth were sharp and long—how had I never noticed this before?

And I convulsed. Before my vision burst into a field of gray, followed by unconsciousness, I saw a malicious smile spread across Father Thomas's face.

Abraham
Atlantic Highlands, New Jersey
January 2, 2019

WHEN I WOKE up in my coffin, Victoria was curled up on my feet... as usual.

The coffin was, admittedly, a bit of an affectation. I could sleep in a bed as long as the curtains were drawn—it's about avoiding sunlight. The problem was that I appeared dismayingly dead when I slept. No one wanted to sleep in a bed with me, trust me. The cats usually avoided me, too, and when I had a dog, the dog would try to wake me up... with his teeth. But Victoria knew that even though I *looked* dead, I would wake up in the evening, and she always wanted to sleep with me. The coffin was tucked into a small storage area in the basement, behind the wall with the washer and dryer.

I blinked, and stretched, and sat up, and she gazed up at me with her huge, attentive, intelligent golden eyes. I'd left the lid off for her, like I always did. She sat up so she could kiss me on the lips, then closed her eyes and kneaded her paws on my chest while I petted her. I glanced at the clock and realized that it was later than I'd thought. I swore, and Victoria gave me a disapproving stare.

I had a finished basement, but it was still dark... all the better to not wake up in a pool of sunlight. There were spiders, but I'm not arachnophobic. They eat things that are grosser than they are, and the cats think they're cat toys. I occasionally find dismembered spiders on the basement floor. I wonder if I have some sympathy for spiders as fellow blood-drinkers, come to think of it. Not enough sympathy to deny the cats their toys...

I was only warm after I fed, but Victoria always wanted to sleep with me, or to be on my lap, anyway. She followed me from room to room unless we had company over. Most cats have a certain dignity to them, but if Victoria did something that made me laugh, like chew on a candle and then make a comical face of dismay, she'd try to do it again to make me laugh again.

I picked her up and kissed her on top of her soft, warm, fluffy black head, then put her down and went upstairs. Victoria trotted along behind me, my furry shadow.

I purchased this house in 1962 from a little old lady who was a bit of a Luddite. I'd renovated it gradually over the years, but I'd kept the wooden floors, the tin ceiling in the kitchen, the original wallpaper... and the kitchen was last updated by the aforementioned old lady in the 1920s. I'd been living in the city for decades and had a craving for the Queen Anne style and trees. I hadn't felt motivated to renovate the kitchen, so it appeared as it had when I bought it—complete with a blue gas stove and an icebox. You can't get appliances like that nowadays. They're practically indestructible.

Destiny was in the kitchen, wearing jeans and a t-shirt that read, "Life is great! Pets make it better!" She pulled a frozen vegetarian meal out of the microwave—a recent addition to my kitchen, which she had brought with her when she moved in. Unlike with sectional sofas, I didn't mind the microwave. I don't eat, so the kitchen should be functional for my wife. Ironically, I cooked more frequently than she did. We did have to upgrade the wiring when she moved in.

I yawned and walked into the living room, sat in my favorite brown leather chair and picked up my book. Victoria hopped into my lap. I petted her.

Victoria shivered and shuddered. "Are you all right?" I asked her.

Victoria jumped down onto the floor, onto the Persian carpet, but her front leg crumpled under her. She stared at her paw curled back on itself, then gamely tried to walk away on her wrist. She stopped after a few steps, appearing confused.

"Destiny? Destiny!"

Destiny put her food on the coffee table and kneeled on the wooden floor and examined her for a moment. Victoria didn't seem distressed, more disoriented. "She can't unclench her paw. Did she injure herself?"

"No."

"We need the emergency vet to confirm. I don't have the equipment to be sure, but..."

I picked Victoria up, and she gazed up at me with her usual cheerful curiosity. It was after dark, so I ignored my sun gear and headed out in my shirtsleeves. Yes, I should have used a cat carrier, but I was in a rush, and it wasn't like she could run away in that state. It was pouring down rain, and I was grateful that there *was* an emergency vet. A few short decades ago...

We left the house, locked the door. As we walked across the porch towards the car, Destiny said, "It's either a neurological event or a blood clot, which..."

That was when Victoria went limp and peed all over me. Her eyes were open, but she wasn't alert.

"Victoria?" I stared into her golden eyes, but despite her still being alive, I wasn't sure anything was staring back. *I'm not ready, I'm not ready!* I glanced at Destiny, hoping she could fix it.

"Emergency vet," Destiny said.

We rushed to the car—I drive a nondescript silver Toyota—in the freezing rain. I held Victoria while Destiny drove. We went to the same emergency vet where she'd had her $6,000 emergency perforated ulcer surgery, the one with the feline oncologist and the feline cardiologist and the feline neurologist. She meowed mournfully from time to time, and I held her close. "Come on, baby, stay with me." I gazed into her eyes again. "Can you hear me?"

She didn't react at all. *Fuckity fuckity fuck fuck fuck.* If we could get to the clinic, maybe it would be okay. I'd pay anything. Six thousand for emergency surgery? Been there done that would do it again if only she would stay with me. Stay with me!

The rain was violent, and Destiny was grim, silent, driving faster than I would have dared. It sounded like buckets of ice water were being continuously thrown onto the windshield, complete with the ice. I smelled like cat pee.

"Hang in there, baby," I said. "Hang in there. I'm here. Hang in there." She felt so light and limp in my arms. "Stay with me." It became a chant, a plea, a prayer: "Hang in there. Stay with me."

As we pulled into the parking lot, she made some weird growly exhalations. "Victoria?" I was shaking now and trying to avoid shaking Victoria. *I can't...*

We rushed over to the square concrete building and rang the bell. I did my best to shelter Victoria from the rain with my body, hunching around her with my back to the torrential downpour. It *felt* like buckets of ice water, too. The door buzzed open, and we rushed in. Destiny said to the desk clerk, "We need a resuscitation."

What? I glanced down at Victoria, limp in my arms. She wasn't breathing anymore. Not my sweet angel girl, I wouldn't accept it, they had to fix it!

The clerk called someone and a woman with tawny gold skin and sleek black hair, wearing blue scrubs, rushed out and looked at her eyes, touched her chest, and said, "Do you want us to resuscitate her?"

"Yes!"

The woman in the blue scrubs took her out of my arms and rushed her into the back, and the clerk said, "I need you to sign some forms before we can try."

I signed everything, waved my credit card around, and resisted the urge to bare my fangs at her. She was only doing her job. And then I stood still off in the corner and silently freaked out. People compare pets to children, but Victoria was more like a mother. Sensitive to my moods, washing my hands like I was her kitten. If the food or water dish was empty, she'd ask me to fill it and let the other cats eat or drink first. Always there with a gentle purr or a comic antic when I was down. Twenty-five years isn't a long time for my kind, but for a cat...

"Abraham?"

Destiny approached, but I shook my head and she backed off. I intentionally tuned out the painted cinder block walls, the television playing HGTV, and the other pet owners shifting uncomfortably on the fake leather benches and pacing the beige linoleum floor. The

whimpers of an injured dog, a cat yowling in a carrier...
I hugged myself and shivered. I was drenched, but the
rain hadn't washed away the smell of cat pee.

I don't know how long it was before the vet tech in
the blue scrubs came back out, her face sad and grim,
and said, "I'm so sorry. Do you want to see her?"

I gave the only possible answer. "Yes."

They ushered Destiny and me into an exam
room—more beige cinder block and linoleum and metal
and an industrial cleaner smell, and silence broken
only by very faint muffled barks coming from farther
inside the clinic—and a tech came in with a small
bundle wrapped in a white towel. She laid the bundle
gently on the stainless steel exam table and pulled the
towel away from her face.

Victoria was clearly dead, but her eyes and mouth
were wide open, like she was screaming, and suddenly I
was making keening sobs and Destiny was holding me
and the tech was crying. The tech quickly covered
Victoria's face again. She appeared worried. I didn't
care; I was in a place beyond dignity.

"It's okay," the tech said. "You can stay with her as
long as you want. Do you... Do you want to be alone
with her?"

I nodded.

The tech left, and Destiny pulled the towel back from
Victoria's face and kissed her gently on top of her head.
She was crying, too.

Destiny turned to me. "Do you want to say goodbye?"

"She looks like she's screaming," I said, but I also
wanted to say that she wasn't even *in* there anymore,
that she didn't even look like herself without the sweet
expression in her eyes. I've been present for cat

euthanasia before, but those always end up in calm, sleepy cat faces, not... this. She was barely recognizable as being Victoria. I scooped her up in my arms. Fuck death, fuck mortality, fuck the short lives of our best and truest companions.

"She's not screaming, sweetie," Destiny said. "They intubated her, to resuscitate her."

There was a timid knock on the door, and the tech came back with a box of tissues. She smelled of disinfectant soap. She handed them to me and said, "I'm so sorry. I know it's hard."

I went and stood in the corner with my back to them, clinging to Victoria. I couldn't lose control... okay, more than I already had. I was fantasizing about going out in the sun. I couldn't go out in the sun; I had a wife and it wouldn't be fair.

Also, Victoria wouldn't want me to.

When I finally calmed down enough to talk, the tech asked us about "aftercare"—meaning what we wanted to do with her corpse—and whether I wanted fur clippings or paw prints. Individual cremation, and fur clippings and paw prints felt undignified, so I said no. I didn't want someone pressing my sweet girl's dead paws into clay or ink or whatever they had in mind. The very idea of someone manipulating her body without me to supervise made me want to scream, or cry, or attack someone.

Destiny had to drive me home. I sat in the passenger seat of my car and shivered. I still smelled like cat pee. When we got home, I drank an entire bottle of Merlot and climbed into my coffin—alone—while Destiny did a poor job of pretending she wasn't hovering. When I woke up, Destiny had placed a book of Mary Oliver poetry on the table, right where I would see it when I got up... almost certainly for "In Blackwater Woods."

———————— ⌘ ————————

Destiny
Atlantic Highlands, New Jersey
January 3, 2019

I WOKE UP AFTER NOON—alone, alas, except for the cats. Inanna was curled up next to my head, and Ivan had his head on my feet. I slid out from under them and wandered into the kitchen.

I supposed I could have had vow renewal leftovers for lunch, but I had Uber Eats bring me a veggie burger from Good Karma instead. It smelled amazing—grains and greens and mustard.

I was eating my veggie burger when Abraham wandered in, appearing groggy, and headed towards the icebox. "Good morning. Are you okay?"

"No," he said, his voice wistful. He pulled a wineglass out of the cupboard and opened the icebox. He poured blood from the carafe into his glass. He sat opposite me and took a sip from the wineglass.

Perhaps I should deliberately change the subject. "Will you play for me after lunch?" I knew he'd played violin in the Victorian era. He owned a Stradivarius.

He smiled, but the smile was subdued. "If you like."

"I like," I said. I adore classical music.

I ate, and he drank, but he finished before me. He rinsed his glass out thoroughly, set it to dry on a dish towel, and vanished into the other room. He returned with the violin.

He placed the case on the kitchen table and opened it. From the first note, as always, I was mesmerized. I sat there, veggie burger forgotten. I had an odd sense—probably my imagination—of an old-fashioned Victorian stage, an audience's adulation. And sadness; it was as if I felt his grief for Victoria myself.

I don't know how long he played, but my delicious veggie burger was noticeably cooler. "You play like a god."

"Hear, o Israel, the Lord is your God, the Lord is one," he murmured as he put the violin back in the case and closed it.

Was that a rebuke? It didn't sound aggressive, more a statement of modesty. Still, it felt appropriate to change the subject, perhaps to a related topic. What was it about death that always led to religion? "Are we going to have a funeral for Victoria?" I took a bite of the veggie burger. "What's Jewish tradition on that?"

He sat in a chair and stared at his violin. "If she were human, I would say a special prayer, the Kaddish, every day for thirty days with a minyan of ten Jews, but I'm not supposed to say Kaddish for an animal."

I chewed, swallowed. "No offense, but I kind of hate that."

"So do I," he admitted. "You and the cats are my family, my only community."

"You could break the rules," I suggested.

He shook his head, but I thought I saw tears in his eyes. "I'm not supposed to say Kaddish alone, either."

I hated to see it, but of course it was a healthy reaction. "One thing that makes mourning an animal hard is that people dismiss your grief. If it would bring you comfort, I don't think God would mind."

He let out a shuddery breath. "I know, but there are already so many Jewish things I can no longer do. I hate to add another way I'm missing the mark to the list."

I took his hands in mine and squeezed them. He gazed down at my hands, lifted one, and kissed it. His lips were soft and warmer than his hands.

"Thank you," he said.

"Will you tell me another story?" I asked. "I know it's not bedtime, but tell me about your first cat."

———⌒◇⌒———

Abraham
Wreschen, Prussia
2 Av 5593 (July 18, 1833)

THE KITTENS WERE a variety of colors. I expected them to all look like their mother—black, orange, and white—but there was a brown striped one, a couple of orange and white ones, and one that had colors like her mother but stripes like the brown one. They were all under a bush in our garden. I reached down and touched the tiny babies. The mother watched me, wary, but I petted her as well. I decided her name was Malkah, meaning "queen."

"Avrahom!" my mother called. "It's time for dinner!"

"Mamme, can we keep them?" I asked.

My mother stepped outside and fanned herself in the July heat—and, of course, she'd come from a hot kitchen. "We don't keep animals in the house."

"But, Mamme!"

My father stepped outside. "I think she performs a valuable service, keeping rats and mice away, and, as such, we should let her stay."

My mother shot him a sour glance, but I rushed to my father and hugged him. "Thank you, Tatti!" I ran to get a crate and a blanket.

As I passed my parents, my mother was glaring at my father, and my father shrugged. "He's a sensitive boy, Rivka. It's a good thing. We want him to be refined, cultured, polite..."

My mother made a face but didn't argue with him as I put the mother and her kittens in the crate. I carried them into the house and up to my room.

"Avrahom!" she called. "Dinner!"

I came back downstairs and said, "But, Mamme, the Torah says I'm supposed to feed my animals before I feed myself!"

My parents exchanged a proud smile, and my mother gave me a cat-sized serving of fish to feed the cats. "Don't forget to wash your hands!"

# Metamorphosis

Abraham
Atlantic Highlands, New Jersey
January 14, 2019

The two a.m. alarm went off on my cellphone. I put my book—*On Wings of Song: a Biography of Felix Mendelssohn*—down on the nightstand. I stood and walked over to the nest box of two-week-old kittens on the guest room dresser, with a heating pad cord peeking out from under an old faded towel. I lifted the towel and peered inside. Three kittens, two black and one brown tabby. They were in a sleepy, peeping heap. I replaced the towel. Destiny works with a rescue organization named "Furkids" and sometimes brings home "bottle babies." Furkids had resources for kittens of adoption age, or older adoptable cats, but it's hard to find someone to care for neonates. They'd all go back to the rescue once they were adoptable age, which was both happy and sad at the same time. I wondered if Destiny had taken them home and assigned me the task of feeding them to help me cope with Victoria. It helped a little. It had been twelve days since Victoria died... not that I was counting.

I padded down the hall in my bare feet and pajama bottoms to the kitchen in the dark—trying not to clatter or creak on the wooden floorboards and thereby wake up my wife—and poured kitten formula into a coffee mug from a vet conference and put it in the microwave for ten seconds.

I tested the formula temperature on my wrist. I generate little body heat, but I've done this enough times that I can tell whether the formula is too hot.

I tiptoed back to the kitten nursery—"guest room," but we should really call it what it was—and picked up one of the black kittens. I lifted the tail and peered underneath. It was the male; the other black kitten was female. It's almost impossible for most people to tell at that age, but I've had cats for over almost two hundred years, and most of that was before the era of spay/neuter, so I've had a lot of practice. I weighed the kitten on a digital kitchen scale and wrote the weight in the black spiral-bound notebook Destiny had provided. I carried the kitten back to the blue armchair next to the window. There was a towel draped over the foot of the bed, blue, contrasting with the white and pink floral bedspread. I put the towel on my lap, then placed the kitten on top of the towel. I picked up a needle-less syringe from the side table, drew some formula into it, and slowly, so slowly, allowed the formula to dribble out into the kitten's mouth.

It's important to be careful with kittens that young. It's easy to choke them. Fortunately, I had heightened senses. I could feel the kitten's heartbeat, smell the scent of vulnerable young animal and milk. I knew exactly the amount of pressure to apply to the syringe.

I repeated the weighing and feeding procedure with the kitten's sisters. They didn't have names yet. I found it easier to wait until either names suggested themselves to me, or they passed an age where I felt confident that they would survive. I put the towel on the bed and padded silently to the kitchen. I stored the rest of the formula back in the refrigerator and returned to the guest room. As I passed the master bedroom, Destiny snorted and rolled over. I wondered what she was dreaming about. I didn't have to look to know that her long red braid would be flung across the bed.

Victoria had had the cutest black-on-black stripes as a kitten—she grew out of them—and would trot up to any vet or vet tech and charm them completely. On one occasion, I heard an entire exam room full of loud squeals and cooing, followed by a tech coming out and asking me, "Do you just love on this kitten all the time?" Well, *of course* I did; isn't that what cats are for?

I tucked my hair behind my ear, sat back down in the brown armchair, and picked up my book. Sometimes I wished I could cut my hair. It had been this length since I was nineteen years old. But I couldn't alter my body. My hair and fingernails didn't grow. They didn't break off from normal wear and tear, either. I once tried to give myself a trim, and the hair slid right out of the scissors, and eventually the screw holding the blades together broke. No, I'd just have to keep what Destiny called my Romantic Poet hair.

It was absolutely not Romantic Poet hair. I was familiar with men's hairstyles of the period, and this was not that. Instead, I had plain shoulder-length brown hair that I sometimes wore in what modern people called a ponytail, and what the Prussian army called a soldier's queue. I was *so grateful* when the 1960s came around and made it socially acceptable for men to wear their hair long again. There had been an unfortunate incident in which I drank some would-be queer-bashers. One can't be leaving evidence like that around. It's bad for anonymity. I'd started wearing a wig whenever I left the house.

Government IDs aside, I was thin and androgynous. I could pass for anything between a young adult man and a tomboyish teenage girl based on clothing and attitude, but I only really used the girl thing as a disguise if I was desperate.

I read until the five a.m. alarm went off and repeated the kitten feeding.

I finished my book and checked the time. Six thirty a.m. I walked to the kitchen and cooked breakfast for one—eggs and toast with coffee with cream and two teaspoons of sugar. I'd replaced the icebox with a modern stainless steel refrigerator for Destiny—I turned a tidy profit on it by selling it to my antiques dealer—but I was pleasantly relieved that she didn't mind my not replacing the 1920s blue gas stove. The model I learned to cook on was similar. Destiny's rice cooker, the vegetable steamer, and the microwave suited her needs—she didn't really cook. I enjoyed cooking more than she did, and I also didn't work and barely slept, so why not?

The kitchen faced north, thank goodness, so I didn't worry about stray sunbeams. And the entire first floor had a wrap-around porch, so sunbeams were rare even on the east and west sides downstairs. I could see the Jersey shore, the city, and the lower New York harbor from the second floor, so it seemed a shame to block off such a view with blackout curtains... not that it was always safe. I was very aware of the way the sun moved through the house.

Destiny shuffled blearily into the kitchen wearing a blue bathrobe and bunny slippers, and grabbed a cup of coffee. "You're an angel." She slurped noisily, sniffled a little and grabbed the plate of food. Adorable. I washed the pan, but could hear the sounds of eating behind me.

"Sit with me, silly," she said, so I did.

We sat in companionable silence at the small, square kitchen table with the white lace tablecloth for a while, and then she said, "How are the babies?"

"Gaining weight," I said. "You should check in on them before you leave for work."

"Good, I will," she said, and took another sip of coffee. "I'm such an addict."

I smirked at her and took that as a compliment to my coffee-making skills. Victoria wouldn't be offended for me to note that even without her, there were good things in life and Destiny was one of them. Outside, a bird chirped.

"They're supposed to deliver Victoria's ashes to the clinic today."

I closed my eyes, turned my head away, and pressed my lips together hard. My chest was heavy.

Destiny reached across the table and took my hand in her warmer one. "In the faith I was raised in, it's left as an exercise for the individual to decide whether you believe Victoria has gone to a better place, or is going to be reborn on this earth, or whether she just returned to some over-arching soul pool. Whatever you find most comforting, I suppose."

I glanced over at Destiny. Her green eyes were full of tears. For Victoria? For me? For both of us? Either way, I appreciated it. I tried to smile and failed. "Just as long as no one sends me any more of those accursed Rainbow Bridge cards."

If you're not familiar with the Rainbow Bridge, it's all the rage in pet death circles nowadays. People send you cards about how your pet is now young and healthy and happy again and waiting in a sunny field outside heaven for you, and when you die, you'll both go to heaven together. It sounds sweet! But what about the homeless pets? What about *my* pets?

Destiny blinked. "I... kind of find those comforting."

I tried to smile again and failed again. "You can. It's just that... I don't want Victoria to wait for me. It'll be a *very* long wait."

Destiny sniffled, but she smiled. "You're very kind."

I shrugged and looked away. Victoria deserved the better place now, not after waiting for an accident to befall me.

"What happens after death in the belief system you were raised in?"

"You go to remedial life lessons. They take about a year, depending on how much you have to learn. Then you move on to the better place." Victoria was already a perfect soul, in my opinion, and deserved to be in the better place now.

"I like that," Destiny said. "Would you mind if I adopted that?"

"Not at all," I said. We held hands for a moment. I reached across the white lace tablecloth and took her other hand. She was soft and warm and here, and it made me feel better. I wondered whether I should ask her to take the day off from work.

Ivan chose that moment to come in and meow for his breakfast. "How are you handling things?" I asked Ivan.

Ivan didn't answer, of course. So I stood up and opened some Fancy Feast for him.

"The good stuff?" Destiny asked. We fed them some of Destiny's holistic kitty health food, but whenever their appetites flagged, it was Fancy Feast time.

"They've had a rough week." Neither of them were eating well without Victoria. They missed her, too.

Inanna rushed into the room to take Ivan's dish—she must have heard the can—so I rolled my eyes and opened a second can for Ivan.

"So much tortietude," Destiny said. She cocked her head at me and said, "I imagine you want your breakfast, too."

I smiled. "I won't say no."

Destiny extended her wrist across the table, so I sat back down, took her arm in both my hands, and bent over to bite. I heard the sharp intake of breath...

*No one* tasted as good as Destiny. Vegetarian diet? Clean living? I didn't know, but with the steak-like iron taste, Destiny had... almost a floral note, like jasmine.

I'd miss it if I turned her, but I was willing to make that sacrifice if it meant she wouldn't die.

I only took a little. I didn't want to make her sick, or weak, or anemic. She used her vegetarianism as an excuse to be tested for anemia regularly, and my saliva had vein-closing and healing properties, or so Flora told me.

"Is that enough?" Destiny asked. She pressed a paper napkin to her wrist, hard.

"I'm expecting a delivery today," I said.

"Okay," she said, and stood up. "I'll check the babies before I go." She paused in the doorway. "I'll bring your girl home tonight."

*You'll bring home a little tin, but she won't be in there. Not really.* "Thank you."

The thing about Victoria that made her Victoria wasn't her leftover calcium. It was the sweet, clever expression in her bright, attentive golden eyes. Her sense of humor. Her compassion. The way she would stand between me and the front door and meow plaintively to ask me not to take Ivan to the vet. But that's all I would have: her leftover calcium in a little tin with flowers painted on it. That and memories.

"I'm still not convinced that she was a cat and not some kind of fae," Destiny said. It was an inside joke that Victoria was a fairy or pixie or some similar creature masquerading as a cat for her own mysterious purposes. Destiny sniffled. "Smartest cat I ever met, and I swear she understood English fluently." She moved her chair closer to mine, sat in it, and put her arm around me. "Are you all right?"

I didn't answer. I don't enjoy lying to my wife, and I wasn't all right.

Destiny squeezed my hand. "I'm so sorry. I'll see you tonight."

———————— ⌁ ————————

Destiny
Atlantic Highlands, New Jersey
January 14, 2019

WHEN CONFRONTED WITH DEATH, what you really need is life. The answer to death is babies.

I stood next to the box of bottle babies and picked up Abraham's black notebook. I read his notes in his meticulous hand. Sometimes his handwriting resembled a Victorian lettering guide, but sometimes, when taking notes for himself, he did it in Yiddish cursive letters. He hadn't done that because he knew I'd be reading his notes.

I approved of the kittens' weight gain, but I picked up each individual kitten, one by one, and examined them—their little white baby fangs, their little blue eyes, their unfurling little ears. I gently palpated their soft, round little bellies while they peeped in protest. They all smelled like milk, although perhaps that was partly because Abraham had wiped them clean and tossed the tissues in a wastebasket. They were looking like normal, healthy kittens, although kittens at their age sometimes "fail to thrive," as we vets say. I hoped that wouldn't happen here; I'd brought them home to distract poor Abraham, not to rub salt in the wound! I knew how much it hurt; Victoria was my cat, too, and I saw people going through the same thing all the time at work.

I replaced the stained, faded towel over the top of the cardboard box. Kittens that age can't regulate their body temperatures and need a heat source. I left the guest room, carefully closing the door behind me. I didn't think Ivan or Inanna would bother the kittens, but they were too little to vaccinate.

I walked down the hall and heard running water in the kitchen. Abraham was doing the dishes. I kissed him on the cheek, and turned and walked out the door.

I missed Victoria, too. I supposed Queen Titania needed to go back to the fae realm to check on her subjects. I'd keep an eye out in six weeks or so for her return. Okay, okay, Victoria probably wasn't Queen Titania, but she seemed like something... more than a cat, like one of the Fair Folk pretending to be a cat for her own mysterious purposes.

If Victoria was indeed one of the Good Neighbors, would she come back to my darling husband?

———————⧜———————

Abraham
Atlantic Highlands, New Jersey
January 14, 2019

I STOOD IN THE living room that evening, wearing jeans, sneakers, and a plain black T-shirt. I was warming myself in front of the fire when Destiny came in and handed me the little tin of Victoria with flowers painted on it, then hugged me. "I'm so sorry."

"I hate death." The carved wooden mantel framed the fire as I stared into it. My grief hurt, physically; my chest ached, and I fought back tears.

"I know, sweetie, but it's a normal part of life." She hugged me again. I could smell the health-food-store shampoo she used—lavender—and hear her breathing. She was so warm and soft. She was wearing her vet scrubs with the violet paw print pattern.

I pulled back a little—the full body contact was comforting, but I wanted her to understand—and gazed into her beautiful green eyes. "Not for my kind, it's not."

I sat on the sofa, still holding the little tin. We now had one of those ubiquitous sectional sofas in front of a gigantic television, in red, because I don't like sectional sofas but do like red. They're comfortable, but I don't think they'll age well, if you know what I mean. I could be wrong; antiques dealers a century from now might do a brisk trade in sectionals, but some instinct of mine insists they'll be kitsch. Perhaps that's harsh; sometimes it feels like everything kitsch becomes classic again... unless it's forgotten.

Destiny sat next to me. "Do you want to do anything with them?" She curled her legs up under herself. "I don't know. Turn them into jewelry, sew them into a little pillow..."

"Ugh!" I shuddered. After I'd refused fur clippings and paw prints at the vet, the pet crematory had called to offer them to me. No. Those types of morbid souvenirs were common in the Victorian era, but I've never liked them. They felt disrespectful. Perhaps this was a Jewish thing, as there's a strong emphasis on treating a corpse with respect, as it used to be the vessel for a soul.

I suddenly felt very guilty for cremating Victoria and not saying Kaddish for her. I knew that was illogical, but the Talmud tells us that the dead mourn their own bodies for seven days. We're not allowed to eat or pray in front of a corpse, as the dead can no longer do those things and that makes it feel like we're taunting them. Of course, Maharsha explains that the soul mourns the body because it learned Torah and did mitzvot with it, and Victoria was a cat. That said, if she had still been here in a form I couldn't see, I could still have offered her some comfort or kind words.

"Well," she said, still talking about the souvenirs, "people do."

"No, thank you. Yuck." I stared at the tin some more. It was black, and shiny, and covered with tiny pictures of flowers spaced geometrically, and mass-produced. Victoria deserved better.

There was a pause before Destiny said, "We could get her a prettier urn, if you like."

I took a deep breath. "Please don't take this the wrong way. I'm not angry with you. But what I want is my fucking cat back, and since I can't have that, I don't know what I want yet."

"That's okay. You have time to decide."

For some reason, that struck me as funny, the kind of funny where you're crying and something sets you off and makes you laugh as well. Yes. Yes, I had time. Lots and lots of time. All the time. What I didn't have was Victoria. Or Flora. Or Samuel. Or Miriam. Or John and

Eliza. Or Shayna. Or Rebekah, Jacob, Rachel, and Reuben. Or, someday, Destiny.

I hate death.

What I ended up doing with her ashes: as a temporary solution, I placed the tin at the bottom of my coffin and added a pillow to simulate her weight on my feet.

It didn't help.

Abraham
Atlantic Highlands, New Jersey
January 29, 2019

MORNING. THE SUN SHONE on the snow outside the window. Icicles hung from the porch roof, sparkling. It was lovely, but I was ready for spring... not that I could enjoy the light and the color of spring except from behind a pane of glass. I should have preferred the shorter days and longer nights, but winter always felt gloomy to me. All the dead, bare trees, and all the plants dead and buried under a layer of snow.

I made oatmeal for Destiny. And coffee, of course. I served the oatmeal in the blue stoneware bowl she'd bought at a college art sale, and the coffee in the mug from the local Ren Faire with little flowers painted on it. She shuffled in wearing her bathrobe and bunny slippers, and smiled when I placed them on the lace tablecloth, next to a vase full of roses. I walked over to the boombox on the kitchen counter and turned on

Handel's *Israel in Egypt*, very low volume. I'd promised my wife food in the ketubah, and I enjoyed making good on that promise.

As she sipped her coffee, she said, "I googled Wreschen."

I shrugged and sat across the table from her, pushing the vase of flowers to the side. I wanted to see *her*, not the flowers.

She took another sip of her coffee. "Wreschen, not Września?"

"It was Wreschen when I lived there."

Destiny appeared to consider that. She took another deep sip of coffee. "Tell me about your children again. Were they from Wreschen, too?"

"No. Flora and I took in some orphans."

She raised her eyebrows at me.

"It was a long time ago. They're all dead."

"I'm sorry," she said, and started on her oatmeal. "But presumably they had children. Why haven't I met their descendants?"

"They… didn't."

She tilted her head at me, but I didn't offer an explanation and she didn't ask. For which I was grateful. It wasn't a cheerful topic.

After a moment, she added, "Flora?"

"I told you I've been married before," I said. After a moment of silent eating, I added, "She… was indiscreet."

"Does that mean she told people you were a vampire, or that she cheated on you?"

I laughed a little. "She didn't cheat on me." It wasn't funny, though. "She decided that the best disguise would be a vampire-obsessed actress who specialized in playing vampires in trashy stage plays. Imagine if Elvira was a vampire. People would laugh at you if you suggested she really was one."

"Clever," Destiny said. She looked like she meant it, like she was wondering why I didn't do it myself.

"It only takes one lunatic with kerosene and some matches."

"Oh." She appeared appropriately appalled. In fact, she was pale, ashen, and her hands trembled. I hadn't intended to upset her...

There was an awkward pause, and I was done volunteering information for the day. Sometimes I can still smell the smoke and hear the screams. I listened to the spoon scraping the bowl, the coffee being slurped, but I didn't look up.

"Does it ever stop hurting?"

I gazed up into Destiny's soft green eyes. They looked like Flora's, I realized. "You get to where you're fine most days, and then it hits you again. Those days just start coming farther and farther apart." After a pause, I added, "It takes longer if you don't engage with it, but some days you just... can't." On those days, there's the full bottle of Merlot, or beer, or similarly unhealthy non-coping, but... see above about *can't*.

It hadn't stopped hurting in the twenty-seven days since Victoria died... not that I was counting. I was taking this poorly... but, of course, it was the cumulative effect of losses combined with isolation. Knowing that didn't make it hurt less, though.

Destiny squeezed my hand, and I stared at the blue gas stove, but I squeezed her hand back. "I don't want you to die." I've had enough death in my life, too much.

"I'm hardly decrepit," she said, and laughed. "You'd be bored after the first hundred years."

"I doubt it," I said, and squeezed her hand again. I took both her hands and stared at them. But I would never tire of Destiny, just like I'd never tired of Flora. I wondered if the Kabbalists were right, if sometimes souls did return to earth.

"You don't enjoy talking about your past."

I looked Destiny in the eye. She deserved the truth. "I've been lying for a long time. I don't want to lie to you."

"Lying?"

"Pretending to not be what I am."

There was a comfortable silence, with Destiny holding my hands, and then she said, "What was the first lie?"

"To study music at the Berlin academy," I said. I squeezed her hands again and said, "They didn't allow people like me to attend."

Her brow furrowed. "Vampires?"

"No." Destiny's brow failed to unfurrow, so I specified, "Jews."

"Oh!" She blinked and gazed at our hands again and bit her lip. "I'm sorry."

"Thank you." I considered the matter, and added, "I told you before: There's someone I don't want to find me. That's why I don't perform publicly anymore."

"Oh!" she said. "Are you... are you safe?"

I shrugged. "He hasn't found me yet."

There was another silence, and she stood up, and I was grateful that she didn't press the subject. "I'll check the babies on my way out." She paused in the doorway. "You can't hide forever, you know."

I could try.

---

Ludwig
Rosenheim, Bavaria
October 13, 1762

WHEN I WOKE, I was lying on the floor, and Father Thomas was gazing down at me. "Are you all right, my child?"

I sat up and crab-walked backwards away from him. "You hurt me!" My blond hair flopped over my face, and I shoved it back and glared at him. I wasn't certain what he'd done to me, but it wasn't spiritual. He'd enjoyed it, in a way that felt vulgar.

Father Thomas appeared wounded. "My dearest boy, I would never do such a thing! I should have warned you that hallucinations were common during the initiation."

I opened my mouth to protest—I had not hallucinated!—but he interrupted me.

"Satan doesn't want you to join us, you see. He must have been very upset. I hope the visions weren't too disturbing."

This was rubbish! I frowned and reached up to touch my savaged neck.

It felt smooth and unblemished. I lifted the shoulder of my vestments to peer at the unbruised skin beneath. I blinked a few times, then examined myself visually and found blood near my clavicle, where it might have fallen during the attack. I gazed up at him, awaiting an explanation.

"Your nose bled during the initiation. Not to worry, I cleaned you up." He sat next to me and daubed at my vestments with the clean side of a bloody rag.

"But—"

"Don't worry, you're all right. You have some different dietary needs now, but I'll see to those."

"Different? But—"

"Don't worry, child. Just go back to your room and get some rest. Tomorrow is a special day; someone important is coming, someone I'd like you to meet."

"But—"

"You're very fortunate! The initiation has given you eternal life. You will never age or die."

Eternal life? Beyond the spiritual metaphor? I wasn't certain how I felt about that. It would become an issue if, God forbid, something happened to my elder brother, Friedrich. "What? I didn't agree to—"

Thomas went on at length about my good fortune. Soothed by his words, I went upstairs and lay down on my cot.

———————— ∞ ————————

Destiny
Atlantic Highlands, New Jersey
February 1, 2019

I HAD THE DREAM AGAIN, but this time I was wearing massive, heavy, old-fashioned skirts and was trying to escape a burning house with children. I couldn't see the details of the house, just... flames everywhere, and crying children.

I woke up with a start. Inanna gazed up at me, concern on her sweet face, so I kissed her on her soft, furry head and padded off to the kitchen to make some hot cocoa, hoping the warm milk would put me back to sleep.

Abraham was reading a book and didn't appear to have noticed that I was awake.

I eyed the stove warily. It was possible that I'd played too much *Sims,* wherein it's common to set your house on fire cooking. I could make hot cocoa in the microwave, but the stuff from the stove turned out better. I took a deep breath, squared my shoulders, pulled out a pan, and filled it with milk, cocoa, vanilla, sugar... I placed it on the burner and cautiously turned the dial. A giant gout of blue flame shot out and licked up the side of the pan.

"Trouble sleeping?"

I jumped and dropped the spoon on the floor.

He came over and wrapped his arms around me. "Hey, hey..."

I put my head on his shoulder and tried to relax. "Bad dream. It happens." After a moment, I admitted, with some embarrassment, "I've always had a phobia about house fires."

"Oh!" He squeezed me closer, petted my hair, kissed my cheek.

"Sorry," I mumbled.

"Don't be," he said. "Would you like me to finish the cocoa?"

I nodded, and he pulled out the chair for me to sit at the kitchen table. I watched him pick up the spoon and drop it into the sink, then get a new one to stir with and add the cocoa, and finally he poured it into a mug. He put some marshmallows and a stick of cinnamon in it and brought it to me. He sat across the table.

We sat in companionable silence while I drank the cocoa. He said, "Would you like me to sit with you while you sleep?"

I nodded, and he got up and grabbed his book, then led me down the hall to the master bedroom. One of the few ways Abraham isn't perfect is that he doesn't sleep in my bed. I've always found sharing a bed comforting. But he sat on the bed with his back against the headboard, and I climbed in and curled up in a ball with my pillow, and that was enough for me to sleep.

---

Abraham
Atlantic Highlands, New Jersey
February 17, 2019

I WAS SITTING on the red sectional sofa in front of the big screen television watching the movie version of *Interview with the Vampire*—I couldn't help it; two of my weaknesses        are        classical        music        and        vampire media—when Inanna hissed at Ivan and backed away. That was unusual; she was tolerant in a bored sort of way, or, on rare occasions, growling and swaggering. "Ivan?"

Ivan stared up at me. His eyes were worried and his nose was twitching, but he walked away as there was crashing and shouting on the television. I assumed Ivan's odd behavior was a reaction to the interpersonal conflict.

He started meeping—little abbreviated meows.

I turned off the television and walked over to where he was—next to the fireplace. He was lying on his side, and only his upper body was moving. Inanna was staring at him with a horrified expression, hissed again, and backed away. He tried to stand up and ended up dragging his lower body behind him before flopping down again. *Not Ivan, not now. Not Ivan!*

"Ivan? Ivan!"

Destiny called from somewhere down the hall, "Abraham?"

"Ivan collapsed!" I rushed over and scooped him up.

"Let me see." She arrived in a towel, with her hair wrapped in a second towel.

We rushed Ivan over to the kitchen table, and I laid him on the lace tablecloth. Destiny looked at his eyes, his breathing, touched his feet.

"Okay," Destiny said, but her voice wasn't okay. It was grim. "I think he's thrown a blood clot, and it's blocking all blood flow to his lower body. It's called a saddle thrombus."

"Are you sure?" My chest ached, and my voice was high, almost hysterical. It couldn't be; I wouldn't accept it. Ivan was lying on the table, nose twitching. He reached out a paw towards me, and I gave him my hand and petted him with the other.

Destiny tilted her head, then she rushed out of the room and came back with a needle and some glucose testing strips. "I was going to teach Marsha how to do this at home. I hope she doesn't mind if they're used."

I had no idea who Marsha was, nor did I care. Ivan remained bravely silent, but his nose continued to twitch and his eyes were anxious and pleading. Destiny pricked his ear. He flinched but tolerated it. She tested the droplet with the strip and the glucose meter and wrote the number on her hand with a pen she spotted on top of the microwave. She pricked one of his paw pads on his hind foot and squeezed, then tested that drop of blood. She compared the number on the meter to the number she'd written on her hand. "I'm sure." Blood from Ivan's ear dripped onto the lace tablecloth. "Look, not only is his blood sugar radically different on opposite sides of his body, but his foot isn't bleeding." She picked up a cotton ball and pressed it to his ear.

"How do we fix it?"

Destiny sighed. "I'm going to be straight with you, Abraham. He has about a thirty-three percent chance of surviving. He may or may not regain the use of his legs. If he survives, he probably has six months before it happens again. Right now there are toxins building up on the other side of the clot and if it loosens up, they'll flood his body and might kill him. The clot might break loose and lodge in his heart, or his lungs, or his brain. We can test to see if he's also in active heart failure, which is common—that'll be bloodwork and imaging at the clinic—but either way... it's not good." She examined Ivan again. "He's not struggling to breathe, at least. But this is a very painful condition, like a permanent muscle cramp."

I said nothing. I knew what she was going to suggest, and the answer was no. I knew he wanted to try—or was I projecting?

"We need to put him down. He's not complaining, because he's incredibly brave, but he's suffering."

"I'll take the thirty-three percent," I said. I'd pay any amount of money.

"You need to think about what's right for Ivan," Destiny said. She took in a sharp breath, sniffled, and wiped under her eyes with the back of her arm.

I leaned over and kissed him on the head.

"Abraham." Her voice was a gentle rebuke, but also compassionate. "At the very least, he needs pain medication, but... we need to let him go, Abraham." She reached out a hand to stroke his head. "Victoria almost certainly threw a clot, too."

Victoria. I could see, in my mind's eye, another little black tin with flowers painted on it, another series of Rainbow Bridge cards. It was one month, two weeks since Victoria died, and *yes,* I was *fucking counting.* Too soon.

No. "I can't do this again."

Destiny made a sympathetic face and left the room.

I glanced away for a moment, at the black and white checked floor tiles. I looked Ivan in the eye. "Do you want to try something radical?"

Ivan didn't answer, of course, but from his body language, his twitching nose, his pleading eyes... he wanted me to fix it.

"Trust me," I said, and kissed Ivan on the head... and bit him, on the back of the neck, near the scruff.

He peeped in surprise, and Destiny gasped—she'd returned with a cat carrier and wet hair, wearing her robe. Ivan's blood was revolting. It wasn't actively lumpy or anything like that, but I could taste disease. I couldn't tell you how I would define the taste of disease, but... I knew. It was almost tinny, is the best description I can come up with. I swallowed and grabbed one of the kitten feeding syringes from the kitchen drawer where we kept spares.

"...Abraham?"

"I'm trying something radical," I said, and bit my wrist. I suctioned my blood into the feeding syringe and squirted it into Ivan's mouth. I didn't know that it would work, and never would have tried it on a healthy cat, but... Ivan clearly didn't have anything to lose.

Ivan drank.

There was a moment where I wondered if anything would happen, and then Ivan convulsed. I braced his back against my arm and used my other hand to soothe him. "It's all right."

Ivan yowled, and his hind legs jerked. I supposed that the change was breaking down that clot. I gave him some more of my blood. Destiny gasped again, and there was the clatter of the cat carrier falling to the floor, but I couldn't spare her my attention at the moment.

It took about half an hour, and then his bite wounds and blood-test needle pricks closed up, and his fur became sleek and glossy. He opened his eyes and gazed up at me with the same adoring look he'd given me when I opened his infected eyes as a baby. He sat up and glanced around the kitchen, then stood.

Destiny had backed all the way up against the farthest kitchen counter and was holding her hands over her mouth, her eyes wide. Her wet hair hung loose. "What did you do?"

"It's okay," I told her. "I know what he needs."

I had some chicken livers in the bottom drawer of the refrigerator, where Destiny never put her food. My emergency stash. I grabbed my blender—not Destiny's new blender, the one I'd purchased in 1972 and barely used—and dumped the livers in. I plugged it in and pressed pulse. There was a grinding sound and an explosion of red in the blender. It smelled *delicious*.

Destiny made a sound of disgust. She was still backed up against the kitchen counter, watching with wide eyes, but now she was clinging to the counter with both hands.

I grabbed Ivan's food dish and placed it on the table, pouring the raw bloody liquid into it. He lapped it up enthusiastically. He spilled a little, but it was hardly the first bit of blood on the tablecloth tonight. It was ruined.

Destiny walked over slowly and touched Ivan's tail, his hind feet. "They're warmer, but they're still cold."

Ivan flicked his tail at her and kept lapping up his treat.

"He'll only be warm after he feeds, like me," I said.

We watched him finish his meal. Destiny tapped the edge of the table. "Ivan?"

Ivan walked over to her like nothing had happened. He sniffed her and gazed up at her, expectant, until she petted him. "It's a miracle. At the very least, scientifically improbable to the point of... Abraham?"

My eyes filled with tears, blurring the vision of my newly healthy, newly immortal golden cat.

"Abraham?"

"Victoria deserved a miracle, too. I should have... I should have..."

I should have thought of that.

———————⌀———————

Destiny
Atlantic Highlands, New Jersey
February 17, 2019


OKAY, SHIT JUST got real.

Intellectually, I knew Abraham was a vampire. I'd even seen him drink blood out of the fridge and let him drink from my wrist. I wore long sleeves to hide the bite marks. Well. Usually it was just light bruising.

I'd never seen him make another vampire. Nor had I thought this was something that he could do to a pet. I mean, there was a movie called *Dracula's Daughter*, but there wasn't a movie called *Dracula's Dog* or *Dracula's Cat*. I think they'd go with the alliteration...

*Bunnicula*?

I... should I worry?

I ran myself a bath with a lavender bath bomb in the clawfoot Victorian tub, with the white tile everywhere. I got in with a nice cup of green tea. It was warm, and smelled wonderful, and I *love* the grassy taste of green tea... Clawfoot tubs don't have a convenient place to set down mugs, so I put it on top of the closed toilet lid, which was kind of gross when I thought about it but I had more important things on my mind. For a moment, I missed the bathtub at my old apartment, which had space for a mini altar. I'd decorated it with sea shells, rose quartz, and a little statue of Aphrodite.

I suspected a nice Jewish boy wouldn't want to bathe with Aphrodite.

Once I was in the tub, it was calm and quiet, with only the occasional bath-related splash or drip from the tap.

On the one hand, Abraham had cured saddle thrombus, a painful condition that left cats maimed or dead, the vet's worst nightmare condition. On the other hand... what was Ivan now? Was this *Pet Sematary* or *The Monkey's Paw*? How did I end up in a horror movie?

I'd married a vampire. That's how. I was even doing the horror movie bathtub scene, I realized, and smiled. I didn't quite have a laugh in me.

Abraham wasn't a demon, nor a shambling undead monster. As near as I could tell, he was the person he'd always been, only without the ability to eat normal food or go out in the sunlight. Abraham had human reason, however. Ivan, as adorable as he was, was a cat. Abraham couldn't explain to the cat what he'd done to him.

Was this fair? And what would happen if a bus hit me tomorrow? Should I run?

I thought of those vast, deep, soulful brown eyes. I had to believe that he'd done what was best for Ivan.

---

Abraham
Atlantic Highlands, New Jersey
February 24, 2019

WE WERE CURLED UP together on the red sectional sofa. Very well, I admitted to myself that it was more comfortable than my beloved horsehair loveseat, or even a chaise longue. I stretched out my legs under a blanket and leaned my head against Destiny's.

Sweet Ivan had been clingy since the change and watched conversations closely... and also television. It was almost as if he understood English fluently now. He was sitting on my lap facing the television and purring.

Inanna had threatened the sofa delivery people, much to my amusement. I'd had to lock her in the bathroom while she growled at me, sounding like a Doberman. She was still angry that I'd allowed the intrusion and sat on the other side of the room, giving me the occasional dirty look.

Sadly, our bottle baby kittens were now six weeks old and almost prime adoption age. I was preemptively devastated. They were wrestling and pouncing on each other, while Ivan was determined to wash them. Perhaps Destiny would bring home more bottle babies at some point. Destiny had named them Aral, Alys, and Cordelia after Bujold's Vorkosigan Saga.

Destiny was flipping channels again—why could moderns not select a channel and watch it? Attention spans really weren't what they used to be! She settled on, alas, the news again. There was some Academy Award speculation, and then...

"Internet personality and independent presidential candidate Thomas Hopkins was thrown off the crowdfunding platform IndieCause today for violating their terms of service."

The balding head with a fringe of frizzy hair and serene face of the man I knew as simply "Thomas" were back on my screen. "This is outrageous," he said. "The terms of use are simply that one may not impersonate others, use copyrighted material without permission, or be 'vulgar, offensive, or inappropriate.' My fundraising is none of those things. It's simply that IndieCause doesn't care about free speech!"

They showed a solemn-faced black man in a suit—DeShon Roberts, the president of IndieCause. "The terms of service says that it's up to the platform to decide what is vulgar, offensive, or inappropriate. IndieCause finds Mr. Hopkins's material offensive and inappropriate and chooses not to host him any longer. I have no further comment."

I had further comments, but most of them were profane. "Can we change the channel?"

Destiny gave me a concerned sidelong look—eyebrows drawn together, lips pursed—and changed the channel to a rerun of *I Love Lucy*.

Abraham
Atlantic Highlands, New Jersey
February 25, 2019

I SAT IN MY wood-paneled study and did some research on the internet—I'd purchased a new PC when my wife moved in. She had a MacBook Pro, and I'd replaced an aging Dell with a newer model after she gave me a quick speech about computer security and out-of-date software. This was fair; the older Dell ran Windows Vista and the new one, Windows 10. Lucy, Destiny's tech, was dating an IT guy.

I hadn't discarded the elderly machine; I intended to find a different purpose for my faithful friend. My kind can be sentimental about familiar objects and outmoded technology. Computers were a new skill for me, but a person needed something to do when stuck indoors all day, after all. I made a mental note to research "best use for an old computer" after I finished my current search.

My study was a small, warm, brown space with a desk, a desktop computer, and a guitar and piano. Despite being "a Mac person," Destiny would often use my PC for quick tasks rather than pull her laptop out of its case. My Stradivarius traveled from room to room with me in case I had a sudden urge to play it—which I often did. I'd had my Stradivarius for over a hundred and... twenty? thirty? years, and it was a priceless instrument that I should have kept locked in a vault. Well. Not *priceless*; similar violins sold at auction for twenty million dollars. Each Stradivarius is unique, and not even modern science can figure out how to create a new violin like it.

That said, locking a musical instrument in a vault felt wrong. Musical instruments want to be played!

I researched Thomas. The usual suspects: Google, Wikipedia, news sites... It wasn't like him to be a political candidate. He preferred to act in the shadows, sending others to do his dirty work. Then again, it was unlikely that an independent candidate would win.

Thomas Hopkins was called things like "the most dangerous man in the US." His "church," the Foundation for a Safe America, was at the top of the Southern Poverty Law Center's list of booming hate groups and received regular scrutiny from the Anti-Defamation League. His "church" had lost its nonprofit status for endorsing political candidates. Good. A string of prisons had fired him for his views, and he was currently making his living running the "church," as an internet personality, and as a political candidate.

I had what modern Americans call "dirt" on Thomas Hopkins. Unfortunately, I didn't think I could share it without sharing "dirt" on myself. No, outing Thomas wasn't my job. Besides, would his followers even care?

I'd spent all night on my research. Destiny wandered over in her bathrobe and peered over my shoulder. "Why are you torturing yourself reading about that loser? Who cares what he thinks?"

"I know him." I glanced up into her surprised eyes. "He's a vampire. And I don't want him to find me."

Ludwig
Rosenheim, Bavaria
October 14, 1762


I WOKE UP ravenous and desperately thirsty. The only food in my room was a dry crust of bread on a plate next to my ink and quills and scraps of calligraphy practice. I devoured the bread and promptly had to rush to a chamber pot to vomit it back up. Was I ill? I clearly needed more guidance on those "dietary requirements" Father Thomas had mentioned. I did successfully swallow a cup of water, but it didn't satisfy my thirst. How odd.

There was a knock at my door. One of the younger boys told me that Father Thomas wanted to see me, so I followed him downstairs.

There was a disturbance in Father Thomas's office. I went in and glanced around.

A tall, thin, pale, sandy-haired priest was staring angrily at Father Thomas. "Imposter! Boy, did you know this man was an imposter?"

"What?"

"He's not Father Carl from Bern!"

I was confused. *Of course* he wasn't Father Carl, he was Father Thomas!

"You must be mistaken," Father Thomas said, serene as always. "This has been my flock for years."

"I am not mistaken! The Vatican sent me here! To check on Carl, who hasn't reported back since being stationed here two and a half years ago!"

"How do you know I'm not Father Carl?"

"Carl and I attended seminary together," the priest said through gritted teeth. "Are you even a priest?"

"They betrayed me!" Thomas thundered. "In 1505, they defrocked me, solely because I refused to obey a political order to release a prominent Jew in exchange for money! I, who had discovered entire covens of witches, who had found nearly a hundred Jews who had claimed to convert, only to practice their filthy ways in secret! And when I refused, when I defended my important work, they dared to excommunicate me! They dared! And you dare to question me?"

I was horrified. Torture was no longer considered enlightened, although it had not been abolished. And he was an imposter? All our sacraments for the last two and a half years! Had our dead all died unshriven? Were our babies all unbaptized? Were our weddings invalid? All our confessions...

Had he truly said 1505?

The sandy-haired priest stared at Thomas, open-mouthed. "You're mad."

Father Thomas tilted his head at the priest for a moment, then lunged and bit him. He shoved him up against the wall, just like—I was certain of it—he'd done with me.

"What are you doing?" I squeaked. "You can't... he's a priest!" *And you're not!*

Thomas glanced at me, holding the priest against the wall with one hand pressed across his mouth. "So, dear boy, about your new dietary requirements..."

I made an impatient sound in my throat. This was not the time to discuss that. "Please, Father, don't hurt him."

Thomas smiled at me. "I won't hurt him."

I breathed out a sigh of relief.

"You will." He smiled again, a malicious smile. "Feel your teeth."

I poked my teeth with my tongue. They felt oddly sharp. I tilted my head in confusion.

"You're a vampire."

I... what? Vampires were supposed to be oversexed undead things that killed indiscriminately. I stared at my hands. They appeared normal, if pale. I felt my face, and it felt like my own. I didn't feel dead, or undead. Nor did I feel lewd or violent.

What had he done to me? I hadn't agreed to this!

"Bite him," Thomas ordered.

I crossed my arms and backed away. "He's a priest!"

"And you promised to obey me," Thomas said.

"I also promised to defend the Catholic faith! I will not harm a priest." I backed all the way to the opposite side of the room.

Thomas rolled his eyes and muttered under his breath, and made a gesture at me—thumb and fifth finger extended out, others curled like claws, almost like he was controlling a marionette—then beckoned. Suddenly, I felt more like the shambling undead of legend. As if asleep, I walked over. I stood next to him, frozen, trapped in a nightmare.

"Bite him," Thomas ordered.

My body obeyed the order, but tears sprang to my eyes. I bit the priest's neck, and blood poured into my mouth. To my horror, I found it delicious.

"Swallow," Thomas said, sounding exasperated.

I drank, and I drank, and I kept drinking until the poor priest fainted, and still I drank, following his body down to the floor. I drank until there was nothing left to drink. Finally, Thomas released me.

I curled up in the fetal position on the floor next to the body of the priest, put both hands over my mouth, and moaned, "I'm going to hell..." I cried for the poor slain priest.

"Now that you've murdered a priest," Thomas said, his tone dark and malicious, "I think you need to ask your parents for some money so we can move to another city."

I stopped crying—shocked out of my grief by anger—and sat up to glare at him. Had he done this to me merely to gain access to my family's money? I hadn't killed the priest; he had used me as a weapon. "You made me do it! Perhaps I will get money from my parents, but I'll leave without you!"

"I admit," he said, sounding grudgingly impressed, "you have more spine than I initially credited you with." Then he explained I knew nothing of vampire life and still needed him, and that he'd only done it for my own good, so I would fully understand my new nature and its darker side. I was still angry, but he did somehow convince me to take him with me when I left. Not that I remember how he did it.

# Where I Began

Ludwig
Berlin, Prussia
October 31, 1762

**M**y new rooms were adequate, if plain. I lived over a bakery, so it was always warm in the winter and smelled divine. Sadly, I couldn't eat their products. I patronized a local butcher—I love the early sunsets of the darker months of the year—saying that the blood was for my cook to make blood sausage. It occurred to me that perhaps I could eat blood sausage myself, but this wasn't the case. I tried it raw and cooked, both with unpleasant consequences. It both lessened my thirst and made me vomit up the parts that weren't blood, concentrated into small balls like owl pellets. Revolting.

What had Thomas done to me? All my plans for my life, gone. All the people I knew would grow old and die without me. Would I ever see my parents or brother again?

I supposed that the only bright spot was that my hair was safe, though it no longer grew. I collected rings, but I only had so many fingers on which to wear them. I supposed I needn't dress humbly anymore, either. I indulged my vanity, thinking that if this was my worst sin, I was doing quite well under the circumstances.

I invested in and collected art. It turned out that I had a knack for it, even if it was distressingly like trade. I prospered, and Thomas eventually came around to visit, discuss theology, and, occasionally, borrow money.

He also taught me the ins and outs of being a vampire, although he laughed at me when I asked if there were any books on the subject. He impressed upon me at length the importance of only giving the gift of eternal life to the best and most worthy individuals. This was flattering, but he didn't have my devotion to the arts. "Imagine," I said, "if one were a painter, or a composer, or a performer with centuries available for practice!"

Thomas merely smiled, indulgent. "I fear that's your passion, not mine. But keep an eye out for those you consider worthy."

I didn't *like* Thomas, but I felt like he knew things I needed to know. Sometimes we would fall into our old patterns of him being a teacher and an authority. I wasn't certain how to change that.

---

Abraham
Atlantic Highlands, New Jersey
February 27, 2019

WE FELL INTO A ROUTINE where I would feed Ivan things like cow's blood or raw bloody chicken livers liquefied in "the cat's blender" for every meal. Inanna sniffed his dish a few times, appeared confused, and went back to her own. Mmm, the scent of iron.

By the way, it was almost two months since Victoria had died. I still cried every time I saw a picture of her. I didn't want to forget, but remembering hurt so much...

"I'm sorry," Destiny said one morning as Ivan lapped up blood enthusiastically, "but that's... yucktastic." She winced and poked at her scrambled eggs, her lip curled. I tried not to find this comical.

I'd replaced the lace tablecloth with one with a floral pattern. She was wearing the cozy blue bathrobe and bunny slippers again. Well, I supposed the bathrobe was warm; the house could be a little on the drafty side with the high ceilings and aging windows. I was wearing the same jeans and T-shirt I'd worn the day before, and thought I should change, on principle.

I smirked at her. "We all have our dietary restrictions, it seems."

She snorted out an almost-laugh. "So, what made you want to be a vampire?"

She'd asked me this before, and I'd given her a glib answer with a hand wave. Destiny was my wife now and deserved a proper answer. I sat down at the table next to her, and Ivan finished his breakfast and climbed into my lap. "It wasn't my choice."

She glanced up at me, surprised, fork suspended in midair. Her head tilted, making her long red braid visible between head and shoulder. A car that needed muffler work drove past the house. Destiny took a sip of coffee, ate another bite of eggs. "What happened?"

"What do you know about kashrut?" I asked, looking up at her.

"I'm not sure I know what that is."

"Kosher."

"Oh." Destiny bit her lip. "No bacon double cheeseburgers?"

I laughed at that and reached over to squeeze her hand again. "Good start. How detailed do you want me to get?"

She shrugged. "As much as you want to tell me, but at least enough for me to understand the point you're trying to make."

I looked her in the eye. "Blood is not kosher. The process of kashering meat starts with it coming from a kosher animal and being killed in a kosher way, but you have to remove all blood from the meat, by rinsing and soaking in water, then salting, then rinsing several times. Also, if an egg contains blood, you're not allowed to eat it. You don't just crack an egg into a bowl of ingredients; you crack it into a different container first so you can check it for blood. No blood. Not even fish blood, which isn't considered actual blood, so it's not technically *treif*, but you don't want to give the appearance that you're consuming blood." I bit my lip and petted Ivan some more. This was a bit, as the modern Americans say, "heavy," but I remembered Destiny's question and smiled. "Also, no bacon double cheeseburgers. Or cheeseburgers."

"Okay," she said, sounding thoughtful.

I hugged Ivan, who was looking back and forth between us, almost as if he could understand the conversation. "I considered going to a rabbi and asking if it was covered under *pikuach nefesh*, but I was too afraid he'd say no."

"Peh... what?"

"*Pikuach nefe*sh. The principle that preserving human life overrides any other commandment. I was afraid that he'd say that no, I was no longer human and that if I really wanted to uphold *pikuach nefesh*, the least I could do is never feed off a human." I avoided biting the innocent, for what it was worth. If I got a little snack in the course of self-defense, however... "I was probably being dramatic. It's allowed to eat non-kosher food if it's necessary to sustain life or cure an illness. But blood is extremely taboo." I sighed. "And then there's blood libel."

"I'm sorry." Destiny smiled, looking sheepish. "I don't know what that is, either."

I loved her innocence. It almost felt wrong to explain, but I did.

"People believed Jews made Passover matzohs with the blood of Christian children. It was used to justify violence, often around Easter, since Easter and Passover are so close together." One year, they even burned my neighbors' house to the ground. I could hear them screaming. My brother Samuel played with their son...

"That's stupid," Destiny said. "How could people believe anything so dumb?"

"People believe an astonishing array of dumb things." I scowled at the table, then petted Ivan again when he glanced up at me. I didn't want to upset Ivan, but it felt like every antisemitic stereotype was either a role they forced us into—moneylending had been considered "usury" until recently and a sin for Christians—or the exact opposite of the truth—see above.

"You don't talk about this very much," she said. She sounded surprised.

No. No, I don't. I was conflicted. For what are obvious reasons. I couldn't walk to synagogue in the daylight—short distances only, like from the house to the car in an emergency, and then only if I completely covered my skin with SPF-rated fabric and if I didn't stay out too long. I wore gloves, a scarf, an enormous hat, sunglasses. I looked like a cross between a beekeeper and the Invisible Man, and sometimes told people I suffered from porphyria, if they asked. With those items, I couldn't stroll around the block, but I could drive. Without, I needed to run indoors at vampiric speed. In other words, I couldn't participate in religious services any more.

And even if I could walk to synagogue, Kohanim are forbidden to have contact with a corpse in Leviticus 21:1, so would my presence force them to pray somewhere I wasn't? Do I need to explain what a Kohen is? A Kohen is a descendant of the sons of Aaron who still have specific honors and restrictions, including blessing the congregation at some services. They wouldn't know unless I told them, but *I* would know.

I hadn't davened—prayed—Shacharit or Mincha, the morning and afternoon prayers, with a minyan of ten Jews in over a century because I would burst into flames walking to the synagogue on Shabbat. It felt like another life ago. I suppose it was. I could have joined a Reform or Conservative congregation, which allows driving on Shabbat, but I was old. The Reform movement started during my lifetime. Before the Reform movement, people were just plain Jewish. I didn't identify with any of the modern movements. And frankly? I could accept reformed liturgy, but drew the line at organ music. Also, I would need to park very close to the building, and suspected that if I called a rabbi and asked for his halachic position on vampires joining, I might find myself having an awkward conversation with a mental health professional. Also, there was the matter that the dead are released from all obligations, including keeping kosher. Was I dead?

Animal blood is treif—not fish blood, but fish blood is *disgusting* and also doesn't quench my thirst; I tried!—and it's also not very tasty, but it was better than attracting the attention of modern law enforcement. Bullets hurt, and you had to fake your death, assume a new identity, move... No, best to avoid the whole thing. I'd managed some actual human blood with a forged doctor's prescription to treat a blood disorder—I supposed I did have a blood disorder of sorts—and claimed I had a private nurse to administer it. I had an in with a sympathetic blood bank employee, as blood is only good for transfusion for three to six weeks, but I could still drink it after that. I'd told the blood bank employee it was for my dissertation research. I also felt like anyone who physically assaulted me was fair game—for a small snack, nothing too serious—but people were so law-abiding these days. Placing myself in harm's way felt like entrapment.

That said, the United States was absolutely the best place for a vampire to live. All Castle Doctrine this and Stand Your Ground that and self-defense. But again, best not to attract the wrong sort of attention. Shoot an attacker with a gun, yes, but bite him with your fangs? Too much explaining to do.

I scratched Ivan's ears, and he gazed up at me with bright, sweet, attentive bronze eyes and purred.

"So you understand," Destiny said.

I glanced up.

"My vegetarian thing."

Destiny's vegetarianism isn't religious, but... "It was... an adjustment," I admitted. I spent a lot of time under bridges starving, subsisting on rats, only drinking people who attacked me. I wouldn't wish that on my wife, but it wouldn't *be* like that for her if she became a vampire. She would have me.

"You can admit it without undermining your case," Destiny said, smiling.

I smiled back. "All right. Yes, I understand. It was an adjustment for me, too, but I still don't want you to die."

"I know, sweetie," she said. "The cycle of birth and death is holy in Wicca, but it also sucks balls."

I laughed. I couldn't help myself.

"At least, the death part does, and you can't have birth without death. You have to have death to make room for new births." She tilted her head. "If it's true that vampires are infertile, is that why the world isn't overrun with them?"

Well. It was true that vampires are only created one way, and that way wasn't birth, but we're not indestructible and I don't consider vampire overpopulation to be an argument against turning. In fact, Flora told me most of us don't make it past two hundred.

There are arguments for turning sooner rather than later that I won't use because they're, as the expression goes, hitting below the belt. My previous girlfriend broke up with me after a date where I swore spectacularly when the waiter spilled my drink on me and he answered, "Dude, don't talk like that in front of *your mom!*" We'd been together for twenty years. I still remember the way her face went into a slow fall. I don't want Destiny to even imagine how that would feel. No. These days, if I like it, I put a ring on it, as the modern Americans say.

In fact, the idea of Destiny dying of old age made me want to go sunbathing, but that's *not* a fair argument and I refused to use it. I try to be an ethical person, despite my condition.

"So," Destiny said, "tell me about it. How were you turned?"

———————⟨✍⟩———————

Abraham
Berlin, Prussia
February 10, 1841

AS THE LAST LINGERING, sweet note from my violin echoed through the dark room, my patron clapped. Baron von Dunn dressed in an ostentatious, old-fashioned style and refused to go out during the day, citing the need to keep his complexion pale. He wore expensive rings on all of his fingers, including his thumbs. His golden hair was pulled back into a soldier's queue and tied with a ribbon. His apartment over a bakery was well appointed, if not to the latest style, and he lived alone (aside from a servant, of course) despite the occasional efforts by matrons on behalf of giggling young women who found him attractive. Sometimes I thought, from the way he looked at me, that those young women had the wrong idea entirely, but it wasn't my place to judge.

Especially because I was a liar. The academy wouldn't accept Jewish students. I'd stammered out the lie that I was a convert when I stumbled over my new name—my teacher had been standing right next to us—and I felt guilty about this, and also had no idea how the baron would react if he learned the truth.

I'd probably imagined those looks, anyway. I knew that I had classmates who were rumored to be romantically involved, but we'd never actually discussed the matter. In other words, what did I know? I still remembered the scarlet cheeks of the older man I was studying with at the Yeshiva. "Young Avrahom, you are both very innocent and quite the radical!" Oh, sure, the passage in Leviticus is usually translated as *You shall not lie with a man as you do with a woman, it is an abomination*, but the original Hebrew is ambiguous, in my opinion. Loosely *Not underage male woman's lying-down*. I believe it's a reference to our ancient Greek neighbors.

He wasn't the wealthiest or most sought-after patron in Berlin—in fact, many thought him very odd indeed—but he liked my playing and I didn't mind if he was odd, as long as he paid. To be honest, I was too sick to play, but I needed the money.

This night, he had a friend over: a tall, balding man with a fringe of frizzy dark hair whom the baron introduced simply as Thomas. Thomas watched me gravely, with something in the position of his eyebrows and the wideness of his eyes implying I'd unwillingly impressed him.

My hair, unfashionably long, flopped over my face. But my father had died. You're not allowed to cut your hair during the shloshim—the thirty days after the funeral—which I'd missed, of course, because of travel. I received word that my father would die and rushed home. I'd arrived on the last day of the Shiva, the seven days after the burial where you wear torn clothes and weep, and your friends come by to feed and comfort you and say the Mourner's Kaddish with you. I stayed for the shloshim with my mother and my brother, Samuel, before returning to Berlin. Berlin felt cold and unwelcoming after visiting home. I loved Berlin—the hustle, the music—but it's hard to pretend to be someone you're not, and mortality reminds you of who you are.

"That was lovely," Baron von Dunn said. "You're very gifted." He had the faintest hint of Bavaria in his vowels. I wondered how long he'd lived in Berlin, and if he had tried to moderate his accent like I had. Of course, I was a native Yiddish speaker, which was a bit more... *fraught*... than Bavarian.

I bowed. "I'm glad I pleased you, Baron."

He stepped forward and pressed a bag of coins into my palm, which I pocketed without counting, and I thanked him again. "Don't you think he's gifted, Thomas?"

"He plays beautifully," Thomas said, sounding reluctant, "but you know that, unlike you, music isn't my passion." His voice was soft, quiet. The rooms were over a bakery, so it was warm and everything smelled of bread and cake. Despite being rented rooms, they were still luxurious, with dark-paneled wood walls and rich red carpets and sofas and heavy draperies, and a glittering chandelier. Thomas stood in the shadows, as if he didn't want to be noticed.

I coughed, filling my handkerchief with blood. My hand was full of wet, red cloth. I kept enough self-control to put my violin in its case rather than dropping it. My chest ached, and I was tired and dizzy.

When I looked up, the baron was watching me, blue eyes glittering. "Are you well, Abraham?"

I was most definitely not well. On the way back from Wreschen, I had caught consumption. I mumbled something about how I would be fine and straightened up... and had another coughing fit. A bit of blood escaped the handkerchief and dripped down my wrist. I thought I might faint and placed my clean hand on a table to steady myself.

The Baron watched the blood drip down my arm and land on the thick, red Persian carpet with an expression I couldn't parse. He licked his lips, swallowed, with his eyes locked on my bloody hand.

Was he angry? "Forgive me," I said.

He lunged at me, almost faster than my eyes could make out... or was that my dizziness? Either way, quicker than I could react. I had a strange hallucinatory vision of long, pointed teeth rushing at me, followed by a sharp pain in my neck and the press of his body against mine as he held me up. The room spun, darkened, and I reached up to cling to him in a desperate attempt to stay on my feet. I was cold, and the room was getting darker and darker. My last impression was of a lock of blond hair brushing my cheek.

When I awoke, I was lying on the floor with blood in my mouth—had I coughed up more blood? bitten my tongue?—and Baron von Dunn was kneeling beside me. I was tired, disoriented, and thirsty. Colors appeared more vivid, noises louder, and the room brighter, but I thought that was from passing out. The room spun, majestic, slowed, stopped. I found myself staring at a gold and crystal chandelier, about four feet tall and three feet in diameter, crystals glittering in the gold and rainbow candlelight. I'd never seen anything so lovely. How had I not noticed it before?

Thomas stepped out of the shadows and eyed me, one eyebrow raised.

Had I fainted? Why was I lying on the floor? How embarrassing! I moved to sit up, but I was still dizzy.

"I'm afraid you're going to need to forgive me, Abraham," the baron said. "I couldn't bear the thought of the world losing your talent."

"What?" Clearly the most brilliant thing I could have said. I rubbed my face with my hand—the one that wasn't bloody—and glanced around. The room was still colorful, bright. Baron von Dunn's clothing had a subtle pattern in it I hadn't noticed. I could hear voices outside, almost well enough to make out the words. I'd never fainted before; perhaps imagining that I had heightened senses was a result.

"Well," he said. "It was presumptuous of me, but I've cured your consumption."

I sat up and felt my neck, which was smooth and dry. Had I imagined him attacking me? "I don't understand."

"Of course you don't," the baron said, and smiled. Had his teeth always been so sharp-looking? Had I ever seen him in so bright a room? "It's all right, my dear boy. You know how, through transubstantiation, wine becomes the literal blood of our Lord Jesus?"

I nodded, although as a nice Jewish boy, I didn't believe a word of it.

He smiled. "The cost of the cure is that you need to drink more literal blood."

This was a cure I wasn't aware of, but of course I'd thought there was no cure. "How much blood do I have to drink?"

The baron laughed at me. "I've made you a vampire, you silly boy."

Like the Polidori novel? Was this a joke?

I stood up to leave, but staggered to the rich blood-red couch instead. I was so thirsty, thirstier than at hour twenty-five of the Yom Kippur fast. "Can you have someone bring me a glass of water?"

Thomas made a sort of irritated grunt and rolled his eyes.

The baron laughed again, but he rang the bell. A frightened-looking maid came in, a young woman with frizzy blonde hair, and he said, "Greta, offer your wrist to Abraham."

What?

The maid walked over, timid and thin and sad, and rolled up her sleeve. Pale bruises covered her wrists, with a single set of puncture wounds near her hand. I could see the pulse point in her wrist under the faint light green and lavender bruising. She held out her wrist to me and watched me, her eyes expectant. She smelled like fresh-baked bread—or perhaps that was the bakery downstairs.

"I don't understand," I repeated.

"You're being obtuse," the baron said.

"With respect, Baron," I said, "I don't understand this joke and think that I should go." I tried to stand, but I was so tired and so thirsty...

"You don't believe in vampires," he said.

"I don't," I answered. They were a Christian cultural concept, mostly familiar to me from my Christian neighbors, or from literature translated from English. Our custom is to sit with a body, never leaving it unattended until it's safe in the ground, and to put them in the ground as soon as possible. We would know if one got back up and walked around. Okay, there was the alukah, but I was clearly not one. They're described in the *Sefer Chasidim* as a living human being that drinks blood and can shapeshift into a wolf. Also, they're usually female. And not undead, whatever that is.

"I would pick a rationalist," he muttered, and moved with inhuman speed to stand next to Greta and bite her wrist. He offered it to me.

I recoiled in disgust.

Baron von Dunn grabbed her bloody wrist in one hand and held my shoulder down with the other, and shoved the wrist at my mouth. I fought. Blood is not kosher, and human blood... revolting. But some of it got in my mouth, and to my horror it was as delicious as Shabbat dinner. I thought of home, of my mother's fish with raisin sauce, followed by soup, followed by a meat course, all with wine and challah bread... Would I ever be able to share Shabbat with my family again?

"It's all right," he said. "It's just like taking communion. Feel your teeth, boy!"

I put my fingers in my mouth, and yes, my teeth were longer and pointier than they'd been. I stared at him.

Thomas stepped closer, and the maid recoiled visibly at the sight of him.

"Go on, boy," the baron said. "It's all right. I pay her well for this. Just like communion."

I drank a little because I was so thirsty, but I cried a little too. I didn't want to harm the girl, and it also appalled me to be drinking something so unbelievably treif. I was nineteen and had never broken kashrut before. Not even as a poor student; I always had an excuse where I claimed I had food at home, or would only eat a whole fruit or vegetable.

"It's all right, silly boy," the baron said. "See? She's fine, and so are you. Blood is a constant presence in our faith, not only in communion but also in our art. The more pious, the more bloody, it seems. It's what binds us together as Christians. The Eucharist, and Christ's blood, is our connection to our neighbors, our fellow parishioners, and all of humanity. Please tell me you're not a reformer."

"I'm a Jew," I blurted out. "We don't drink blood."

The Baron drew back. Thomas hissed and crossed himself. Even Greta appeared shocked, the shock driving the sadness from her eyes.

"You told me you converted," the baron said, his voice wary. Thomas glared at him; I don't think he noticed. His eyes were locked on me.

"I lied," I admitted. "I just wanted to attend the academy…" I knew it was a mistake as soon as I said it, but it was a relief to not lie anymore.

"I'm going to ask you to leave and never return," Baron von Dunn said, his voice quiet. "Still, I'm glad that the world didn't lose your gift with the violin."

Yes. There was no point in explaining anything. I was sad but also felt a lot less guilty about my lie. Clearly, the truth had been a mistake.

I stood. "Thank you for your past patronage." I nodded to Greta. "Thank you for…." I picked up my violin and headed towards the door.

"You're just going to let him leave?" Thomas asked. His eyes glittered malevolently, but his voice stayed almost serene, which somehow was more threatening than shouting would have been.

The baron closed his eyes for a moment, exhaled slowly, and said, "Yes." Then he stared at me with eyes that were both sad and worried, and that frightened me even more.

Thomas growled, and I gathered up my things and left quickly. I didn't know what the alternative was to their letting me leave, and I didn't want to know.

As I descended the stairs, I heard Thomas say, "The gift of eternal life is only for those who believe. 'And whosoever liveth and believeth in me shall never die.'"

The baron responded, "That's a spiritual reference, not a reference to our kind," as I passed out the door and beyond the point where I could hear them... which was much farther than it had been before.

When I got back to my lodging, I counted the money the baron had given me. A gold mark, three silver thalers, and a handful of groschen. Enough to go home and ask Rabbi Mendel what to do about this conundrum.

On the other hand, one should never ask a rabbi a question if one doesn't want to hear the answer. The rabbi is there to offer his scholarly opinion, not to tell you what you want to hear. Did I want to go to the rabbi who'd trained me for my bar mitzvah and tell him I'd become some kind of monster and wanted his halachic opinion on the most observant way to be a monster?

Yes! But also no, because I thought I wouldn't like the answer. The answer being, of course, that drinking blood is wrong, if possibly covered under pikuach nefesh, and drinking human blood is worse than wrong, and that drinking human blood until someone dies is murder.

Perhaps I could merely ask him if I was an alukah, but I didn't want the answer to that question, either. I wondered if I could turn into a wolf. I closed my eyes and concentrated, but if I had that ability, I had no idea how to use it.

I was exhausted, so I slept.

Abraham
Berlin, Prussia
February 11, 1841

SLEEPING WAS A MISTAKE. I woke up ravenous, and when I peered out the curtain, I burned my fingers on the drapes. I couldn't leave my boardinghouse, and I was hyperaware of the other tenants. I had a loaf of bread on my dresser, so I tore off pieces and devoured them... and promptly vomited them back up, violently enough that I felt motivated to not try again.

I knew the cellar had rats, so I went downstairs. It had previously been cold and dark and damp, but I no longer felt the chill like I used to, and saw better in the dark. Was I dead? I didn't want to be dead!

There were indeed rats, and there was also a quiet peeping noise in a remote corner. I grabbed and drank a rat. I couldn't bring myself to say the blessing for a meal over rat blood. Still starving, I went to investigate the soft sounds in the corner.

A brown striped tabby cat was nursing three very tiny kittens. She hissed as I approached, but I offered her the rat remains and she accepted the gift, gnawing hungrily at the carcass. Her kittens were so slight and helpless, little blind fluffy things.

The landlady—a sallow, sour-faced older woman with graying hair—came downstairs. "What are you doing?"

"I was looking for some charcoal to draw with," I lied.

"Oh no, you didn't! Again?" I thought she was talking to me, but she headed towards the cat.

The cat hissed and drew itself up, hackles raised.

"What are you doing?" I asked.

"I can't believe she had kittens again," the landlady said. "She's here to eat rats, not to populate the cellar with cats. I'll have to drown them."

"What?" Judaism forbids cruelty towards animals. We're allowed to eat meat, but kosher slaughter is intended to be humane. We're not supposed to take eggs while the hen is sitting on them, and if you ask twenty Jews to explain the prohibition against mixing milk and meat seventeen will say "Because the Torah says so," one will say it was a pagan ritual, one will explain that it's insensitive to mix symbols of life and death so cavalierly, and one will suggest that you should think about how the poor mother goat would feel to know that not only had you killed her baby to eat it, but that you were cooking it in the milk she produced to feed it. Drown kittens?

"Drown them. I've drowned dozens of them. What, do rich music students' families not drown unwanted kittens?" She curled her lip at me and reached towards the nest of kittens. The mother cat snarled and slapped her hand away with her claws. Rich red blood bloomed under the scratch marks, smelling deliciously of iron. She swore.

"I'll be leaving this evening, and taking the cat and her kittens with me," I said with as much dignity as I could, even though the smell of her blood was making me salivate.

She laughed at me. "Such a ridiculous soft thing you are! Take the cat, if she'll let you. Good riddance! But you're paid through the end of the week and I won't be giving a refund." She reached a hand towards the nest. "Let me drown just one, as payment for the scratch..."

I grabbed her hand and glared at her face, very aware of the delicious smell of her and the blood dripping onto the floor. My stomach growled. We stared at each other for a moment, and her expression changed—eyes wide with the whites showing around the edges, pale cheeks. I didn't want to hurt her, and hated frightening her, but I wouldn't let her hurt the kittens.

"You'll leave now," she said.

"I'll leave tonight."

"Let go of my hand! I'll call the authorities and have you removed."

I'm not proud of it, but it was the desperate hunger and the threat of the authorities, along with the smell of blood, that did it. I bit her. I didn't kill her, but I left her lying unconscious and bleeding on the cold floor and suspected death would come for her soon enough. I hid her behind some boxes.

I needed to leave, to hide. If I was arrested, well. Jews had only been citizens since 1812.

I walked over and kneeled in front of the mother cat. "Trust me?" I reached out slowly and stroked her head. I think she understood that I'd defended her and her babies, because she let me pick them and her up and put them all in an old crate. I draped a blanket over it and took them upstairs.

I packed rapidly, watching the light under the window fade, and after sunset I headed out with everything I owned. We moved into a dark place under a bridge. I named the cat Rebekah, and I hunted for her and her babies until they were old enough for her to teach them to catch their own food, a hilarious process involving Rebekah doing little pantomime ballets with dead or mostly dead rats and mice for her kittens. I named her children Jacob, Rachel, and Reuben. I slept in a pile of crates during the day and kept blankets for Rebekah and her kittens.

It was a far cry from my life in Wreschen. Despite what the landlady had said, I wasn't rich. I had a small inheritance from my grandfather that wouldn't last long. Part of me thought that life under a bridge was what a monster deserved. I thought about my mother and my brother, Samuel, often, thinking of evenings at home by the fire, comfortable chairs, delicious food, and unconditional love. Well. I supposed I had unconditional love from Rebekah and her kittens, but I longed for human companionship.

I was desperately hungry, but I was never tempted to drink my only friends. I drank from rats, and from bandits far from my bridge, and longed for home, but what if I lost control like I had with the landlady and bit a relative? I wanted the company of humans but felt as if, as a monster, I didn't deserve it.

One night, a man followed me under the bridge, slow and stealthy. I thought he was a thief, although something felt familiar about him. I was going to attack him, but as he stepped closer, I realized he was wearing ostentatious, old-fashioned clothes under his cloak, and was extremely pale. Rings glittered on all ten fingers.

Baron von Dunn and I stared at each other for a moment, awkward.

He burst out laughing. "Abraham! I can't drink you, can I?"

"No," I said, "I suppose you can't." I was smiling, though. I was having so many emotions, including anger that he'd done this to me and abandoned me, but I was so lonely that I was also relieved to see a familiar face... and it *was* funny.

"Ah, Abraham," he said. "You have no idea how hard this has been for me. No one has your talent with the violin, no one!"

Oh yes, it had been hard for *him*.

"I even broke ties with Thomas over it. He thought we should kill you, but destroying your gift would be the greatest sin imaginable in my eyes. God gifted you for a reason!"

Lovely. I supposed I should be grateful that he thought I should live, but I was having trouble feeling gratitude here under my bridge. Besides, I didn't know who Thomas was, besides the baron's friend.

"And then poor Greta died unexpectedly."

Had she really died unexpectedly? I supposed he didn't seem the sort to waste his favorite food source.

He shook his head. "Play for me one last time. Like you used to. Please, Abraham."

I was so desperate for human companionship—even his—that I pulled out my violin and played. The most difficult pieces were simple, natural, although the violin felt brittle under my fingers. I put the sorrow of being separated from my people, the death of my father, my longing to go home, into the music. Even Rebekah and her kittens couldn't resist and sat at my feet, enchanted.

Baron von Dunn wept, tears flowing down his face, silent sobs shaking his body.

The last note faded away.

Baron von Dunn stood transfixed, still weeping. Then he blinked, as if waking up from a nap.

"Scheherazade," he breathed, "you could tempt me to stay here until dawn."

"Why would I want to do that?"

He laughed and pulled out his coin pouch. Instead of removing money, he removed all his rings and his pocket watch and put them in the purse and handed it to me. "Don't live under a bridge. You're destined for greater than this."

I took the money and said nothing.

He stared at me, tears drying on his face. Things were awkward again. He adjusted his collar. "Take care."

I bowed with a flourish that might have had a sarcastic edge. When I straightened up, he smiled at me, tipped his hat, and left. When I thought he was out of earshot, I muttered, *"Heng dikh oyf a tsikershtrikl vestu hobn a zisn toyt."* Hang yourself from a sugar rope and you'll have a sweet death. I opened the coin purse. It was full of marks and thalers. The rings were even more valuable.

I invested the lot in my brother's bank's new Berlin branch.

———————⸿———————

Abraham
Atlantic Highlands, New Jersey
June 11, 2019


OVER BREAKFAST—DESTINY was eating eggs and toast this morning, from the Ren Faire dishes, as it was getting to be Ren Faire season, while Inanna ate her kitty health food and Ivan ate a dish of pureed chicken liver—Inanna glanced up from her dish and gave Ivan a long, appraising look.

I tensed, ready to stand.

"Abraham?" Destiny was wearing an oversized T-shirt advertising the Indigo Girls this morning.

Inanna swaggered towards Ivan.

"No," I said. "Inanna, no."

Inanna looked me in the eye with an irritated expression and butted Ivan away from his dish, maintaining eye contact with me.

Of *course* she did. Of *course*. If only cats understood rude gestures. It was probably inevitable, based on their previous relationship, and I suppose we were fortunate that it had taken four months for her to try it. Fortunately, Ivan was such a sweet boy that it seemed unlikely that he would do anything about it...

I stood. There was a tense moment while Ivan watched Inanna eat his breakfast, and then, with preternatural speed, he slapped her with his claws out.

Inanna sailed across the room at high speed, leaving a bloody spray behind her and hitting the blue stove with a wet thud and the scent of iron. Blood pooled on the black-and-white checkered floor and sprayed up towards the ceiling.

Destiny screamed and rushed to her cat, grabbing a dish towel to press into the wound. Ivan appeared confused and distressed. He stared down at his bloody paw, then at me.

"I can fix it," I said.

"I think you've done enough," Destiny sobbed. She picked up Inanna, still applying pressure to the wound, and glanced around. "Carrier. Oh, gods, it hit the jugular..."

"He didn't realize his own strength." I stepped closer. "I can fix it."

"I'm sorry," Destiny said, holding Inanna in a towel and pressing the wound. "Ivan is a monster." I felt a moment of hurt, protective rage, but she continued, "He might violate dangerous-dog ordinances. If the county knew..."

In a flash, I was standing between Ivan and Destiny. Behind me, Ivan meowed plaintively. "I'm a monster," I reminded her. A scary monster who used to lurk under bridges and creep out at night to hunt criminals and vermin in the dark. Was that really what she thought of me—*her husband*?

"Abraham..." She was uncertain now, her voice rising as if in a question, as if she understood the insult she'd given.

Some of my anger bled away at her uncertainty, leaving exasperation. "Let me help!"

She laid Inanna on the table, moaning, "This is a mistake. This is a mistake!" I don't know whether she wanted to atone for her faux pas, or if it was a moment of weakness because she didn't want her cat to die, but... time was of the essence.

I bit my wrist and used the feeding syringe to drip my blood into her mouth. I could have bitten her, but I thought she had already bled enough for it to take. The transformation is more likely if there is an injury or ill health involved.

This was a calmer transformation, as these things went. She shuddered rather than thrashed. Well, there was no blood clot to dissolve. Where Ivan took about half an hour, she took about ten minutes.

She stood and gazed up at me, and glanced at Ivan, and then sat and started washing her bloody fur energetically while her wounds closed.

"It's a mistake," Destiny said. "If the county finds out, they might try to put them down."

"That would be a bad idea. They can't just give them an overdose of anesthesia," I said. "They'd sleep it off. The only way would be to cut off their heads."

Destiny stared at me in shock.

"And I remind you," I added, my voice sounding uncharacteristically cold even to my ears, "that Ivan is *my* cat and I will not allow that." *God help Animal Control if they try to take my cat. My wife has never seen me kill, but if anyone tries to harm Ivan... I'd have to change my name and move, of course, to avoid Thomas, but I'd risk that for Ivan.*

"I love Ivan, too." She stared down at Inanna. "And I love Inanna, but this is a mistake. She's a *bitch*, Abraham. The sweetest cat in the world, but she won't do what she's told and attacks landlords and delivery people, and you gave her super strength and a taste for blood."

"Well," I said, "on the upside, since they now eat the same thing and she might have a newfound respect for Ivan, at least I don't expect cat fights."

"Oh gods," Destiny said.

"Yeah, don't break those up," I said. "Leave them to me."

I stared down at Inanna, who gazed back at me with a shocking deficit of sass in her bronze eyes. "From now on," I told her, "you do as I tell you, young lady."

From Destiny's expression, she was thinking something like it was a good thing that cats don't speak English. What she didn't know—and what I didn't tell her because I didn't think it would further my cause of turning her—is that I have some sway over my fledglings. I don't know the exact depths because my maker never explained it, and I'm not an asshole, but… it's enough. Inanna attacking people from this point on would no longer be cute, and I wouldn't allow it, so it would only happen if I weren't at home.

I loved Inanna, but if I were to choose my forever companion, it would have been Victoria. Victoria and Ivan. It had been five months and nine days since she died, and true to what I told Destiny, I had gotten to where some days I was fine and then it would hit me out of the blue that my sweet, precious girl was gone, that she had died in my arms when I was too stupid to notice, that no amount of money could bring her back…

Ivan started lapping Inanna's blood off the floor.

Destiny
Atlantic Highlands, New Jersey
June 11, 2019

I'd put my foot in it this time.

I carried Inanna into the bedroom and shut the door. She wriggled loose and glanced around the room, curious, like she didn't understand why we were in there.

It was clear from his expression—the compressed lips, the flash of hurt in his eyes—that Abraham considered my calling Ivan a monster the same thing as calling *him* a monster. I don't think of Abraham as a monster! He's a person with human reason who understands his condition.

Ivan is a cat. *A cat.* He's adorable, but he hurt my sweet girl, Inanna, because he's *an animal* and *doesn't* understand his situation.

And my apology for calling Abraham a monster was to let him do the same thing to my darling Inanna as well. Turn her into... whatever Ivan was.

By the way, Inanna was a precious angel baby with me. She hadn't warmed up to Abraham yet, but lots of cats are one-person cats and I thought Inanna was one of them. She's such a sweetheart that when my landlord said she'd lunged at him, I assumed he had a cat phobia! But multiple people had said the same thing. When I was home, she calmly watched the repair people or whatever. She was a darling at the vet. My cat was only aggressive if I wasn't there to tell her it was okay.

I... I needed to commit. I mean, I was committed to Abraham. We were *married*, but I needed to fully commit to having a vampire husband. Like, he wasn't an unusually soulful Goth with a medical condition; he was a *vampire*. He was an immortal being who'd come to terms with his state, more or less. A vampire who seemed to hate being a vampire in some ways and consider it a nifty cure for disease in others, rather than seeing it as a disease. If Abraham didn't see it as a disability, neither should I.

I lay down on the bed, on top of the white comforter, and Inanna curled up on my chest and purred like nothing had happened. I kissed her on her soft head and told her she was a good girl.... even though she'd left bloody paw prints on the bed.

If Inanna was going to outlive me now, I hoped she planned to warm up to Abraham, eventually. I even envied her eternal life with him for a moment. Unfortunately, the cost was still more than I wanted to pay.

# Ludwig's Tale

Ludwig
Berlin, Prussia
May 28, 1840

I attended a concert at the Academy of Music. Late, because I had to wait until after sunset. My footsteps echoed on the beige stone floors despite my attempt to be quiet, but no one appeared to notice.

The violinist was a lovely young man, with the androgynous beauty of an angel—neither completely male nor completely female. His thick, dark hair fell into his face. When he played, he sometimes closed his large doe-like eyes in bliss, and it was simultaneously profoundly spiritual and like the descriptions I've heard of carnal ecstasy. I felt like he'd permitted me to see something intimate, not in a crude way, but as a gift.

I approached him after the concert, while he was talking with a teacher from the school, a stern-looking older man. I bowed and introduced myself. "Do you have a patron?"

He smiled shyly. "I do not." He spoke with a gentle voice and had a thoughtful quality. There was nothing of the vulgarity of some performers about him.

"Tell me about your financial situation."

He bit his lip. "My tuition is paid; I used an inheritance from my grandfather. My parents gave me money for an apartment, and it's enough to cover my rent." He smiled. "As long as I don't eat extravagantly."

So, better than some, worse than others. I pulled out my purse and counted out some coins and handed them to him. He thanked me and bowed.

"What is your full name?"

His eyes darted around the room, and he stammered, "Abraham... B-Braun."

I laughed. "Are you certain?"

He chewed on a fingernail and stared at the floor. Finally, he admitted, quietly, "I'm a convert."

His teacher patted his shoulder, comforting and fatherly, and walked away to talk to another student.

"Oh." I blinked and considered this. I'd never actually met a Jew before. I patted his shoulder comfortingly, much like his teacher had. "I'm glad you told me."

He shuffled his feet, appearing miserable. A flush colored his tawny, pale skin.

I leaned closer. "Am I making you uncomfortable?"

He blushed and nodded.

"We will speak no more of it," I said. "Forgive me, I can be... well. We will speak no more of it." I was never good at dealing with people.

"I'm not offended," he said, but his cheeks were very red.

"Do you feel able to play a little more for me, or are you too fatigued?"

"I can play."

I led him back to my home, to my drawing room, and gestured for him to play. He took out his violin and played, and without the other instruments, it was even more sublime. I'm a harsh critic; I have supernaturally enhanced hearing and trained for music early in my life, but this... The sound was luxurious, like the rarest silks and velvets, colorful and bright like a stained-glass window, rich and heady and addictive like the finest wine. This was a beauty that would haunt my dreams.

He finished, and I sat there, breathless.

He glanced up at me with his huge, soft dark eyes, and asked, "Did my playing please you?"

I huffed out a quiet laugh. "It was transcendent."

He smiled, a genuine, flattered smile, and for a second my heart stopped. I pulled out my purse and handed him more coins.

"Come back tomorrow," I said.

He blinked in surprise, but all he said was, "If you like."

.

Ludwig
Berlin, Prussia
May 29, 1840—February 10, 1841

ABRAHAM CAME BACK the next night, and the next. I couldn't get enough. I had found the recipient for my first gift of immortality. I wanted to ensure that this wonderful young man could play for me long after his contemporaries had died. No one was more deserving of the gift. I told Thomas that I had someone whom I intended to make one of us, and he said he wanted to meet this person. I told him that Abraham was a brilliant musician, but as to his being a convert? Thomas didn't need to know everything.

Sadly, Abraham's father was deathly ill, and Abraham had rushed home. I waited patiently for over two months for him to return so I could offer him eternal life.

His playing the evening of his return was magnificent, as always, although he appeared a little pale and needed a haircut... to be honest, I liked his hair long. Once his bow touched the strings, I barely avoided weeping at his music. His exquisite playing was a tangible thing, like a wave, like a brush of fingers.

"That was lovely. You're very gifted."

Abraham bowed. "I'm glad I pleased you, Baron."

Abraham coughed, and his handkerchief filled with blood. He still managed to put his violin away. He coughed again. There was so much blood that it escaped and dripped between his fingers, trailing down his arm to the elbow and onto the carpet. The scent of it was intoxicating, but I knew what it meant: Consumption. Consumption and death.

My family raised me knowing that a nobleman, a leader, must sometimes make the difficult decision. I wasn't Abraham's baron—his *Freiherr*—but I saw no reason to let him die. Quite the contrary.

So, I bit him. I took him into my arms, as if he were my bride, and buried my teeth in his neck. My lips brushed his soft skin in what was almost, but not quite, a kiss.

He was delicious, despite the consumption. Sweeter, more subtle and complex than the finest wine—what I purchased at the butcher's was swill next to this. He was warm and yielding—or perhaps too ill to fight me off.

I was determined that he wouldn't suffer during the transformation. I drank until he passed out, then gently lowered him to the floor. I brushed his overlong hair out of his eyes, bit my wrist. I dripped my blood into his unconscious mouth, pressing my wrist to his pale lips, trusting his instinct to swallow.

Thomas watched, impassive.

I remembered convulsing when I turned, but Abraham merely kicked weakly and shuddered. His transition was quick and gentle; he must have been very ill. I'd turned him just in time.

When he awakened, I said, "I'm afraid you're going to need to forgive me, Abraham. I couldn't bear the thought of the world losing your talent."

"What?" He blinked his beautiful eyes at me.

"Well," I said. "It was presumptuous of me, but I've cured your consumption." Surely, he would be pleased that I'd saved his life.

He sat up and felt his neck, as I had done. "I don't understand."

"Of course you don't." At least, I didn't think he'd guessed my nature. "It's all right, my dear boy. You know how, through transubstantiation, wine becomes the literal blood of our Lord Jesus?"

He nodded.

"The cost of the cure is that you need to drink more literal blood."

He still didn't seem to understand. "How much blood do I have to drink?"

Finally, I resorted to, "I've made you a vampire, you silly boy."

And then he asked for a glass of water, of all things. As if that would do him any good.

I rang the bell for the maid, with whom I had a financial relationship regarding my dietary needs. I've never cared for hunting. "Greta, offer your wrist to Abraham."

"I don't understand," he repeated.

I offered him Greta's wrist. He drank—not as much as I would have liked—but he also cried. Thomas grimaced, and despite feeling more sympathetic, I had to agree with Thomas's dismay. This was not how I had pictured this going. I'd pictured welcoming Abraham into a new vampire family, moving him into my home. I'd pictured him being grateful that I'd saved his life.

"It's all right, silly boy. See? She's fine, and so are you." I rhapsodized about the role of blood in art and liturgy, but he merely looked dismayed. I was finally driven to adding, "Please tell me you're not a reformer."

And then he destroyed everything with a couple of sentences. "I'm a Jew. We don't drink blood."

Thomas hissed and crossed himself. I felt like the floor was falling away from my feet.

"You told me you converted."

"I lied," he admitted. "I just wanted to attend the academy…"

He'd lied.

"I'm going to ask you to leave and never return." I sighed. "Still, I'm glad that the world didn't lose your gift with the violin."

"You're just going to let him leave?" Thomas asked.

I closed my eyes. Thomas would harm him, kill him. Thomas would destroy his gift. I couldn't allow that. I took a deep breath and said, "Yes."

Abraham gathered up his violin, thanked us, and left. I think he grasped the danger he faced.

Thomas said, "The gift of eternal life is only for those who believe. 'And whosoever liveth and believeth in me shall never die.'"

"That's a spiritual reference, not a reference to our kind," I said. Thomas had proved that by pretending to be a cleric and murdering a priest. He was a poor excuse for a Christian.

"There cannot be a Jewish vampire!" Thomas said. "My family died of plague! My grandmother's family, all gone, she was the only survivor… only to die of the Black Death a generation later, along with my parents! We all know the plague was a Jewish plot, caused by poisoned wells! They all confessed under torture; they always do! And you would make a Jew an immortal?"

"I didn't know!"

"Go! Go to his lodgings and bring him back!" He made the marionette-controlling gesture at me.

I had no idea where he lived. He'd always come to me. I probably could have found him, but I clung to the technicality and I stood still, staring blankly at him while inwardly sighing in relief.

"It's been over three hundred years, and I still have the charm my grandmother gave me to protect me from witches. It's all I have left of her. Do you know what I went through in the hospital for orphan children? I was better off on the streets! There cannot be a Jewish vampire!"

I felt pity for his loss, but not enough that I would willingly find Abraham. It took a long time for him to release me.

I told Thomas that I didn't think we could be friends anymore, and he agreed with insulting enthusiasm.

<hr />

Ludwig
Berlin, Prussia
February 11, 1841—March 26, 1841

A RICH, LUXURIOUS SOUND haunted my dreams, with memories of dark hair falling into huge dark eyes. Eyes closing and lips parting in ecstasy as he played. The memory of his fingers caressing the strings of his violin pervaded my dreams, and I craved more. I attended other performances, saw other musicians, but no one had Abraham's gift. Worse, I was obsessed with his sad eyes as he left the last time I saw him. I prayed for guidance.

One night, Greta came over to offer her wrist, but she was pale and smelled oddly.

"Are you well?"

"No, Baron, I am not." She swayed on her feet.

"Well, I can't drink from you in this state," I said. "Why don't you rest, and we'll see how you feel in the morning?"

"I... thank you, Baron, I will do that." She wobbled off to her room and closed the door.

I read and practiced the piano all night, trying to take my mind off returning thoughts of a particular violinist. I wasn't completely successful, perhaps because I was just good enough at the piano to understand why I would never be great. My musical abilities were part of a nobleman's education, nothing more.

I was also getting thirsty, so when Greta didn't come downstairs the next morning, I went to check on her. The first thing I noticed was the stench of chamber pot. It was lying in the middle of the floor and had a vile white fishy-smelling substance in it. Her washbasin was full of a clear fluid that wasn't water.

Greta was unmoving on the bed. Her eyes were open and sunken, the skin on her face and hands was wrinkled, and she was most thoroughly dead. I wouldn't say that I considered Greta a friend, but her passing saddened me.

I went downstairs to the bakery and asked them to please summon an undertaker and a priest, and to send a message and a small bequest to her younger sister Ingred, of whom I knew she had been fond.

Arranging Greta's funeral took most of the day, and I grew thirstier and thirstier. Night fell, and I was forced to go out hunting. As I've said, I don't enjoy hunting... but I dislike it enough that it bears restating. I wandered out into the cold spring rain, looking for someone to bite. The butcher shops were closed, and I was getting dangerously thirsty.

I found myself thinking of Abraham, of the delicious taste of him. As I remembered, I found myself drawn to the underside of a bridge, for reasons I didn't fully understand. It was dark, and dirty, and cluttered with old crates falling to pieces, but there was a golden glow peeking out of the shadows. There were fewer rats than expected at such a location. There was a dark figure beneath the bridge that might have been stalking me.

It was Abraham! And, further, he was the source of the golden glow... but only when I closed my eyes, or concentrated. Was this the gift Thomas had promised so long ago? I was so relieved to see him, I babbled. "Play for me one last time. Like you used to. Please, Abraham."

He indulged me, for whatever reason.

He'd been gifted before, but the change! His new vampire senses, the speed of his fingers. It was richer than gold and gems, sweeter than honey, as clear and bright as the sun I haven't seen since the day Thomas turned me, sunlight sparkling on water. It was somehow both intensely spiritual and almost overwhelmingly sensual. And the grief of it! It was both crushingly sad and so astonishingly gorgeous that I felt like I'd seen and heard an angel. Tears streamed down my face, but I kept myself from sobbing aloud so I wouldn't miss a note. The sound drew even a colony of cats, who sat at his feet, and his lips quirked up at the sight of them. I was mesmerized.

As the notes faded away, I let a few sobs escape. I was trembling. I felt like I was waking up from a very sad dream. Finally, I whispered, "Scheherazade, you could tempt me to stay here until dawn."

"Why would I want to do that?"

I laughed. Why indeed? I gave him everything I had on me: all my money, all my rings, my watch. I wished I had more. I handed him the purse, telling him, "Don't live under a bridge. You're destined for greater than this."

He bowed, but it was an angry, sarcastic bow. Well, he probably believed I had wronged him. Had I?

On the way home, there was a man smashing the glass front window of a Jewish bakery, so I bit him and drank. I didn't kill him, and of course I didn't give him any of my own blood, so he would merely wake up in a dirty alleyway with a sore neck.

———⁓∞⁓———

Ludwig
Berlin, Prussia
May 12, 1841

I WAS SO TROUBLED by all this that I went to my priest and explained the situation—omitting vampirism, of course—and asked him if he thought I had done the wrong thing in cutting ties with Abraham. We sat in his office, in heavy chairs at a solid desk, surrounded by stone walls and floor and aging carpet. Father Markus was a young man with dark hair and thick glasses, and he leaned forward on his desk and focused as I spoke.

"Well," Father Markus said, "it depends on your conscience, and while it's unfortunate that your former protégé now lives under a bridge, you aren't morally obligated to continue your patronage if you choose not to, although one should always strive to be charitable. That said, perhaps your violinist is a good Jew. They exist."

I blinked. This wasn't an opinion that Thomas—or anyone else—had ever expressed to me.

"If you would like to know more, I would recommend the work of Moses Mendelssohn. While I don't agree with his faith, his philosophical work is irrefutable, and his is reputed to have been a man of excellent character. If you haven't read his books, you should."

I considered this. "Do you... do you think it would endanger my belief to do so?"

Father Markus smiled at me. "His works do not sway the reader to Judaism, although they do advocate for a better position for Jews in society. As to his thesis that the state has no right to interfere in the conscience of its citizens, well. If the Crown tried to force you and me to become Protestants, we would agree, wouldn't we?"

Yes. Yes, I would. The law that required all children of mixed Catholic and Protestant marriages to be raised as Protestants was bad enough.

"Thank you," I said. "I'm always pleased to have more books to read."

"I hope that I've given you some comfort," Father Markus said.

I wasn't sure that was how I would have described it, but I smiled at him and stopped at a bookseller on my way home.

———————— ⌘ ————————

Ludwig
Berlin, Prussia
May 28, 1841

SADLY, MENDELSSOHN'S *On the Civil Amelioration of the Condition of the Jews* and *Jerusalem* did not ease my mind. Quite the contrary.

Father Markus was correct that Mendelssohn's work was irrefutable. A sample:

*Brothers, if you care for true piety, let us not feign agreement, where diversity is evidently the plan and purpose of Providence. None of us thinks and feels exactly like his fellow man: why do we wish to deceive each other with delusive words?*

Abraham had lied to me, but he had lied to attend an academy that would have barred his magnificent talent based on his faith. I believe that Abraham would have preferred to openly be the man he was with no dissembling. I played back our conversation repeatedly, remembering his blushing discomfort and what I now realized was his deep shame.

Much like the shame that I now felt.

But not a shame that would permit me to miss a performance. He played publicly now, and I would always find him, always, and weep at the beauty. Both at the beauty of the music, and at a possible beautiful friendship that prejudice had caused me to let slip from my fingers.

After some years, he moved to London. There was nothing for it but for me to move to London as well. I refused to miss a single performance.

Perhaps eventually I would find the courage to approach him.

# Too Much Attention

Abraham
Rumson, New Jersey
October 17, 2019

The dog patio at Garden State Pizza was cool and windy, but Ivan sat on the table, glancing around and enjoying the night, much like he had on other visits. I wished I had brought Victoria here, but she'd been dead for over nine months. Also, she wouldn't have enjoyed it. But we—and Ivan—were regulars. He was a rare cat that enjoyed outings on a leash.

I loved the sound of the wind in the trees, and the foliage was at its prettiest. It's a shame that I can only enjoy the fall colors from indoors or after dark. It's my favorite season. Watching it on television, or at the movies, or on YouTube, wasn't the same. There wasn't the wonderful changing-leaf smell, or the crisp air. I could get those at night, but without the color, which is the best part. I supposed some lovely red and yellow leaves had landed on the patio, but they'd raked most of them away.

The waitress put down Destiny's pizza. She'd topped her previous most outrageous eyeshadow: cheetah spots. Instead, she'd painted her lids in sunset colors and drawn little trees in eyeliner tonight, and was wearing an excessive amount of perfume. A few moments later, the manager delivered my beer, a Märzen from Germany. I prefer an amber one in the Munich style, by the way. I inhaled the lovely, crisp aroma from the beer and took a sip. Yes, I can drink. It doesn't sate my thirst, but I can drink.

The gate to the patio squeaked open, and a man's voice shouted, "No! Freddy, no!" A medium-sized, short-haired black and white dog raced towards Ivan while a man tumbled after him. A woman rushed inside the fence, calling "Freddy! Freddy, no!" She was a pale woman with dyed blonde hair with gray roots.

I stood and interposed my body between the dog and Ivan, but couldn't move as fast as I'd have liked without outing myself as something preternatural. The dog tried to race around me, and I grabbed him. We wrestled for a moment before he slipped out of my grasp and caught Ivan in his mouth. *You motherfucker!* As the modern Americans say.

Destiny screamed. Ivan struggled to flail around in such a way as to get his claws into the dog, but the dog shook its head in that backbreaking motion. There was an iron scent and a splash of blood... I should have been faster, and to hell with the consequences. *Ivan!*

I gripped the dog by the collar and glared into his face. "Give me my fucking cat right now, *Schweinehund,* or I'll snap your neck." Then I seized his mouth with my other hand.

I didn't hurt the dog, of course. I only applied a little pressure to the lower jaw, but it was enough to surprise the dog into letting go. Destiny rushed over to Ivan and started examining him. She removed her sweater to press against the bite wound. It reminded me unpleasantly of Inanna's turning.

"What the hell? Let go of him!" the dog's owner, a man with graying brown hair and ruddy beige skin, said. "What kind of idiot takes a cat to a dog patio?"

I didn't release the dog's collar. I was too angry to speak English, so I stared at the dog as I cursed his master. *"Er zol vaksen vi a tsibeleh, mit dem kop in drerd!"* He should be buried like an onion with his head in the ground!

The dog gazed up at me and whimpered. *Good,* I thought. *You stay there and don't move until we leave.* I hesitantly released his collar, and the dog only moved to shrink back from me.

I glanced down at Ivan, who was eyeing the dog with a speculative, almost satisfied expression, but made no move to attack—although, as a vampire, he absolutely could. The dog stared back at Ivan, appearing disconcerted, like he knew Ivan's reaction wasn't that of prey. I shook my head at Ivan, who started washing his paw, then licked the blood off his back, acting very much like a cat who wasn't seriously injured. Apparently, Freddy the dog was smart enough to know when he was outclassed. I felt sorry for him, even though I was still furious that he'd hurt Ivan. I picked Ivan up and examined his wounds. They would have been serious if he weren't a vampire.

"Your dog attacked our cat," Destiny said, her voice shaking. "We had permission to be here. Leash your dog!"

"If you've hurt my dog..." The man knelt and examined his dog's neck and jaw. "He seems to be okay." He glared up at me. "Fuck off, shorty."

I'm *not* short. I'm a perfectly normal height for a man in 1841. In other words, about five feet five inches tall. And to think that in 1841 I assumed it would be my thinness that would provoke comments for all eternity, but then people had the absolute temerity to become freakishly tall. Ugh.

Oh, I understood I was supposed to feel my masculinity was being threatened. Sadly for him, I was raised that a manly man is clean, moral, and—assuming education and leisure—well-read on matters relating to Torah and Talmud. Even today, the "nice Jewish boy" is polite, studious, and gentle. By such standards, this rude, sweaty, shouting idiot was the opposite of manly.

I replied with the finger—so much for polite, but when in Rome... Ivan hissed at the man and his dog over my shoulder. The dog didn't move until the gate was closed, and then he crept under a table opposite the exit.

"I'm so sorry," the man's wife said. "You're right, we should have had him on a leash. We just weren't expecting cats."

"I understand," Destiny said, although she still sounded shaken. "It's all right. I'm a veterinarian and have had a lot of pets. Come on, Abraham."

I headed for the car with Ivan.

"That said, please be more careful in the future," Destiny said, her voice sounding more stern, with more of a vet's authority. Apparently, she had come to the same conclusion I had. "You should always leash a dog with a high prey drive. Next time he could chase another animal into the street and be hit by a car, or something."

"Yes, of course you're right," the wife said.

"It's a *dog patio*," the man shouted after us. I rest my case.

"They could call the police," the wife hissed back.

We couldn't call the police. There was someone looking for me. Too much attention.

The waitress and the manager were watching us leave with matching shocked expressions. Destiny shoved a couple of twenties into the manager's hand. The manager tried to argue with her, but Destiny was rushing to the car.

Ivan's wounds were already closing up. He would have died if he were still a mortal cat.

I was shaking, mostly with anger. "I don't think we can go back." I gazed down at Ivan, who was probably sore from the mauling. "At least we can't bring Ivan anymore, which makes it a lot less fun." No, we should never go back. Staying in one place rather than running away from Thomas was one thing; attracting attention at pizza parlors was another. I didn't know what I'd been thinking. I supposed I *hadn't*.

Destiny shook her head. "I don't blame the dog, I blame the owners. In particular, the husband."

"As the modern Americans say," I said, "fuck that guy."

Destiny laughed.

Ivan made a motion with his head that might have been cracking his neck back into place.

We got all the way home before I realized I hadn't even had the chance to finish my beer.

———————————⌒⌒———————————

Abraham
Berlin, Prussia
June 20, 1841

I STOOD ON STAGE in a pool of limelight, in a wood-paneled concert hall. As the concert ended and the house lights—candles and kerosene lamps—came up, I realized the baron was in one of the expensive boxes. He'd been to all of my public performances. I didn't know whether to be flattered or annoyed.

I also noticed a balding man with a thick, scraggly fringe, and prominent eyebrows in one of the cheaper seats. Thomas was also attending one of my concerts, and I didn't like it one bit. Neither did the baron, judging from his expression. The baron had said Thomas wanted to kill me, so I slipped offstage. I was finished for the evening, and knew the concert hall well.

I sidled out a side door and was met by a lovely blonde woman, tall and pale and willowy and dressed entirely in black. Her dress, while otherwise proper, plunged daringly at the neckline, showing a lot of décolletage. Wisps of pale hair escaped her bun and fell artfully over her face. She smelled of roses. She smiled at me and said, "I was hoping to catch you."

"Forgive me," I said. "I'm avoiding someone."

Her smile broadened, and I glimpsed fang. She was one of my kind. How had the concert hall attracted so many vampires? Was it me?

"Come with me. Those of us who are performers need to stick together." She spoke with a British accent. She gestured and led me to a carriage, where a waiting footman opened the door for us.

I don't know why I trusted her, but I did. I got in. So did she. The footman closed the door, and we headed down the street at a stately pace. The interior of the carriage was fine wood and plush velvets, but it was too dark to judge the color. Or perhaps the velvet really was black.

"I was told that you were extraordinary, and it's true!"

I murmured my thanks.

"Whom are you avoiding?"

I considered whether to tell her. I bit my lip.

She reached over and took my hand, and the gesture disarmed me.

"The man I'm avoiding was there when I... became what I am. He didn't want my... the one who made me a... he didn't want him to let me leave."

The beautiful woman's eyebrows drew together. "He... wanted your sire to take responsibility for you?"

"I think he wanted him to... unmake me, or something."

Her jaw dropped, and she blinked.

"Because I'm a Jew," I added.

She tilted her head at me. "I see." She considered this. "My maker was similarly concerned about faith." She rolled her eyes. "If I don't accept the religious authority of the Pope, why should I accept the religious authority of the king or queen? I can read now."

I liked her. She was her own woman, in an age that didn't encourage women to be their own people. I smiled at her. She smiled back.

Still, something I'd said was bothering me. "Can he?" Could I be human again, live a normal life with my family? I thought longingly of home, of my parents... of being able to keep kosher...

She squeezed my hand. "I don't understand what you're asking."

"Can he... unmake me... somehow? I might... if that's all he wants, maybe I should let him catch me."

The lovely blonde grasped my hand in both of hers and looked me in the eye. "No, Abraham. There is no cure."

That was incredibly disappointing. I closed my eyes for a moment. Time to change the subject. "What's your name, by the way?"

"My goodness," she said. "Where are my manners? I've been most shockingly forward." She released my hand and extended hers to me. "I'm Flora." She smirked. "I should probably introduce myself as Miss Lawson—as I am now the eldest surviving daughter because of what we are—but I've just pulled a strange man into my carriage."

I kissed her cool, pale hand.

"I'm here to play a vampire in a stage play." She made spooky hand gestures and giggled. "Who better?"

I was simultaneously alarmed and amused. Was she really so open about what she was? I supposed she wasn't avoiding anyone.

She smiled at me. "Let's find somewhere quiet to talk."

I was torn. I felt like I shouldn't lead her on if I had no intention of marrying her, and the Torah forbids interfaith marriages. On the other hand, what nice Jewish girl would tolerate my new dietary restrictions? I wouldn't be able to use any of our dishes or utensils for my food without treifing them (making them render *her* food non-kosher)—did that apply to the icebox? I supposed I didn't use the stove... And watching my wife grow old and die, and our children grow old and die? Perhaps I should seek a compatible vampire wife instead. I'd have to think about it.

I was getting ahead of myself. What can I say? She was incredibly attractive. Still.

My cheeks were warm. Surely I wasn't blushing. "Talking might be nice."

---

Abraham
Berlin, Prussia
July 8, 1841

ONE NIGHT, AS I LEFT the theater, there were four men waiting for me outside the door. They dressed like they had come for the cheaper seats. One of them said, "You have to come with us."

I crossed my arms. "I think not." I gave them a long, scornful look and turned to walk away from them.

One man grabbed me from behind, and I easily flung him off me. I turned to fight.

They were surrounding me now. One pulled a set of chained manacles from among the rubbish and swung them like a sling before striking me with them. He aimed for my face, but I raised my arm to block the blow.

Another pulled a wooden club from the alley. Another had rope.

I'd never been in a physical fight before, and I'm not a physically imposing man. That said, the man who'd grabbed me had been no match for my strength. I eyed the men, sizing them up.

In the shadows, a man approached. A man with a bald pate and a frizzy, dark fringe of hair, strong eyebrows, deep calm eyes. Thomas.

"I told you," Thomas said, "that you need to decapitate him. That, or burn him."

All right, now I was frightened. The air suddenly went cold. I didn't understand his enmity, but...

The man with the manacles said, "What, this skinny little thing?"

Oh, for... *fine*, yes, I had consumption when I was turned... I rolled my eyes and pondered that I was going to be privileged to enjoy an eternity of derisive remarks about my slim build.

"You can't join the order if you don't obey," Thomas

said. This caused a bit of an uproar among the men, and I took that opportunity to run away as fast as I could.

*"Dio mio!"* Thomas said, sounding frustrated, and raced after me.

Thomas and I tore through the dark streets, faster than any horse. I was a little faster, because I was running for my life. I ran into the dark places, under bridges, through alleys, and finally found a place to hide: next to a rubbish bin in an alley.

Thomas ran right past the entrance to the alley and kept going. When I could no longer hear his footsteps, I climbed up the walls—it was easier than I expected—and sat on the roof.

So, Thomas was sending thugs after me, and was giving them instructions on the most effective way to kill me without telling them I was a vampire.

Perhaps it was time for a change of scenery.

———————⌘———————

Abraham
Atlantic Highlands, New Jersey
November 6, 2019

I WAS SITTING on the red sectional in my pajamas with Ivan and Inanna, stream-bingeing *What We Do in the Shadows*—one can only practice violin so many hours a day, after all—when Destiny returned from work. She took off and hung up her puffy coat. She sat down next to me, still in her green vet scrubs; paused the show; and said, "Well, I had a day."

I raised my eyebrows and waited. She'd trailed a couple of fallen leaves in with her, and Inanna hopped down to sniff them. Destiny still smelled like disinfectant soap.

"A woman called in to ask if any of the vets were regulars at Garden State Pizza. Her dog has developed some disturbing symptoms, including a seizure, sun sensitivity, and vomiting, and she wanted to find out if Ivan was sick, too."

*Fuck.* So much for keeping a low profile. We really needed to stay out of police reports. "I didn't think the dog had consumed enough blood to turn!"

"What? Is that even a thing?"

"Drinking vampire blood is always risky. Draining the blood first increases the odds that it'll take, but..." Attention True Blood fans: vampire blood is not a drug. It won't make you high, but it might make you undead... depending on how well your body fights it. Perhaps Freddy had an undiagnosed medical condition... well, he had one now. If they'd tried to, as the moderns say, "put him down," he almost certainly woke up in a refrigerator. Poor thing!

Destiny covered her face with her hands. "I'm not a good liar, Abraham. I told her Ivan wasn't sick, but she could probably tell that I knew more than I was saying."

I sighed. "Offering to take Freddy off her hands would probably be suspicious."

"Very." She grimaced.

That poor dog. His owners would have no idea what to feed him.

I gazed down at Ivan, who was watching me with his large copper eyes. "We can leave town."

"Leave town? Over the dog?" Destiny's voice was high, almost squeaky, so I glanced into her ashen face. Her faint freckles stood out more prominently against the situational pallor. "That seems... excessive."

Perhaps, but it wasn't like I hadn't done it before, many times. I'd gotten comfortable here, which was a mistake. "I don't want anyone looking too closely at Ivan's health." Nor did I want anyone—particularly Thomas—looking too closely at *us*. The UK was calling to me again...

Destiny bit her lip. "My family is here! And my work."

"You don't need to work unless you want to..."

Destiny made a face. "You know I want to."

"...and I can arrange for you to have vet credentials under a new name, or even a practice of your own..."

Destiny stood and paced a little. "I don't want a new name! I want the nice, normal life I have now!"

Only Destiny could call having a vampire husband and two vampire cats a normal life. This was what made her the perfect wife for me. I smiled and almost laughed, despite the stress of the moment, and said, "Is your life really so good that you wish for nothing more than what you have?"

Destiny blinked at me and blurted out, "I want children."

We'd discussed this before, of course. I'd told her I couldn't, that perhaps we could adopt when the time was right. I supposed she'd decided the time was now. "And I'd like you to live forever. With me."

"That's your way," Destiny said. She sat next to me. "The human way is to have children. That's our immortality."

I fidgeted and stared at my hands. "My kind can't," I reminded her. "Flora and I adopted instead."

"That would be good enough," she said, "but a selfish part of me would like to carry the baby. My mothers did the artificial insemination thing..."

"What's the rush?"

"I'm twenty-eight, Abraham. Women's fertility declines around thirty-two, and I want two children... I've just always wanted the normal life my mothers fought so hard for."

I tilted my head at her.

"Lawrence v. Texas happened when I was eleven years old. When I was thirteen, my mothers flew to Canada to get married, and they could finally legally marry in New Jersey when I was twenty-two and in vet school."

I winced and made a mental note to hug Morgan and Bridget the next time I saw them.

"Yeah," she said. "I overheard them talking one night when I was ten. If Morgan had died, the state might have sent me to live with my grandparents instead of leaving me with Bridget, because Bridget and I weren't legally related. Bridget was legally *my roommate*."

*Ouch.* Maybe Bridget needed *two* hugs.

"Yeah," she said. "'Family Values' my ass."

I sighed. This wasn't the time, not with the accidental vampire dog situation. I suspected this could go badly. On the other hand...

Perhaps it was time to commit myself to the mortal life Destiny wanted. I had my immortal pets; I should give my wife her mortal children. Marriage. Compromise. "If we get through this unscathed, we can do whatever you want."

Destiny already had her mouth open to argue with me. She stopped, closed her mouth, blinked. "Really?"

"On the condition that we do an infant conversion and raise the child as a Jew," I amended. "Complete with Hebrew school."

"Conversion? What?"

"According to Orthodox and Conservative halacha, only children born of a Jewish mother are Jewish. Everyone else needs to convert." I took her hand. "I'm assuming, of course, that you don't want to convert. You've never expressed an interest before."

Destiny smiled a regretful smile and squeezed my hand. "No offense."

"None taken," I said. "In that case, the baby would need to convert. Otherwise, if they decide to be Jewish, they would have to study with a rabbi for a year and then go to the mikveh, while a baby conversion is just going to the mikveh."

"Mikveh?"

"It's a ritual bath. There are a lot of rules, but it's kind of like Christian baptism, only no one dunks you, you dunk yourself. For a baby, it's one second completely underwater. They can still change their mind and renounce their conversion later. This just keeps their options open."

"All right," she said.

I squeezed her hand. "Did you have your heart set on raising children in your tradition?" My previous children had come with their own faith, alas.

Destiny shrugged. "Wicca isn't exclusive; we don't care if you're Wiccan and something else." She blushed. "I honestly care more that they be a vegetarian."

I couldn't help but smile at that. "I have no problem with that." If the child was going to end up keeping kosher, which I would have preferred, being a vegetarian would honestly make that easier. Most kosher rules involve meat. "We're settled, then, although we need to see how this dog thing plays out."

"Do *you* want to have children now?" Destiny asked.

I did, Hashem help me. I closed my eyes for a moment. "I enjoyed being a parent."

---

Abraham
London, England
September 12, 1898

AS THE LIGHTS CAME UP—fully electric! So modern, and no more greenish tint—I bowed to the audience. The hall was round, with red and cream arches and decorative spandrels. I couldn't help but notice that once again, one of the plush boxes held a pale blond man with rings on all ten fingers. He had a season pass and never missed a performance. Sometimes he brought friends, sometimes he came alone. He always wept.

Tonight's performance was a recent work with a larger symphony, *Scheherazade* by Rimsky-Korsakov, which prompted a standing ovation at the end. We did a curtain call. People, including whatever Baron von Dunn was calling himself these days, threw roses at the stage. I bowed and picked up some roses for my wife with a smile. Flora also had a box and was holding court there with some of her fans. I bowed again, and left, and came back and bowed again... all very flattering. Of course, I'd had a lot of practice. I'd been playing violin for almost seventy years at that point.

I worked my way through the crowd and up to Flora's box and handed her a rose. Some of her lady friends giggled.

Flora Lawson was pale and blonde and willowy and astonishingly beautiful, and she wore all the latest fashions, only all in black. I didn't know if her charm and wit were some sort of vampire power, or if she'd used the centuries and observation to hone her social skills to perfection.

"Mrs. Lawson, you simply must come to my daughter's birthday party. She adores you!" one woman said to Flora—a wealthy woman, based on her clothing, but I didn't recognize her. Not that my not recognizing her meant much. Flora always teased me that I only had eyes for my violin.

"Oh, Lady Wallace, you know I'd love to, but as I've explained, Abraham and I can't go out in the sun because of our... condition." She smiled and winked, and the ladies all laughed. "I'd be happy to attend something after dark, of course."

I was uncomfortable with this line of wit, but Flora had been around longer than I had and had actually had a sire who taught her lore, so I deferred to her on matters of vampirism. Flora had known Queen Elizabeth; she'd mopped her floors, but had avoided the dreaded pox that led the queen to her heavy use of Venetian ceruse to cover the scars.

Vampires, or vampyres, had been the subject of literature in England since at least Polidori's *The Vampyre* in 1819 and Le Fanu's *Carmilla* in 1872, but they were enjoying some popularity post-Stoker, particularly in the penny dreadfuls (although nothing topped the popularity of the *Varney the Vampire* serial—1845-1847) and theatrical farces and extravaganzas. Flora not only made a big show of relishing such roles but also engaged in a lot of winking claims of being a vampire herself, intending that she would be disbelieved. My role in this little drama was that of the patient, long-suffering husband who played along. I'd read all of those vampire books, of course. There's something about seeing yourself represented, even if it's negative.

I was equally uncomfortable with my growing fame, but Lawson wasn't the name Thomas knew me as, after all, and Flora believed firmly in hiding in plain sight. Thomas had said music was the baron's passion and not his, and to the best of my knowledge, he was still on the continent.

The well-dressed woman—Lady Wallace—turned to me and smiled, clasping her hands in a show of delight. "Mr. Lawson, your playing was divine tonight! You're very gifted."

I bowed and murmured that she was too kind. I don't need to point out that the name they gave me at birth isn't Lawson, do I? That was Flora's choice of name.

"Please, bear upon your wife to make an exception just this once!" Lady Wallace continued. "The two of you would be the hit of my daughter's birthday."

I smiled. "Thank you, Lady Wallace, but my wife and I are on a strict evening schedule as performers. The constant late nights wreak havoc with one's sleep schedule." I glanced into the back of the box, where two children—a dark-haired boy and a blonde girl—were curled up asleep on the floor. "Speaking of late nights..."

John and Eliza were unrecognizable as the street urchins we'd taken in. They were clean, healthy, and dressed in the finest clothes money could buy, and we had a governess for them. John was eight and Eliza was five. Despite not really having a schedule, they would still fall asleep during my concerts. I was teaching them both music. I loved them with all my heart. My only regret was that I wasn't raising them as Jews, but they already had a faith when we found them. My people believe that the righteous of all faiths—or no faith, for that matter—have a place in the World to Come, so my regret was grounded in, as the Talmud says, a desire to replace myself on earth and continue the traditions of my father and mother, rather than any kind of fear for their immortal souls. Then again, what with the horrible situation in France with poor Dreyfuss, perhaps it was just as well that they were Christian.

"Yes, we should put them to bed," Flora said. "My apologies, ladies, but motherhood calls."

I handed Flora my Stradivarius in its case and picked up Eliza and held her in one arm, and held John's hand in the other. Eliza sleepily wrapped her arms around my neck, and John yawned and blinked. Flora and I took the stairs down to where the carriage was waiting.

When we got home, I took them upstairs to the spacious nursery with all the dolls and toy trains and put them in bed. Flora tucked them in, and we headed downstairs. A brown tabby, Ruth, was waiting on the sofa for us. Ruth, believe it or not, was a direct descendant of Rebekah. She immediately climbed purring into my lap. Her latest batch of kittens pounced and wrestled on the floor, occasionally squeaking if a sibling accidentally bit too hard in play.

We had servants, of course, including a ladies' maid and a valet. We pretended for them and went to "bed" late every evening and "slept in late" every morning in a huge four-poster bed Flora had draped in black for the mystique. There were coffins, hidden in a locked room in the basement, but we don't need a full eight hours a night. In fact, we nap only rarely. There were no maids paid to let us drink blood, like the baron had had. Our home was free of rats, for which we credited Ruth and her progeny. Sometimes someone would try to rob us while leaving a theater or concert hall, much to their sorrow. New vampires need more blood than older ones, so this sufficed. We couldn't simulate full chamber pots, but the staff was too well-mannered to question us on this point.

It was Flora who told me, on one of those nights, we couldn't have children of our own. Some human women claimed to have had children by a vampire, but Flora insisted they were all covering for affairs by blaming their pregnancies on their dead husbands. She said this is also the origin of the myth of the sexually insatiable vampire. In my experience, we have the same sex drives we had as mortals, although some of us grow curious or jaded over the centuries. That said, I can still picture the pale curves of Flora's hips and breasts in the moonlight, bright against the black velvet coverlet. I remember the silky-soft feel of her bare skin under my hands, the taste of her lips, the faint scent of perfume, the brush of her loose hair across my face and chest. Lying in bed with Flora, whispering conversation all night while we pretended to sleep, was my favorite part of the day. Judaism considers marriage to be the ideal state, and I agree.

That night, high-pitched child screams interrupted our time alone. We threw on dressing gowns and raced to the nursery. Eliza was sobbing in her bed, while her governess, Miss Robinson, a short, stout, square-faced woman, stood over her with crossed arms.

"Do stop, you ridiculous child! You're not allowed to wake the entire household. Hold out your hand." She produced a ruler from her pocket.

John got out of bed, stood between the governess and his adopted sister, and crossed his arms. He stared up at Miss Robinson with a grim resignation.

"What's going on here?"

"Mr. Lawson, I'm so sorry! Your daughter woke the household for no reason, is all. I'll take care of it."

I walked over to Eliza and hugged her. "What happened?"

"I don't want to die!" she whimpered. Tears streamed down her face.

I pulled her closer and kissed her on top of her head. I'd make sure nothing happened to her.

"Eliza had a nightmare," John said.

"It's all right." I gave Eliza another squeeze. "You're not going to die."

Eliza sniffled. "The little girl in the book Miss Robinson read to us died!" Her lower lip trembled, and another tear slid down her cheek. Her mother had died of consumption, coughing up blood and wheezing and gasping for air, clutching her chest... in front of Eliza.

I gazed at Miss Robinson, who drew herself up and squared her shoulders. "It's a perfectly normal book intended to elevate the spirits of young children."

"She's going to punish Eliza for having a bad dream." John had run away from an alcoholic home to escape beatings and wouldn't stand for them, not for himself nor for other children. I admired his courage.

"Miss Robinson," Flora said, her voice heavy with disappointment. "We discussed this with you when we hired you. We're very opposed to corporal punishment." We'd been opposed since the Eastbourne manslaughter case, in which a teacher had beaten a teenage student to death. That had been forty years previous, so Miss Robinson wouldn't have followed the case.

"Children won't learn without correction," she replied. "I'm sorry, but no one can actually teach under these conditions. With respect, you and your request are highly eccentric."

Flora stared at her for a moment, then burst into loud peals of laughter. This was apparently not the reaction Miss Robinson expected.

Since Miss Robinson didn't appear to understand the joke, I elaborated. "My wife likes to tell people we're vampires to promote her career, and as such we don't go out during the day, refuse to attend religious services, avoid garlic, and leave the curtains drawn tight at all times, but asking you not to beat our children is what makes us 'highly eccentric'?"

Miss Robinson scowled at me.

I skimmed the book on the nightstand. It was a gruesome description of a pious child dying, so I threw it on the fire. "We'll have no more of *that*."

Eliza appeared surprised and grateful. Miss Robinson opened her mouth and closed it again.

"Miss Robinson," Flora said, using her most charming voice, "I agree! We're highly eccentric! But I believe that the rate at which you're compensated and the quality of your living quarters and meals should make our odd demands more palatable."

"Yes, I have no objections to any of *those* things," she said. "I apologize, but I really must—"

"Your services are no longer required," I interrupted. "Please pack your belongings and leave. I'll have your final pay in the morning. In the meantime, I must ask that you no longer interact with our children."

John was staring at me with immense, grateful eyes, his lips slightly parted. I smiled at him, and he rushed forward and hugged me. As far as I was concerned, John and Eliza were perfect in every way.

"Thank you, Miss Robinson, that will be all," Flora said, her voice firm. She stared at Miss Robinson until she had left and closed the door behind her. "Of course, now we have to hire a new governess or send them to school. Education is the law."

"I won't be sending them to one of those dreadful boarding schools where the pupils are gnawed by rats, and Miss Robinson might be sadly correct about the prevailing philosophy of education in day schools, so we'll have to hire someone."

Flora glanced over at John and Eliza and said, "Can you sleep?"

Eliza nodded, her expression solemn. John eyed the door for a moment and nodded.

We wandered off back to bed.

"Can we turn Eliza, if she's that afraid of death?" I whispered.

"No," Flora whispered back. "If we do it now, she'll never age. We can give her that choice when she's fully grown."

We went downstairs earlier than usual to pay Miss Robinson and see her off, and for "breakfast," which comprised tea and bits of kipper sneaked to the cats when the staff weren't watching. Once John caught me in the act, and I pressed a finger to my lips and winked at him. He giggled.

Flora arranged for an advert for a new governess. "Eccentric couple opposed to corporal punishment seeks philosophically aligned governess for two children."

––––––––\~\~\~––––––––

Destiny
Atlantic Highlands, New Jersey
November 19. 2019

WE WERE HAVING a baby.

Okay, I wasn't pregnant yet. But I'd always wanted children, and the life that Morgan and Bridget had fought so hard for. They'd had so much paperwork—medical power of attorney, house in both names, bank accounts, wills, living wills—to simulate what heterosexual people got when they got married.

When I was a girl, I always wanted baby dolls. My Barbies got married, and I used Skipper as Barbie's daughter rather than her sister. When I played *The Sims*, I would always try to have big happy families and my Sims were all Family Sims. I went through a phase where I would dream that I was pregnant. I guess my biological clock went off early and often? Sometimes I would dream that I'd adopted children off the street.

Not that I'd wanted to drop out of vet school, or whatever, but you know. Um. Also, my previous partners were often but not always women. I didn't discriminate; I was an equal-opportunity dater.

I curled up on my side, and Inanna worked her way under my arm and pressed her back against my chest. Such a sweet girl.

---

Abraham
Atlantic Highlands, New Jersey
November 20, 2019

DESTINY SLEPT. I'd finished bingeing *What We Do in the Shadows*—vampire orgies! I'm sure that there are vampires who attend orgies *somewhere*, but all the ones I know are ridiculous fuddy-duddies. I was always shy. I suppose that if Flora had had a burning urge to attend one, I might have considered it...

Yes, I still love Flora. Still. Always. I'm not being unfaithful to Destiny, nor am I unfaithful to Flora in loving Destiny. I think I've heard it attributed to Isaac Bashevis Singer, but I just searched online and apparently it's Romain Rolland: "Everyone, deep down within, carries a small cemetery of those he has loved." My graveyard is full. It would take me a very long time to enumerate the losses, but I remember them all, from the first—my grandfather—to the latest: Victoria. I still miss the late nights talking with Flora, still sometimes have a flash of sense memory of being enclosed in a curtain of blonde hair moving over me, but that's gone forever, and I have to commit to the now. I don't begrudge Destiny her need to sleep, only her mortality.

I thought again of the idea that before I was born, my soul mate and I were a single soul that was shattered into two. I always found that idea romantic until Flora died. Declaring either Flora or Destiny my bashert—the word literally meant "destiny," I suddenly realized—felt like infidelity to the other in a way that two marriages over a century apart didn't. Could a person have more than one soul mate?

I pulled out the cat fishing pole. Inanna blinked at me lazily, but Ivan leaped around the room with vampire speed... and tore the feathers off. He trotted away holding them, looking proud. I took them back when he lost interest and tied them back onto the pole. He'd been an impressive little athlete before, but now... He broke the pole a second time. He dropped the feather bundle and headed to the back door, then gazed at me, expectant. I walked over and peered out the glass.

A medium-sized, sad-eyed, filthy black and white dog

sat on our back porch. He was so dirty that only the vague sense that he was like Ivan told me he was the dog from Garden State Pizza. "Hello, Freddy," I said, and wondered if his idiot owner was looking for him.

I opened the door, letting in a blast of freezing air, and he walked in, whimpering, head hanging, tail between his legs. He smelled appalling, like he'd gotten soaked and rolled in a pile of rotten roadkill. I could tell he was thirsty, so I closed the door and offered him a dish of cow's blood, which he lapped up. Then I said, "Well, Freddy, you stink, and it's time you had a bath."

Freddy stared at me for a moment, then followed me to the cast-iron clawfoot tub, where I washed him. I dried him with a towel, and patted him. "You're a good boy."

He responded by thumping his tail a few times. I wouldn't say he relished the bath, but he appeared relieved to no longer smell like enthusiastic decomposition.

Ivan came in and gazed up at Freddy, who lowered himself onto his belly and gazed up at Ivan. They sat like that for a moment, and then Ivan bumped noses with Freddy and licked him briefly on the face. Ivan is the best boy. Having a cat sire is a dog's worst nightmare, but Freddy had lucked out. Inanna would have made his life a living hell.

"What are you doing here, Freddy?" I asked. But I knew. On some level, he knew we knew what he needed, and his instincts had brought him to Ivan for help. Just like I can always pick out Baron von Dunn in a crowded room. He seemed to always find me when I was performing publicly, no matter where I was or what name I used.

We still had a dog bed from our last foster, and I set it up for Freddy and patted it. He jumped in, appearing grateful, and slept. I tied the feathers back onto the cat fishing pole and put it away.

If his owners—his previous owners—assumed he'd run away, this might be the best possible solution. I would take responsibility for my grand-fledgling, like I took responsibility for all my fledglings.

When morning came, I would tell Destiny we had a dog again. I hoped Freddy would be friendly to Destiny's mothers next week over Tofurkey. I'd have to pretend I had a non-contagious stomach malady, of course.

———————⌒∞⌒———————


Abraham
London, England
December 14, 1899


I'D RECEIVED AN UNSIGNED note asking me to meet, so I'd left my violin locked in my dressing room and was standing out in the park in the snowy dark, next to a fountain. I knew, somehow, who my correspondent was, so I was unsurprised when the man I knew as Ludwig von Dunn came out of the shadows. We stared at each other for a moment. He still wore his blond hair in a soldier's queue and had rings on all ten fingers, but had finally adapted to modern clothes—ostentatious, expensive-looking ones, in a bright royal blue.

"Abraham." He bowed.

"Baron." I didn't.

There was an awkward silence, and then he said, "I've been very proud of you, Abraham."

I stared, surprised.

He shook his head. "I realize now that I have wronged you, but you've done magnificently for yourself despite me and my failings. I hope that you'll consider forgiving me."

I tilted my head at him.

"I've come to realize..." He blew out a large breath and continued. "I'm not saying this as an excuse, more of an explanation. I'd never met... anyone of your faith before and had nothing but the prejudices of my youth to inform my reaction. After observing your behavior, and reading your Moses Mendelssohn, and much personal reflection, I've come to realize those attitudes are... incorrect." He bit his lip. "More than incorrect. Immoral."

There was an awkward pause. On the one hand, I genuinely appreciated the apology. On the other, he still couldn't bring himself to say the word "Jew." Finally, I said, "It's our tradition that you make amends first and then ask for forgiveness."

"Tell me what I need to do to make amends, then."

I bit my lip in thought. "It's a fair question," I admitted. "I honestly don't know the answer."

We stared at each other for another awkward moment. Curiosity warred with exasperation, but both had the same question. "Why now?" I asked. "You don't even like me!"

"How can you think that?" He took a step forward

but stopped. He stared at the ground. "I *love* you, Abraham. If I could have adopted you as a son, I would have. And your gift! I was simply... shocked."

"Adopt me?" What? Those sidelong glances he'd given me when he thought I wasn't watching were *not* paternal. "I was just a man who played violin for you!" Also, I already had a family. The baron appeared to be my age... but of course he was much, much older, I realized.

"There's a gentleness, intelligence, and sensitivity that comes out in your music," he said. "And you've always been modest..."

"With respect, Baron, you don't know me. You just admire my playing, which is kind of you, and flattering, but is not the same thing as being my friend."

He rocked back on his heels, but he said, "I understand your point, but that is again my failing as a man. Please give me permission to call on you at your home sometime."

"I..." I sighed, capitulating at the insistence of my better nature. "You may, but please arrange a time first to ensure that we aren't busy."

"I will, thank you," he said. "Thank you for being more reasonable than I deserve."

It was perhaps indelicate to ask at this juncture, but hopefully he would understand. "Have you... heard from Thomas lately?"

"He's up to his usual rabble-rousing in the slums," the baron said, and curled his lip.

So closer than I liked, but no sign of him yet. I'd discuss it with Flora later. "Thank you."

We tipped our hats to one another, and I turned towards home.

There was a faint orange glow in the house's vicinity. I glanced over my shoulder at the Baron, who walked over behind me and looked.

I hurried in the house's direction. The glow grew brighter as I walked. A fire engine pulled by a team of horses and escorted by barking Dalmatians raced down the street past us. I picked up the pace. If the house on fire was close enough to ours, we would have to evacuate.

There were bright orange sparks shooting up into the sky, and shouts and screams. Was it the Wilsons, who had children who played with John and Eliza sometimes? If one of our neighbors lost their home, Flora would offer to let them stay. Or the Smiths. Were the Smiths watching all their possessions going up in smoke?

As I rounded the corner at a run—well. It was not the Wilsons, nor the Smiths.

It was *us*. Our house. Our home was a barely recognizable nightmare mass of orange light and black charred wood. Sparks shot up into the sky. The roar of flames, men shouting, and the hissing of water pouring onto the fire dampened the sound of screams. Some perverse part of my mind tried to identify each scream. That was a child's scream. A woman screamed; I think it was sweet Miss Nussey, the governess, whose sister had died of abuse at a boarding school. That scream was probably a cat. There was a scent like cooking meat, but buried under the stench of burning wood and gas and kerosene and other acrid scents. The house was immense, and we had gas-lights. The heat from the fire and the steam were unimaginable. It was exactly as I've heard the Christian hell described.

For a moment, all thought, all comprehension, completely shut down. I stared dumbly at the blaze for several seconds, and then reason rushed back in. *Where was my wife?* I needed to get to my wife! I'm not a large man, but it took four adult men to hold me back. One of them grabbed my face. "You can't go in there!"

"Flora!" I shouted. "Has anyone seen Flora? Where are my children? Flora!"

A wild-eyed man walked over and shoved a crucifix into my face. "Your wife is in hell where she belongs, vampire! And those poor children are in heaven, safe from whatever evil plan you had for them. I know what your people did in Whitechapel! We all know! The head of our order told us what you were going to do to those children..."

*Where were my children?* My hands balled into fists. There were more screams, screams from women and children, coming from the house. They weren't dead, not yet. At least, the children weren't.

I broke free and put both hands on his throat and squeezed. "Where is my wife?"

"Upstairs," he said, and laughed. "Why don't you get her? Just turn into a bat and fly up there!"

There was something in his voice that...

He was lying.

I looked again, looked closer. Listened. There was a voice, almost inaudible over the roar and hissing of flames and water, so I let go of the man and darted towards the side of the house, pursued by a neighbor who stopped before he got too close to the blaze. Someone had piled heavy wooden beams against the cellar door. I ran to the door and started pulling the beams away in a blind panic, my vision tunneling to nothing but the beams. I was moving as quickly as I could, but that still felt like it was too slow...

"Help! Please! Help us!" It was Flora's voice! A child was wailing, and Baron von Dunn was beside me, helping me move heavy beams in the scorching heat.

"Flora!" I shouted, heaving beams out of the way. "Flora!" We moved the last beam and flung open the door.

My heart leaped. Flora stood inside, coughing, holding a screaming, crying Eliza in her arms. John stood beside her, his face streaked with soot and tears and his arms around her waist. I beckoned to them. "This way! Hurry!" I could almost touch them.

"Children first!" she said, tugging on John's arm. "This way!"

A gas pipe next to the door exploded, throwing me and the baron back against the fence and Flora and the children back into the house. Then the entire house collapsed in on itself. In the bright orange haze, I could make out burning wood falling on dark, screaming, writhing figures that were almost certainly Flora and the children.

I let out a banshee shriek and threw myself at the house, but hands with rings on all ten fingers were pulling me away from the fire, and a voice murmured into my ear, "I'm sorry, I can't allow you to go in there..."

"Let me go! Let go of me!" I screamed, but I wasn't able to break free of the Baron's grip as he dragged me towards the front of the house while I shrieked like a madman. My vision blurred, tunneled, turned into a sea of red as I fought to get to my wife and children, to be where they were...

Several other men held the wild-eyed man down on the ground, but he laughed. If Baron von Dunn had let go of me for even a moment, I would have committed murder in front of all those witnesses. I wanted to tear him apart with my bare hands. I struggled to escape the baron's grasp, but he was too strong...

I remember little else, but I found myself in a bedroom in a strange home with a woman I didn't know wiping my face with a cool, wet rag. I didn't care. I couldn't feel anything at all, no emotion, and my memory of everything after the fire was a blank, because nothing mattered without Flora, John, and Eliza.

Eliza, who had been so afraid of death. Brave little John, clinging to Flora's skirt, tear-streaked but still standing. And my beautiful, beloved immortal wife, my Flora, dead. Also, presumably my sweet Ruth, the last of Rebekah's line, and probably her kittens as well.

Baron von Dunn came into the room carrying a box. "You're awake." He sat on the edge of the bed. "I know it's soon, but... It's presumptuous of me, as always, but I brought you some things."

Things. I couldn't care less. I couldn't even bring myself to turn my head.

He opened the box and pulled out a violin case. "I brought your Stradivarius, in case that might bring you some solace." He placed my concert hall dressing-room keys on the nightstand.

I knew I should thank him, but speaking took strength I didn't have.

"I'll put it here, on the floor, next to the bed. Also, I thought you might like this." He pulled a tiny kitten, orange with white feet and chest, out of the box. "I remembered you like the creatures. I don't know how to care for them myself, so you'll have to help..."

I reached out and took the kitten. It was a girl, definitely old enough that she was probably weaned. She mewed and curled up on my chest and purred. She was sweet and adorable, and obviously I was going to keep her, but she wasn't my poor darling Ruth. If he'd asked first, I would have said no, not yet.

I cried.

# Life and Death

Abraham
London, England
December 15, 1899

Baron von Dunn said, "Forgive me for disturbing you, Abraham, but the undertaker wishes to know how you would like to handle the burial." He stood in the bedroom doorway, like he was poised to leave if I told him to go.

I didn't know how long it had been since the fire, but probably not more than a day or two. I glanced up from where I had curled up into a ball on my side around the as-yet-unnamed kitten. "Flora and the children were Christians, so you would know better than I." I noted I had reverted to German, but it didn't matter.

"Really?" He came in and sat on the edge of the bed. "You didn't want to raise the children as... your faith?" He had switched to German as well.

I sighed and looked back down at the kitten, kneading her paws on the blue and white quilt and purring in a low buzz. Devorah, I decided, would be a good name for her; it meant "bee." "I did, but they already had a faith, so I respected their existing beliefs."

"Ah." One foot fidgeted in what might have been embarrassment. After a moment, he added, "Would you like me to deal with the funeral arrangements?"

"Please."

"I will, then. But is there anything else I can do for you?"

I thought about it for a moment. "I would like for you to find me ten Jewish men who will come here and say the mourner's prayer with me. Preferably daily for a week."

Baron von Dunn blinked, paled, and appeared to grow more uncomfortable the more he thought about it, but all he said was, "I'll do my best."

I got out of bed, sat on the floor, and tore my shirt. "Thank you."

He left, and I rang and asked the maid to bring Devorah some raw fish. I watched her eat, and then she climbed back into my lap. She climbed up my chest and bumped noses and lips with me, did her buzzing purr some more, and curled up in my lap and fell asleep.

Ludwig
London, England
December 15, 1899


I WAS FAIRLY CERTAIN Abraham hadn't caught it, but I had. The man who set the fire, the man who thrust a crucifix into Abraham's face, had said *the head of his order* had told him what they were going to do to those children.

Thomas, despite—or because of—being a charlatan, always found others to do his dirty work, and always offered membership in an exclusive religious order as a reward. He'd offered it to me, after all. I was certain that the fire was the work of Thomas, my maker, and equally certain that Abraham *could not* know. He wasn't strong enough for that information.

I could protect him. I have a gift for hiding. All vampires have gifts; Thomas's is to influence the minds of others, and mine are hiding and seeking... among others. I always know the location of other vampires, if I concentrate. Abraham could board a boat to China and I would know to find him there—not by location name, perhaps, but a sense of direction and distance.

I... Abraham was still the only Jew I'd ever met, and his request that I find Jewish men to pray with him...

I knew Jews lived in Whitechapel, a poor part of town. In fact, the area was well-known for its overwhelming population of Eastern European Jewish immigrants, fleeing pogroms. I took a carriage there, through loud and dirty streets, and stopped at a building covered with Hebrew signage that I presumed was likely a synagogue, from the sheer proliferation.

It was a shop selling pickles.

The shopkeeper gave me directions, however, in exchange for a purchase of pickles that I couldn't eat. I thought that perhaps my housekeeper Martha might like them.

The actual synagogue was a more discreet building, with one small sign above the door. I stepped inside. It was somewhat like a church, clean and open, with wooden benches and an altar, only full of men wearing odd hats and shawls, mumbling and swaying together in a way that was both exotic and alien to my Catholic ears. One of them stopped and approached me as I came in, and the others trailed off and watched me with wide eyes and ashen faces, poised like they might flee.

Had they recognized what I was?

The man who approached me had thick glasses and dark hair, and a warm complexion like Abraham's. He paused and visibly straightened himself, took a deep breath, and kept approaching. He stopped out of arm's reach and asked, "Can I help you?"

I blurted out, "I'm a Christian!" It was stupid, but I didn't want them to think I was there to pray with them, I suppose.

The man pressed his lips together for a second and said, "Yes, I assumed that was the case. How can we help you?"

I felt astonishingly stupid and awkward, so I babbled. "My friend is Jewish and his house burned down with his wife and children in it."

The man blinked. "I'm sorry for his loss."

"He, um..." I took a deep breath. "He wanted me to find ten Jewish men to say a special prayer with him. For... the dead."

The man looked away, silent, lips slightly parted, with a slight crease in his forehead. Then he gazed back at me, his eyes gentle.

"Did I... remember that correctly?" I was still unsure about the social norms, about what I should and shouldn't say.

"Yes," the man said, his voice reassuring.

"Can... can you help me?"

"I can," he said, sounding very confident. "Where is your friend right now?"

"He's staying at my home. What do you need from me? Will these men help me as well? Are there ten of them?"

"There are indeed ten men here—a minyan—it's ritually important... as you might have guessed from your friend's request."

"Oh," I said. "Yes, that makes sense, yes."

The man nodded, but he shuffled one of his feet a little. "I... presume you do not live in Whitechapel, sir."

"No, but I can arrange carriages if you need them." I bit my lip. "Also, there's no need to call me 'sir' when you're doing me a great kindness! Mr. Weiss will do." I offered the man my card.

The man accepted my card gravely, reading, then looked up into my eyes and said simply, "This is what we do—usually for members of our congregation, but I'm very sorry to hear about your friend, alone and without other Jews, trying to mourn such a terrible loss. I'm glad he has a friend like you who is willing to help him."

I could only hope to be worthy of such kind words.

———————— ⌒∽⌒ ————————

Abraham
London, England
December 16, 1899

BARON VON DUNN RETURNED a few hours later. "The funeral will be tonight; will you attend?"

I nodded. Speaking took strength I didn't want to waste.

He kneeled on the floor next to me and brushed my hair out of my eyes. "Chin up, man, you're having visitors!" But his voice was gentle.

I tilted my head at him.

"The men to pray with you." He laughed, but it was an awkward rather than humorous laugh. "I went into the synagogue in Whitechapel, because I knew a lot of your people live there. You should have seen how they looked at me! Like I had come to murder them all! But when I explained what I needed, they were very kind." He smiled, a sad smile, and patted my shoulder. "Clean up, man. Sit in a chair!"

"They'll expect me to be dirty and sitting on the floor in torn clothes," I said. "It's our way."

Baron von Dunn appeared puzzled and dismayed.

"In fact, I'm not allowed to wash or wear clean or new clothes for a week."

There was a pause.

"I... I suppose your people don't go in for the British stiff upper lip, do you?" He tried to smile and failed.

"No, not in the face of death." I picked up Devorah and stood. "That said, I should receive them in a more public part of the house." Devorah gazed up at me, adoring, and purred.

"As you say." He stood. "Follow me."

We went downstairs to a wood-paneled sitting room, and I sat on the floor, on a plush, colorful patterned carpet in reds and browns. I wondered if the blood-red sofa was the same sofa he'd had in 1841. My kind can be sentimental, so it was possible.

I set Devorah down on the floor. She scampered around the room in a bouncy, bounding movement.

The doorbell rang, and a maid rushed to answer. Ten men in black wearing black hats came in, with two women carrying enormous dishes of food. It smelled *amazing*, like all my memories of home gathered up into savory dishes. It was so sweet of them to bring food that I wished I could eat it, and it smelled like it was expensive food for people who lived in Whitechapel. They placed the food on a heavy mahogany table.

One man, a young, grave, dark-haired man with glasses, sat on the floor next to me. He said nothing but patted my hand. I started crying, wordless, and he hugged me.

The woman, who had a scarf on her head, said to Baron von Dunn, "I'm Sarah. I brought brisket, and Chava made a cholent for you." I realized I was probably being offered their Shabbat dinner and tomorrow's lunch, but refusing it would have been an insult. Their accent reminded me of home; they were likely from the same part of the world as my family.

"Thank you," he said.

Chava looked at the mantelpiece, and quietly removed her shawl and draped it over the mirror there. It wasn't because vampires don't have reflections, by the way. We do; that was an invention of Stoker's. It's a Jewish tradition to cover mirrors when someone dies. Some say that it's to allow us to focus on mourning, but the Kabbalists say it's because when a soul leaves this world it leaves a void that attracts demons and evil spirits, and covering mirrors prevents you from seeing them, as they're not visible to the naked eye. Don't dismiss this as rubbish; the ghosts that haunt mourners are our turbulent emotions, our grief, our anger, or our despair. It was also superstition in both Britain and Germany to cover mirrors in a house where someone died so the spirit of the deceased wouldn't be trapped in them, but, of course, Flora and the children had never been here.

Based on their accent, I could tell my visitors were Yiddish speakers, so I thanked them in Yiddish. *"A sheynem dank."* They nodded at me, their eyes kind.

Several of the men sat on the floor with me, but none of them tried to engage me in conversation, which I appreciated. After I finished crying, the solemn young man closest to me said, "Are you ready to say Kaddish, or do you need a moment?"

"I'm ready."

He led us through the entire service in Hebrew. He had a lovely singing voice. The baron stood on the sidelines and looked like he was curious but trying not to stare. When the time came, I sobbed my way through the Kaddish.

By the way, if you've ever wondered what was in the Jewish prayer for the dead... nothing about death or the afterlife. It's a 2000-year-old prayer in Aramaic and opens with the line "May the great name of God be exalted and sanctified" and various forms of it are part of each service. There are debates about how this prayer became the prayer to say for the dead, but some explanations include that you're saying the prayer for the dead person, who can no longer say it themselves, or that you're saying it as a sort of character witness for the dead. You're supposed to say it daily for thirty days for a spouse or child and eleven months for a parent, but after the seven days of shiva I was supposed to go to them rather than them visiting me at home. The only change from the version they say as part of normal services is that the mourner's version removes the line about "may all our prayers be answered," as they deemed it too heartbreaking to expect a mourner to say that.

After, the leader patted me on the back and said, "We'll be back for the evening minyan." They shuffled out. Chava took her shawl, but spoke to the maid about covering the mirror before she left. Devorah came out from under the sofa and bounded over to me, her tail in the air, and climbed into my lap.

I picked her up and walked over to the table, closed my eyes, and inhaled, filling my nose with the scent of home. I so wished I could eat it, but my stomach would rebel if I did. "Can we give it to poor children in honor of John and Eliza?"

"I think that's a good idea," he said, his voice soft. "I'll have Martha take care of it."

"Thank you." I took a spoon and put a drop of the cholent on my tongue. Just like my mother used to make.

———⦿———

Abraham
London, England
December 16, 1899—December 24, 1899


THE FUNERAL WAS very Catholic—a Mass. Flora was a non-conformist, and the children were Church of England, but if I had wanted to be particular on those points, I should have been more specific. The baron did his best, and I was grateful. One advantage was that it was in the evening, so we could attend. The seats were hard wood, uncomfortable; the walls were golden beige stone, and the windows were dark, but I'd seen the stained glass as we approached. There was a faint burned smell under the abundance of flowers. The music was gorgeous, with a choir, piano, organ, and a young boy on the violin. Technically, I shouldn't have been listening to music during mourning, but I decided this was a funeral, not a concert, and therefore didn't count. It was in Latin. I wish I didn't speak Latin. I know that speaking Latin and Greek were considered the mark of being educated, but Latin reminded me of pretending to be Christian in Berlin so I could attend the academy, which I now considered a shameful sin. Besides, what would I use Latin for? Medical texts? I don't get sick. Reading ancient works? The Romans mistreated the Jews. I mainly used it when playing Christian religious music for money. I supposed there were some interesting scientific texts in Latin. I also speak English, German, Yiddish, Hebrew, and a smattering of French and Aramaic, and I have less fraught feelings about those. I was more interested in the music and moved my fingers along with the violin. I cried silent tears during the eulogy. I sat when everyone sat and stood when everyone stood, but drew the line at kneeling. Fortunately, that seemed polite enough.

The baron took communion. I questioned him about it later. He said it was the only thing he could eat without vomiting and attributed this to its divine nature. My people, despite having endless holidays with family meals, don't really do divine food, but I decided I wasn't one to question. I expected him to accept my religion, after all, so it was only fair to extend him the same courtesy.

On the seventh day after the funeral, I took a bath in the baron's enormous cast-iron clawfoot tub, much to Devorah's dismay. She sat next to the tub and meowed piercing cries; perhaps she thought I might drown. Because I had no other clothes, I put on the same clothes I'd been wearing for a week and returned to the sitting room and the blood red sofa.

"Do you need me to buy you new clothes?" the baron asked. In German, of course.

"Not until thirty days after the funeral," I said in the same language. "But if you have some second-hand clothes that aren't freshly cleaned, those will do."

The baron appeared dismayed at this, but all he said was, "Perhaps we could go to a concert tonight."

"I'm sorry," I said, and I meant it. "I can finally leave the house, but I'm not allowed to go to concerts until thirty days after the funeral."

He looked like he'd swallowed a lemon but said, "I'll see if I can find you some clothes, and perhaps we can go for a walk in the park, then."

"I'd like that, Baron."

"Please call me Ludwig. *Ich bin* Ludwig."

I blinked. We'd known each other for over fifty years, and this was the first time he'd invited me to use his given name. "As you wish." I added, to try out the new pronoun implied by the offer to use his given name, *"Wenn du willst."*

He smiled and shook my hand, then vanished into his rooms, returning with somber black clothing, shirt and trousers. I took them into my own room and changed. Devorah rolled around on my dirty clothes and purred, and I laughed my first laugh since the fire. If Ludwig heard me, he didn't comment.

We wandered out together to the park. It was a beautiful winter night, all white and bluish in the moonlight. Snow crunched under our feet as we walked. I inhaled the fresh new snow scent, like rain, but colder.

I gazed up at the moon, at the falling snow, at the dark cloudy skies and bare branches with white nestled in them. "Thank you for letting me stay with you. I don't know where I would have gone." I breathed in the cool night air. "Under a bridge, perhaps."

"How are you feeling?"

I shrugged.

"Don't you know?"

"I'm done with lying."

He winced and patted me on the shoulder. We crunched forward, past bare trees reaching up into the sky.

"Once the shloshim is over, I'd like to go back to Berlin."

"After the what?"

"Thirty days after the funeral."

"Ah." The snow scraped under his feet. "I was hoping you would return to the stage."

"I'm understandably nervous about attention at the moment."

"Reasonable."

In the distance, I heard a hoot and a soft flutter of wings. We passed a fountain with a crust of ice around the outer edge. "London was Flora's city. I was happy here because she was here, but now I don't feel safe."

We walked together in an almost silent world of snow for a moment, our footsteps the only sound, until a horse and carriage on the road broke the spell. The air chilled my lungs, but it was a good chill, a chill that felt like I was alive.

"It seems a shame for the world to lose your gift. Perhaps you could start over with a new identity."

"I suppose." The snow started falling heavier now, in big fat flakes. I closed my eyes and raised my face to it, letting them land on my cheeks and nose.

"You don't want to be naughty and cheat the rules and attend a concert?" His voice was wistful.

"I'm appreciating having time to mourn." I tried to smile at him and probably produced something pitiful. "My heart wouldn't be in it. Not yet." I was gradually returning to the world, and the prescribed pace was just about right.

He appeared very disappointed but said nothing.

"You could go without me," I suggested. "I'll be fine at home with Devorah."

He shrugged. "I might."

We crunched our way back to his house. Early the next morning, I took an enclosed coach and donated generously to the synagogue in Whitechapel that had been so kind to me.

---

Abraham
Eatontown, New Jersey
March 13, 2020

I FIDGETED IN the brown vinyl and wooden chair next to Destiny as our reproductive endocrinologist flipped through paper records in a green folder. The nameplate on her desk read Dr. Olga Gogol, and everything was white, blue, and brown, with a tasteful modern painting of a pregnant woman, a vase full of fresh tulips, and a quantity of plants. The plants almost covered the hospital smell. I had to sit on the far side, away from the window and its view of cherry blossoms.

Dr. Gogol had ivory skin, brown hair she wore in a bun, and a faint Russian accent. She was wearing an N95 mask, because of COVID, but the current recommendations were that civilians didn't need them. I certainly didn't. "Your tests all look very promising, Destiny. So, can you tell me why you've decided on donor intra-uterine insemination?"

Destiny shrugged. "I'm a product of IUI myself, so... it worked for my moms." She smiled. "I was conceived here, in this very clinic."

The doctor glanced up from her chart and appraised the two of us. "I was asking about the donor part."

I would have thought that was obvious, but I spelled it out for her. "I've been assured that I... can't." I only resented her making me say it a little. I mean, it was not something of which to be ashamed, especially not for my kind. Vampires don't reproduce sexually.

"It's standard procedure for us to test both partners first, just to make sure." She gazed at me, expectant.

I wondered if I could refuse without jeopardizing our chances. How incriminating could a sperm sample be? I glanced over at Destiny, who appeared hopeful. Curiosity finally got the better of me. "You're wasting your time, but I suppose I can humor you."

She offered me a cup. "Would you like a magazine?"

I performed the maneuver commonly referred to as a facepalm, much to their amusement.

Dr. Gogol showed me to a private room. Suffice it to say that a sample was produced and returned. Technically, sages can't agree on whether the sin of Onan was masturbation or coitus interruptus, but since the main gist is that he was refusing to provide a baby that might disinherit him, this was clearly something not worth nitpicking in this context.

The doctor took the cup and a little dropper and examined the sample under a microscope. "Wow." She moved the dial. *"Wow.* No offense, but I see what you mean. *Terrible* motility. It's like they're all dead."

I wasn't surprised. I'm two hundred years old, and arguably dead as well. "Do they have fangs, too?" I whispered to Destiny.

Destiny giggled and whispered, "No, but they're all shaped like tiny bats."

I giggled back.

Dr. Gogol didn't glance up, but she asked, "What?"

"Nothing."

The doctor kept peering into the microscope. "Interesting." She straightened up. "Sorry." She walked back to her desk, sat down, and made a note in Destiny's records.

There was an awkward silence while she wrote.

I launched into my prepared spiel. "My family is from Września, in Poland, and spent some time in Berlin. They're all Ashkenazi Jews. If you have a donor with a similar background, perhaps one who's musical..."

The doctor laughed. "My family is from Odessa, in Ukraine. They used to say there that if you see a Jewish boy on the street and he isn't carrying a violin, he must play the piano."

I laughed. "I play the violin." Note to self: a faint *Ukrainian* accent.

She smiled. "Well, I have to admit that it's challenging, but it might be possible to try with yours, despite the motility issue. It might come to a donor, but... we'll see what we can do."

Destiny appeared delighted.

"The cost would be significant. We'd have to do IVF. I'm going to recommend ICSI, where we manually introduce the best sperm we can find into the egg with a needle to combat the motility issue, and perhaps surgically extract the sperm, but if you're willing to bear the cost, we can try."

I hated to disappoint Destiny, but Flora had been very insistent that it was impossible. "I'm very pessimistic."

"Please?" Destiny wheedled, drawing the word out.

I put my hands up. "Fine! Fine, if you want to waste time and money on negative pregnancy tests, who am I to stop you?"

Destiny squealed and leaped out of her chair to hug me. She was so warm, and her hair was down today, so a silky curtain of red hair that smelled of lavender surrounded me. I closed my eyes and breathed in the soft scent of her. I *loved* her hair. I loved *her*. I loved her enough to throw money at the impossible, just because she wanted it. I felt guilty for letting her get her hopes up, but she wanted to try it this way first...

"One question," Dr. Gogol said. "If we're successful, the procedure can cause multiple viable embryos, or twins, so... do you prefer a boy or a girl?"

Without a second thought, I answered, "One of each, God willing." As the Talmud says, to replace ourselves on earth... although I'm not going anywhere, come to think of it, so a girl?

———————⌒∞⌒———————

Destiny
Eatontown, New Jersey
March 13, 2020

DR. GOGOL WAS THIN, muscular, and tall, with androgynous features. She wore her hair in a severe bun. *Very* attractive. Hey, I'm married, not dead!

Dr. Gogol pulled me aside and said, in her Ukrainian accent, "Do you need me to show you how to give yourself an injection?"

I burst out laughing. "I've never given myself an injection before, but I'm a veterinarian. I guess it's time to become my own pin cushion."

"All right," she said. "Show me."

I shrugged and took the needle. "Where? Butt? Belly?"

"Belly," she suggested.

So I did. I had a lot of practice with cats and dogs, so I didn't hesitate, or wiggle the needle, or anything. In and out. Bam. Sure, it was a sudden sharp prick, but because I was the one doing it, I expected it. Even easier than a flu shot.

Dr. Gogol laughed. "Yes, you are a professional. If we ever want someone to teach classes, we will call you."

I grinned at her and glanced over at Abraham, who looked queasy. Which was *adorable*.

I headed to the car, started it, and drove to pick up Abraham, who was waiting at the door.

I'd always assumed that we would use IUI, which wasn't a problem! It worked for my moms, and if I'd married a woman instead of a man, that's what we would have done, but... for some reason, the idea of Abraham's genetics...

Like I've said, he's *beautiful*, and plays the violin like a god, and he's smart. I wouldn't have objected to having a musical genius child! Okay, fine, that's not how genetics works, but let me dream!

I knew from my reading that the egg harvesting was likely to give me cramps in my side, but if that was the price for having a baby with Abraham, it was worth it. If Morgan could have had Bridget's genetic baby...

*I could be a mother this time next year.*

The "family values" set always talked like heterosexual couples have a monopoly on healthy families and caring for children, but knowing the efforts my moms went through to have me, and being treated as a family... it made me want it all the more.

I wondered about Flora, Abraham's first wife, and what she would have given for the opportunity I had now. Something told me she would have been thrilled.

————⚬⚭⚬————

Abraham
Eatontown, New Jersey
May 4, 2020

I'M SKIPPING THE egg harvesting, which gave Destiny aches in her side, and let's not even discuss what they did to *me* because it was embarrassing and involved needles in sensitive places. Suffice it to say that they had what they needed to attempt fertilization. I was willing to go through the motions for my wife because I loved her, but Flora had said it wouldn't work, and Flora was usually correct on vampiric matters.

The doctor called us in. I geared up in my Invisible Man beekeeper suit, with the SPF-rated hat and SPF-rated sunglasses and SPF-rated shirt and pants and SPF-rated scarf and gloves. And our N95 masks, of course, although I was immune to COVID. I ran to the car, and when we arrived at the clinic, Destiny dropped me off at the door, then parked the pollen-coated car. We shuffled back to Dr. Gogol's office together, with the painting of the pregnant woman and the plants and the scent of hospital disinfectant.

Okay, I shuffled and Destiny bounced. I was expecting bad news, to be honest. If it was good news, why not tell us over the phone?

We sat in front of the desk, where Dr. Gogol was reading on her computer. She smiled at us. "So, the needle worked."

Destiny squealed and grabbed my hand and squeezed, her hand soft and warm. I blinked and let out a surprised breath.

"We manually fertilized seventeen eggs, and two of them actually became blastocysts." She smiled, but there was a sympathetic edge to it. "Hopefully they'll implant all right. It's common to try more than once, so if they don't implant, we might have to try again."

Ugh. I did *not* want to deal with the needle again, nor did I want my wife to deal with the egg harvesting again. I would have been perfectly happy with using a donor, or adopting, but Destiny wanted *my* genes for whatever reason, and I was smitten.

"What now?" Destiny asked. "Do we try right now?"

"No, you need to take hormones to prepare your uterus. They were hard enough to get that I want to make absolutely certain that they implant. We'll freeze them. Sometimes they don't survive that, but almost ninety-five percent do."

"Right, of course," Destiny said. She bounced a little in her chair.

"As we discussed, I tested them for common genetic diseases, especially considering your odd sun sensitivity. They seem healthy. No porphyria, no Tay-Sachs, no cystic fibrosis, no HBOC... none of that bad stuff. So that's good. I'm going to recommend assisted hatching. I want to make sure they have every advantage, since, you know, no one wants to go through this again."

Tay-Sachs. I wondered if I was older than that particular mutation. If so, we had that to be grateful for. I made a mental note to look that up later.

I might be a father this time next year. I might be a father to my genetic child. I still had trouble believing it. Flora had said I couldn't, and she'd never been wrong before... but what if they simply hadn't had the technology?

"So we're having twins?" Destiny asked.

"No," Dr. Gogol said. "They're common with fertility procedures, but we try to avoid them because twins are a riskier pregnancy. We don't want you losing either of them. You can carry them one at a time."

Destiny nodded, then bounced up and down in her chair, which creaked on the floor tiles. "So, when do I come back?"

"Make an appointment at the desk."

We did, and then we returned home and watched *Only Lovers Left Alive*. After, I took out my Stradivarius and played the bright, sweet, rapid tones of the Paganini Caprice No. 5 myself, much to Destiny's delight. "I want you to play that while I'm being implanted."

I laughed out loud. "We'll ask if they mind."

She giggled. "So, what do you think of some celebratory TMI?"

I kissed her hand and said, "Your wish is my command... not to mention my husbandly duty." I waggled my eyebrows at her.

She stood and beckoned to me, and I followed her into the bedroom. I would follow her anywhere.

---

Abraham
Eatontown, New Jersey
June 3, 2020

WE WENT TO THE clinic—of course, I needed my sun gear, now referred to by Destiny as my beekeeper Invisible Man cosplay—for them to implant the first one, and Destiny was all but vibrating in excitement, which was *adorable*. I was glad I didn't feel the heat like I used to, because it was hot and humid that day and I was covered with SPF fabric from head to toe.

The room where the procedure was going to happen was white—white walls, white floors—and smelled of disinfectant, and they gave Destiny one of those dreadful hospital gowns in a slate blue that was almost gray. Everyone was masked, of course. The staff thought my bringing a violin was odd but were patient... until I played. I played the entire Paganini Caprice no. 5 with the staff frozen, spellbound, the only other sounds medical beeps.

There was silence after, and Dr. Gogol said, "I now see why she insisted on you rather than a donor."

I felt my cheeks warm. Surely I wasn't blushing. My kind usually doesn't.

"I wanted that playing while I was being implanted," Destiny said, her voice sleepy. They had given her a Valium, after all.

I switched to Mozart's Violin Concerto No.4 in D major.

"But..."

"This might be less distracting."

"No offense to Mozart, but I want the Paganini!"

What's an adoring husband to do? I played the Paganini again and followed it up with some of the violin solos from Rimsky-Korsakov's *Scheherazade*. *Scheherazade* had been my signature piece since 1899. That year was also a time when I had two adopted children and loved them with all my heart. Judaism, like my wedding to Destiny, explicitly wishes for children. At my bar mitzvah, my father was told, "...and may you be blessed to bring him before the wedding canopy..." Having children is a mitzvah. I'd always assumed I'd have children until I was told I couldn't, and then I assumed I'd adopt children. Apparently, with enough assistance, I could have my own.

And then the procedure was over.

Dr. Gogol came to stand next to me. "Do you play professionally?"

I tried to smile, but I suspect it came out sad. "Not anymore."

"You should."

I shrugged.

"Seriously," she said, emphatic in her faint Ukrainian accent. "You should."

The nurse added in a southern twang, "I don't even like classical music, but that was... wow, you might have changed my mind. At least where you're concerned." She wore her red hair in almost a beehive style.

Destiny sat up and scratched her nose, then stretched. "When do I take a pregnancy test?"

"Twelve to fourteen days, and I don't want you peeing on any sticks until then because they won't be accurate yet. Make an appointment." She helped Destiny stand. "Take your progesterone. Have a lot of sex."

My cheeks were warm, but Destiny grinned wickedly and said, "Well, if it's *doctor's orders...*"

I drove home, but Destiny had to pull the car up to the door and switch seats for us to do it. I held my breath while she did it, but she managed. Fortunately, we'd found a close spot.

We binged more vampire media, including *Blade*, which wasn't the best choice when we were trying to conceive. And, of course, followed Dr. Gogol's instructions.

———————⚯———————

Abraham
Eatontown, New Jersey
June 19, 2020

ON THE BIG DAY, I bundled up in my cosplay yet again. We drove to the clinic, where Destiny dropped me off at the door and I waited for her to park. We went upstairs together. I was nervous, but she was happy and energized. I fidgeted in the white, blue, and brown waiting room with photos of their "success stories"—adorable babies—while they drew blood, and they called us back to Dr. Gogol's office, to sit under the modern painting of a pregnant woman again. If this drew out too long, I could grow to resent that painting, feeling like it was taunting me. Soft jazz played in the background. I could smell that Dr. Gogol had freshly watered her plants. Part of me was still afraid that something would go wrong, that the embryo wouldn't implant.

"Congratulations," Dr. Gogol said with a happy crinkle in her eyes over the mask. "It's a girl, by the way. We can implant her brother next time."

*One of each, God willing, to replace ourselves on earth.* The minimum requirement for fulfilling the mitzvah of being fruitful and multiplying was a boy and a girl. As Maimonides says, anyone who adds a soul to the Jewish people, it is as if he has built an entire world.

Destiny squealed, climbed into my lap, pulled down our masks, and kissed me. She was warm and soft in my arms.

I was almost two hundred years old, and had been told over a hundred years ago that this was impossible. I'd made peace with the idea. I was only going through the motions to make my wife happy, and always assumed that we'd have to fall back on a donor, eventually. I tried to picture what our daughter would look like, trying to imagine our features mixed. I hoped she would have Destiny's beautiful hair. So I said the blessing for firsts: "*Barukh atah, Adonai Eloheinu, Melekh ha'olam, shehecheyanu, v'kiy'manu, v'higiyanu laz'man hazeh.*" Blessed are You, Adonai our God, Sovereign of all, who has kept us alive, sustained us, and brought us to this time.

"I recommend not telling many people until a couple of months in," Dr. Gogol said. "Just to limit the number of people you would have to tell if things didn't work out. We tell people not going to fertility clinics the same thing, by the way."

It's what Jewish superstition says, too. *Bli ayin hara! Ken eina hara!* No evil eye!

"I understand," Destiny said, "but I'm absolutely telling my moms!" She pulled out her phone, and there was the electronic click and ding of texting.

I was already considering names. It's the tradition in Ashkenazi Jewish families to name children after the dead, to keep their names alive. That said, it's also considered bad luck to name them after someone who died young and tragically, so maybe I shouldn't name the child Eliza. Maybe Eliza could be her middle name.

Abraham
Atlantic Highlands, New Jersey
October 14, 2020

WE WERE LOUNGING around on the red sectional, bingeing *True Blood* with Ivan, Inanna, and Freddy. Destiny had a craving for cheese, so she was nibbling on cheese and crackers and rubbing her rounded belly.

Freddy lifted his head and stared at the door. I stood and looked out the window. The trees outside were a riot of color, but that's not what caught my attention.

Freddy's former humans were stepping out of a car parked in our driveway. "Shit!"

"What?"

"You answer the door and see what they want, and Freddy, Ivan, and I are going down to the basement." I patted my legs and inclined my head, and they obediently followed. I led them into the dark, musty room with the concrete floor and the coffin and shut the door with one last "Stay," then headed back up to the top of the stairs, which a previous homeowner had carpeted so my feet made no sound.

Idiot Husband was saying, "Where's your cat?"

"He's around here someplace."

Idiot Husband's wife said, "We wanted to let you know we had to put poor Freddy down. He attacked Frank when he tried to take him for a walk."

Yeah, I'll bet he did. Poor Freddy! Ivan hadn't tried to sunbathe since the first time he put a paw on the windowsill. That said, euthanasia drugs wouldn't have worked. Freddy would have woken up in a refrigerator. I thought of Freddy arriving with the stench of death on him and shivered.

"I'm so sorry," Destiny said. "I'm sure that was hard."

"Has your cat shown any unusual symptoms?"

"No, he seems fine. I'm so sorry to hear about your dog, really."

Destiny is such a good, kind woman. Her voice was full of absolute sincerity.

"I wanted to know if your cat had his rabies vaccine," Idiot Husband said.

"I'm a veterinarian, so yes, all my pets are up to date on their shots. I do it myself."

I came out of the basement and headed into the hallway. *Of course*, they weren't masked.

"What's the breakthrough infection rate for vaccinated cats?" Idiot Husband asked.

"Did your veterinarian think Freddy was rabid?" Destiny's voice was full of deep concern.

"No," Idiot Husband's long-suffering wife said. She'd cut her hair into a bob since we last saw her.

I headed into the living room. "I'd like for you to leave."

"Is your cat in there?" Idiot Husband started for the hallway. He was wearing jeans and a shirt with what I suspected was a football-related image—I don't follow sports.

I stepped in front of him. "Leave now." I'm not a physically imposing man, and Idiot Husband sized me up. I sized him up back. He was bigger than I was, and had presumably been fit once, but he was softening and graying around the edges with age. I could absolutely take him—I could pick him up with one hand and throw him—but he didn't know that. Besides, the police might come, and bullets hurt, and then you have to fake your death and move and change your name. Better to not cause any trouble. Best of all to not end up on television for Thomas to see.

"Frank, we should go," the wife said. "Freddy didn't have rabies, and these people's cat doesn't have rabies."

"Freddy was fine until he bit that cat!" He glared at me.

He might have been an idiot, but even idiots occasionally have a point. That said, the point might have been on top of his head. "Freddy was arguably a dangerous dog who attacked other animals... and you." I crossed my arms and raised an eyebrow.

We stared at each other for a while, and then Idiot Husband said, "Come on, Clara, let's go!" Like it was his idea. I somehow resisted the urge to roll my eyes at him.

Inanna watched them leave from her perch on top of a bookshelf, her head tracking their progress. Part of me wished she would attack Idiot Husband, but that would have been terrible. We're trying to convince people that we have normal, healthy, non-aggressive pets, after all.

Was it too late to keep a low profile and avoid Thomas's notice?

I listened to the car drive away and let the pets out of the basement, dog paws clattering on the wooden floor. Freddy seemed subdued, and I gave him a hug. Then I called my attorney. Maybe I was overreacting, but I knew what they did to rabid pets. Believe me, no one thought Freddy had rabies.

My attorney, by the way, was Ludwig of course.

———————⚬❦⚬———————

Abraham
London, England
January 15, 1900—1934

ON THE THIRTIETH DAY after the funeral, I told Ludwig, "As far as I'm concerned, you have made your amends and I forgive you completely and without hesitation. If I have wronged you in return, please let me know so that I might make amends to you as well." And those weren't just pretty words. I meant them. Forgiving people whether or not they deserve it is a Christian Protestant thing; Judaism does not require you to forgive those who wrong you.

Ludwig appeared surprised and pleased, and only said, "Thank you. You've done me no harm, of course."

Ludwig and I boarded a boat for Berlin, with Devorah and my Stradivarius, of course. We didn't live together, but we rented rooms near each other so we could visit. We spent many nights with me playing the bright, sweet notes of the violin, or us going out to hear music together.

I had a new name, but by 1919 it was a golden age for Jews in Germany. I spent the years performing, changing my name every decade, attending the theater (in memory of Flora), donating to causes involving poor and homeless children, attending the symphony with Ludwig, and enjoying the new medium of film. Prussia's constitution had made us full citizens, and they rescinded all the unfair taxes and regulations. It was the age of equality and secularism, and we thrived. Berlin had been the center of the Haskalah, the Jewish Enlightenment, and we moved out of the ghettos and into normal, secular life. We built new synagogues, wrote music, plays, screenplays. We went into the professions from which the law had previously barred us. Antisemitism was also on the rise, a growing rumble, but we believed that if we assimilated and committed to being Germans, the law would continue to protect us.

My brother still had descendants—he lived to be shockingly old—and I introduced myself to them as the son of a cousin, and then another, younger cousin. Miriam was the youngest, and I adored her. She reminded me of Eliza. So sensitive and imaginative, with long brown curls and intelligent eyes. I watched her grow into a thoughtful young woman, marry, and have a son of her own while I pretended to age—a process involving costuming and an altered walk. I wasn't the best actor, but I also hadn't lived with a popular actress for nothing.

Life became good again.

# The Rule of Law

Abraham
Atlantic Highlands, New Jersey
October 18, 2020

Ludwig came in and waved to Destiny. Then he did a double-take. "Abraham, what have you done?" He held his hands over Destiny's belly. "May I?"

Destiny nodded.

"My God." He laid both hands—bearing his trademark rings on all ten fingers—on Destiny's baby bump, clad in a green maternity dress. "It's a miracle."

"It took some effort," I said.

"And needles in sensitive places," Destiny added.

I winced.

"Kinky, but I'm not here to judge," Ludwig said. "I'm here to provide legal advice, such as it is. Tell me everything."

We sat on the red sectional together, and I explained at length about Idiot Husband and about his insinuations that Ivan was rabid. Destiny sat next to me, smelling of lavender and watching with interest.

"Is your cat rabid?" he asked.

I made a sound of disgusted dismissal and called, "Ivan!"

Ivan trotted silently into the room with his tail in the air, all golden and friendly, and walked across the wooden floor to Ludwig for the petting that was obviously his due. He gazed up at Ludwig with bright bronze eyes, expectant.

Ludwig shot me a sharp look. "Your pets? Seriously?" But he petted Ivan enthusiastically, and when Freddy trotted over, too, claws clicking on the wooden floors, he patted him with equal glee. "Hello, kitty, I'm your grandsire. And, puppy, I'm your great-grandsire." He pointed at Destiny's belly. "I have no idea how to describe our relationship." He turned back to me. "Anyway. He's *adorable*, but can you prove he's not rabid?"

"Rabies spreads via saliva," Destiny said. "Freddy bit Ivan. Ivan didn't bite Freddy. Ergo, QED, STFU."

"I like her," Ludwig said. "Keen legal mind. Have you considered a career in law?"

"I like being a veterinarian."

Ludwig shrugged. "I'm thinking a restraining order. One hundred feet at all times. After all, the man is clearly unhinged."

Destiny said, "He's just sad that he lost his dog."

Ludwig stared at her for a moment. Then he turned to me. "I see." He turned back to Destiny. "I know, my dear, but we just want to make certain that he doesn't cause issues for your cat."

"I'm not an idiot."

"No one said you were. Quite the contrary, I should think."

"Hmm," Destiny said.

"Either way, I don't think it will come to this, but if he convinces county officials that there's a rabid cat around, give them my card and a copy of the restraining order and decline to surrender your pet without first consulting your attorney." He placed his card on the table and sat back in his seat. "As for payment..."

"You know I can afford it."

"Oh, Abraham, you *know* I don't want your money." He glanced at the ceiling for a moment and smirked. "Our firm's annual year-end party is coming up, and it would be such a coup if I could secure your services as entertainer..."

I winced yet again.

"Oh, how lovely!" Destiny beamed. "I keep trying to convince him he should play for more people than just me."

"I knew I liked you." Ludwig turned to me. "So, of course, in order to protect your darling offspring slash pet, you'd be thrilled to perform for us."

"You're just... profoundly insensitive sometimes."

"You know you love me just the way I am." He beamed at me. "Your restraining order will arrive soon; I'll have one of our minions drop it by." He stood. "We should all go to the symphony together at some point."

He pulled me aside and said, "May I ask you a question in private?"

I made an elaborate shrug, then told Destiny, "Excuse us," and led Ludwig back to the kitchen, with the black and white tiles and the blue gas stove. We sat at the kitchen table.

Ludwig lowered his voice. "Your pets, and not *your wife*? I assume that you're planning on turning her after your odd reproductive experiments?"

I sighed. "So far she's said no."

Ludwig raised his eyebrows.

"She's a vegetarian." As if that explained everything. Perhaps it did.

In the other room, Destiny turned on the television.

Ludwig considered this for a moment. "Do you want me to...?"

"No!" I said, then lowered my voice. "No. Thank you."

"Are you... not attached to her?" he whispered.

"The opposite." I sighed and stared at the floor. It was the eternal paradox of my life. The best, kindest companions aren't the sort to choose this life. Flora had also been turned by someone who didn't ask permission, for what it's worth. She'd even told me she'd never liked meat because she had always felt sorry for the animals.

Hmm. I have a type. Can a person have more than one bashert? Of course, any sort of predestination has some inherent theological problems, but I supposed I still found the idea of a soul mate hopelessly romantic.

There was a long pause, and then he said, "You and your mortals. I can't let myself get attached to mortals anymore. They're so fleeting. It hurts too much."

I didn't really have anything to say in response to that. What would I say? I thought of Flora suddenly, the scent of her hair, the sound of her laughter, and the wave of it was almost overpowering. Maybe Ludwig was right.

He patted me on the shoulder and walked towards the door, bundling up in his hat, gloves, scarf, and sunglasses, which were odd with his expensive suit. Was his suit SPF-rated? "I'll tell people we met at our support group for people with extreme sun sensitivity."

"Bye, *Lou*," Destiny said.

---

Destiny
Atlantic Highlands, New Jersey
October 18, 2020

I WAS CERTAIN Ludwig was gay, and I was raised by lesbians and went to Pride every year as soon as I could walk, and was bi myself. Okay, he could have been a swishy straight man or a product of changing standards of male behavior over time or something, but based on the way he looked at my husband...

It was overt enough to me that I suspected some women might be jealous, but... it wasn't my way. I trusted my husband. Besides, I was four months pregnant. That meant I wanted to adopt every animal I saw, cried at the drop of a hat, and couldn't find my car keys. Also, sometimes I was horny, but mostly I was exhausted and oversentimental and forgetful. Also, all dairy products smelled like feet. This was unfortunate, as only a few weeks ago I had craved dairy products. Speaking of feet, my feet hurt. Also, my back. I was more inclined to ask someone to rub my feet than throw a jealous fit.

I lay down on my side and nibbled on my latest craving—walnuts—and turned on the television and started flipping channels. I missed my TV buddy, Lucy. We were trying to be responsible—pandemic and all—but really, we spent eight hours a day together at the clinic, so how bad could it be? I'd Zoom call her later.

I thought of Abraham's previous wife, Flora, again. I think that despite the mood swings, she would have wanted to do this, too. I don't know how I knew that, but... I just knew. It was probably more pregnancy hormones.

Abraham and Ludwig left the kitchen, and I could almost hear the anime-obsessed manga girls from my college dorm squealing about "bishies"—*bishonen*—
beautiful boys. Ludwig was stunning, by the way. Like Marilyn Monroe gorgeous, only with no apparent awareness of his sex appeal.

Hmm. Maybe he was less gay than I thought. He was the only person on earth who didn't realize how handsome he was.

"Bye, *Lou*," I called, and he did a shy little wave. *Definitely* a manga boy.

Abraham
Berlin, Germany
May 31, 1939

"I CAN GET YOU fake identity papers if you want them." Ludwig appeared nervous. He always looked nervous these days. To be fair, I probably did as well; I'd been anxious ever since Kristallnacht. He dressed like a Hollywood leading man, with the suit and the hat covering his impeccable blond wig.

I scowled at him. "I'm done with lying."

Ludwig scowled back, and we glared at each other. Then I rolled my eyes and stared at his wallpaper. It was a floral print, with enormous pink pseudo-oriental blossoms and twining green vines. He'd sold his beloved antique red sofa and purchased a pink one. Why? Because it was worth a ludicrous sum of money, and he was tired of hauling it around whenever he moved. The wooden end tables and the like were all painted green to complement the wallpaper. The apartment was in town, and we could hear the cars and the sound of voices downstairs.

Finally, he said, "I assume you have no interest in attending Wagner's *Tristan and Isolde* tonight."

"I don't forgive him for his essay 'Judaism in Music.' If you genuinely admire my so-called gift with the violin, surely you disagree with it." Seriously, if you haven't read it? It's incredibly offensive. Stuff about how Jews don't have "a German soul" and are therefore incapable of producing true music. Also, we can't speak

European languages properly and therefore we can't express genuine passion.

"Of course I disagree with it!" he said. "Lots of artists say stupid or offensive things! Even Mozart, who was the greatest composer in history, adored toilet humor and enjoyed signing letters 'Lick my ass'!" He shuddered theatrically. "There have also been prominent artists, writers, and musicians in history who were devotees of the Greek sin, and we don't throw out *their* work, either!"

"Hmm," I opined. Toilet humor and homosexuality were a lot less offensive to me than antisemitism. The sin of Sodom isn't "sodomy" in the Jewish tradition, it's hoarding resources and exploiting the poor. More than one blushing older man at the yeshiva tried to argue with my interpretation of the passage in Leviticus—you know, the one I think referred to the Greeks. Eventually one whispered, "I believe that you are mistaken, Avrahom, but I'm too embarrassed to explain why!"

But I digress. In short, Wagner could 'lick my ass'... not that I was going to say that to Ludwig. So instead, I limited myself to another "Hmm."

"Exactly!" Ludwig said. "Judge the artist's work, not the artist. His work is divine, even if his views are repugnant."

Ludwig, I thought, was deeply repressed. "I'd prefer to not attend. I encourage you to go, however. You love his work."

"I will then," Ludwig said, prissily.

"Then do that," I said.

"I will!" he answered.

"Good," I said, and picked up Ludwig's spare violin to practice.

Ludwig
Berlin, Germany
May 31, 1939

IT BROKE MY HEART to see Abraham so degraded. Oh,
he was still beautiful, of course. But he looked tired
and resigned, and I hated it.

Of course, I hated all the laws about the Jews. All
the Jews that I had met were kind, upstanding people.
But it hurt more with Abraham. I hoped music would
take my mind off things. So I went to the opera, despite
Abraham's regular condemnations of Wagner ringing in
my ears.

He hadn't condemned homosexuality, I noted, but he
hadn't exactly enthusiastically endorsed it, either.
Which was as to be expected! The rules against it came
from Leviticus, a text that Christianity and Judaism
shared. Also, Abraham clearly preferred the company of
women. I'd watched him with his wife Flora from afar;
they had been surprisingly affectionate in public.

Not that I was certain why I cared. It was merely
romantic friendship, after all. Unlike Abraham, I had
never married, and I had never engaged in anything
carnal myself. Vampires don't reproduce sexually, so
there was no need.

I sat in my box seat and waited for the opera, with
the red velvet and the scent of cigarettes.

To my intense annoyance, the men in the next box were talking. During the opera! I wondered if it would be better or worse to lean around the wall and hush them. I did my best to ignore them, but I heard, "We can round them up, send them to work camps, away from the prying eyes of the foreign press."

Then I heard the deep voice of my maker. Not God, of course. *Him.* Thomas. I considered fleeing mid-opera, despite how rude that would be, but I needed to know their plans. I took a deep breath and listened, despite my mounting horror. Thomas asked if they could place him in charge of one of the camps, saying that he had a history in the penal system that would be of use. They discussed the camps they were talking about building, and of course Abraham couldn't work in direct sunlight; he would die.

We needed to leave.

The opera forgotten, I listened to the men in the next box talk through the rest of the performance. After, I waited until I thought they had left, then stood. I knew Thomas was in the lobby, and he shouldn't have been aware of me in the same way that I was aware of him. That wasn't his particular gift, it was mine. He wasn't leaving, so perhaps he had spotted me on the way in. Rather than wait all night, I walked out of my box and towards the exit.

In the lobby, a tall, balding man with a frizzy fringe of dark hair stopped me. Thomas, of course. Wearing a Nazi uniform.

"Hello, Ludwig," he said, and the various soldiers around him became more interested in me.

"Hello," I said politely. I didn't use a name because I didn't know which one he was using.

Thomas clapped me on the shoulder and pulled me aside. "How have you been?"

I mumbled I was fine.

"Wonderful, wonderful." He steered me away from the crowd, out of earshot, and lowered his voice. "Can you believe? This bunch of ridiculous pagans might actually do it! Of course, once they succeed, we'll have to be rid of *them*—they're practically witches and should all be burned at the stake!—but... marvelous!"

I was appalled, but muttered something polite and searched for the exit. If I'd been mortal, my heart would have been racing.

Thomas lowered his voice. "Can you see your way clear to giving me another loan?"

This irritated me out of my fear. I pursed my lips. "The term 'loan' implies that you intend to pay me back."

Thomas rolled his eyes at me. "How much cash do you have on you?"

"No," I said. "You'll have to make me here, in front of all these people."

Thomas scowled at me. "The older you get, the more irritating you become."

I tipped my hat to him. "I'll take that as a compliment." I edged out the door and slipped into the shadows, trying to prevent him from following me.

I took a very roundabout way home.

Abraham
Berlin, Germany
June 1, 1939

LUDWIG RETURNED FROM yet another Wagner opera, still in his fancy opera finery, but this time, instead of glowing, he was anxious. "Abraham, I think the two of us should move to America." He paced a little and sat next to me. "I... *heard* things... at the opera."

I was sure he had. "I should hope you heard an opera," I said. Outside, there were passing cars. The scent of exhaust drifted in through the open windows. Ludwig and I weren't neighbors anymore. They had forced me to move from Ludwig's building into a much worse one reserved for Jews. I'd been living with a sense of creeping dread for months.

"Be serious!" He sat next to me on my cheap blue sofa and lowered his voice. "The Führer requires his officers to attend Wagner operas. Which they hate because they're all philistines, so they chatted throughout the performance in the box next to me. At first I was angry that they were talking during a glorious performance and ruining it, but then I realized they were talking about.. imprisoning all of you." Then he added, as if I were too dense to understand, "All the Jews."

I'd known what he meant. Horror and irritation did battle within me, and irritation won. "All of us? There are, what, thousands—tens of thousands—of us?" I stood, and it was my turn to pace on the threadbare beige carpet. "Really, Ludwig. You've been watching them systematically strip away all of my rights, they've burned and smashed and seized Jewish businesses, we've been barred from most professions, they're arresting us for no reason, people are chanting 'Protect Germany from the Jews' on the street and painting the word 'Jude' and six-pointed stars on our homes and remaining businesses, we can neither be doctors nor receive medical attention, I can't walk down the street without people glaring or shouting harassment... but it's opera gossip that frightens you?"

Ludwig leaned over and put his face in his hands. "You're infuriating." He'd asked me to leave the country months ago with him, after Kristallnacht. I didn't want to leave without Miriam. This had turned into debates about logistics: precisely how many family members we could bring with us. Miriam's husband David hadn't wanted to leave his aging parents. They didn't want to leave David's brother, and David's brother's children, and David's wife—Miriam—and David's late brother's wife... I wished we could bring them all! It was agonizing to have to choose. I wanted to airlift the entire Jewish population out of Germany and couldn't. Ludwig agreed, but also felt that the larger the group, the more likely we would be caught.

"Fine," I said, defeated. "Get paperwork for Miriam and her family and I'll go. Shanghai is the only place allowing Jewish refugees. We can go there." I felt a vast, swelling wave of bitter resignation. I was a German! This was my country, too, and I resented being forced to flee my home. The sense of betrayal was complete.

"I don't *want* to go to Shanghai. I want to go to New York, and they'll let you in even if I have to forge paperwork naming myself president of the United States." There was a long pause, and then he said, "I saw Thomas, too."

I stopped pacing at that.

He looked up and ran his fingers through his hair, mussing it. "He hates the Nazis. He thinks they're a bunch of pagans and heretics, practically witches, but they're close enough to his views on your people that he's working with them. And if Thomas is involved, we need to go. He knows me." He met my eyes. "He *turned* me."

"I see." I supposed Thomas had been his mentor... much like Ludwig hadn't been mine in the early days, for which he was still trying to make amends. I knew from Flora how important that relationship was.

"I'll get those papers," he said. He had an air of determination about him. I supposed tonight was the night.

---

Abraham
Berlin, Germany
June 2, 1939

I WENT TO VISIT Miriam that evening, intending to take her to Ludwig's basement for our future trip to America. It was Shabbat, and I had a standing invitation to Shabbat dinner. Obviously, I never joined them for dinner, as I can't eat, but I sometimes came after dinner to play card games and dolls with Miriam's children Shlomo and Ruth, and to make silly faces at little Shayna. I could see my brother in Shlomo's features, especially the family's prominent nose, and they all had my family's coloring—pale tan skin, dark hair. I'd been going more often since their bank was "Aryanized," which meant that the government seized all their assets and handed them over to non-Jews. Miriam's husband David had committed suicide when they took his livelihood, so I was supporting them.

Yes, my brother's bank, the one he founded in 1841, was Aryanized.

The door was open, and no one was at home. There was no sign of a struggle. Just a dark house with empty spaces where furniture had previously stood, and children's rooms full of toys, and silence. I could smell a single glass of wine in the sink and the waxy scent of the Shabbat candles. I didn't know what to do. Scour all the jails?

I went home, deeply anxious. Two soldiers were waiting for me inside my apartment. "You're under arrest."

The other one swung the butt of his rifle, striking me in the head with a loud crack and knocking me to the floor, and his partner started kicking me in the ribs. Isaac, my handsome tuxedo cat, hid under the sofa. Good, he was safer there. He was a direct descendant of my darling Devorah, by the way.

I grabbed the man's foot and flung him into the far wall with a crash, then stood and grabbed the other man and bit him. I drank, even when there was a loud bang and a sense of force to my back from the direction of his friend. I turned and lunged and grabbed him by the throat. "Where were you taking me?"

"What are you?" He tried to maneuver the rifle to point at me.

I slapped it out of his hand. Any regrets I might have had about taking a human life flew out of my head. Perhaps it was time to act like the monster I was. "Maybe you should have asked that before you shot me." I drank. I needed the blood to heal. Then I asked, "Where were you taking me?"

"Train station. Work camp. Poland."

I snapped his neck and ran through the dark cobblestone streets, and found a small crowd of maybe twenty people at a train station, under guard. I counted the guards. There were only six or seven. If they'd been closer together, I would have known that I could take them, but they were spread out. I was likely to be shot again. I could take multiple bullets, but what about the children? Miriam stood in the center, holding little Shayna. Shlomo and Ruth stood next to her, clinging to her skirt. There were young men, alert, like they were looking for an opportunity to escape, and venerable old people, and small children, all standing on cobblestones next to train tracks in the moonlight.

I sneaked up behind the first guard and silently broke his neck. I felt nothing. I was cold, perfect, and distantly aware that I should have been be feeling emotions, but survival took precedence. I took his weapon and crept up behind another guard.

I could hear the train in the distance but had no idea how far away it was. I snapped the neck of the second guard and headed towards the third. I didn't think they'd noticed yet.

As I approached the third, the lead man told Miriam, "I don't think your baby is worth a bullet. Hold still, so I can use only one for both of you."

Miriam turned her back on him, clutching six-month-old Shayna to her chest and shaking, tears running down her face. "Please. Please don't. Please." She walked away, towards the edge of the crowd. "Please don't. She's just a baby."

I pointed my stolen weapon at him and aimed. He fired. There were screams, and a spray of red and the scent of iron, and blood-soaked children crying for their mother.

"Miriam!" Faster than any mere mortal could track, I shot the lead man. I had a sense again that I would have feelings as soon as the situation was over, but that was a problem for future me.

There were more of them, and they turned their guns on me. The prisoners screamed and ran except for Shlomo and Ruth, who sat on the ground next to their mother and sister and cried and shook their mother. My feelings gave one final sob and curled up into a whimpering ball, one that I could easily ignore for the time being.

I lost count of how many bullets hit me. I was no longer human. I was a thing of teeth and speed and I killed as many as I could. The first few bullets barely hurt, but the later ones felt like red-hot pokers. I ignored them and kept killing. I snapped necks, gnawed out a throat or two. I left their blood cooling in puddles on the ground, undrunk. I had no time for that.

When I killed the last one, there were five or six people huddled in the street, and little Shlomo and Ruth crying next to their mother's body, and the little ball of bloody cloth that was their baby sister. I took their hands and called to the people to follow me, and led them through dark, deserted streets into Ludwig's basement. I rushed up the stairs at inhuman speed to Ludwig, to ask him to forge papers for them. "We need exit papers. Lots of them."

His eyes widened at the sight of me. "How many?" he asked.

I didn't know. I stared blankly at him.

He rolled his eyes at me and followed me to the basement, radiating impatience.

When he entered the room with the people I'd rescued, he stopped in his tracks. He counted—two elderly couples, a sickly-appearing young man with thick glasses, and Shlomo and Ruth, who were still covered in blood. He spoke to them, quiet and gentle and reassuring, asking questions. He washed the blood off the children with a damp cloth from upstairs. He took notes and gave them clothing, backstories. Had he been storing clothes for Miriam and the children?

I could feel an emotional storm approaching. I shoved it away, clinging to the icy perfection, and stared after him, silent.

He went back upstairs and fussed over papers for about an hour, then stepped out. He returned with passage out of Germany for seven: two to Dublin for the elderly couple that was willing to pretend to be Catholic, two to Shanghai for the couple that wasn't, train tickets to Calais with boat tickets from Calais to London for the sickly man and the children. He handed out the paperwork and the train and boat tickets, and told the young man to pretend that Shlomo and Ruth were his children, and to meet us at the docks in

London. He walked them all to the boats or the train station himself and returned home calm and satisfied.

He said, "It's time for us to leave."

"They shot Miriam. And Shayna." I was shaking now, but I wasn't sure whether it was rage or fear or despair.

"All the more reason to leave."

"I'm going to kill them. All of them." Sure, the Talmud forbids taking revenge, but I didn't care at that point. I was ready to fight the entire army. They'd taken on the wrong monster. I wondered how many I could kill in a single night. And if they managed to kill me? Well, that would stop the approaching storm, wouldn't it?

Ludwig gave me a sharp look and sighed. "I'm sorry." He made a gesture in front of my face—thumb and fifth finger extended out, others curled, almost like a child with a marionette—and I couldn't move. "Come with me."

Golem-like, I followed him to the living room. A strange calm spread over me. My bullet wounds were closing up, and there was the occasional sound of something metal hitting the floor. He shuffled through a pile of papers, scowled, and burned a few, finally settling on some he appeared to like. He wiped the blood off my face, neck, and hands, threw my clothes in the fire, bandaged my wounds, and dressed me in a girl's pink frilly dress, including styling my hair with pink ribbons, and girl's shoes. I don't know where he got them or how he knew they'd fit. He thrust papers into my hands.

"My cat," I said.

"Oh, for..." He sighed, and made the marionette gesture again. "Stay here."

I sat on his sofa, the new pink one, and wondered if I was dripping blood on it. After a while, I realized I wasn't bleeding, but my body was expelling the bullets, one by one. They landed on the sofa, the floor... I sat in silence, with only the occasional sound of metal bouncing off wood.

After some time, he returned covered with blood, carrying a yowling Isaac by the scruff in one hand and my Stradivarius in the other. He handed me the cat, who immediately calmed.

He stared into my eyes and made the gesture again. "I need you to be a young girl, one who doesn't necessarily respect her father. Roll your eyes a lot, but don't talk to anyone. These papers aren't invented identities, they're *stolen* identities, and I need you to play your part. Your name is Bettina Weber, by the way."

I rolled my eyes at him and stood, and a few bullets fell out of my dress. He washed and changed, and put on the attitude of an older man... something in his posture, perhaps. Flora would have been envious of his transformation. He examined me carefully before we left. I definitely wasn't bleeding anymore.

We boarded a Norddeutscher Lloyd ship headed to New York via Cork with Ludwig handling the paperwork, the luggage, and the Stradivarius and me holding the cat and rolling my eyes a lot. A German soldier tried to flirt with me, but I just looked bored and stared silently at him until he slunk away. Aside from the flirty soldier, no one glanced at us twice.

The spell wore off halfway across the channel, and I stood up. I walked over to him, shaking in rage, and said, "I'm going back as soon as we land." Fuck my homeland, fuck humanity, fuck everything.

Ludwig gazed at me with an expression of pure pity and said, "I'm sorry, but you're not," and made the gesture again.

Damn him. My emotions calmed again, so at least there was that, but I wanted to kill. I wanted to tear my way through the German army and leave nothing but gore in my wake. I wanted to die in an orgy of destruction.

We disembarked at Cork—despite Ludwig's having purchased passage to New York—and boarded a Cunard White Star liner to London. When we arrived in London, the young man with the glasses was waiting for us, holding Shlomo and Ruth's hands. Ludwig gave him a giant roll of money. I was still wearing the pink dress. Shlomo and Ruth didn't seem to notice.

"You are one of the righteous among the nations," the young man said, weeping, and hugged Ludwig. Ludwig was stiff and awkward with the hug, but his expression was soft.

Ludwig asked Shlomo and Ruth, "Are you hungry?"

They shook their heads, silent.

He asked me, "Would you like to visit Flora's grave while we're here?"

I just stared at him. I wanted to kill.

We took a carriage to Kensal Green cemetery. There were weeping angels over Flora's and the children's graves in white marble. I handed Isaac to Ludwig and placed a rock on each tombstone. Christians do flowers, we do rocks. Shlomo and Ruth watched, silent.

The angels were weeping for Miriam and Shayna—not these stone angels, the actual angels. I was shaking again now, and I let out a shriek of rage and grief that would have had heads turning our way if it weren't the middle of the night. I flung myself onto Flora's grave. Ludwig quickly made the gesture again and shushed me.

I didn't want to be calm, but I had no choice. "We're bringing the children with us," I said.

Ludwig made a face. "I suppose I forged them paperwork."

We returned to the docks and boarded a boat to New York a few hours before dawn—also Cunard White Star. We loaded Shlomo and Ruth onto the boat with us, allegedly the teenaged girl's cousins. I switched my identity back to a young man once we boarded, much to my relief. I hadn't enjoyed being "Bettina Weber."

I curled up in the fetal position on the bunk, shaking, and refused to respond to Ludwig's questions. He placed a cool hand on my shoulder and murmured, "I'm here." I don't know how long we sat like that. Isaac curled up next to me, for which I was grateful.

As the sun rose outside, he shook me gently and asked, in a soft voice, "Abraham?"

I made a rude gesture at him.

He patted my shoulder and said, "Are you hungry, children?" There was a pause, and then he said, "I think you should eat whether or not you're hungry. Let's go up to the dining room together."

They left, and while they were gone, I pulled myself together. If it was morning, it might be time to say Shacharit—and the Mourner's Kaddish. I wanted to pray for Miriam and Shayna.

I missed the kind people of the synagogue in Whitechapel and arranged a prayer group on the boat. I didn't have a prayer book on me, but some of the other passengers did. I realized I knew most of it by heart at the end of the first service. Unfortunately, there weren't ten Jews on the boat, so we couldn't say Kaddish. The children were too young to count for a minyan.

Neither of the children spoke a word the entire voyage.

———————— ⌘ ————————

Abraham
Manhattan, New York
December 21, 2020

IT WAS A "year end" party, but they might as well have called it a "Christmas Party" because they played Christmas muzak before the party and had decorated with Christmas trees, tinsel, and balls. They covered the tables with white tablecloths and silvery place settings. Nary a token Hanukkiah in sight—not that it was still Hanukkah; that had ended three days ago. Nor was any other winter holiday represented. Speaking as a religious minority, if your only accommodation to non-Christians is to say "holiday" instead of "Christmas," just say "Christmas." You're not fooling anyone—except, perhaps, yourself.

Joke: "What day is Hanukkah this year?" "The same day it always is! The twenty-fifth of Kislev."

I played my way through the classics, opening and closing with Paganini. Ludwig's legal firm seemed to appreciate my playing based on the smiles, foot taps, and applause. Destiny sat in the front row, beaming and clapping enthusiastically whenever I paused playing. She was wearing a sparkly purple maternity evening gown. Who even knew such a thing existed? And a mask, of course. Most of us were masked if we weren't actively eating and drinking.

"Curtain call!" Ludwig shouted.

"Yes!" Destiny shouted.

I wondered for a moment what I should play. "I think I know just the piece. Have you ever wondered what a legal contract would sound like on a violin?"

I could pick out, by the smiles, who here was Jewish.

"This is a legal contract with a traditional melody from the Jewish tradition, Kol Nidre." I played.

The story goes that during the era of forced conversions, many Jews felt so guilty about converting that they needed absolution from this, and to be released from their vows on our Day of Atonement. Kol Nidre means "all vows," and in it we preemptively apologize for any vows in the next year that we cannot keep. It fell out of favor with the rabbis in the nineteenth century and Reform synagogues tried to ban it because it was taken out of context and used to slander us as faithless and liars. With my history of pretended conversion, it resonated with me. The attempt to ban it failed, partly because it's haunting and sad and beautiful and partly because Jews don't give up traditions easily.

Afterwards, I went to the open bar and ordered red wine (because my beer options were all boring). Two teenage boys giggled next to me. They both had beers, and they both looked too young to have beers. The bartender, a young man with visible tattoo sleeves under his uniform shirt, kept giving them a sour glance. I wondered what the story behind that was but didn't feel it was my place to ask. I didn't want to get the bartender in trouble if he was involved somehow.

The first boy, who had acne and braces, said, "My SS name is UnterWaffenHussenLahder." He was wearing too much body spray under his ill-fitting suit.

The second boy, who was dark-haired and dressed in an expensive suit with the tie untied and top shirt button unbuttoned, answered, "My SS name is UberWaffleHattenRobberHussan."

They burst into giggles.

*Hilarious.* I found Ludwig's eye across the room and gave him my most annoyed look. He winced and came over. "Are you enjoying the party?"

I glanced over at the boys and then rolled my eyes.

Ludwig put on his most avuncular smile and asked, "Hello, boys, are you enjoying the party?" The smile went well with the suit. You can take the man out of the rococo era, but you can't take the urge to peacock yourself about in something wildly expensive out of the rococo era man. He even still had his habit of wearing rings on all ten fingers. He also wore a wristwatch that cost more than most people's cars.

The boy with acne put his beer behind his back and bit his lip. The other boy said, "It's okay for old people."

I took my wine from the bartender, took a sip, and said in what I thought was a very mild and patient voice, "The Holocaust isn't funny."

Ludwig's eyes became enormous, but he said nothing.

"Are you Jewish?" the dark-haired boy asked. The boy with acne blushed.

"Yes," I said.

There was a brief pause, and then the dark-haired boy rallied. "Then why aren't you laughing? I thought Jews were supposed to be funny."

"I guess I didn't get the memo," I said with passive-aggressive false calm. I took another tart sip of wine.

"Are you sure you're Jewish? You don't have any Jewish traits! I bet you don't think the site Cats That Look Like Hitler is funny, either."

I raised my eyebrow at him and took another sip of wine. Not enough that they thought they were driving me to drink, but enough that—hopefully—they knew I didn't consider that comment worthy of a response. *Little boy, I've been needled by far more obnoxious people than the likes of you. Unsatisfactory effort.*

"Excuse me," Ludwig said. "Who's your father?"

"My *mother* is Mary Richmond," the boy answered. "Maybe you've heard of her. She's a partner. What, are you going to talk to her about whether I'm sensitive enough to *the help*?"

In the background, the bartender scowled. I gave him a sympathetic glance.

"No," Ludwig said, "I'm going to discuss whether you're being polite to *my guest*."

"What, are you gay?" the boy asked.

Ludwig smiled, the smile where his eyes went dark and you could see a faint hint of fang. There was a moment where they stared at each other, the dark-haired boy looking like a rabbit who was staring into the eyes of a fox.

"Uh," he said. Certainly the wittiest thing he'd said all night.

Ludwig gave him a hard stare and waved his hand at him, and the boys scattered.

Destiny waddled over with her hand on her belly and kissed me on the cheek. "You were inspired, as always."

I smiled and murmured thanks.

"If you'll excuse me," Ludwig said, "I need to speak to Mary for a moment. I'll be right back." He rushed away.

"Is something wrong?" Destiny asked.

"Just some teenagers who think they're funny," I said.

Destiny scanned the crowd and noticeably picked out the boy with acne, nervously standing behind his mother, and the dark-haired boy watching Ludwig beeline towards his mother with an expression of chagrin. The woman Ludwig spoke to—presumably Mary—scowled toward her son and mouthed something that looked suspiciously like *You're in big trouble.*

Ludwig headed back to hover protectively at my side, which was equal parts endearing and annoying. He leaned over to the bartender and asked, in an almost conspiratorial tone, "What's the best wine you have back there?"

We both gave him enormous tips.

# A New Life

Abraham
New York, New York
June 6, 1939

New York City looked more like the movies than I'd ever dreamed possible. Our boat pulled into the harbor in the dark, and yet it was all tall buildings and glittering lights. Even the children—depressed as they were—appeared awed. We rushed to the front of the line, hoping that we would get indoors before sunrise. The air was all the scent of brine and exhaust fumes.

There was some awkwardness at Ellis Island, where the desk clerk issued Shlomo's paperwork under the English version of his name: Solomon. I supposed the papers didn't list the name I was born with either, but I felt bad for little Shlomo. At least they got Ruth's first name right. We registered under the name Horowitz.

I noticed they hadn't renamed Ludwig's alias. He was, however, questioned as to his views on Hitler. "It's difficult to answer that question without using language unbecoming to a gentleman," he said, turning up his aristocratic nose.

They also gave us literacy tests. I channeled Bettina Weber and rolled my eyes extensively while reading their samples as quickly as possible.

When asked about the Stradivarius, I handed Isaac to little Ruth and played Paganini for the immigration officer. This caused a visible change in his attitude, and they allowed us into the United States.

That unpleasantness over, we went looking for food for the children and purchased a newspaper so that we could find an apartment.

———————— ⌒⌒⌒ ————————

Abraham
New York, New York
July 1, 1939—July 1, 1943

WE SETTLED INTO an apartment in upper Manhattan. I enrolled the children in public school and Hebrew school on the weekends. It was cheerful and bright, with the sounds and smells of passing cars at all hours. Isaac spent his days sunning on a windowsill, and would come when called so I could stroke his soft, sun-warmed fur. I tried to go say Kaddish for Miriam and

# Immortal Gifts

Shayna—at a small group that met in living ru
rather than a full synagogue—but I had missed th
entire month. I told God repeatedly in the presence of
less than ten Jews that it was my sincere wish to say
Kaddish for my loved ones, but not enough people had
arrived for me to do it. One can only say Kaddish in the
presence of ten other Jews.

My first attempts to cook for Ruth and Solomon...
well, I didn't poison them, so I considered it a minor
victory. The children were unimpressed with my skills,
but that was fair. We ate at restaurants a lot until I
improved.

I didn't make them call me Abba or Tatti because
they already had a father—he was dead, but he had
existed—but as far as I was concerned, I was their
parent now. Ludwig helped, in an allowance-giving,
homework-assisting paternal style. We were Onkel
Avrahom and Uncle Ludwig to them.

My investments were at an unusually low point
because some assets had been seized by the Nazis, but
still livable. Ludwig's were doing well. So neither of us
had to work, although I did the odd violin concert
under an assumed name. Ludwig paid a doctor to have
us declared exempt from the draft because of ill health,
which was just as well because obviously we couldn't
march outdoors. We bought war bonds to make up for
it.

We also leaned into our old British accents and did
our best to avoid speaking in German because of anti-
German sentiment... at least in public.

Ludwig and I did the masquerade for the children,
much like Flora and I had done for John and Eliza,
which was stupid because they'd witnessed my attack

on the Nazis who killed their mother. We pretended to eat, or told them we'd eaten while they were at school, and fed any table scraps to Isaac. When they were home and awake, we flushed toilets randomly. We "went to bed" and stayed up all night reading. Ludwig took the largest bedroom with a view of the Chrysler Building, of course, but I took one with a lovely view, and the children shared. They seemed to prefer that. Little Solomon was wildly addicted to The Lone Ranger on the radio and would sometimes shout "Hi ho, Silver, away!" right before bed.

We also took the children to stage plays, concerts, and movies. We helped them with their homework. They were exemplary students, but they had to be. Many American universities, including Harvard, Yale, and Columbia, had rigid quotas on how many Jewish students they admitted. One dean of Yale instructed his admissions department, "Never admit more than five Jews, and take no Blacks at all."

If the children noticed that Onkel Avrahom and Uncle Ludwig weren't aging, they said nothing. Nor did they ever discuss what happened the day their mother died. I wasn't certain they remembered, to be honest. Surely they did, but they never spoke of it, gave no sign of it. Perhaps trauma had erased their memories.

———⟨∞⟩———

Ludwig
New York, New York
July 1, 1939—July 1, 1943

# Immortal Gifts

I HAD REMARKABLY little experience with children. I'd never intended to have any and even when I was a child myself, I spent little time with children who weren't my brother Friedrich. Abraham had parented before and I did my best to follow his lead. Not that I cooked, mind you. His attempts went from smelling dismal to smelling quite appealing, but of course, neither of us could eat it. We always had an excuse for the children, however. I wasn't sure why, since I was fairly certain they knew, but again, I followed Abraham's lead.

Alas, Friedrich, dead these many long years. It dismayed me to realize I seldom thought of him these days. But I had been a spare—Friedrich was the heir—and they had shipped me off to the church as soon as Friedrich reached his majority. On the rare days that I thought of him, I missed him terribly.

It was... oddly satisfying to help Solomon and Ruth grow and succeed. All right, Abraham's disapproving expression when I bribed the children to clean their bedroom was... less satisfying. Oh, the scolding I received! "Bad for their characters," etc.

Next time, I'd wait until Abraham was out.

It saddened me to not share a room with Abraham. It wasn't like we slept, after all. I merely wanted to have a conversation partner for those hours. But for propriety's sake, and appearances, and to further the illusion of ordinary mortal humanity for the children... well. One wouldn't want to give the wrong impression about our relationship. There might have been consequences. We hadn't shared a room except on the boat across the Atlantic, so perhaps he was pleased to have his own space again.

I was further saddened that times had changed so as to savagely curtail perfectly innocent physical affection between men. Men used to hug and hold hands and the like and never be thought less manly, let alone be accused of indecent behavior! But now it was as fraught as interactions with women had been in my youth. Ironically, they were fraught for the same reason: sex. Sex, and fear of people thinking that you might have it inappropriately.

I would never understand the obsession with sex, and I sorely missed hugs and hand-holding. But in deference to the times, I never held Abraham's hand in front of the children, however much I might have wished to do so.

---

Abraham
Atlantic Highlands, New Jersey
March 3, 2021

I WAS READING in my study—a biography of Leonard Bernstein, if you're interested—when Destiny came in. It was late—two a.m. or so. I tilted my head at her.

"The baby's head dropped, my water broke, and my contractions are about three and a half minutes apart."

My brain refused to process this information. I stared at her.

"I'm in labor," she said, sounding mildly exasperated.

I leaped out of my chair so quickly that I startled her, rushed around the room at vampiric speed gathering up the things she had packed for the hospital and my

sun gear, then asked her, "Do you want me to ca.
you to the car?"

"I—" She clutched her stomach. "Let me try."

I rushed to the door and opened it for her. She
waddled down the stairs, and we piled into the car and
drove to the hospital. The trees were still bare, but the
snow was gone. I dropped her off at the door and
parked the car and ran to meet her in the ER, quickly
enough that I didn't show up on any cameras.

As I saw it, my job was to wait on Destiny while she
did all the hard work. I held her hand; I mopped her
brow. I supported all of her pain medication decisions.
She squeezed my hand and moaned, and I kissed her
cheek and told her she was doing a great job.

It irresistibly reminded me of death, which might
sound odd. There was something momentous in the air,
a sense that the number of souls in the world was
changing. I thought of my father, of Flora and the
children, of Victoria. Also, I realized Destiny might die,
although maternal mortality rates were much better
than they had been in my youth. The realization still
caused ice in the pit of my stomach. Destiny was fine;
I'm not sure what I would have done if she hadn't been.
The nurse took her readings at one point and said, "Uh
oh," and I had a moment of wondering if I was going to
create a new vampire right then, but it all came to
nothing.

Either way, I knew that my life was changing forever.

When our daughter finally emerged, it was shocking
and bloody. I'd never been present for such a thing
before. Okay, I'd been there when my sweet Devorah
had her kittens—she'd insisted—but it was so much
easier for cats that I found myself unprepared. Or

perhaps it's partly that cats are incredibly stoic and liars about whether they're in pain. I hid my discomfort and anxiety and told Destiny that she was amazing.

The smell of iron was overwhelming and was making me salivate and my fangs protrude, so I clapped my hand over my mouth and caught her eye. She smiled and nodded, and I rushed out to the men's room to control myself. I returned, calmer, with the nurse trying not to smile at me. I suppose she thought I'd vomited at the sight of blood, and found that somehow cute.

And then we—I—we had a crying baby girl. They cleaned her off and handed her to Destiny, who was glowing. I wondered what she was. Was she human? A vampire? Something new? I'd known her for less than five minutes; how did I already love her with all my heart? I said the blessing for firsts again. "*Barukh atah, Adonai Eloheinu, Melekh ha'olam, shehecheyanu, v'kiy'manu, v'higiyanu laz'man hazeh.*" Blessed are You, Adonai our God, Sovereign of all, who has kept us alive, sustained us, and brought us to this time.

"What do you want to name her?" the nurse asked.

Destiny gazed at me, and I suggested, "Miriam Eliza?" While we traditionally don't name babies after someone who died young and tragically, there's an exception for martyrs.

Destiny smiled and nodded. She kissed Miriam on the forehead and said, "Oh yeah, I could do that again."

The nurse laughed and said, "You were a champ."

Destiny
Red Bank, New Jersey
March 4, 2021

WE HAD A private hospital room to share with Miriam, which was lovely. I held Miriam, who was perfect, and Abraham sat on the bed next to us. "How are you feeling?" he asked.

It was the happiest day of my life, or at least tied with my wedding, but... "My hoo-hah hurts." I burst out laughing at his mortified expression. "I'm happy, but yeah, that hurt like a..." I trailed off and glanced down at little Miriam. Did I need to censor my language for a newborn? "Like a matron fornicator."

Abraham gently laid a hand over Miriam's ear and murmured, "Innocent ears!" but he was grinning.

I laughed.

"Seriously, can I help?"

I considered this. "I'd really like a cup of tea and maybe some chocolate."

He hopped up. "Easily done." He kissed my forehead and walked out. Behind the blinds, I could tell the sun was rising.

The nurse came in. "Good morning, Mrs. Levy." Before I could say anything, she opened the blinds, leaving Miriam and me in full sunlight.

I stared down at Miriam in a panic, but she didn't react to the sun at all. Not a vampire, then. I mean, Ludwig had said she wouldn't be, but I what if he'd been wrong? I glanced up at the nurse, who was staring at me. "My husband has a sun sensitivity, and I didn't know if our daughter inherited it or not. Please close the blinds again for her father?"

The nurse asked, "Sun sensitivity?" but she closed the blinds.

"Like porphyria," I said. I'm not a good liar, but that was enough that the nurse's eyes widened and she stared down at Miriam in alarm.

Abraham came in with a paper cup full of tea and a candy bar. He'd found Lindt.

The nurse eyed Abraham, but all she said was, "I was actually here for your daughter, for tests."

I surrendered my daughter, and Abraham helped me sit up—ow—and drink tea. I only ate a few squares of chocolate, but I drank all the tea. Then I said, "I think I'll lie back down, if you don't mind." I didn't want to sit any more than I needed to. Parts of my body were well aware that they had recently passed a baby.

He helped me settle back in. He was stronger than he appeared, but I supposed that was to be expected with his condition.

The nurse bustled back in. "Here's your little girl! We didn't close the blinds and she didn't react, so she's fine. What condition does your husband have again? Did you say porphyria?"

Abraham's eyes went wide and his jaw dropped. He took Miriam out of the nurse's arms and turned his back on her.

"Thank you," I said. "Please keep the blinds closed."

"We didn't hurt your baby, sir," the nurse said.

That was when my mothers arrived. "Let me see that baby!" Morgan insisted, and Abraham handed her over.

Morgan held the baby and bounced a little. "Aren't you precious? Yes, you are!" Bridget leaned in and kissed Miriam on the forehead.

The nurse returned with my lunch, which wasn't vegetarian, so I made her take it back.

————————⁓◯∽∽◯⌒————————

Abraham
Red Bank, New Jersey
March 4, 2021—March 6, 2021

OUR EXPENSIVE private room wasn't particularly private. People were coming in and out at all hours of the day and night to take Destiny's blood pressure, check the baby, etc. And even though we'd said that we wanted to "room in" with little Miriam, they kept whisking her away for tests and exams. I held her and cuddled her while Destiny slept, and was keen to go home—not least because the staff kept coming in and trying to open the blinds. All that said, Miriam was worth the inconvenience and the effort we'd gone to to get her. She was perfect. She cried and slept a lot, but I think she recognized us and would cry when the staff came and took her away. I had never imagined I could love anyone as much as I loved Miriam.

When we could finally go home, well. Those couple of weeks were a blur. Thank goodness we had no bottle baby kittens.

At first, Destiny lay in bed, and I brought her meals on a tray, and brought her little Miriam whenever she cried. Then Destiny started moving around more. She intended to go back to work once her maternity leave was over, so I was going to take primary responsibility for baby care once that happened. I read up on the topic.

Not needing sleep was an advantage in infant care. I could let Destiny sleep while I fed and diapered little Miriam.

I put Miriam back in her crib after a feeding, and Ivan came over and hopped into the crib. He sniffed her all over and then gazed up at me.

"Yes, she's a baby," I said.

Ivan tilted his head at me. I again had the sense that Ivan understood English now.

"What?"

Ivan lay down next to Miriam and wrapped a furry "arm" around her. He purred. Maybe he was warm; he became warmer after he fed, just like me.

Freddy trotted into the room and lay down in front of the crib, as if he were guarding it.

Miriam seemed perfectly satisfied with breast milk, by the way. I wasn't surprised. Despite what I had been told about vampires' being infertile being untrue—we just needed a great deal of modern technology to make it happen—Ludwig continued to insist that vampires were only created one way.

---

Destiny
Rumson, New Jersey
April 28, 2021

THE SHORT, PALE woman wearing an elaborate headscarf ushered me and Miriam back to the changing room introduced herself as "Elisheva, the mikveh lady." She led us into a luxurious changing area, with a shower-tub combo and brown, cream, and stone tiles. Fluffy white towels sat waiting on a granite counter.

"No necklace, no wedding ring, no scents. Nothing you weren't born with," Elisheva said in a practiced tone. It was probably her regular spiel. No masks, either; they'd asked for our vaccination status instead.

"It's Miriam who's converting, not me." I smiled at her, even though I felt a slight twinge of guilt at feeling like I was being disloyal to my faith. But we don't care if you're Wiccan and something else, so Miriam could decide for herself when she got older. According to the Internet, this was even a thing: "Jewitch."

"Oh!" Elisheva bit her lip. "Well, do shower, to keep things clean in the mikveh, including between your toes and under your fingernails. You can wear your bathing suit, but Miriam can't wear anything she wasn't born in."

"Including her diaper, I presume."

Elisheva nodded. "And take her into the tub with you, so you can wash between her fingers and toes. Do you want me to hold her while you change?"

I nodded and handed Miriam to Elisheva, who smiled and spoke gently to Miriam. I ducked behind a door and changed into my bathing suit. When I came out, Elisheva had her back turned, which was nice. "All done."

Elisheva handed me the baby and said, "I'll be outside. Knock when you're ready."

I climbed into the bath with Miriam and examined her fingers and toes for dirt. When I was convinced that Miriam was as clean as a baby could be, I climbed back out, wrapped Miriam in a fluffy towel, and knocked.

"Ready?" Elisheva asked through the door.

"Yes," I said, and opened it.

Elisheva smiled at me and led me out through another door into a room with a deep pool of water, where Abraham and Rabbi Kaplan and Dave the accountant waited. Abraham was so beautiful—huge brown eyes, long brown hair, delicate features... For a moment, I stopped and stared at him.

Elisheva nodded at me, and I handed her Miriam's towel and descended the steps into the warm, soft water. It wasn't my particular tradition, but it still felt deeply holy to me. Hey, I'm eclectic. I don't think my tradition has a monopoly on holiness. My initiation included a bath in my mothers' massive tub with rose petals and incense, so... the same, but different, I supposed.

---

Abraham
Rumson, New Jersey
April 28, 2021

DESTINY AND I brought little Miriam into the community mikveh together for her conversion ceremony, and Destiny went to shower and bathe little

Miriam. I sat with Dave and Rabbi Kaplan from Temple Emanu-El and fidgeted in the waiting area. He was a pale man with thick red hair and horn-rimmed glasses wearing a kippah. He would oversee Miriam's conversion today. Next to me, my accountant, Dave, fidgeted. On the other side of Dave, Destiny's friend and vet tech Lucy looked around curiously.

"Do I need to do anything special to be respectful?" Lucy asked.

Rabbi Kaplan smiled at her. "You're fine, but thank you for asking. If it were Destiny converting, the men would be outside and you would turn your back when she dropped the towel, but that's not necessary for a baby."

Lucy tilted her head. "Thank you."

Rabbi Kaplan turned to me. "You know your baby would be Jewish in our congregation, without conversion?" Rabbi Kaplan said. Yes, I'd gone Reform after Rabbi Kaplan informed me services were Friday nights and assured me Sunday mornings were a High Reform thing. He also promised a lack of organ music, saying they tended more towards acoustic guitar—which is still a *no* if one is Orthodox, by the way, but... it wasn't an organ. I'm sorry, organs are just too... churchy.

"I know. I want her to be recognized by Conservative and Orthodox congregations as well. I was raised Orthodox."

"Of course."

"His parents were super frum. Sent him to yeshiva and everything," Dave added.

I gave Dave a quelling glance and added, "Unfortunately, they're no longer with us."

"I'm sorry to hear that," Rabbi Kaplan said. "May their memory be a blessing." There was a pause, and then he added, "We'd love to see you in our services."

"I have an unusual sun sensitivity that makes me not want to leave the house during the day."

"Oh, is that why you're not the one taking the baby in? Not wanting to take forever scrubbing off the sunscreen, only to put it back on?" Rabbi Kaplan smiled at me, his expression sympathetic.

I'd actually done it out of respect for the mikveh itself, but I nodded. I didn't know if I counted as dead or not, but if a corpse got into the mikveh somehow it would have to be drained and refilled. It didn't matter whether they knew or not; *I* would know.

Of course, the dead are released from all obligations as well. Was I dead or undead? How did that affect halacha? I wished that I'd gone to ask Rabbi Mendel about it after all, back in 1841, as I had considered doing. I thought perhaps I should create a throwaway email address and ask a few rabbis. I wondered if they would assume I was a crank and ignore me.

"Well," he said, "I wish you'd come for Passover last month; that was at night. Maybe in the fall, when the days get shorter, you can come see us on Friday nights. At the very least, I expect to see you for the High Holy Days. I mean, you're an Amud member..."

He meant I paid dues at a higher rate to support the synagogue. "We'll see." I wanted to attend High Holiday services, badly, but was still concerned about whether all the Kohanim would have to leave because I was arguably dead. The Kohanim bless the congregation, so I could deny my entire community blessing. Would my very presence nullify the blessing?

Yes, I'd fully adopted Ludwig's definitions of vampires and rejected the idea that I might be an alukah... although if I were, I would definitely not be dead. Hmm. That said, Ludwig had chuckled when I asked if we could shapeshift.

"Also, I assume your wife is secure in her particular tradition, but please make sure she knows she's welcome to study with me and join the tribe as well, if she likes. No pressure, of course."

I smiled. This was, without a doubt, the loveliest reaction I'd ever received to my mixed marriage. "I will. Thank you."

Destiny came out wearing a bathing suit with the baby wrapped in a towel, followed by the mikveh lady in her lovely tichel.

The mikveh itself is a small pool with enough water to cover the entire body. There are seven steps down into the water, and most modern mikvaot are lovely. This one was no exception; all blue and cream sandstone-like tile. It looked like a luxurious spa. We'd been told that this water was clean and purified and warm, and on the other side of the wall was natural rain water, and when someone went into the water the waters would "kiss," which fulfilled the commandment that the mikveh be natural water. It was slightly over Jacuzzi-sized across, but five feet deep. It smelled fresh, unchlorinated.

Dave stood up and turned his back to give Miriam privacy. If she were older, we would have waited outside and relied upon the mikveh lady to say things were kosher.

Destiny took Miriam out of the towel and walked down into the water with the naked baby. The waters came up to her shoulders. She smiled up at me. "This is nice." She bounced Miriam in the water.

"Hold her out away from you," Rabbi Kaplan said. "In order to be kosher, nothing can touch her but the water."

Destiny appeared uncertain but held Miriam out at arm's length.

"All right," Rabbi Kaplan said. "In my experience, they cry. There's a moment of surprise, and then they cry. Blow in her face first, and then let go."

Destiny winced.

The rabbi smiled, a gentle smile. "Isn't that the hardest thing for any parent? Letting go?"

Destiny glanced over at me, and I nodded. She blew into Miriam's face and let go. I felt a moment of panic—oh no, what if we lost Miriam in this tiny space—but surely it was safe? They wouldn't allow this if it weren't.

Miriam scrunched up her face before disappearing under the water, and I made the blessing for her. "*Barukh atah Adonai, Elohenu Melekh ha'olam asher kid'eshanu b'mitzvotav v'tzivanu al ha'tevillah.*" Blessed are You, O Lord, our God, King of the universe, who has sanctified us with Your commandments and commanded us concerning the immersion.

"*Kasher!*" Rabbi Kaplan said, and Destiny caught the baby and pulled her close. Miriam cried, as expected, but mostly seemed startled. And then we all sang "*Siman Tov u'Mazel Tov*" to her, the song for weddings, conversions, and other joyful events. Destiny kissed Miriam on the cheek and she quieted.

My baby was a Jew, and I was so grateful to Destiny for being so generous as to do this with me. When

Destiny brought the baby out, I kissed her on her tiny head, and Destiny on her cheek. It wasn't Sukkot—sometimes called Zman Simchateinu—but it was very much the season of our joy (the literal translation of "zman simchateinu").

---

Abraham
Atlantic Highlands, New Jersey
August 2, 2021

THE KNOCK ON OUR front door came around three p.m. on a hot August Sunday.

Destiny got up and carried Miriam on her hip to the door. I craned my head around the hall to see who it was.

It was, alas, two Atlantic Highlands policemen, Idiot Husband, and Long-Suffering Wife. One policeman stood a little in front, and the other stood behind, writing things down in a little notebook. The man in front was bigger and darker—dark hair, terra-cotta suntan—and had a colossal mustache, while the one in the back was thin and pale and fair-haired. It had been about nine months since we'd seen them last. Had Idiot Husband really spent all that time agitating for something terrible to happen to Ivan?

"Can I help you?" Destiny asked. I was already picking up a copy of the restraining order and Ludwig's business card.

"May we come in?" the officer asked. Behind him, Long-Suffering Wife rolled her eyes almost audibly.

I walked over to stand behind Destiny, paperwork in hand. "I have a restraining order requiring Frank here to keep 100 feet from us at all times," I said, handing the paperwork to the officer. "My attorney's card. Do you mind if I call him?"

"Hopefully that won't be necessary," the officer said. "Sir, ma'am, do you have a rabid pet?"

"No," Destiny said. "I'm a veterinarian, by the way. My cats are both fully vaccinated. Do you need to see my vaccination records? I have them here in the house..."

"My dog was fine until he bit her cat!" Idiot Husband said.

"Rabies spreads via saliva," Destiny said. "His dog bit my cat. My cat didn't bite his dog." She turned to Idiot Husband and said, "I'm so sorry about your dog."

"His dog attacked my cat," I emphasized. "This is harassment."

"Have you tested your cat?" the other officer said.

"The only test for rabies involves decapitating the pet, so no. But I can provide my proof of vaccination, and he's shown no rabies symptoms. If he were sick, he would have manifested symptoms in the first thirty days, usually more like a week..." Destiny paused, then added, "It's standard practice to quarantine them for thirty days, watch for symptoms, and conclude that they're uninfected if they show no symptoms during that time."

"Their cat isn't rabid," Long-Suffering Wife said, in a long-suffering monotone.

The one who did most of the talking asked, "May I see him?"

I didn't like where this was going, but Destiny called, "Ivan!"

Ivan trotted into the room on his silent little cat feet. The talkative officer walked over and offered Ivan his hand. Ivan sniffed it, then gazed up at the man, expectant, awaiting petting.

The officer grabbed Ivan by the scruff.

"No!" Destiny said, rushing forward. "What are you doing? Stop!"

I was bracing myself to grab my cat away and leave town after, because an altercation with the police would attract Thomas's attention. I needed to either talk him down or act so quickly that things didn't have time to escalate, because if they did, my wife and baby might be harmed. I had a quick, visceral mental flash of Miriam senior, little Shayna, and the single bullet. I walked towards the officer, both hands up, trying not to appear threatening. "My cat is fine. Please put him down."

Inanna swaggered towards the officer and growled, a threatening large-dog-worthy sound. The officer glanced down at her, uncertain, then looked back at Idiot Husband, as if he was wondering if he had the wrong cat. Inanna stared up at the officer and growled again. There was the slightest shift in her weight in her hindquarters, like she was thinking about leaping.

Ivan was doing what cats do when you scruff them and was holding still, but his eyes were preternaturally intelligent and calculating. There were clattering claws down the hall, and Freddy burst into the room and launched himself at the officer, who dropped Ivan in surprise. Ivan raced out of the room, a golden blur, and vanished. Freddy did a little dance on his hind legs at the officer, as if the body-slam were friendliness.

Inanna washed one of her front paws, appearing decidedly smug.

"Freddy."

Frank the Idiot Husband had fallen to his knees on our Persian carpet and was staring at the dog. Freddy stared back at his former owner with huge, sad eyes.

*Oh, crap.* People no longer believed in vampirism. Were we about to be the proof for the modern era? That would *absolutely* attract Thomas's attention.

"Sir, I thought you said you put your dog down."

"I did," he breathed. "I was there. The vet declared him dead."

"This dog showed up on our doorstep, and we have sucker written on the outside of our house in both cat and dog," I said. I intentionally kept my voice light and casual, and besides, it was the truth... just not the whole truth.

The officers stared at each other, looked at Frank, and looked at us.

"Was your dog put to sleep at her clinic?" the quiet officer asked.

"No."

"Is your dog microchipped?" the first officer asked.

"No." And then Frank did the unthinkable and cried.

"So you can't prove this is your dog."

"No." He sobbed.

Clara, the Long-Suffering Wife, stared at Freddy. "He looks exactly like our Freddy, but our Freddy is dead, so it can't be him."

I grabbed a box of tissues and handed it to Frank in silent sympathy.

The officers stared at each other again. The one with the restraining order placed it on the coffee table. "We're sorry to bother you, Mr. and Mrs. Levy. Mr. and Mrs. Cranshaw, it's time for us to go."

Destiny and I glanced at each other, and she handed Miriam to me and kneeled in front of Frank. "Do you need a glass of water first?"

Frank shook his head. He stood shakily, with Destiny's help, and walked towards the door. The man stared at the dog again. "He looks *exactly* like Freddy."

Clara let out a long breath and blinked, like she was holding back tears.

And then they all left. I went searching for Ivan—I knew he was in his favorite basement hiding spot behind the coffin—and petted him and apologized for the mean man grabbing him. Ivan let me pick him up and carry him upstairs and give him a treat of chicken liver puree, which he graciously shared with Freddy.

"Should we give him back his dog?" Destiny asked.

"We can't." I frowned. "We'd have to explain his new dietary needs, and that he can't go out, but that's okay because he doesn't need to, and..."

Destiny looked like she didn't see a problem and was mildly exasperated with the explanation. I supposed it must have sounded like normal discharge instructions to her.

"We can't tell them about Freddy's condition without telling them about mine."

Destiny did a one-armed shrug around the baby. "You have a medical condition. So does Freddy." It was naïve of her to think she could trust Idiot Husband and his wife with that kind of information, but I loved her for it. The answer was still no.

"Last time I told someone about my condition, they contacted mental health professionals on my behalf. I left town and changed my name."

Destiny sighed. "It sounds like you do that a lot."

I bit back a bitchier reply as unfair and settled for "Yes, there's a dangerous bigot out there that I don't want to find me, so sometimes I have to move."

Destiny nibbled her lip and stared at the floor. Then she said, "I still don't want to move. We'd have to bring Miriam's brother with us, and my mothers. That said, you'd let me know if it was too dangerous to stay, right?"

It was my turn to shrug. "Assuming I accurately judged the danger, yes." Thomas was, I was reasonably certain, after me specifically—because I was a Jewish vampire. Miriam was Jewish, but not a vampire. Destiny was neither.

Destiny eyed Freddy. "Do we need to dye the dog?"

I burst out laughing. "I think the damage is done." I gave Freddy a comforting hug but wasn't sure whether I was comforting him or me.

# Family Reunion

Abraham
New York, New York
June 9, 1953

Ruth entered the apartment with a strained expression. "Onkel Avrahom? Uncle Ludwig?" The windows were open because of the heat, and there was a faint scent of hot garbage wafting up from the street. Downstairs, children squealed, splashed, and laughed as they played in the water from the open fire hydrant.

"Is something the matter?" I asked as Ludwig stuck his head out of his room with a book in one hand.

"This is awkward," she said, "so please sit down and let me get it over with as quickly as possible."

Solomon glanced up from his university homework at that. "Ruthie?"

Ludwig and I sat on the long, red, square, modern sofa side by side. Was Ludwig missing his red Victorian sofa? Ruth didn't sit; she paced.

Finally, she said, "So, good news and bad news. The good news is that I'm engaged."

"Mazel tov!" I said.

Solomon was silent. I glanced over and he was watching her with an expression of concern.

"The bad news," she said, "is that my future in-laws are very religious and don't approve of... your lifestyle."

Ludwig and I shared a confused look. *Lifestyle?* Did they know we were vampires, or did they think we were...

"I told them you didn't share a room and that I've seen nothing... untoward. They applaud your discretion but are only willing to allow us to marry if... if you and I put some distance between one another."

"Your uncle and I have *never*..." Ludwig said, with some heat.

"They don't care, Uncle Ludwig." She sat in a chair opposite the sofa. "Appearances. You know."

Ludwig scowled. "I'm uncertain you should marry a young man whose parents have such dirty minds."

Dirty thoughts are not a sin in Judaism. You have to act on them inappropriately in order for it to be a sin. Not that this was the time to offer this information. Besides, that didn't mean they were blameless. Telling a young woman to cut ties with her parents was unkind. I hoped the young man in question was nicer than his parents.

"You've never... they did their best to raise us and you're ungrateful!" Solomon said.

"I am not!" Ruth said.

"You've always kept them at arm's length, even though they saved our lives!"

Ruth rolled her eyes and made a disgusted sound, looking for all the world like the eighteen-year-old she was.

I raised my hand. When I had everyone's attention, I asked, "Do you love him?"

With tears and a sappy smile, Ruth nodded.

"Then I support you and will do what I can to help you," I said, even though I thought my heart would literally break.

Ludwig stood and stormed out of the room, slamming the door. I winced. I glanced over at Solomon, who was glaring daggers at Ruth.

"Thank you," she said. "And if I might be so bold, um, while I'm incredibly grateful that you're paying for my brother's college, please consider whether you're ruining his marriage chances as well."

"Butt out!" Solomon said.

"You know Ludwig and I are just friends, and not...?"

"It's none of my business," Ruth said, with a firmness that brooked no further argument.

———————⸎———————

Abraham
New York, New York
April 30, 1956

SOLOMON STARED AT the sheaf of letters he'd spread out on the dining table, his shoulders slumped. All rejection letters from colleges. "New York University is an excellent school," he said. They had rejected him from Yale, Columbia, Cornell, Pennsylvania... all medical schools with Jewish quotas. Solomon had a perfect A+ average in premed from Brandeis and excellent testing scores. The scent of brewing coffee wafted in from the kitchen—a necessity for all of Solomon's studying become entrenched habit.

Ruth had married the nice young man from Brooklyn. I'd even met him once, not that his parents knew that. He was quiet and gentle and well-spoken, and I approved. Solomon was postponing everything in favor of his med school dreams and didn't even date. All he did was go to class and study.

Ludwig had chosen not to meet Ruth's spouse. He found her in-laws' accusations hurtful in a way that I didn't. I found the requirement to cut ties with us more painful than the reason and didn't really care what her in-laws thought of me. Ludwig cared. His feelings were his own and were valid.

Ludwig glanced over the pile of letters, his expression dark and his lips pressed together. "What school would be your first choice?"

"It's fine, Uncle Ludwig. New York University is fine."

Ludwig walked over to the white telephone and picked up the receiver. "Operator, I'd like to talk to Columbia admissions. Thank you, yes, I'll hold."

Solomon stared at Ludwig, his mouth slightly agape.

"Yes, thank you. My name is Louis Weiss, and I'm interested in making a generous donation to your university." Ludwig was a well-known philanthropist in his current persona, so I'm certain that got their attention. "I'm thinking around a hundred thousand... oh, I'm sorry, this is admissions and not fundraising? How silly, the operator must have misunderstood me..."

Solomon waved his arms and shook his head.

Ludwig moved the receiver away from his mouth. "What's that, dear? You didn't get in? Oh. Well. That changes things, doesn't it?" He lifted the receiver to his mouth again. "I'm sorry to have wasted your time, but I hope you have a lovely day... what? The name of the student?"

Ludwig smirked at Solomon, who buried his face in his hands.

"Solomon Horowitz. Yes, he's the son of a dear friend... Oh, will you? That would be lovely. Let us know what you find... Yes, thank you, and have a wonderful day." He placed the receiver back on its cradle.

"Uncle Ludwig, they might throw out someone else if they let me in!" Solomon said.

Ludwig all but placed the back of his hand on his forehead as he radiated martyrdom. "You're welcome?"

Solomon put his head down on the table and moaned, "Thank you."

———————⌒∞⌒———————

Abraham
Atlantic Highlands, New Jersey
September 5, 2021


DESTINY ANSWERED the door, and the man who came in was white-haired, stooped and shrunken, and almost as thin as he'd been as a teenager. "Please, come in," she said. The foliage outside was beginning to turn olive drab.

The old man came in slowly, leaning on a cane, but when he saw me, his eyes lit up. "Onkel Avrahom."

"Hello, Shlomo." I wouldn't have recognized him if I hadn't been expecting him. I'd watched him from afar but hadn't seen him this old...

He shook his head and laughed. "We always knew. Always. In the beginning, Ruth and I would whisper to each other about whether you were going to eat us, but as time went on, it became obvious that we'd been rescued from the true monsters by something with a paternal instinct."

In retrospect, perhaps Ludwig and I should have been more forthcoming.

"Is Uncle Ludwig around?"

"We don't live together anymore, but he's around."

"But you're vampires."

"Yes." He was so old. I was suddenly unbearably sad that I'd let him get this old, but this wasn't a life he would have chosen. I could have offered him the choice. I could almost taste the bitter regret. Of course, after one of his girlfriends—as the moderns say—"ghosted" him after meeting me and Ludwig...

"Well," he said, "let's see this baby!"

We led him over to the sectional sofa and put Miriam in his lap. He pulled out an ancient stethoscope and listened to her little heart, examined her eyes. "What's her name?"

"Miriam." I held out a finger, and she grabbed it in a warm, chubby hand.

He glanced up at me, surprised.

"Your mother, and you, are direct descendants of my brother, Samuel."

He smiled. "So you're really my uncle, sort of. My mother once said she met him, when she was tiny and he was ancient. Everyone thought you'd died of consumption."

"I almost did. It's why Ludwig turned me." I made a face. "Without asking."

Solomon laughed. "Yes, that sounds like him." He gazed down at Miriam and said, "What am I looking for?"

"Is she a normal baby?" Destiny and I thought she was a perfectly normal human baby, but parenting was a more anxiety-inducing exercise than I had expected. I wanted reassurance, but also I was curious.

"She looks like one. Why wouldn't she be?"

"She's mine," I said. "As in, genetically mine."

"It took some effort," Destiny said. "The best reproductive assistance money could buy."

"Hmm," Solomon said. "You should probably ask Uncle Ludwig instead of me. Despite my upbringing, I don't really know much about vampires."

I pulled out my cell phone.

———— ⌘ ————

Abraham
Atlantic Highlands, New Jersey
September 5, 2021

LUDWIG RUSHED indoors under a heavy hat and cloak, and, when the door was safely closed, removed them. He eyed the elderly man on the sectional sofa with interest.

"Uncle Ludwig," Solomon said.

"My God, Solomon." Ludwig sat next to him on the sofa. "How... how have you been?"

Solomon laughed. "I had a good life. Married a wonderful girl, had three darling children, seven sweet grandchildren..." He smiled. "I had Onkel Avrahom call you because he asked *me* if this was a normal baby, and I thought you would know better than I."

"Only time will tell for certain. Most of what I know is legend, since I don't think a baby like Miriam has been born in my lifetime, and I'm almost three hundred."

"I'll take legend," I said. I stretched out my legs, putting my feet on the coffee table. Ludwig picked up a pillow and swatted them with it. I glared—it was *my* coffee table, and I'd put my feet on it if I liked! Solomon, sitting further down on the red sectional sofa, chuckled. Destiny, sitting on the other side of Ludwig, put her feet on the coffee table in solidarity and gave Ludwig a defiant smirk.

Ludwig looked at Destiny, looked at the pillow in his hands, and placed it beside himself. "Well," he said. "It's possible that she'll stop aging when she reaches adulthood."

Destiny blinked. Her feet came off the coffee table as she sat up.

"Or she might be a perfectly normal human baby. Only time will tell."

"I'm... hoping for that," Destiny said. I was hoping for the other option, of course. Because fuck death, that's why.

"One thing she isn't is a vampire," Ludwig said. "Those are only created one way."

"Flora told me that if we turned Eliza, she wouldn't age."

"Very true," Ludwig said. "Miriam appears to be developing at a normal rate for a human baby, so I wouldn't worry about that."

Ivan trotted into the room and sniffed Solomon thoroughly, then gave me a quizzical look and hopped up onto the sofa next to him.

Solomon smiled and petted Ivan. "Of course you still have a cat."

I smiled back and petted Ivan, too. His fur was so silky, but he was one big muscle underneath. Not like Inanna, who was massive, soft, and chunky.

"If she takes after you"—Ludwig smirked at me—"she won't have our sun sensitivity or our strength, but she might have our speed. She might also have a different random ability." Ludwig shrugged. "Or she could be mortal."

Solomon glanced over at Destiny. "You're not a vampire."

"No." She smiled at him.

"Vampires can't conceive," Ludwig said. "But that's not how new vampires are created, anyway."

"Vampire women don't menstruate," I said.

"Tell me that next time I'm having horrible cramps and you might make some headway," Destiny teased.

Solomon glanced from me to Destiny and back, then gave me a sympathetic look. He was always a perceptive boy. He handed Miriam to Destiny and then stood and beckoned. I followed him into the kitchen.

"You're in anticipatory mourning. I can tell." He smiled at me, his eyes gentle. "Don't mourn her until she's gone. You'll miss being happy now."

"Your lives are so short," I whispered. "You were a child a blink of an eye ago."

"I've had a wonderful life." He shook his head, causing his thinning white wisps of hair to shake. I remembered his thick head of brown hair with some sadness. "Don't mourn me either until I'm gone, and even then, know that you and Uncle Ludwig gave me a good life. Maybe get to know my children and grandchildren. They're your line, too."

I nodded, looking away.

Solomon patted my arm and started walking towards the door, leaning heavily on his cane. I followed most of the way. At the door, he made the thumb-and-pinkie phone gesture and said, "Uncle Ludwig, Onkel Avrahom? Call me."

Destiny beamed at him.

"I hope I did that right," he said. "My grandchildren do it all the time."

Destiny gave him a cheerful thumbs-up, and he smiled back, then left.

---

Destiny
Atlantic Highlands, New Jersey
September 5, 2021

I... DIDN'T want my baby to be immortal. I loved Miriam with all my heart, and that was why I wanted her to be a plain old regular mortal human baby. Immortality didn't appear to make Abraham happy, after all.

There was no point in borrowing trouble. I'd deal with things when there were things to deal with.

I liked Solomon. I suppose I shouldn't have been surprised that I liked a man my husband had raised. So far, Abraham seemed to be a wonderful father. Abraham had let Solomon stay a normal human man, which boded well for me and Miriam. I wondered if Abraham and Solomon had discussed it. It felt rude to ask.

I added Solomon's cell phone number to my phone—I got it from Abraham—and texted him, saying, *This is Destiny. I enjoyed meeting you! Please stay in touch.*

He texted back a thumbs-up emoji, which made me laugh.

———— ⌒⟨∞⟩⌒ ————

Ludwig
New Jersey
October 1, 2021

THOMAS WAS HERE, in the New York metropolitan area.

Worse, Thomas was not *here* as in Manhattan, Thomas was in Atlantic Highlands, where Abraham was. I wished the thing about bats were true; I could have flown across the harbor to Abraham's. Instead, I had to drive. I didn't know why Abraham wanted to live in *New Jersey*, of all places. I supposed it wasn't a stereotypical vampire hangout.

New reality television concept: *Vampires of New Jersey*. I wished I could sell it. What can I say? Sometimes I viewed rubbish during those long nights not sleeping. Let us speak no more of it.

Instead, I was stuck driving for an hour—I *despise* driving—to Abraham's. I was fairly certain that Thomas wouldn't be able to sense him, as his gifts tended more towards subtle hypnosis, but my ability to hide and seek... I wanted to be next to Abraham. I put my classical playlist on shuffle and drove. I had the windows tinted to prevent UV light but was also wearing sun gear.

I should have taken the ferry. I hadn't wanted to wait.

Very well, the countryside was picturesque, and driving there was better than driving on the busy Manhattan streets. But not even the autumn leaves and Itzhak Perlman could soothe my anxiety. Abraham knew Thomas had tried to kill *him*, but he still wasn't aware of Thomas's hand in Flora's and the children's deaths. I would spare him that knowledge, if I could.

I had devoted my life to Abraham and his safety for over a hundred years. Sometimes I was overcome with his physical beauty, although Abraham seemed unaware of this. I sometimes dreamed of his huge, dark eyes, his soft and sensuous lips, his delicate hands, his hair falling into his face as he played. Sometimes I feared my feelings might cross the line into... something else.

One anxiety at a time. I didn't have room in my head for more than one.

I parked my black Rolls-Royce Phantom V—I had bought it new, but now it was "vintage"—next to Abraham's boring silver Toyota, and rushed to the door.

————————⟨∞⟩————————

Abraham
Atlantic Highlands, New Jersey
October 1, 2021

THE NEWS WAS FULL of live feeds, of course. It wasn't every day that the "alt-right"—read "Nazis"—came to Atlantic Highlands. Ludwig dropped by to check on us, and he, Destiny, and I watched, in fascinated horror, images of mostly young white men as they swarmed the streets in the night with tiki torches, shaking their fists and shouting. They passed by Temple Emanu-El—my and Miriam's synagogue—and waved their torches threateningly at it while chanting, "Jews will not replace us!" Counterprotesters stood around the synagogue protectively, with signs reading "Punch a Nazi" and "Keep NJ Safe from Hate!"

Destiny held Miriam closer and shuddered. Together, they smelled like lavender, baby powder, and that new-baby scent. This almost certainly felt different to Destiny than it would have before she had a Jewish husband and baby.

I felt a surge of trauma-related panic, but covered it with logic. "That's so stupid," I said. "We're a tiny minority, less than 2.4% of the US population, and way less worldwide." At Destiny's questioning look, I said,

"After we lost six million in the Holocaust, I look up numbers every couple of years."

Ludwig lowered his eyes and crossed himself.

When the police around the synagogue told the crowd to disperse—they would have done this even if Rabbi Kaplan hadn't volunteered as a chaplain with them, but I'm sure it didn't hurt—the Nazis continued down the road to a park, screaming ethnic slurs and chanting about how Jews wouldn't replace them. I had googled this at one point and my IQ had reduced by several points.

At the park, in the torchlight, a familiar figure took the podium. He wore long red robes that looked like a cross between Inquisitor robes and a Klan uniform, and wore a huge wooden cross around his neck. He was tall and balding, and pulled back the red hood to reveal a frizzy fringe of dark hair and intense eyes. Seeing him again, especially in this context, was both unexpected and a bitter shock—although I suppose it shouldn't have been.

"Hypocrite," Ludwig spat. "How dare he dress like an Inquisitor? I know for a fact that they defrocked him in 1505."

The man—it was absolutely Thomas Hopkins, also known as Thomas of Toledo—raised his arms to thunderous applause and shouts and waved torches. Then he held up a single hand, and the crowd fell silent. "It's always been my truest mission to protect and purify," he said. His voice was still incongruously soft and serene. "This nation is a Christian nation, one nation under God, and yet there are Jews and witches working against you as we speak, seeking to undermine your values and way of life. They're using every means at their disposal, including control of all the world's financial markets, control of the media, and the blackest of black magic. Their goal is nothing less than your genocide, and our government does nothing! Not even questioning obvious Jews and witches. The government doesn't care, or was bought off by the Jews long ago."

This started another chant of "Jews will not replace us!"

I rolled my eyes. "Boring. Stop recycling your own material from the 1930s. Or even 1888 and the Goulston Street graffiti blaming us for the Jack the Ripper murders: 'The Juews are the men that will not be blamed for nothing.' Same old boring rubbish."

"How can people believe this garbage?" Destiny asked.

"Unfortunately," Ludwig said, his voice almost a whisper, "he has some demagoguery abilities. Mind control. They don't even realize it's happening."

"Jews control the world!" Thomas shouted.

I burst out laughing, much to Destiny's and Ludwig's dismay. I turned to Ludwig and said, "How many Passovers did you celebrate with me, Solomon, and Ruth, and how many of those went smoothly? How many of those did we all agree on what we wanted to include? 'We can't use this Haggadah because it doesn't have Miriam's cup!' 'I want to do the Four Questions, too, it's not fair to only let Ruth do it!' 'This Haggadah is too long!' Yes, that's precisely the type of organizational skill required to run the world." I crossed my arms and tilted my head with a smirk.

Ludwig covered his face with his hands. "Be serious."

"If I'm serious, I might cry," I said, and meant it.

"There is only one true solution," Thomas said. "Only one."

Hmm. What could that possibly be? I was fairly certain that I knew...

On the television, a police officer walked up onto the stage and said, "May I see your permit for this demonstration?"

"I don't need a permit," Thomas said. "This is well within the bounds of free speech and peaceable assembly." He didn't quite do the Qui-Gon Jinn Jedi Mind Trick wave, but he might as well have.

"I'm afraid you do," the officer said. "The maximum occupancy of this park is a hundred people, and we don't have an exact count, but you appear to have more like three hundred. That's a health and safety violation, and you need a permit."

"So says the Jews' sock puppet!" shouted someone in the front row.

"Is he here because you two are here?" Destiny asked.

Ludwig and I exchanged an uneasy glance as the crowd on the television started chanting, "Free speech! Free speech!"

―――――― ∞ ――――――

Abraham
La Paz, Bolivia
May 13, 1977

STILL NAUSEATED from the airplane, and profoundly grateful that we'd landed after dark, I wandered through dimly lit streets. I wasn't as affected by the altitude as I would have been if I had been mortal, but it still felt... unfamiliar. My Spanish was terrible, but adequate to the task of asking after German immigrants from a particular era. Ludwig's Spanish was better than mine, but I'd left him at the hotel, washing up after the flight.

Bolivia had expressed an unwillingness to extradite certain Nazi war criminals. Flying to Bolivia was a lot of effort to go to for a meal, but if it prevented the inexplicable evil of the Shoah from ever happening again, it was worth it.

I spotted the man under a streetlight, rushing through the streets with a brown paper bag. I followed him back to his home, where his wife looked both ways before shutting the door behind him. Ludwig appeared at my side, silent; somehow he always found me.

I opened up the file folder in my hand and compared the couple with the pictures of them paper-clipped to the sheets inside. Oskar and Helga Clauberg had worked in the camps and done medical experiments on Jews.

Ludwig and I peered in the windows side by side. It turned out that the paper bag contained liquor. The man opened a bottle and poured two glasses. They drank together.

They didn't *look* like monsters. They looked like an ordinary elderly couple. I glanced back down at the folder to confirm their identity and my eyes landed on "attempted to create conjoined twins by sewing twins together, leading to gangrene and death," "allowed women to be raped to study sterilization efficacy," and "intentionally infected children with tuberculosis," and my heart iced over.

"Are you still nauseated?" Ludwig asked.

"I could eat," I said, and closed the folder.

---

Abraham
Eatontown, New Jersey
October 1, 2021

WE PULLED UP into the driveway of Destiny's childhood home after dark, with the child seat and the pets. The leaves were turning.

I didn't think Destiny had shared "my little problem" with her mothers, but somehow I wasn't sure it would have fazed them. They were, for lack of a better descriptor, hippies, and appeared to believe in all kinds of things that most people didn't. Their home was full of bright furniture, occult-themed paintings, crystals, and, on one wall, a broom wrapped in colorful ribbons. Destiny told me it was her mothers' "wedding broom" and they'd jumped over it at their handfasting—their non-legally binding religious wedding—which they'd had a couple of years before Destiny was born. The entire house smelled of sage and incense.

We brought the baby in, and Morgan greeted us at the door wearing jeans and a t-shirt from her dojo with, "Oh, precious, blessed be!" She kissed both Miriam and Destiny on the cheek and smiled at me. She gave the pets a dismayed glance, and added, "They're not destructive, are they?"

As if in answer, Freddy wagged his tail cheerfully, Ivan trotted into the room with his tail in the air, and

Inanna turned up her nose and wound herself around Destiny's ankles.

"No, Mom," Destiny said, sounded a bit like a teenager when she did. I recognized the tone from raising Ruth and Solomon, and it made me smile.

"Blessed Be!" Bridget called from the kitchen. "I'm just finishing up some tea. I need a nice chamomile after watching all the craziness on the television."

"Tell me about it!" Destiny said.

Morgan said, "Let me hold that baby!"

Destiny laughed and handed Miriam to Morgan, who sat on the sofa and stared at her. "Those eyes! She's an old soul, like her father."

I smiled, even though I was reasonably certain Morgan didn't know how old my soul really was.

Bridget bustled in wearing a long skirt and beaded blouse and carrying a tea set, and sat next to Morgan, setting the tray on the coffee table. She'd done something new with her hair: metal rings and bits of purple woven into it, and pulled into a side ponytail. She poured herself a cup and glanced over at Destiny, who nodded. "Oooh, baby!" she cooed. "Take a lot of photos. They grow up in the blink of an eye." She smiled at Destiny. "I remember Morgan and me standing by your crib and crying because you were going to grow up." She handed Destiny the cup of tea and poured herself a second one.

Destiny laughed, but it was a sympathetic laugh. I couldn't join in because I felt it too keenly. Mortal life was too short, and if Miriam was a normal human, I would offer her what her mother had thus far refused when she was old enough. I sat in an overstuffed chair, and Freddy lay down at my feet. Ivan hopped up onto the chair arm, and I patted him. Inanna sat next to Destiny, silently watching Morgan and Miriam like she was going to intervene if she didn't approve.

The tea smelled delicious, like daisies, but I didn't ask for any. Bridget gave me some anyway.

Bridget smiled at me, and I smiled back. Then Bridget turned her attention to Ivan. "Who's this handsome fellow again?"

"His name is Ivan," I said.

Ivan tilted his head at me, then hopped down and walked over to Bridget with his tail in the air.

Bridget petted him and said, "My goodness. Is this a cat or a fae?" She glanced up at me. "Is this your familiar?"

I laughed. The fae thing had been Destiny's recurring joke about Victoria, but I supposed it suited Ivan, too.

Bridget patted the couch, and Ivan hopped up next to her for more petting. "Those eyes! Are you sure he's not a pixie pretending to be a cat?"

"I've had him since he was five weeks old, so the substitution would have to have happened before that," I said.

"Look at *these* old eyes," Morgan said, and Bridget leaned over with her head practically on Morgan's shoulder.

"Oh, my, you're right," Bridget said, leaning over and putting her head on Morgan's shoulder. "Hello, darling. How are you?"

Miriam, of course, said nothing, but she gurgled a little.

"My turn with the baby?" Bridget asked her wife.

"In a minute," Morgan said.

Bridget rolled her eyes and turned back to Ivan. "Will you give your regards to Titania next time you see her, my prince?" She scratched his ears.

Ivan purred for her.

We drank tea and carefully didn't discuss the news. Sad to say, Eatontown was feeling safer than Atlantic Highlands after we'd seen Thomas there. He'd gone to the park instead of our house, and the police were on high alert, but I was still worried.

———————— ∞ ————————

Abraham
New Brunswick, New Jersey
November 14, 2021

IT WAS TOO COLD TO hold a family reunion outdoors, although it wasn't yet snowy. Solomon had rented a ballroom in a local hotel and invited his children, his grandchildren, a great-grandchild, Ruth's children and grandchildren... Solomon introduced us as distant cousins. They were all friendly, and I could see some family features in them, especially around the eyes and nose—the prominent family nose, the large dark eyes, the pale tan skin and brown hair. The room was all nubby ochre industrial carpet, thick sepia drapes, and tables covered with food. In the corner, a bartender tended an open bar. Solomon had asked me to bring my violin. Upon hearing this, Ludwig had wrangled an invitation.

I was devastated to learn that Ruth had died of pancreatic cancer only a year previously. I'd just missed her. At my expression, Solomon patted my shoulder and told me, "Eighty-six is a good run." I didn't feel any better. In fact, I felt like I could have saved her... like I should have saved Victoria.

Miriam was eight months old, nearly eighteen pounds, and was at the age where she was crawling around—although she wasn't yet very good at it, thank goodness—and would put things in her mouth. She could sit up by herself, and Destiny was developing enormous biceps from carrying an eighteen-pound baby everywhere she went, although we switched off carrying her. She'd had to get a new vet uniform because the sleeves on the old one were too tight. Everyone cooed over her. Solomon introduced us to so many children and grandchildren and nieces and nephews and... I couldn't keep track of all the names, but Destiny was thrilled. She asked almost everyone if they were musical, which made Solomon smile.

"Play for us, Abraham," Solomon said, so I did. The entire room, previously a hubbub of chatter and laughter, fell silent as I ran through the repertoire I did for Ludwig's company holiday party the year before. Destiny appeared delighted. The various children and grandchildren and nieces and nephews gathered around. Well, I'd been practicing for about a hundred and eighty years at that point, so if I wasn't any good by then... The only one who didn't stop what they were doing was Miriam, and even she tilted her head at me while rhythmically moving her fists to the music. Ludwig stood in the corner, blinking back tears. I had introduced him as an old family friend.

When the last sweet notes faded, Solomon had tears in his eyes, too, but he was smiling. He leaned over and whispered into my ear, "I'd almost forgotten. Almost."

"I see why your wife asks everyone if we're musical," Solomon's daughter Rivka said. She laughed, and added with a blush, "I sing in the shower, but that's about it." Rivka had Miriam's—Miriam Senior's—nose almost exactly, but her hair had bleached streaks in it and hung down to her shoulders in a bob.

Rivka's son Michael added, "I played in a band in college. Electric guitar."

Someone turned on dance music on the other side of the room, and Ludwig headed that way.

I'd never tried an electric guitar, but I'd dabbled in acoustic guitar for a while. Maybe I should try it. I'm really more of a classical music person, though. One thing that happens when you get very old is trends feel like they move faster and faster, and it's better to not try to keep up. I'd master, I don't know, punk or hip-hop in time for it to fall out of favor. In fact, wasn't punk already out of favor? Am I proving my point? Perhaps two hundred years old or whatever is too old to chase trends.

That said, Ludwig was an excellent dancer, if a little... Bob Fosse meets punk rock. Perhaps it was simply that Ludwig was cool, and I wasn't. He was dancing oh-so-dramatically over on the dance floor, and all the girls were trying not to swoon. One waiter stopped to watch Ludwig dance, apparently forgetting the tray of dirty dishes he was carrying.

I smiled and leaned over to Solomon and whispered, "I missed you, too." And I had. I didn't know why I'd thought it so important to stay away. I'd seen some glances and whispers after Ruth's engagement, and Solomon had trouble dating until he got his own apartment, but... I should have asked his wife's opinion rather than assumed.

There was a microphone, and Solomon walked over to it and said, "I know you've all heard the story, but I'm going to repeat it. My sister Ruth and I were scheduled to be deported on a train, and Nazis shot our mother and sister Shayna in front of us."

I tensed. Surely he wouldn't. Surely he wouldn't out me in front of his—our—entire family. That couldn't possibly go well.

"We would never have escaped if it weren't for my Uncle Abraham. He whisked us away from the soldiers, and he and his friend smuggled us out of the country to raise us together. None of us would be here without my uncle Abraham and his friend Ludwig." His watch beeped, and he held up his finger and took a pill.

Destiny gave me a sidelong glance, and I tried to keep my expression calm and ignore the sinking feeling in my stomach. I glanced over at Ludwig, who had a single raised eyebrow and was watching me out of the corner of his eye.

"Obviously, I can't thank my uncle Abraham personally—I'm eighty-eight years old and he's my Uncle—but you just heard his grandson play. Uncle Abraham, if you can hear us in the World to Come, thank you, and know that this family reunion is because of you and is, as the kids say, the ultimate finger flip to the Third Reich. They tried to kill us, they failed. Look at us now!"

I let out a long-held breath. Around us, people clapped and raised glasses in a toast.

Destiny leaned over and whispered into my ear, "See?"

My heart sank.

Destiny
New Brunswick, New Jersey
November 14, 2021

The family reunion was *everything*. Absolutely everything. I wished my moms could have one, but of course Morgan's family disowned her when she came out—family values my ass—so it would only be Bridget's family. Her father was a conductor, so they were proud of her musical accomplishments—although they sometimes appeared to be going to great lengths to avoid commenting on her personal life.

But here I was, surrounded by Abraham's family in an astonishingly brown room, and it was everything I'd ever wanted. I just wanted it for my moms, too.

The distant family was... interesting. It disappointed me that more of them weren't musical, but they were friendly and kind and just plain *nice*, and very welcoming to the distant cousin's wife and baby. Also, some of them had Abraham's coloring, especially around the eyes.

Abraham's playing was mesmerizing, as always. Even little Miriam liked it, and people came up to me after to say that they saw why I kept asking people if they were musical.

Ludwig's dancing... he should TikTok that shit *immediately*. He'd be internet famous! Boys, girls love it when hot boys dance, I'm just saying. Of course, the more time I spent with Ludwig, the more I thought he was oddly innocent. He appeared to have no awareness of his hotness.

(He was *smoking* right now. Half the room was captivated.)

Solomon gave his little speech about Abraham and Ludwig saving them from the Nazis. I hadn't actually heard the whole story! I'd known that Abraham raised them in the city after they'd escaped, but... poor Solomon and Ruth! But his conclusion, that the Nazis had tried to kill them and failed, and look at how they had prospered... this was what being human was all about. And it was all made possible by my husband and Ludwig saving them, and letting them be human. They'd done this!

I leaned over and whispered into Abraham's ear, "See?" Then I handed him Miriam and rushed over to hug Solomon. "I hadn't heard that story!" I murmured into his ear.

"Oh yes," Solomon said. "Ruth and I were nonverbal on the boat. Uncle Ludwig made certain we ate and slept, but it was Onkel Avrahom who dried our tears when we finally broke down—which we did randomly for a while. He was traumatized as well, but he would ask us questions and watch our facial expressions for answers, and made certain he understood our preferences that way. It was how he realized Ruth hated pink and yellow and liked blue and green—they had to buy us new wardrobes—and that I loved radio shows, especially westerns. He bought me little toy horses and trains." His eyes grew soft. "Of course we had the excuse of not knowing English, so he engaged a tutor and told her we were shy and afraid of making mistakes, and kept us out of school until we were verbal."

"My goodness," I said.

He glanced both ways with a glint of mischief in his brown eyes and lowered his voice. "We were a little afraid they might eat us, but it was hard to be afraid of such an incompetent cook."

I burst out laughing.

"He got better. Our first Passover, though, my goodness..."

———————⁜———————

Ludwig
New Brunswick, New Jersey
November 14, 2021

I ADMIT, I quite enjoyed the family reunion, despite the wine being mediocre. Everyone was friendly, and it was interesting to see Solomon again after all these years. Honestly, I wasn't certain why we'd stayed away, but again, I'd followed Abraham's lead. I wished I could accept Solomon's thanks, but of course, well. Vampires were not a thing people believed in anymore.

Tragically, I am old enough to remember the Great Male Renunciation and Beau Brummell, a pox upon his name. And Lord Byron with his insistence on black tuxedos, he bears some blame, too. Do moderns, with their insistence upon men wearing dark, subdued colors and casual attire, really look upon portraits of Louis XIV without seeing something that is ineluctably masculine, regardless of the long curls, high heels, and furs? It's the nature of the male animal to strut, and yet I cannot find expensive formal clothing not in somber colors. How am I to strut when dressed as if in mourning? Thank goodness I have an excellent tailor, although we do often quibble. Our compromises make excellent fashion, in my opinion.

A woman thrust a folded napkin into my hand. It had her phone number on it. I wasn't sure what to say to that—I had no use for her phone number but didn't wish to be unkind—but she headed for the door and I put it in my pocket for lack of a better thing to do.

A man in a suit walked over and handed me his business card. I read it. He was an OB-GYN. I glanced up at him, confused.

He made the thumb and pinkie phone gesture at me and said, "Call me." He leaned closer and whispered, with great drama, "Socially."

I had no idea what I'd done to provoke this response, so I murmured something polite, put the card in my pocket, and walked over to stand next to Abraham.

Abraham lowered his voice and asked, "Is something wrong?"

I whispered back, "Your relatives are quite... libidinous!"

He burst out laughing. Damn him. I scowled at him.

Destiny, hearing the laughter, came over to see what was happening. Abraham's explanation, "Apparently people are hitting on Ludwig," provoked similar unwarranted merriment.

I spent the rest of the evening glued to Abraham's side, which made the entire event much more enjoyable. I even convinced him to play again.

———————⌀———————

Abraham
Brooklyn, New York
April 15, 1986

I CREPT INTO THE back of the auditorium and found a dark corner to watch as they awarded the John Park Award. It was a lovely venue, all red curtains and soft red velvet seats and gold filigree walls, and the scent of people in seats. There was a lot of talk about advances in pediatrics and the nomination process, and then they called up Dr. Solomon Horowitz, my little Shlomo, to accept the award.

"Thank you," he said. "The hardest thing for any doctor is needing to tell a patient they're terminal, but when the patient is a child..." He paused and bit his lip, a habit he'd had since he was a child himself. "Some people believe you should tell the parents and let them handle it, and that's heartbreaking enough, but I always ask the parents if they would like me to help them explain. It depends on the child's age, of course, but I explain to them in words that they'll understand that they're not going to get better. That I really wish I could make them get better"—his voice broke here—"but sometimes we don't know how to do that no matter how much we wish we could." He took a moment to shuffle the papers he hadn't glanced at once. "It's heartbreaking, but even though I always cry, I always think it's important for me to help the parents explain, if they want me to.

"My work in pediatric cancer has given me a lot of experience in explaining terminal disease to young children, and, as a father myself... It's the absolute worst." He took another moment, breathing deeply with his eyes closed. "There's no right or wrong answer for every family, but... I always start by asking the parents what they think their child knows about their illness." He winced. "It's important to respect their culture as well. It ties into what they think makes a good parent, or a good child, or how they view death."

My face was wet, thinking of little Shayna.

"In closing, I would like to thank my mamme, and my onkel Avrahom and uncle Ludwig, who raised me after she died. Onkel Avrahom played the violin, and he created such beauty that I always think of his playing when I think of the World to Come. May their memory be a blessing."

---

Abraham
Atlantic Highlands, New Jersey
November 22, 2021

THE PHONE CALL CAME at 2:47am. Because that's when these phone calls always come: the middle of the night.

I tiptoed into the dark bedroom and woke Destiny as quietly as I could so as not to disturb Miriam. "I need to go to the hospital."

Destiny blinked at me, looking confused. "What?"

"It's Solomon," I said, my voice as heavy as my heart. "Heart attack. They don't expect him to survive."

"I'll come with you," she said, rolling out of bed. She put on a pair of old gray sweatpants and a faded Hard Rock Café T-shirt, stepped into flip-flops, and picked up baby Miriam.

Miriam cried.

"I know, honey," Destiny said, kissing Miriam on the forehead.

I grabbed Miriam's diaper bag, and we headed out to the car together. There was a light layer of snow on the ground as we left the house and loaded up the car, reflecting the moonlight. With Miriam strapped into the baby seat, we headed out.

We pulled into the parking lot and found a fairly close space.

"Go ahead," Destiny said. "We'll catch up."

I ran. I can move fast, faster than the eye can see. I doubt I appeared on any security cameras as I raced up the stairs to room 429, Intensive Care.

Rivka was waiting outside the door, as was her son Michael, and Rivka's brother Elias and Elias's two teenagers whose names I'd forgotten. Rivka kissed me on the cheek. "You're cold!" She rubbed my hands in hers, adding, "Thank you for coming."

"Of course," I said. "May I...?"

"Absolutely," she said, "but I should warn you he has a lot of tubes and ports coming out of him and you might find it distressing to see him like this. Just... prepare yourself."

I nodded, squeezed her hands, and went inside. It had that hospital smell: disinfectant and bleach. There was a ventilator hiss, and medical equipment beeping, and occasional voices over the intercom.

Solomon did, in fact, look terrible. He had a breathing tube taped into his mouth, and the aforementioned tubes coming out of his arms, and they'd restrained his hands. I gave the nurse a sharp glance.

"He kept trying to pull out his breathing tube," she said, sounding defensive. She had warm copper skin and glossy black hair pulled back into a bun.

"He's a doctor," I said, crossing my arms and scowling at her. "Perhaps he should make his own medical decisions."

"Are you immediate family, sir?" she asked.

I wanted to introduce myself as Solomon's father but restrained myself. "I'm family."

"If you're his son, you can make his medical decisions, otherwise you'll have to take it up with his daughter. She seems to be handling everything."

I wondered what happened to the wonderful girl Solomon said he'd married and realized that it was the same thing that had happened to Ruth.

Solomon made a noise. I walked over and took his hand, and he jerked his hands against the restraints. A tear slid from one eye down to the side of the mask.

"Do you want a pencil and a piece of paper?" I asked.

Solomon tried to nod and squeezed my hand. I glanced around and found a yellow pad and pencil in a box hanging from the back of the door. I brought them to him and untied his right hand.

The nurse glared at me and watched us like we were about to do something terrible.

I held the paper and his arm so he could see what he was writing, and Solomon wrote "thank you for" before dropping the pencil.

Fuck death, fuck disease, fuck the human body, fuck the passage of time. I kissed him on the forehead, like I had when he was a child and I was putting him to bed.

———————— ∞ ————————

Abraham
New York, New York
October 31, 1941

THE SCREAMS WERE coming from the children's room.

I rushed in, turning on the lights. Ruth was rubbing her eyes, and Solomon somehow appeared both frightened and ashamed. They had dolls and toy planes and cars, and their fuzzy flannel bedding was printed with stars and planets. Their little violin sat in the corner, sadly unloved, alas. Outside, there was the sound of busy city traffic and the scent of exhaust.

I sat on the edge of Solomon's bed. "Are you all right?"

Solomon nodded, but it wasn't very convincing. "Just a bad dream, Onkel Avrahom." His big dark eyes showed white around the edges from fear.

Ludwig stood in the doorway. "Was the scary movie for Halloween a bad idea?"

Solomon shrugged.

I thought it was the newsreel footage of Nazis before the movie myself. I'd found it upsetting as well, although part of that was seeing someone I thought looked like Thomas in the background of one shot. Perhaps that had been my imagination.

"You're safe here," I said. "I won't let anyone hurt you."

Solomon considered this for a moment, and then he hugged me. He was still shaking.

We sat like that until he stopped shaking, and he lay back down and I tucked him in. "Would you like me to stay until you fall asleep?"

Solomon nodded.

I glanced over to Ludwig and nodded, and he turned out the lights and left the door cracked open. A sliver of light spread across the floor.

I waited until Solomon's slow, even breathing convinced me he was asleep. I kissed him on the forehead and tiptoed out.

---

Abraham
Red Bank, New Jersey
November 22, 2021

"HE WANTS YOU TO remove the tube," I said.

"Are you immediate family?" the nurse asked.

I rolled my eyes at her and opened the door to the hallway. Destiny was sitting in a chair by the door with Miriam sleeping on her lap. I told Rivka, "He wants the tube removed. He wants to communicate."

Rivka nodded, and walked into the room and told the nurse, "Unless it'll kill him, remove the tube."

"I'll get Dr. Altimira," she said, and left.

I stood next to his bed and held his hand, and we waited. A few minutes later, a dark-haired, olive-skinned woman in a white coat wearing thick glasses came in, read his chart, looked at his vitals, and said, "Do you want me to take out the tube, Dr. Horowitz?"

He nodded.

She removed the tape, disconnected it, fiddled with it for a moment. "Take a deep breath, then cough." He did, and she gently removed the tube.

He was breathing slowly, but he was definitely breathing on his own. "Thank you," he whispered. "Hate that thing."

The doctor smiled and said, "Yeah, if you need it, you need it, but it's not very comfortable. Have the nurse call me if you need anything else from me."

"Do you want me to call your family in?" I asked.

"Actually, I wanted to talk to you alone first." His voice was scratchy and quiet, which made my chest ache.

The nurse said, "Press the call button if you need me, and the desk is watching your vitals." She left, closing the door behind her. Dr. Altimira followed her.

"I just wanted to thank you again for saving me when I was six," he said. "They would have shot me, like Mamme and Shayna, and instead I had eighty good years."

The tears were warm on my face, but Solomon's eyes remained dry. His lip did tremble when he mentioned his mother and sister, however.

"I knew I had to be a doctor," he said. "Partly because the Nazis said I couldn't, but I wanted to save lives, too. I know now that if there'd been a doctor at the scene, they wouldn't have been able to save Mamme and Shayna, but I've done a lot of good in my life, saved other lives."

I didn't know what to say to that, so I squeezed his hand gently. I might have been able to save Miriam Senior, depending on how bad the bullet damage was, but it was unlikely. There's a point where it's hopeless. The change requires a relatively intact heart, one strong enough to move vampire blood through the body. And, of course, anything involving decapitation is too much.

I couldn't have saved Shayna.

I squeezed his hand again.

He smiled at me. "It's not that I want to live forever—especially in this condition!—but I wish I was going to see what kind of man Michael's boy was going to grow up to be, and your daughter... Perhaps I will, from the World to Come." His smile turned wistful. "It's like life is both too long and not long enough. Too much and too little."

"Do you want me to...?" I couldn't finish the sentence from his expression.

"What, eternal life in a hospital bed?" He laughed, but it was a gentle laugh. "No, thank you."

It wouldn't *be* eternal life in a hospital bed. There would be no aches, no pains. He would be strong and fast and healthy. He'd still *look* old, but... I opened my mouth to say all that, but...

"Call the family in, please," he said.

I did as he asked me, and everyone shuffled in except Destiny, who still had a sleeping baby on her lap.

"I just wanted to tell you all that I love you," he said. "That's all."

Rivka burst into tears, and her son put his arm around her and sniffled.

"We love you, too, Zayde," the teenage girl said, with tears in her eyes.

"All right," he said. "Sorry to be maudlin and then ask you to go, but I'm exhausted and might nap, now that the damned tube is out. Hate that thing. Couldn't talk with it in."

We all started shuffling out, but Solomon grabbed my hand and said, "Stay with me until I fall asleep."

I nodded and sat in the chair next to him, holding his hand.

"*A sheynem dank, Onkel.*" His eyes closed.

There were a few peaceful minutes with the heart rate monitor doing its slow, steady beep beep. I didn't want to let go of his hand and leave, so I sat by his bed while he slept. Why had I stayed away all those years? To avoid gay panic? To give him a normal life? How could his life be normal after what happened to him? Orphaned by the Nazis, whisked away to be raised by vampires...

And now I had only had him back in my life for a few short months, and was about lose him forever.

It had been almost three years since I lost Victoria, and it still hurt sometimes. I still had the horrible little tin with flowers painted on it in my coffin, still had her sweet face as my phone's lock screen. It had been over a hundred years since I lost Flora, John, and Eliza, and so long since I'd been to Kensal Green to visit their graves, but I still lit Yahrzeit candles for them every year. I remembered their faces perfectly; I thought perhaps I should commission portraits. Then again, the portraits might hurt, like my phone lock screen hurt—but I couldn't bring myself to change it. The very idea felt like a betrayal.

The beeping sped up, and Solomon's eyes fluttered open. His hands clutched at his chest. "Hurts," he gasped. "Hurts." And then, in an almost childlike voice, "Make it not hurt."

I knew it was wrong when I did it. He'd specifically said no less than an hour ago. I knew it was wrong, and I bit him and offered him blood from my wrist. He drank.

I wish I could say that I did it out of some kind of noble desire to preserve human life at all costs, or out of some parental instinct. Maybe it was parental, a little. But the main thing was that I couldn't bear it. I couldn't stand there and let someone I'd raised as a child die after he asked me to make it not hurt. It was too much. I couldn't. I couldn't watch him die. I wasn't strong enough. I couldn't save Flora, or John, or Eliza, or Miriam and Shayna, or even Victoria, but I could save Solomon.

The beeping became faster, more irregular as he convulsed, and a voice on the loudspeakers said, "Code blue, repeat, code blue. Room four twenty-nine, code blue."

The door slammed open as Dr. Altimira came in with nurses and a crash cart. The beeping became even more irregular, almost random. She started doing CPR on him. "Defib," she said, and the nurses turned on the electric paddles. Behind them, Solomon's family crowded in. The teenager wailed, and her father hugged her.

I had no idea what effect defibrillation would have on the change. I supposed I was about to find out. What had I done?

"Charged," the nurse said.

"To me," the doctor said, and they handed her the paddles. "Three-two-one... clear!"

Solomon's body did the television jump, and the beeping stabilized a little, then became erratic again.

Destiny came into the room—alone. She must have left Miriam with someone—and stood behind me. I looked around and saw Rivka's son Michael standing behind the glass with Miriam.

The paddle device made its fully charged noise again, and the doctor said, "Three-two-one... clear!"

Solomon jerked again, and his heart rate stabilized to something normal-sounding. The bite marks on his neck, which I didn't think anyone had noticed, closed up. His color improved, though he was still pale. He had thicker hair. His breathing stabilized.

"Why is he so cold?" the doctor said. "I need an electric blanket in here, stat."

Solomon opened his eyes, glanced around. The look he gave me was accusing, but he didn't say a word.

Destiny whispered into my ear, "What did you do?"

# Fallout

Abraham
Red Bank, New Jersey
November 22, 2021

The nurse tucked the electric blanket around Solomon. "If you need anything, press the button, and we're watching your vitals."

Solomon nodded, and everyone left except for me and Destiny. There was a moment of dimly lit quiet, only broken by the beep beep of the medical equipment.

Once everyone was gone, Solomon exploded. "Of all the selfish, inconsiderate…"

I hung my head and said nothing. I knew it was wrong when I did it, and I deserved his anger. The enormity of my offense made an apology feel like the wrong thing to say, like I was looking for an unjustified easy out. I didn't deserve forgiveness. I only hoped that in time he would come to decide that I'd done the right thing. I hoped I had, at least.

He sighed. "I thought you were the sensitive one and Uncle Ludwig was the one who did things without permission, but apparently..." He made a face and scowled down at his pale hands. "I've taken an oath to do no harm, and you do *this* to me?"

"It's not like that!" I said. "You don't have to bite people without permission..." I trailed off as I realized perhaps I wasn't in the best position to discuss consensual biting. From his expression, Solomon caught the gaffe as well. I persisted. "Expired blood bank stock is perfectly drinkable and I have an in with an employee, and there's animal blood, which isn't kosher, but..."

Solomon put both his hands over his face and groaned. "Why would you raise me to be observant and then do *this* to me?" The tubes and hospital gown sleeves hung over his chest, and the beeping increased in speed. He seemed more dismayed than angry, but I knew Solomon and he wasn't a man to express anger lightly, and there could very well be an explosion coming.

"I never meant to... I wanted to give you a normal Jewish life!" The rescue, the masquerade, separating households with Ludwig, the staying away so his wife and/or in-laws wouldn't go into a gay panic, the staying away so he wouldn't notice I hadn't aged... it was all trying to give him a normal life.

Destiny's head was moving back and forth between us, a shocked expression on her face.

Solomon tried to cross his arms, but all the needles and tubes got in his way. He bared his teeth at them, showing a hint of fang. "I'd made peace with death, even though it was hard, even though life on earth is a divine gift to be cherished! I told myself I would see Mamme and Shayna again, and now..."

"Listen," I said. "It'll be all right. I'll bring you something to drink, and then I'll show you the ropes. I can—" I owed it to him.

Solomon cut me off. "No, thank you."

"This works better with a mentor," I said. "Trust me, Ludwig and I had a falling out, and I tried to go it on my own, and—"

"Fine," Solomon said. "Call Uncle Ludwig and ask him to come and then go home."

"Solomon—"

"For the love of Hashem, why would you wait until I was eighty-eight years old to do this?"

I covered my face with my hands. "I never meant to. I just... couldn't bear it."

Solomon sighed again, sounding exasperated. "How old are you?"

"I don't know," I said. "Two hundred something, probably." After the first hundred years, who cares? Not me, that's for certain.

"Two hundred years, and you haven't come to terms with death?" He made a disgusted noise. "Then again, why should you? It's not your problem, is it?"

I looked him in the eye, letting him see that he'd hurt me, and said, "It's *very much* my problem."

Solomon sighed again, closing his eyes, and said, "Please call Uncle Ludwig. I don't have his number."

I pulled out my phone, with Victoria's sweet furry face and bright, clever golden eyes gazing up at me expectantly on the lock screen, and unlocked my phone and made the call.

———— ⌒⧖⌒ ————

Destiny
New Jersey
November 22, 2021

I DROVE US HOME, through the slow sunrise over snow. This was my worst nightmare.

Well, no, trying to get out of a burning house with pets or children was still worse, as nightmares went, but this... Solomon hadn't consented.

I needed an explanation. I needed to know *why*.

Abraham raised Solomon. Abraham raised Solomon and hadn't respected his wishes in the end. Was it some kind of misguided parental instinct to save his child at all costs? I didn't want Miriam to be a vampire!

And did that make him more or less likely to turn *me* without consent? Oh gods, I didn't want to leave my husband!

Was I really thinking of leaving my husband? It was a pretty serious red flag...

We pulled into the driveway, and he ran indoors, which would have been inconsiderate of him if I didn't know that he might literally burst into flame if exposed to the sun.

I turned off the car and sat like that for a moment, eyes shut, and took a deep breath. I picked up Miriam to bring her into the house. If the conversation went better than I hoped, I could get the diaper bag later.

Oh, gods.

Abraham
Atlantic Highlands, New Jersey
November 22, 2021

IT WAS SUNRISE when we arrived home, the snow turning that faint pink color and the air with that crisp snow scent. I rushed to the door, leaving poor Destiny to deal with the baby, but... sunlight. I hadn't brought my hat or gloves, so it was dangerous.

Once inside, Ivan gazed up at me. He was so sensitive to human emotions now. I picked him up and tried to give him a reassuring hug, and he squirmed out of my arms and stared at me with an alarmed expression, as if he knew I had done something horribly wrong. I tried not to be hurt by this.

Destiny came in with Miriam and vanished into the bedroom. I waited in the living room for the inevitable chewing-out that I knew was my due. It sounded like she was changing Miriam's clothes, so I waited. Then she came back out.

"Do you want to tell me what happened?"

Somehow, it would have been easier if she'd yelled at me. "I just... he said he wanted for the pain to stop, and... the idea of not saving him was unbearable."

Destiny closed her eyes and pressed her lips together. "I see."

I sighed. "It was an impulsive mistake. I just... it hurt too much, and... I did the wrong thing."

Destiny nodded. "And he didn't want to be a vampire."

I winced. "I offered, and he said he didn't want to be in a hospital bed for all eternity, and there wasn't time to explain that he wouldn't be..."

She lowered her head, as if examining the floor. "I see."

"I feel like this is an argument I shouldn't make, because I understand he didn't consent and that makes it academic, but is eternal life really such a terrible thing?"

Destiny looked me in the eye and said, "It's not the eternal life, it's the cost. I became a vegetarian when I was ten years old. I went to school for eight years to be a vet." She paced. "I wouldn't be able to be a vegetarian, I couldn't have more children, I don't know how I would work at a vet clinic having to run from the car to the door every day, what if it was my turn to open the clinic?" She stopped pacing. "And rescue adoption day outside the pet food store. I couldn't do that anymore because it's outside in the sun..." A single tear rolled down one cheek. "I've centered my whole life around loving animals, and then I'd have to choose between drinking their blood and drinking the blood of a human being? I feel like I wouldn't be *me* any more if I became a vampire. At least, I wouldn't be the sum of my choices anymore."

I closed my eyes and bowed my head. That was, as the television show phrased it, her final answer.

"Which is why I need to know *why*. Why didn't you respect Solomon's wishes?" She didn't sound angry, just earnest.

"I made a mistake, an impulsive mistake," I said. "I can't give you a better answer than that."

Destiny nodded and left the room. This seemed to be an insufficient reaction, so after a moment, I followed her into the bedroom.

Destiny was packing a suitcase. She gazed up at me, her expression guilty.

"Where are you going?" I asked, trying to sound casual and, I'm certain, failing.

Destiny stopped packing and came over to take my hands in hers. "I love you, but I need some time to process what just happened."

Process. That was one of those newfangled things people did nowadays. I glanced down at her hands, so warm in mine. "Where are you going?"

"My moms' house."

I swallowed. "How long?" I glanced up, and Destiny was looking at our hands, too.

"I don't know," she said. "Not forever, I don't think."

Oh, *that* was comforting.

"I just..." She looked up into my eyes, took a deep breath, and said, "I no longer trust you to let me die if something happens to me, and I don't want to be a vampire, and I need to figure out if I can live with that."

I opened my mouth to object but couldn't think of anything to say.

She squeezed my hands. "I understand why you did it. I do. If I don't agree with a pet owner's decisions, it takes a lot of self-control to let them do the wrong thing. Sometimes they want to euthanize a pet that can be easily treated, or refuse to euthanize a hopeless case with a miserable pet, and it's their decision. And pet rescue! You can't save every cat or dog, and it hurts! It hurts to lose them, and it hurts to have to say no to taking another one, and it hurts to adopt them out!"

"Then..."

"Solomon and I aren't your pets."

*Ouch.*

She squeezed my hands again, as if to take out some of the sting of her words. She smiled, a sad smile. "And I love you so much that if I stay now, I'll stay forever, so... just give me some time, Abraham."

I closed my eyes and nodded, even though I felt like I might literally die of a broken heart if she left. I again hoped that Solomon would come to terms with my terrible mistake, but it wasn't as if—if he did—I could call up my wife and say *Solomon forgives me, come home!* No, turning Solomon without his consent and leading my wife to think of me as untrustworthy were two separate issues from the same mistake.

She picked up the suitcase and left, presumably to put it in the car, and I stood in the bedroom doorway like an idiot. I could hear the car door opening and closing outside. Then she came back in, walked past me, and picked up Miriam.

"You're taking Miriam!" I suppose I couldn't process.

"You can visit her any time you like," Destiny said. "I want you to be in her life! If this goes on... longer than I expect it to, then we'll arrange some kind of shared—"

"You're taking my baby!"

Destiny cried. "I love you, but I don't trust you not to—"

"I can't change a baby! She'd never grow up! Like me, how I'm permanently nineteen. I can only turn adults!"

"Good to know," she said. "But she's still breastfeeding, even though she's experimenting with solid food, so it's best if she goes with me."

I couldn't argue with the logic, but... "You're taking my baby."

"I'm sorry," she said. Miriam cried, too. I don't think she understood what was happening, but she understood the adults were fighting.

I leaned over and kissed Miriam gently on the cheek. "I love you," I whispered. She smelled like milk and baby shampoo, and I missed her already.

And then Destiny kissed me on the cheek and left. I could hear her opening and closing the front door, the car door, and finally, the car driving away.

<hr/>

Abraham
Atlantic Highlands, New Jersey
November 23, 2021—December 9, 2021

THE VAMPIRE DEPRESSION cliché has its roots in reality. If you live long enough, you've—as the modern Americans say—"seen some shit." Sometimes it's too much, and a vampire will go out in the sun, intentionally. Too many loved ones outlived. Too much *human inhumanity* witnessed. They call us monsters, but look at the things they do to each other and tell me what's monstrous.

Obviously, I couldn't do that, however much I wanted to, however much I knew nothing would ever matter again without Destiny and Miriam... I'd only fooled myself into thinking that things mattered without Flora and Miriam Senior, after all. But there was still the chance that Destiny would come back—not that a measly couple of decades would matter beyond torturing myself with the inevitable pain to come—and I had pets. That might sound trite, but I held on to the fact that Freddy and Ivan and Inanna—yes, Destiny left Inanna with me—needed me. And Miriam couldn't grow up without a father. That wouldn't be fair to her. In short, I had responsibilities, and had guaranteed that I would have responsibilities forever. Duty tra la la.

Not that I dealt with the situation cheerfully or rationally. I drank. Yes, vampires can get drunk, it just takes considerable effort. We're all heavyweights; our metabolism fights off intoxication almost as quickly as we can consume more alcohol, especially with my preferred drink being beer or wine. I drank, and I googled for pictures of Flora and the children. Because I was finished hiding from that particular pain, that's why. It's a good thing that vampire pets don't need a litter box, or to go out. I fed them, and I fed myself, and I googled.

*Everything* is online. *Everything.* Even photos of nineteenth century actresses who specialized in vampire roles. I took a big swig of beer—a Doppelbock, if you care—and reached out to touch the screen.

Flora. I'd had almost fifty years with Flora. I ordered photo prints of some of what I found online. Then I hired an artist to paint a portrait. Why? The noble reason was that I'd made my mistake because I wasn't coping with death and loss, and it was time to actively engage with my grief. The less noble reasons were that I wouldn't have had this issue with Flora because she was already a vampire, and because in an odd way Flora reminded me of Destiny—in a painful, dead-wife way rather than a painful-separated-daddy-wondering-if-his-wife-and-daughter-would-ever-come-home way. I didn't have either Flora or Destiny, but it had been Destiny's choice to leave. Flora had wanted to stay with me.

Or maybe I was simply torturing myself. That felt valid, too.

The photo prints arrived first, of course. I hung them up near the mantel and put the horrid little tin of Victoria's ashes on the mantel next to a photo of her. My sweet furry angel, in a floral-print tin. I should get her something better.

As expected, my throwaway emails asking rabbis questions about vampires had been ignored, but Rabbi Kaplan—my own rabbi!—wrote back to tell me that it's permitted in some halachim (traditions) to say Kaddish for a pet. I cried for an hour after reading that.

Dave, my accountant, came by at one point. He paced around my living room, wringing his hands.

"Will you sit down?" I said.

Dave sat. "Do we really have to give her money? Does Louis know if ketubahs are legally binding in the US?"

The correct plural of "ketubah" is "ketubot," but that's not why I groaned and buried my face in my hands. "Don't even ask that. *Ken eina hara!*" No evil eye!

Dave watched me for a moment, then said, "I know, by the way."

I regarded him sidelong from under my hair and wondered where this was going. If it was extortion, it was unnecessary because he could simply embezzle instead. And Dave—I liked Dave, but... he was no Blade. He was slightly taller than me, but he was basically a short skinny human guy, and I was a creature of preternatural strength and speed.

"Any accountant worth his salt would know. You're at least eighty, and I think you're older. Numbers tell stories."

I snorted. "Ludwig said I was insane to let someone else manage my money."

Dave reacted with a flicker of recognition of a different name for Louis, but didn't address it. "I won't tell anyone. I like my job. Just..." He bit his lip, and his shoulders tensed.

I glanced up.

"If... if my tests come back saying pancreatic cancer, can we talk?"

Fuck. He hadn't been pacing for me... or if he had, he shouldn't have been. Poor Dave!

I patted him on the shoulder. "Yes, I have a cure for cancer. The cost of the cure might be more than you want to pay, however." And I did. I had a cure for consumption, saddle thrombus, heart failure... and cancer.

He nodded and bit his lip again. "Thank you." His shoulders relaxed a little. I looked more closely. He'd lost weight, and his color was bad—almost ashy.

"You'll be all right," I assured him. If he would rather be a vampire than die of cancer, I was more than willing to make that happen for him.

Dave gave me an awkward side hug, then pulled away, appearing embarrassed. Time to change the subject.

"Also," I said, "I'm reasonably certain that ketubot are not legally binding in the US, though I'd pay her anyway, but... don't count us out yet."

Dave nodded. "Okay." And then he left.

I thought about the kitchen, about mornings talking about the meaning of life, about Destiny in her cute blue bathrobe and bunny slippers with her hair tumbling around her, begging to be mussed...

I drank some more. Inanna came over and regarded me with cool bronze eyes, tilted her head, and climbed into my lap and licked my face, which made me cry. I hadn't thought she liked me. She washed my tears away, and I kissed her on her furry head and told her she was an angel.

I was lying around on the stupid red sectional sofa—thinking I should really get rid of the ridiculous thing—when Ludwig came by to see me.

He kneeled by the sofa and brushed my hair out of my eyes. *"Bist du betrunken?"* Are you drunk?

I laughed. *"Natürlich."* Of course.

Ludwig frowned at me. "Well, you've put your foot in it this time, haven't you? When is she coming back?"

I groaned, miserable. "I don't know."

Ludwig made a face. "Sit up, man. In fact, take a shower."

I rolled my eyes at him.

He stood and walked over to where I had the pictures of Flora and the children. He said nothing, but he looked at them. Then he looked at me.

I said nothing back. What was there to say?

"Take a shower," he said. "You stink."

My kind doesn't really produce much in the way of oozy stuff. We only really produce things like sweat and fingerprints after we feed. Maybe you shouldn't ask how I know that. I try to lead an ethical vampire life, but I'm not perfect. It's all right, none of the people in the Bible are perfect, either, and some of them are kind of terrible. We're not the chosen people because we're better than anyone else; the story goes God went from nation to nation asking if they wanted the Torah and the other nations said no thank you. We were the ones who said yes, and that's why we're chosen, because we chose. But I digress, my point is that I didn't stink.

Okay, maybe I smelled like alcohol to another vampire. That was fair. And Ludwig was more of a wine man than a beer man.

"Up you go," Ludwig said, tugging at my arm and pulling me upright. "Up you go," he repeated, pulling me to my feet. "Take a shower." He dragged me into the bathroom.

I shooed him out and showered. When I finished, I realized I hadn't brought a change of clothing, so I wrapped myself in a towel before going into the bedroom. I picked out any old thing—pajama bottoms and a Hard Rock Café T-shirt—and came out, barefooted and wet-haired, to sit on the stupid sectional again. If she didn't come back, I was getting rid of it. I thought longingly of my Victorian horsehair sofa, exiled to the so-called mother-in-law suite.

Ludwig sat next to me. "If she divorces you, I want to represent you."

That was the single most horrible idea I'd ever entertained in my life, and I laughed the most inappropriate laugh in response.

"That's not the response I expected," Ludwig said, "but I'll take it." He quirked up a lip into a lopsided grin.

"I don't want a divorce," I said. "If she asks for one, I think I should move to, I don't know, Sacramento or something and not give her one." Which, really, I shouldn't do; it's considered cruel in Judaism for a man divorcing a woman to deny her a get—a halachically valid Jewish divorce—and not let her marry again, but I didn't want a divorce. I wanted my romance novel happily ever after, and if I couldn't have it, I wanted to sulk in solitude somewhere far away.

On second thought, no. I wouldn't sink that far. The ghost of my mother might come haunt me. In some neighborhoods there would be scathing letters to the editor. Scathing social media posts?

"*Not* Sacramento," Ludwig said. "Maybe San Francisco."

"Why do *you* get a say?" My voice sounded whiny to my own ears.

Ludwig shook his head at me. "And you call *me* insensitive." He made a face at me. "By the way, Solomon is fine. He's adjusting better than you did. No troll impersonations under any bridges, at least."

Well, at least there was that. "Good." I envied Ludwig his chance to mentor Solomon, however. Solomon wasn't taking my calls. But it pleased me that Solomon was doing well. Of course he was; he was a bright boy who succeeded at everything he attempted.

Ludwig gave my shoulders a little shake. "Buck up, man. Stiff upper lip, and all that. Pull yourself together!"

"I'm not going sunbathing," I said. "I have pets."

Ludwig appeared alarmed at this response but didn't offer an opinion.

———⁂———

Ludwig
Manhattan, New York
December 9, 2021

"SACRAMENTO! GOOD Lord!" I paced in my living room—floor-to-ceiling windows, red antique sofas, wine storage… the last the most important, of course.

Solomon, seated on one of the red sofas, glanced up from what he was reading—not a treatise on how to be a vampire—alas, there was still no such thing, it was most likely a medical journal—and said, "That's not very nice, Uncle."

"But I know nothing of their classical music scene, and then I'd have to pass the California bar, and…"

"Where's your sense of adventure?"

Adventure. Bah. "I think I left it at the opera house with my gloves," I said.

Solomon laughed.

I intentionally changed the subject. "What are you reading?"

"Medical journal," he said. "I would love it if there was some kind of kosher vampire dietary supplement, and I'm reading articles on synthetic blood."

I sat next to him, intrigued. "Is there such a thing?" It would make my life easier, assuming it tasted better than animal blood.

"Experimentally," he said. "Many of them are hemoglobin-based and derived from bovine blood, so they would also not be kosher. There are also products based on stem cells and others on perfluorocarbons, which are not water-soluble and require emulsion... "

"I don't know what that means, but it sounds like there aren't purchasable options on the market. Also, we could just drink the cow's blood as is."

"True." Solomon grimaced. "There have been human trials, and one of the perfluorocarbon-based products was approved and subsequently withdrawn. They have approved one synthetic blood for veterinary use."

"Too bad we can't ask Destiny for a sample to see if it's drinkable."

Solomon raised his eyebrows at me. "It's one of the hemoglobin-based ones."

"Ah," I said.

Solomon tilted his head and regarded me for a moment. I waited for him to ask the obvious question.

"Why can't we ask Destiny?"

"She took your side," I said. "Moved out. Temporarily, he hopes. He's taking it badly. Hence, Sacramento."

"Hmm." He raised his eyebrows again and put down the medical journal. "What do you think?"

"About what?"

He rolled his eyes at me. "You know what."

Yes, I did. I stood up, crossed my arms, and gave him my most disapproving look. "It's not nice to play your parents against each other."

Solomon rolled his eyes at me, like he was a teenager again. "Were you two an item?" he asked.

"Good Lord!" Had he really had the indelicacy to ask me such a thing? "You moderns make everything so vulgar!"

"You didn't answer my question," Solomon said, sounding smug.

"No! No, we were not!" I walked over to the other sofa, but I didn't sit. I glared at it for a moment, then gazed back at Solomon.

"Oh." Solomon bit his lip and glanced at the floor, then looked back up at me. "So if you're not an item, why is it he can still do no wrong? You always take his side!"

"It's less that he can do no wrong," I said, "and more that I cannot condemn him for doing to you the exact same thing I did to him."

Solomon blinked. Perhaps that thought had never occurred to him.

I walked over and sat next to him. "Besides, I adjusted better than he did. It's a religious thing, I think. I was raised with drinking the literal blood of my Lord Jesus, and you two were raised that blood is the single most taboo thing anyone can drink."

Solomon put his face in his hands, between his knees, and groaned.

I patted him on the back. "You'll be all right. I promise. I was distraught at first, but now that I've accepted it I can see the advantages. I consider it a blessing now. You'll never get sick, you'll never die, you have all the time in the world to pursue your interests..."

"He should have raised me to be an atheist if he planned to do this," Solomon moaned.

"He didn't plan this," I said, trying to sound reassuring. "He's a sensitive boy, and can be... impulsive... occasionally. All that passion that he channels into his music... Sometimes it overflows." I patted Solomon's hand. "Remember, he's still nineteen, in a way."

Solomon gazed up at me, radiating skepticism. "Are you *sure* you two were never... ?"

"I'm certain." It came out sounding far more sad than I intended, which surprised me.

Solomon considered me for a moment. "Do you want her to divorce him?"

"No." After a moment, I added, "Even if I... were inclined that way... he prefers the company of women." I was proud that I expressed myself so delicately.

Solomon patted my shoulder.

There was a long, awkward pause, and it was Solomon's turn to change the subject. "Nineteen? Do our brains develop after the change?"

"I don't see why they would. No other part of our bodies does."

"Arrested development. Literally."

I could feel my face creasing into a frown. "That's not very—"

"The human brain isn't finished developing until the age of twenty-five or so. Specifically, the prefrontal cortex, which is responsible for making good decisions, planning, and prioritizing." He considered this for a moment. "How old were you when you turned?"

"Twenty-one," I admitted. Why did this feel like I was confessing a terrible character flaw?

Solomon regarded me for a moment. His gaze was so searching that I looked away.

He blessedly changed the subject again. "I wish I understood precisely the scientific nature of our, as you put it, dietary needs. Is it the hemoglobin? The oxygenation? Both? Neither?"

"I don't know the answer to that," I said. "All I know is that we're neither demons nor unholy. I can take communion!"

"So it's a blood-borne medical condition." He picked up a pencil and a notebook, and chewed on the pencil. "That might narrow things down."

"I'm sure you'll figure it out, given time." I smiled at him. "All vampires have gifts based on their passions, and I suspect that this is yours."

---

Destiny
Eatontown, New Jersey
December 9, 2021

I'D LEFT MY SWEET baby Inanna at Abraham's, and I felt incredibly guilty about it. I didn't want to explain her diet to my mothers until I was good and ready, and… I wasn't ready.

Lucy and I had gone out to the movies the previous night. She'd offered to take me to a bar and let me vent, but… I wasn't ready to explain to her, either.

As I came into the kitchen, Bridget was asking Morgan, "How was your Tae Kwon Do last night?"

I poured myself a cup of coffee and started adding cream and sugar.

Morgan snickered. "We had a new guy who saw me and he was like, 'A girl? I bet you're gay, too!' I answered, 'Yup, you caught on to that one quick.' Then Marty had us spar and I kicked his ass and offered him a moist towelette after."

Bridget and I giggled, and Morgan grinned at us.

The three of us sat at the kitchen table, drinking our hot beverages of choice. The silence grew awkward.

"When you're ready to talk," Bridget said, "we're ready to listen." Today, she wore her hair in a dark cloud of curls, held back by a beaded headband.

"And slap a bitch, if need be," Morgan offered. She was wearing one of her Tae Kwan Do dojo shirts, boxers, and a bathrobe.

I laughed. I didn't know what Abraham would do if Morgan slapped him. Probably catch her hand on the way to his face like a ninja, or some other such nonviolent vampire shit. "Don't slap him."

Bridget sat at the table next to me and poured me a cup of green tea. Morgan poured herself a cup of coffee that smelled so strong I was surprised that the spoon didn't stand up.

"Spill," Morgan said.

I looked at the two of them. If anyone would understand what I was about to say, it was them. "Abraham is a vampire."

They didn't react, which felt like an odd response, so I elaborated. "I don't mean that he's a Goth, or that he's a psychic vampire that saps the life out of discussions. I mean, he keeps expired blood bank stock in our fridge because he prefers his food to be ethically sourced."

Bridget raised an eyebrow, but her eyes appeared concerned. Morgan sat back and crossed her arms. Well. Morgan was the more science-y of my two mothers, so maybe she didn't believe in vampires.

"That's why I left Inanna there. She was injured, and he... cured her? ...by making her a vampire, too."

Bridget raised her other eyebrow, and Morgan opened her mouth to object, so I rolled up my sleeve to show the faint bruise on my wrist from a bite. Abraham's bite marks healed fast, but... "I let him drink from me."

Morgan examined my wrist with an expression of growing outrage.

"It was consensual," I said.

"So, what's the problem?" Bridget asked.

I sighed. "He turned someone without permission, and I don't want to be a vampire, so..."

Morgan released my arm to scowl into her cup of coffee. "It's traditional to say that I never liked him, but that's not true."

"'Men all suck' feels wrong coming from us and is also not true," Bridget added, her voice sympathetic.

"Well," I said. "The person in question was terminally ill but also didn't want to be a vampire."

"What did they have?" Morgan asked.

"He was in his eighties and had heart failure."

"Yeah," Morgan said. "He would have died." Her voice was clipped, matter-of-fact.

"I..." I didn't know if that helped or not. I bit my lip, took a sip of green tea, and continued. "I thought I would live a normal mortal life with an eternally young and gorgeous husband, but now I'm afraid he'll make me a vampire, too, and I need to decide if I can live with that."

"I don't go that way," Bridget said, "but he *is* beautiful."

Morgan examined at my wrist again. "I assume he bit you more than once."

I nodded.

"Can he market his saliva as a treatment for wounds?"

I laughed. "You two are taking this well."

"Well," Morgan said. "He wronged someone else, not our baby."

"I'm a polytheist," Bridget said. "If I can believe in the Fair Folk, ley lines, and magic, why not vampires?" She laughed, but it was a gentle laugh. "I always knew he was an old soul. I just assumed his body was younger than that."

"That's why I left Inanna at Abraham's," I said. "I didn't want to deal with feeding her blood."

"Not very vegetarian-friendly," Bridget agreed.

"And also hard to explain to my moms," I added.

Morgan made a sound of disgust. "We both had to come out to our parents. We know firsthand how hard it is when your parents show their ass and make your situation about them."

I took Morgan's hand and squeezed it. I knew Morgan still considered coming out to her parents the worst experience of her life.

"So this is temporary?" Bridget asked. "Or permanent?"

"I... I'm not sure," I admitted, "but I'm hoping it's temporary."

"Well," Bridget said, "we love you and are here for you, no matter what you decide."

⸺⚬⚭⚬⸺

Abraham<br>Atlantic Highlands, New Jersey<br>December 10, 2021

THE KEY TURNING in the lock was probably Ludwig, I thought. He'd been coming by to check up on me often enough that I'd given him a key. I didn't bother to get up; Ivan had curled up next to me, back pressed into my chest, and was purring softly. I didn't want to disturb him, so I stayed where I was and kissed his furry little head.

But it wasn't Ludwig. It was Destiny. Destiny and Miriam.

I sat up and stared at them. Was she coming back? She didn't have a suitcase. Ivan tilted his head at them. She was *so hot*, as the modern Americans say. Even in jeans and sneakers and a T-shirt. Her hair tumbled down loose, exactly the way I like it. She wasn't wearing makeup, but that simply made her cupid's-bow lips look more kissable. Her soft, pale skin with the faintest, cutest hint of freckles cried out to be touched.

"You haven't been by to visit Miriam," Destiny said.

I snuffled and rubbed my face. I didn't have a good answer.

Inanna walked into the room, stared at Destiny, then pointedly turned right around and left the room.

Destiny winced. Freddy trotted into the room and wagged his tail at her, as if to apologize for his housemate's snub.

Destiny walked over to the mantel, where there was a brand new portrait of Flora and the children. The artist had worked overtime; high pay will do that. Despite her initial estimate of a month, she had completed the painting in two weeks.

I'd replaced our ketubah—the decorative Jewish prenuptial agreement—with the painting of Flora and the children. I'd moved the ketubah to the hallway, next to our wedding portrait.

I hadn't included a Lieberman clause promising a get in our ketubah on the grounds that Destiny wasn't Jewish and wouldn't care. The ketubah was for me. I don't know what it says about me that I wanted a document promising my wife food, sex, and a share of my money should we divorce. Our wedding had been at the justice of the peace. Our vow renewal had been small, and interfaith, and presided over by a woman who got her credentials out of an ad in the back of *Rolling Stone* magazine, but I'd wanted *some* part of it to be Jewish.

Destiny said nothing about the missing ketubah. All she said was, "She's pretty. Is that...?"

"Flora," I said. "And the children, John and Eliza."

"Did they..." She stopped and paused before continuing. "Did they all die in... the fire?"

"Yes."

"I'm sorry," she said.

"So am I."

There was an awkward pause.

She gazed at the photo prints next to it. "The artist did a good job."

"I agree."

We stared at each other, silent. I stood up and took Miriam away from her and kissed her on her little forehead.

Miriam gurgled at me and reached up to grab my hair. "Dadadadada."

"Yes," I said, smiling my first smile since Destiny left. "I'm your dada."

"Dadada."

"That's right!" I kissed her on the forehead again.

"She missed you," Destiny said.

"I missed her, too."

"I missed you, too," Destiny said, her voice soft.

I poked Miriam lightly on the nose, making her giggle, and observed, "You didn't bring the suitcase."

"No," she said, and glanced away. She looked like she was going to say something but changed her mind. Then she said, "How long were you and Flora married?"

"Fifty years," I said. "Not long enough."

"I was going to say that was a long time," she said. "How old were you when you got married?"

I didn't know why she wanted to talk about Flora. Perhaps she wanted to talk about anything that wasn't us. "Not very old. I don't know, thirty?" I laughed. "She was over three hundred."

Destiny blinked.

I looked her in the eye and said, "The heart wants what it wants."

She swallowed.

"Fifty years is the blink of an eye, but you've probably got fifty years and if you're willing to give it to me, I'll take it. Under any restrictions you want to place." And I meant it. I'd rather have Destiny for fifty years and watch her grow old and die if the alternative was not having her at all.

"Good to know," she whispered. "I'll take it under advisement."

"Do," I said. "Please."

She took Miriam back and said, "I should go. Visit us."

"Leaving so soon?"

She smiled at me, a sad smile. "Before I do something I'll regret. I think I need a chaperone."

I gave her a long glance. She looked *amazing*, even more beautiful than I remembered. Her gorgeous hair tumbled down loose to her waist, and I had a vivid flash of memory of her pulling me onto the bed and her hair falling all around me like a silk curtain. She smelled incredible, like lavender shampoo and a hint of jasmine. I wanted to wrap up every one of my senses in her, to touch and to taste and... things that were a terrible idea if she was going to go back to her mothers' house. "I'll visit you."

"Please," she said. She walked back to the door and gave me one last look—was that longing, or was that my wishful thinking?—before she left.

I picked up my violin and practiced. The pets gathered around to listen.

———⚬✖⚬———

Destiny
Eatontown, New Jersey
December 13, 2021

WE SAT ON THE lavender sofa together. Miriam was asleep on my lap, and Morgan and Bridget were streaming *The L Word* on low volume.

There was a bang and the front door popped open. Four men came in dressed in black, wearing black ski caps and a black stripe across their eyes. Miriam woke up and wailed a distressed baby cry.

"What the fuck?" Morgan stood and raised her fists.

Bridget squeaked. I handed her Miriam and stood next to Morgan and raised my fists as well, glancing around the room for something heavy.

They said nothing, just moved forward, kicking over our coffee table as they came. There was a tinkling sound as Bridget's glass tea set shattered, and her crystal ball rolled behind the sofa. I grabbed Morgan's softball bat and swung, striking one of them in the arm that he raised to protect his head.

"Fuck!" He grabbed at the bat, and I kicked him in the stomach until he let go of it. Note to self: don't let the thug grab the bat.

Morgan did one of her Tae Kwon Do roundhouse kicks, hitting an approaching thug in the head. She didn't turn her head, but she said, "The strategic thing to do would be to get in the car and drive away."

Behind me, I heard Bridget scrambling towards the back door. Good. I eyed the man in front of me and swung the softball bat meaningfully. He eyed me back, then ran after Bridget and my baby. I chased him.

There was a tall, balding man with a scraggly fringe of hair standing in front of the back door, blocking the path. "Morgan!" I raised the bat and ran at him.

He caught it faster than my eye could track. He was strong, so strong, and I realized he was a vampire. It must have shown on my face, because he smirked at me and tugged at the bat.

I let go of it and backed away.

He pulled a circular amulet out from under his shirt with one hand and pointed at me with index and middle finger with the other. "You witches have no power over me!"

"I think the bitch broke my arm," the thug I'd hit with the bat said.

The vampire rolled his eyes at him. Then he grabbed Bridget and started prying Miriam out of her arms.

*No no no no no no no no no no no no...* "Stop!" I said. "You'll hurt her!"

"Then I'm sure you'll want to cooperate to prevent that," he said, his voice serene.

One man put his hands on Miriam and said, "You pull the bitch's arms and I'll catch the baby."

The vampire let go of Miriam and started pulling on Bridget's wrists. She whimpered, and I had a sudden panic that he still might hurt Miriam, or hurt Bridget in a way that would prevent her from playing the cello. Something in the vampire's attitude told me not to point that out. I was certain that if I verbalized my fears, he would do it. He would *hurt my baby*. My vision darkened at the edges, and I concentrated on breathing. I would *not* pass out!

Morgan stormed into the kitchen, fists raised. "You hurt either of them and you'll answer to me."

"What she said," I said, and opened the silverware drawer and grabbed their sharpest knife.

They pulled Miriam out of Bridget's arms together. Bridget whimpered, but her eyes were defiant. The vampire let go of her and took the baby from his thug. Bridget rubbed her forearms and wrists, glaring.

Morgan's thug stumbled into the kitchen clutching his side but didn't complain.

"Put down the knife," the vampire said. "I'd rather have both you *and* the baby, but I really only need one of you."

I considered my options… mostly whether I believed he'd hurt my precious angel Miriam. The answer, horrifyingly, was yes. My heart pounding, I put the knife back in the kitchen drawer and then crossed my arms and glared at him, trying to look calm and not scream.

The thug I'd hit with a baseball bat punched me in the face. I was more aware of slamming backwards into the kitchen counter than the blow, but I could tell it would sting later. I heard Morgan swear, Bridget sob…

"Did I tell you to hit her?" the vampire asked.

The thug flinched. "N-no, Master Thomas."

So, his name was Thomas. Something nudged at the back of my mind, before… "Are you the guy who led the march?"

He smiled at me and did a sarcastic half bow. "I'm pleased you've heard of me… although you obviously haven't taken my teachings to heart."

I didn't know what this meant because I'm not up on my bigoted psychos, but I suspected he meant Abraham.

The vampire—Thomas—glanced around. "Clean up this mess. We want him inside, where he won't attract attention." He indicated Morgan and Bridget with a tilt of his head. "Tie their hands, gag them, and take them upstairs." He stared at the least-injured thug. "You wait for him."

I had to watch them bind and gag my mothers. Bridget was clearly frightened, but defiant. Morgan was simmering with rage. They led them upstairs and made them lie down on the floor and tied their legs. Then they led me downstairs to a dirty white van parked out front in the snow.

There were men inside with brown button-down shirts. One of them had some kind of shotgun.

"Let me off at the warehouse," Thomas said, "and take them to the hotel."

A hotel? Without the vampire? Hopefully, Miriam and I could escape without the vampire.

———————— ⌇∞⌇ ————————

Abraham
Eatontown, New Jersey
December 13, 2021

MY CAR PULLED INTO Destiny's mothers' snowy driveway around seven p.m., which meant it was already dark. Because it was time to stop wallowing and start acting like someone Destiny might want to come back to, that's why. I let the pets out of the car and they followed me up to the house, bounding through the crunchy bluish snow. It came up to Ivan's and Inanna's shoulders, and halfway to the door Ivan hopped gently onto Freddy's back.

The door was ajar, and the doorknob was lying broken on the ground in front of it. That was ominous. I knocked anyway, and called, "Hello?"

There was a muffled sound from inside, and next to me, Inanna growled. Her hackles were up.

Freddy forced the door open with a leap and charged in. Ivan tumbled gracelessly off Freddy's back, landed on his feet, and tilted his head.

Freddy barked, and Ivan charged in, so I followed.

Ivan led me upstairs, where Bridget and Morgan were lying on the floor next to their bed, tied up and gagged. Bridget was crying—my heart skipped a beat in sympathy—and Morgan looked like raw fury would break her bonds. I ran in to untie them, and a dark shape lunged from behind the door.

I dodged the flash of knife, and the three pets slammed into him, knocking him to the ground. He rolled, scrambled back to his feet. There was an arc of shiny metal followed by a splash of blood and a yap of pain. *Freddy!*

Inanna leaped onto the man's hand in a flash of tortoiseshell fur and sharp claws. The man screamed and dropped the knife. She'd covered his hand in deep, bloody gashes, as if a tiger had mauled him instead of a house cat.

Freddy's wound closed up as we watched. The man's eyes grew wide. Then he stared at Inanna, who growled at him, and Ivan, who hissed. "What the fuck?" He looked like he might run for a moment, but Inanna growled at him, deep and menacing, and Freddy bared his teeth and tensed to jump, snarling, and the man put his hands up, his back to a mirrored closet door.

He wore all black, with a black stripe painted across his face, like a cheap ninja costume without the hood and mask, and a swastika armband. His unkempt hair fell over his pasty face.

I picked up the knife. "Where's my wife?" My accent was distinctly German, I noted.

"Fuck you, and fuck George Soros, and fuck the Jewish space lasers."

George Soros, the Jewish philanthropist that Fox News was obsessed with? And... Jewish... space... lasers? Maybe it was better to not ask. "Oh, come on," I said. "They obviously left you here to give me a message." They clearly hadn't left him for his wit.

"They left here me to kill you!"

I rolled my eyes and used the knife to cut Bridget's and Morgan's hands free.

Bridget ungagged herself first. "They took them. They took Destiny and the baby!" She untied her own feet while she spoke, then sat unsteadily on her bed. They had a silk bedspread painted with astrological symbols. It was almost certainly handmade.

Morgan untied her feet first and stood up before removing her gag. She assumed a martial arts stance next to the dresser, upon which was a small statue of Aphrodite releasing doves, fresh roses, pink candles, and small pink rocks.

Blood dripped onto the floor from the man's hand. It smelled delicious. I tried not to salivate, but I let a hint of fang show when I asked, "Where is my wife?" I didn't really want to frighten Bridget and Morgan and didn't know how much they knew, but...

"It's a trap," Morgan said. "A trap for you, specifically."

I turned my head to stare at Morgan.

"Apparently, the white supremacist doesn't think Jewish vampires should exist," she said.

The idiot thug stared at me. Then he shakily made the sign of the cross. Maybe he'd realized that he was disposable. I rolled my eyes at him, which was apparently not the reaction he'd expected.

I hadn't interacted with Thomas directly since... when? a hundred and eighty years ago? A hundred and seventy? My kind have long memories, but... Perhaps it was a cultural bias, with the Talmud forbidding revenge, but it felt unhinged.

Also, Destiny's parents knew. I'd expected them to take it well, but...

"It's okay, honey," Bridget said. "Our daughter told us everything. You're still the same person you always were, just... older, and with pointier teeth."

"The threefold law is a bitch," Morgan said, but her tone was sympathetic. She turned her attention back to the intruder. "How about you? Are you ready for a little instant karma?" She made a fist. "I'm only an orange belt, but I can still hit pretty hard for an old lady..."

I leaned in closer to the thug, letting him get a good look at my fangs. "Where is my wife?"

"I don't know!" he said. "Some abandoned building in Brooklyn is all I know." The whites showed around his eyes now, and his hands shook.

I was going to need help. I pulled out my phone to call Ludwig. As I did, I could hear Bridget next to me calling the police, much to my alarm. The police were fine for a bunch of thugs, but Thomas would go through them like a knife through warm brie. I hoped the police would be all right and stay out of his way. I had another memory of Miriam, Shayna, and the single bullet to kill them both. I imagined the sound of the gun and the splatter of blood, but this time, it was

Destiny and *my* Miriam. I thought I might vomit at the mental image, but instead I called Ludwig and asked him to come and help.

.

# Room 306

Abraham
Eatontown, New Jersey
December 13, 2021—December 14, 2021

The Eatontown police handcuffed Thomas's thug, blood dripping red and delicious-smelling over the metal cuffs and onto the beige carpet. Judging by their expressions, his cat-induced wounds alarmed the police, but they didn't press the topic.

"Who's a good kitty? You are, yes, you are!" Morgan cooed, and scooped up Inanna. Inanna purred and pressed her head up into Morgan's chin with a blissful expression, apparently loving being praised for violence. I absolutely agreed, but thought Morgan was a dog person. Then again, Inanna had defended her doggie friend, so...

The officers turned the thug towards the bedroom door. "Let's go," one policeman said.

There was a knock, and Ludwig called, "Hello?"

"Come in, we're upstairs!" I shouted down, doing my best to keep my accent American. I could hear the door opening and footsteps heading up the stairs.

"He's a vampire!" the thug said, wild-eyed, spittle shooting out of his mouth. "They're witches and he's a vampire! The dog is a vampire, and there's something wrong with the cats. Maybe they're vampires, too! Maybe they're witches! I'm a patriot! I stormed the Capitol to protect democracy! You can't arrest me. It's a revolution! Fuck the Jewish space lasers!"

"Be careful. I might use them on you." It wasn't a very good joke, but it was either laugh or scream. They had *my wife and baby*.

"Psych is going to have a field day with this one," one officer said.

The other one snickered. "Yes. You've found us out. I hereby, using my powers as a Jew, demand you come quietly before I shoot you with the space laser." He rolled his eyes and gestured impatiently.

"I see he's trying for an insanity plea." Ludwig smirked at the thug. "I hope you can afford adequate representation. Don't look at my firm." He and Solomon had bundled up in heavy coats, but it was still dark, fortunately. Solomon was avoiding eye contact, but I was still glad to see him.

"When the master comes, you'll be sorry! We're going to save this country from the Jews and the witches!" He sneered. "Heil Hitler!"

Behind him, Solomon glared at the man, jaw tightening. For a moment, I feared for the thug's safety. Well. Not feared for the thug, so much as worried that Solomon might do something unwise in front of the police.

One officer—the one not shoving the thug out the door—turned around and asked Bridget and Morgan, "Do you have anywhere else to stay, or do you need us to find you a place?"

Bridget looked at me, then at Ludwig. "We'll... find a place." She reached out and took Morgan's hand and bit her lip. Morgan visibly squeezed Bridget's hand. She glared at the thug.

And then police and thug were gone, and we were alone. There was an awkward silence. Ludwig opened his mouth to say something, glanced at Bridget and Morgan, and closed it again.

"I think they know everything. They know about me, at least."

Ludwig nodded.

I caught Solomon's eye. "Thank you for coming."

He made an irritated face at me. "I'm still angry, but I won't let Nazis hurt another mother and child if I can help it."

Of course he wouldn't.

"I understand that what I did was wrong and hope you can find it in your heart to tell me how I may make my amends to you."

Solomon closed his eyes and pressed his lips together, but he nodded.

"We should continue this discussion at my place," Ludwig said.

We needed to hurry. It was almost sunrise.

———————— ◦⧜◦ ————————

Abraham
Manhattan, New York
December 14, 2021

I HADN'T BEEN to Ludwig's current penthouse before—he'd purchased and renovated it in the past year—but it was, as the modern Americans say, "extra." Bright, patterned wallpaper in black, red, and white; two red Victorian sofas that looked suspiciously like the one he'd had in 1840 (would he really buy the sofa back, along with a twin?); mirrors; a wall of wine fridges. Thick Persian carpets. In the center of the room was an inlaid wood coffee table. He also had an enormous crystal chandelier that would be at home in Berlin's *Hamburger Bahnhof*. I stared at the chandelier, momentarily mesmerized. He also had floor-to-ceiling windows with magnificent views, only slightly hindered by the transparent gray UV-blocking shades. Genius. I might need those for my home, particularly upstairs.

I'd never wanted to go out in the daylight so badly. *My wife and baby* were out there, somewhere.

The pets sat in a row, watching us with preternaturally intelligent eyes. It was as if they understood what was happening and were waiting for us to form a plan.

Bridget set her cello down by the end of one sofa and sat, fidgeting. Morgan called in to the hospital, citing a family emergency, then paced.

"All right." Ludwig perched on the edge of the sofa. "So. We should absolutely let modern law enforcement handle the thugs, but they won't be able to handle Thomas."

"That'll be a job for us," I said. I didn't sit. I was too keyed up.

"Well," Ludwig said. He wrung his hands, and he bit his lip.

I tilted my head at him.

"I can't go up against Thomas, and you know it. Remember leaving Germany?" He sighed and stared at the floor.

I remembered. I remembered being turned into a golem-like creature, dressed in a pink dress, Ludwig tying pink ribbons in my hair like I was a doll, and Ludwig shuffling me aboard a boat.

"What?" Solomon asked.

"Remember Abraham's disguise? He didn't choose it, I did. A vampire sire has mind-control abilities over their offspring, and Thomas turned me, so I can't fight him."

Solomon stared at me, startled. I raised my hands and shook my head. "I wouldn't."

Solomon eyed me thoughtfully. "Could Abraham make me not angry with him?"

"Temporarily," Ludwig said. "And unlike what Thomas does to people, you'd know."

I glanced around the room. "I... I appreciate what you're trying to... Now is not the time! *They have Destiny and Miriam!* We need to get out there and—"

Ludwig stood. He made the marionette gesture at me. "Calm down."

The compulsion felt like a bucket of ice water thrown over me. I closed my eyes and took a deep breath.

"Sit down."

Golem-like, I sat and ground my teeth. I understood that he was making a point, but now was not the time.

"Stand up," he said.

I stood. He'd made his point!

"Do ballet."

I stared at him. I had no idea how to do ballet.

"Right." He considered for a moment, then snapped his fingers at me, releasing me, and turned to Solomon. "You get the point."

Solomon regarded me with a thoughtful expression.

"Really?" I glared at Ludwig.

"What?" He rolled his eyes.

I rolled my eyes back at him.

Morgan crossed her arms. "Will you two just get a room already? My daughter is out there, in danger!"

Ludwig and I turned on Morgan with, I imagined, identical expressions of outrage. I agreed with her wholeheartedly, but was still calmer. Damn him.

"Modern Americans make everything so vulgar." Ludwig sighed. "At least I needn't worry about accidentally upsetting your delicate sensibilities."

Morgan snorted aloud. "'Delicate sensibilities'? I'm an ER nurse. If I had 'delicate sensibilities' I would have died the first time someone came into the emergency room with—"

Solomon stepped between us, much to my relief. I'd heard the stories and thought Ludwig might faint if Morgan continued.

"I understand. Uncle Ludwig was making two points. One, that Onkel Avrahom could hypnotize me into not being angry and is choosing not to because he's more ethical than that, and second, that Uncle Ludwig can't go against Thomas. I imagine Thomas would do something worse than pink dresses and ballet."

"Quite." Ludwig shuddered.

"I thought Inanna had been unusually well behaved lately," Bridget said. She pushed her dark curls out of her eyes.

Inanna started washing one of her paws. Her enthusiasm for the task grew as she found a bit of blood between her toes.

"Well," Morgan said. "I'm not anything supernatural—okay, I've been called a witch, and things that rhyme with 'witch,' and worse—but I can go out in direct sunlight and set things on fire. My understanding is that'll do the trick." She shoved her red hair back with one hand as she paced in her jeans and scrublike shirt.

"It will, indeed," I confirmed. I had a vivid sense memory of the stench of smoke, of overwhelming heat, of screams. I closed my eyes and took a deep breath. We needed to find Destiny and Miriam. My brain kept substituting them for Flora and the children...

"What I *can* do," Ludwig said, "is tell you where he is."

Really? This wasn't something I could do...

He closed his eyes for a moment. "Thomas is in an abandoned warehouse"—he pointed— "that way, approximately twenty-three miles away. Miriam is not with him; she's perhaps three miles away from him in a hotel."

"You know where Destiny is?" Bridget asked, her eyes full of hope.

"Unfortunately, no," Ludwig said. "I have no ability to find ordinary mortal humans."

So... Miriam... wasn't *an ordinary mortal human.* "When we have more time," I said, "you might need to unpack that."

Ludwig looked like he was going to answer, but Morgan interrupted. "Can we just give the address to the police?"

"Alas," Ludwig said, "I cannot give you the address nor the hotel name, just that it is a hotel approximately twenty-three miles away,"—he pointed—"that way."

"If you can find Thomas," Solomon asked, "can Thomas find you?"

"He does not have that ability. And even if he did, I can hide," Ludwig said, looking coy.

Interesting. I wondered if *I* could hide, although considering that I'd never known it was a possibility...

"How did he find Abraham?" Solomon asked, and I wondered how Solomon got to be such a smart boy. All that studying, I supposed.

"You'd have to ask him." Ludwig shuddered.

So Thomas couldn't track other vampires, not even his offspring—or, at least, not Ludwig. Interesting. I wondered where I'd gone wrong, what mistake I'd made to draw attention to myself. I supposed Ludwig had explained how he always found *me.*

"Count me in," Bridget said, but she sounded anxious. She fidgeted a little in her long skirt and blouse. Unlike her athletic wife, Bridget was thin and all her muscle development seemed related to playing the cello, all forearms and triceps and deltoids.

Solomon said, "You can count me in, too."

"I'm so very sorry," I said. I meant it, too, and my voice sounded sad.

Solomon actually looked me in the eye. "I know."

"I understand that now isn't the time, but please think about how I might make my amends to you when this is over." I hoped I wasn't being too pushy.

Solomon shook his head, and an idea appeared to strike him. "You raised us to be observant and yet you never went to shul with us. I always wanted you to come with us when we were little. You even missed my bar mitzvah! I understand about not being able to walk to morning services, but I picked Kabbalat Shabbat, hoping you would come because it was Friday night instead of Saturday morning..." He still sounded hurt, despite its happening seventy-five years ago. I winced.

He really had known all along. I had done the masquerade with him for nothing and missed so much. I shuffled my feet and hung my head. Finally, I admitted, "I didn't know if the Kohanim would have to leave because I was there."

Solomon tilted his head at me.

"Because I'm undead, or whatever. I don't use the mikveh, I don't go to services where I know Kohanim are..."

Solomon shook his head at me and smiled sadly. "You're an idiot, Onkel."

That stung, although I don't know if it showed or not.

Solomon took my shoulders and shook them gently. "*You're not dead.* You were there when I turned. My heart beats. I have brain activity. I breathe." He gave me another gentle shake. "We're not dead!"

I wasn't dead? I'd been proceeding as if I were dead—undead—I didn't know which, but... I felt a soar of hope.

"Well, technically…" Ludwig said, and my hope crashed.

Solomon glared at him.

"What?" Ludwig asked. "Technically, we don't *have* to breathe, we can hibernate…"

Solomon rolled his eyes at Ludwig.

"What?" Ludwig sounded like he really didn't know. I almost wanted to laugh.

Solomon held my shoulders and said, "When this is over, you and I are going to the mikveh together, and then we'll go to services together." He shook me again. "You're supposed to mourn, not fall into despair. We're actually prohibited from mourning forever, because death is temporary! The souls of the departed have gone back to God, and we'll see them again in the World to Come. Stop cutting yourself off from your people! You can only truly be a Jew in community with other Jews." He squeezed my shoulder. "This is how you make amends to me."

I nodded.

"So," Morgan said. "Let's go burn down a warehouse."

"After making sure Destiny isn't in it," Bridget amended.

"Of course."

"I suggest," Ludwig said, "baby first, wife second. If only because I know where the baby is, and the fewer hostages Thomas has, the better."

Despite my anxiety for my wife, I couldn't argue with his logic. *Damn it.*

"Also," Ludwig said, "take a violin. I have one you can borrow."

I stared at him. Why would I…?

"Trust me."

––––––––⌾⌾⌾––––––––

Ludwig
Manhattan, New York
December 14, 2021

THIS WOULD BE FINE. I wouldn't have to confront Thomas at all! I knew precisely where he and the baby were, and we could go in and collect the baby and leave.

If I closed my eyes, I could see almost a light overlay covering the city, with the vampires on it as glowing spots of color. It was barely visible but still there if I concentrated with my eyes open. Marginalia on the illuminated manuscript of life.

Obviously, my penthouse contained two vampires: Abraham and Solomon—five if you counted the pets. Abraham was the ornate capital I of my *in the beginning*, the north on my compass. He glowed like a shining-golden-light version of himself, hair streaming around him like he was underwater, with a faint, barely audible violin note sustained around him, the scent of wine, and the barely remembered taste of honey in my mouth. Solomon was more... a sense of a young vampire in an old man's body. I saw a shining translucent golden image of child Solomon from the 1940s superimposed over the adult form. I couldn't detect a sound until I homed in on the image, and then I had the faintest impression of a coffee pot brewing and the scent of books.

The pets were adorable but less complex. Ivan had a child's classroom slate that read "I understand speech," which, when he realized I could read it, switched to "I'm thirsty." Inanna was a golden mother bear—when I focused on her, Abraham and the other pets became bear cubs—and Freddy was a puppy with a chew toy. I asked Abraham to feed the pets. He headed towards the kitchen, and they trotted after him on little silver psychic leashes.

Thomas was still approximately twenty-five miles away, across the East River, which was a black inky light-sink. Still, he glowed a malevolent dim red in the distance, like some kind of baleful furnace, an angry imp in the margins making a rude gesture at the reader. He wasn't moving, or at least was moving little enough that it wasn't visible at scale. I couldn't hear him from this distance and also didn't wish to look too closely. I knew he wouldn't know, but part of me was afraid that I was wrong about that. Besides, if I was trying to hide myself and Abraham from him, perhaps I shouldn't seek him out. I looked enough to confirm that it was an abandoned warehouse and left.

There were other vampires in the area—pinpricks of light scattered around the city—but they were uninvolved.

And then there was Miriam. I'd spotted her in the womb, a little silver baby-shape of light curled up inside Destiny. Now she was a tiny silver glow twenty-three miles away, and if I closed my eyes and homed in I had a faint, blurry gray-scale impression of a building with a lobby and a lot of rooms and the intellectual knowledge that it was a hotel. Miriam wasn't alone, but I couldn't sense any vampires near her. She had a faint, tingling chime sound to her if I listened hard enough. Also, she wanted to go home, and her baby's distress was like a magnet pulling me towards her to help.

We could do this, as long as Thomas stayed where he was.

———————⌘———————

Destiny
Brooklyn, New York
December 14, 2021

FAMILIARITY BREEDS CONTEMPT, and I was feeling contempt for that sawed-off shotgun and its wielders. Perhaps that was unwise. The shotgun was loaded, and I was certain they were willing to use it. That didn't exactly make them smart—or manly.

The hotel was brown and beige, bland and boring, and I'd been sitting around with these two pasty, basement-dwelling, no-account losers and their BO all day. They wouldn't let me bathe myself or my daughter. Whoever this Thomas guy was, he had terrible taste in henchmen—or perhaps they were disposable.

If I were a vampire, I'd be able to bite them. Well. I supposed I could bite them as a human, but it wouldn't have the same effect. Either way, it would be better than *this*.

I dozed off in a chair at one point, and dreamed I was a lady in massive, old-fashioned skirts—black. Was I in mourning? I wasn't sad. I walked through dark, foggy, smelly streets, and when a man jumped out, laughing and calling, "Look what we have here, lads!" in a British accent, my teeth grew out long and I grabbed him and bit him and drank. The other men ran. I woke up both happy and sad that I wasn't a vampire. Super strength and sharp teeth would have been convenient right now, but I would regret it later.

Not being with Abraham seemed stupid now. I loved him; he loved me. If he understood how important it was that he respect my autonomy on the vampire issue I thought he would, and if he didn't, I could leave him permanently and go make my way in the big city, perhaps trying to invent that Charlaine Harris blood substitute. With Solomon!

I mean, hopefully not! I still wanted my normal human life with my eternally young and gorgeous musical genius husband. Two kids, a dog and two cats, a job, hanging out with my moms... maybe I could see Miriam and her brother get married and have children of their own...

Yeah. When I got away from these losers, I was going back to Abraham.

———————∞———————

Abraham
Manhattan, New York
December 14, 2021

WHILE WAITING FOR SUNSET, Solomon and I went into Ludwig's library, which was a glorious space. He had paintings from various time periods—from 1800 to the modern era—covering the walls. Multiple mahogany bookshelves were filled with antique books. I knew he collected old devotionals, but the crown jewel of his collection was a handwritten copy of the Vulgate kept in a glass case. He also owned a Gutenberg Bible, and two original Douay-Rheims Bibles, one of which was a bit worn from his personal use. Several works called *Lives of the Saints* were shelved together on one bookcase—by Butler, by Baring-Gould, a 1575 Polish version. A gigantic, imposing desk stood in the center of the room, holding piles of musical scores rather than a computer. In the corner, Ludwig had a harpsichord, which I knew he prized, but he also had a piano, a cello, a violin, and a guitar. I play the harpsichord, as well as the piano and classical guitar, but the violin is my first and dearest love.

Thick, plush Persian carpets hushed our steps as we walked together into the room. Solomon laid the tefillin bag on the desk. I noted that Solomon still had the set I gave him all those years ago. My tefillin were back at home, of course. I hadn't used them in a long time, but I couldn't bear to part with them.

"You can borrow mine and go first." Solomon pushed the bag towards me.

It had been... what, a hundred and eighty years since I'd last laid on tefillin, but it felt like yesterday. My hands remembered what to do without me. On second thought, I'd shown Solomon how to do it in... 1945? That didn't really count, though, because I didn't say the prayers. I was only demonstrating. I suppose I'd thought that because the dead are released from all commandments...

Tefillin are a pair of black leather boxes with long straps. Inside the boxes are scrolls with the texts referring to tefillin, which are about the duty to always remember the redemption from Egyptian bondage, the obligation of every Jew to educate his children about this and God's commandments, the assurance that God will reward our observance of the commandments, and the Sh'ma. These are handwritten on handmade kosher parchment by a special scribe. There's a distinct way to wear them; you wrap one around your biceps, pointed at your heart, and wind the leather straps seven times down to your long finger, and wrap the other around your head, like a crown, with the box in the center of your forehead.

I said the blessing and wound. It was the scent of leather, the feel of the straps down my arm, and my body knowing what to do without my telling it. Then I said the Sh'ma. They translate the opening words as: "Hear, O Israel, the Lord is our God, the Lord is One." The rest includes an instruction to bind these words "as a sign" upon your hand and between your eyes—which I had just done, literally. A sense of calm resolve came over me. There are no prohibitions or particular restrictions about laying on tefillin, and they were a profound comfort to me. I should have done this years ago. I used to do it every day.

What I really missed was someone to do it with me. And no matter what, I never stopped loving the Lord with all my heart and all my might.

I unwound them and handed them to Solomon, who repeated my actions. Solomon and I had slightly different accents for the prayers, but it was close enough. After, we packed the tefillin back up, and I closed my eyes and inhaled the scent of old texts.

"You live in a Victorian farmhouse, with 1920s appliances," Solomon said, "and Uncle Ludwig lives here. Why don't you live somewhere like this?"

"Pets are messy." I shrugged. "I think Ludwig would have a fit if a cat scratched his sofa, or worse, one of his rare books."

The corner of Solomon's mouth curled upwards. Behind the heavy curtain—no UV shades in *this* room—I could feel the sun setting.

It was time.

---

Abraham
New York
December 14, 2021

WE LEFT THE PETS in Ludwig's penthouse, with instructions for the doorman about when and what to feed them if we were late returning. If this alarmed him, he showed no sign of it. I suspect he thought we were simply eccentric rich people. It sounded like an odd thing for Ludwig to ask the doorman to do, but perhaps he had an arrangement with him. Hmm, perhaps I should have checked the doorman's wrists...

We piled into Morgan's green Subaru Outback—which conveniently had a child seat that we tossed into the cargo area—and backed out of the parking space. Morgan's red hair reminded me of her daughter, causing a pang in my chest. Fortunately, my nervousness about the city traffic distracted me.

Ludwig sat in the front seat. He closed his eyes, then pointed a finger. "That way. Approximately twenty-four miles."

Morgan sighed and pulled out of Ludwig's parking garage. We turned right onto a one-way street headed another way. Ludwig made a frustrated noise in the back of his throat and pointed behind us. Amid much pointing and instructions, we eventually were headed the right way.

We turned onto FDR and headed towards the Brooklyn Bridge. Morgan turned on the Indigo Girls, and Ludwig reached over and snapped it off.

"Hey! My car, my tunes!" She reached towards the dial again.

Ludwig placed his hand in front of the dial. "I need to concentrate."

Morgan sighed heavily. We sped along in silence, weaving in and out of traffic. I fear that I'm old and will never fully acclimate to city traffic. We crossed the bridge, which would have been lovely if I weren't fearing for our lives. I clutched my seatbelt tightly. I suspected Bridget was smiling at my discomfort but didn't have the energy to be offended.

"Here! Turn here!" Ludwig gesticulated wildly. "Here!"

Morgan glanced over her shoulder, frowned, and somehow got into the right lane after we'd sped past the turn.

Ludwig let out a martyred sigh. Morgan gave him a dirty look. I closed my eyes and hoped we reached our destination alive.

We took the next turn, and he pointed and had her turn left. Morgan turned down a major road, and then Ludwig had her turn right. "We're getting close."

We kept going.

"Right! Right!" He pointed and made a noise of frustration as she zoomed past.

"That's a one-way street," Morgan said. "One-way the wrong way."

Ludwig sighed. "I apologize. I have tracked vampires very little via automobile."

Morgan made a face. "You're no GPS, but I suppose GPS doesn't know where my granddaughter is."

We continued into a modest neighborhood, turning to end up on that one-way street. Eventually, we pulled up outside a dingy hotel, plain and square. Morgan parked on the street and fed the meter.

We walked into the lobby. It wasn't sleazy, but it wasn't particularly nice, either. Beige carpet, brown sofa, long wooden desk. The scent of cheap, burned coffee floated through the air with the sounds of Muzak. Yuck.

"I'll handle this one," Ludwig murmured. "Stand behind me and say nothing."

Having seen Ludwig *handle things* before... better him than me. Under different circumstances, I might have anticipated enjoying this.

A pale, bored-looking young man with stringy dark hair and glasses sat behind the desk, web surfing and occasionally slurping an enormous Starbucks cup of what smelled like one of those sugary burned coffee drinks. Ludwig walked over to him and quietly placed a hundred-dollar bill on the counter. The young man blinked blearily at the money, then at Ludwig. I had to admit Ludwig looked out of place here in his bespoke vicuña suit, his Blancpain watch, and rings on all ten fingers. I fit in better in my jeans and plain gray T-shirt, although the violin slung across my back on a shoulder strap was perhaps an odd fashion choice.

Ludwig smiled, conspiratorial. "You never saw us."

"Uh." The young man glanced around, bit his lip, and reached for the bill.

Ludwig grabbed his hand. "There's more where that came from. What's your name?"

The man gave him a skeptical look. "Troy." He pulled free.

"Well, Troy," Ludwig said, leaning closer. "I'm the attorney in a particularly nasty divorce case, and this man"—he pointed at me—"is the rightful custodial parent of a baby that an anonymous person says might be in this very hotel." He cocked his head for a moment and pointed upwards. "Third floor, that side."

Troy appeared alarmed for a moment but took another large slurp from his Starbucks cup and said nothing. I edged closer, next to Ludwig, and tried to look like a worried parent—which was hardly a stretch.

Ludwig smiled. "How much for a room key?"

Troy opened his mouth, then closed it and bit his lip. He eyed his coffee for a moment, admitting, "You're not the first person to give me money and say that I didn't see them this evening."

Ludwig's smile broadened. He pulled a gigantic roll of hundred-dollar bills out of an inner suit pocket and started laying them on the counter one at a time.

Troy's eyes widened. He glanced at me. I chewed on a fingernail, a habit I haven't had in about a hundred and eighty years, but now was a good time to start again.

Ludwig kept putting down hundred-dollar bills. "Say when."

Troy blinked, as if coming out of a trance, starting. He produced a shiny white keycard, pushed it into the card programmer, and removed it again and handed it to Ludwig. "Room three oh six."

"I admire an enterprising young man," Ludwig said, putting the roll of bills back in his inner jacket pocket. "Lovely doing business with you."

Troy rolled up the money and tucked it into his sock, under his jeans. He watched us walk to the elevators, looking like he expected us to come back and take it away again.

We all boarded the elevator. Once the doors closed, Solomon laughed. "Never change, Uncle Ludwig."

I hugged Ludwig. "Thank you."

"Do stop," he said. "We haven't retrieved your baby yet. There will be time to celebrate in the car on the way home."

Morgan cracked her knuckles. The elevator dinged and opened on the third floor.

Room 306 was directly across the hall from the elevator. Ludwig placed a pale hand on the door. He closed his eyes, and a lock of golden hair fell over his face. He nodded when he glanced back at us.

I was more nervous than I'd been for my bar mitzvah. I gestured, and we all huddled around the corner. I leaned against the dirty cream wall. "We're going to walk right in?" I asked. "Really?"

"I think we need to move quickly," Ludwig said. "I'm fairly certain that there are only ordinary mortal humans in there with her, which means the three of us"—he gestured at me and Solomon—"are faster than they are. We hit them fast and take the baby and leave."

"Which means you two stand back and watch the door," I told Morgan and Bridget.

Morgan frowned. "You brought us all this way to watch the door? What if Destiny is in there?"

"Then she leaves with us," I said. "And if they try to leave with Miriam, you two get them."

Morgan considered this and nodded. "If you're having trouble, I'm coming in to help."

"Hopefully it won't come to that," I said. I turned to Bridget.

"Unlike my wife, I'm not much of a fighter." She squared her narrow shoulders. "But what mother wouldn't fight for her child or grandchild if need be?"

I nodded and patted her on the shoulder.

A baby started crying loudly in room 306. We exchanged worried glances.

Ludwig and Solomon nodded, and together we crept over the brown and orange industrial carpet to the door of room 306. We stared at each other.

Ludwig held the shiny white keycard over the lock. He held up one finger, a second finger, a third finger, then put the card in the lock.

The light turned green, and we opened the door and rushed into the room.

A man's voice shouted, "What the f—" but Solomon silenced him by grabbing him and slamming him into a cream and brown wall. Ludwig grabbed the second man and bit him.

I only had eyes for Destiny and the baby, back in the far corner of the room. Destiny was wearing dirty clothes and sported a black eye and purpling bruises. Bastards! She was standing next to the bed holding Miriam. If looks could kill, the room would have been full of thug corpses.

Miriam was crying, tears leaving tracks down her dirty face. My precious baby! What is it about your child that turns you completely inside out with their tears? I ran and interposed my body between them and any thugs.

The thugs were wearing black T-shirts with red swastikas on them under button-down shirts. Solomon's struggled, but Ludwig's fainted, perhaps from blood loss. I rushed over and took Solomon's thug's...

His sawed-off shotgun. For a helpless mother and baby.

I grabbed the weapon away from him and backhanded him, hard. He sailed into the air, dented the wall with his head, and fell to the floor, unmoving. I kicked him while he was down, snarling.

I rushed back to Destiny and Miriam. "Are you all right?"

Destiny nodded. "Let's get out of here. I'm ready to go home."

The thug I'd backhanded stirred, and Destiny kicked him in the head. He hit the wall with a satisfying thud and went limp.

Destiny turned back to me and said, simply, "I knew what I was getting into when I married you. I chose you. I choose you again." She smiled. "Just let me stay human, okay?"

I nodded. "Okay." I could almost hear a chorus of angels. I put an arm around her. "Come on." We started walking across the nubby brown carpet together. I considered picking her up in my arms and carrying her so we could move at vampiric speed. I was walking on air, and Destiny and Miriam would be almost as light as air in my arms. I stretched out an arm, intending to hand Ludwig the shotgun.

"Oh, God," Ludwig said, turning to face the entrance of the door. From where I was standing, through the open doorway, I could see the lighted number 3 over the elevator.

The elevator dinged, and the elevator door opened.

———————◦∞◦———————

Ludwig
Brooklyn, New York
December 14, 2021

I FELT IT BEFORE I saw it. Like the feeling between your shoulder blades when someone is watching you. I turned my head towards the hotel room door.

Dull, angry red, like a baleful, banked furnace, two floors below and rising. I'd allowed myself to become distracted. I'd missed it when he moved. I supposed he hadn't been that far away... and I'd been very focused on first the desk clerk, and then the room occupants.

I'd have asked how he found me, but he'd expected us to come.

I wanted to run, to hide, but I faced the door. The lighted number above the elevator was unnecessary. There was banked fire on the other side of the door.

He was here.

# Scheherazade

Abraham
Brooklyn, New York
December 14, 2021

Thomas stepped out of the elevator, all black and red Inquisitor robes and calm face. His eyes locked with mine.

Without a thought, I raised the shotgun and fired. I aimed for his heart, but he made a gesture and Ludwig knocked the weapon aside, causing me to miss. The shotgun fell to the floor and skidded over to a stop below the dresser. "*Guten abend,* Ludwig."

Ludwig closed his eyes and shivered. "How did you find me?" He'd slipped into a German accent.

"I wasn't looking for *you*," Thomas said.

This answer didn't appear to reduce Ludwig's anxiety. Quite the contrary. He shivered and shook his head. Shaking off the compulsion, perhaps?

"Fine," I said. "How did you find *me*?"

Thomas laughed. "When I saw a police report about a dog afraid of the sun who drank blood, and the diseased cat that caused the condition, I knew it was you. Only a soulless Jew would give the gift of eternal life to a dumb animal. When a pair of adolescents posted on my Internet forums about a Jew playing violin at a Christmas party and the strangely frightening blond man with sharp teeth who defended him, driving distance from the animals, that only confirmed it."

Ludwig lowered his eyes and let out a slow breath. He looked even paler than usual.

Next to me, Destiny shuddered. I stepped in front of her and the baby. I'd stayed for them rather than run away, as had been my instinct, and I stood by that decision.

"Don't feel bad, Ludwig," Thomas said. "It was only a matter of time before someone made an error." He turned back to me. "Eternal life is a blessing and a reward—a reward for Christian faith. A gift that Ludwig accidentally cheapened and debased by giving it to the unworthy. I've been trying to correct Ludwig's mistake for a long time." He scowled. "Since he refused to reverse his blunder himself."

Ludwig stepped between us. "I told you, destroying a magnificent gift like Abraham's would be the greatest sin imaginable! It would be taking a present from God and throwing it back in His face!"

Thomas spoke around Ludwig, ignoring him. "He wouldn't even force you to convert."

"A forced conversion is meaningless. If one cares for true piety, one must respect freedom of conscience." It impressed me that Ludwig was paraphrasing Moses Mendelssohn, but I feared Thomas would be unimpressed with the source if he knew it. "Besides, any mental influence I used would wear off over time."

"I'm not arguing with you, Ludwig," Thomas said. "I'm finished with you. You've served your purpose. You served your purpose when you provided the money for us to go to Berlin, and since you made it plain last time we met that the bank is closed, I may as well tell you so. You're not unworthy enough to destroy, but you're not worthy of the effort it would take to convince you of your errors. You're a ridiculous, soft, spoiled thing that wouldn't last ten minutes on the streets, and even less time in an orphanage." He laughed. "Even the adolescents on my internet forums thought you had an unnatural passion for him."

Ludwig froze, his body tense. He took a deep breath, then slowly let it out again. He said, his voice defiant, "I have *never*—"

Thomas snorted. "It's better I not know. During the Inquisition, we would castrate and stone men for that." He shoved Ludwig out of the way.

Ludwig stared at Thomas—perhaps processing the implied threat. My fists clenched, and for a moment I fantasized about punching Thomas in the face. Gossip—*lashon hara*, the evil tongue—is a terrible sin in Judaism. You may not speak negatively of others, nor may you listen to this talk. The ancient rabbis likened what we now call character assassination to murder, saying that causing the blood to drain from the face was like spilling blood.

"I seem to recall," Ludwig said, visibly drawing himself up, "that you *enjoyed* biting me... in a way that felt vulgar. Perhaps you should examine your own urges." His accent was back to American.

Thomas looked Ludwig up and down, arms crossed. "It truly is a shame that this country has degenerated to such a point where people like you—sodomites—aren't at least imprisoned. I stand by stoning or burning."

Behind me, Destiny said, "Welcome to the twenty-first century, asshole, where we don't do barbaric things to people just because of who they love."

I love my wife.

"I must say," Thomas said, in an almost conversational tone, "that I don't care for modern women."

I *adore* modern women.

"Of course you don't," Destiny said. "I hear you're not even a real priest. I heard they drummed your loser ass out centuries ago."

Ludwig cringed, like he was expecting an explosion, but Thomas ignored her.

He stepped closer to me. "I never dreamed Ludwig would have enough spine to reconcile with you—let alone on the very night of the fire that was supposed to cleanse away the insult that is your existence. *You* should have died, not those innocent children. At least they're in heaven now." He paused. "I'd regret your wife if she weren't married to you. Shameful. The Nazi term was correct. *Rassenschande*: racial shame."

Time—and all thought—stopped. I could see the nightmarish orange and black skeleton of our home, feel the heat, smell the stench of burning meat, hair, and chemicals. I saw the dark shapes writhing in the fiery glow as the house collapsed in on itself. My vision darkened at the edges to form a tunnel effect around Thomas.

Without intending to, I flung myself at him and wrapped my hands around his throat, shrieking. We sailed backwards with my momentum, but Thomas caught himself in the doorway.

"I don't need to breathe," Thomas whispered, amused.

He might not, but I imagined he'd have some difficulties if I tore his head off with my bare hands. I squeezed harder and roared an incoherent scream of rage. I'd always thought people were exaggerating when they said they were seeing red, but apparently not. His face floated in a sea of crimson, while my ears filled with a rushing and pounding sound. My vision was still dark at the edges as I crushed.

Thomas's smile became broader, and his eyes glittered with malice. "Of course, then I realized how much that must have hurt you, which is why we'll now have a good old-fashioned witch-burning, to take care of your current *Rassenschande.*"

My grip tightened, and I snarled.

Behind me, Destiny said, "Like hell we will! Give me a couple of hours in the vet clinic with you unconscious. You heal fast, but you're not a starfish, and we have equipment that can remove fangs, amputate limbs... decapitate..."

Behind me, Solomon stepped between Destiny and Thomas. I heard what I was fairly certain was him cracking his knuckles. Ludwig stood behind Thomas, watching with worried eyes. I couldn't see Morgan or Bridget and hoped they stayed hidden.

Thomas rolled his eyes. "Modern women. No sense of their proper place. She dies before you. I might keep the baby and raise her to hunt your kind, by which I mean heathen vampires. We can have a new Inquisition and she can be my hammer!"

I bared my teeth and leaned in, intending to tear out his throat. He placed a hand on my forehead and shoved me away, rolling his eyes.

And then I lost control of my body, as Ludwig said, "Play the violin."

I stopped. My vision returned to normal as I stepped back, removed the violin case from my shoulder, and laid it on the bed. A strange, cold, calm rage swept over me, like sinking underwater in the ocean in winter. My mind cleared even as my body obeyed Ludwig's order.

Destiny watched me with a confused expression, then turned her gaze on Ludwig. Thomas's head tilted slowly, as if he were trying to figure out what Ludwig was doing.

I could feel Solomon's sympathetic eyes on me as I pulled the violin out and played Rimsky-Korsakov's *Scheherazade*. It wasn't my best playing, as I was merely a puppet whose heart was set on murder. The violin wasn't my Stradivarius, either; it was Ludwig's loaner. But my body obeyed the order to play, whether or not I willed it, and the familiar notes brought me some comfort despite their icy perfection.

"Yes," I heard Thomas say over the violin. "And you shoot him while he plays, Ludwig." His voice turned mocking. "I hope you at least got what you wanted from him. That was why you wanted to turn him, wasn't it?"

The compulsion to play stopped—because Ludwig was now compelled instead of me—but I continued the piece, trying to cling to whatever solace the violin might bring me. I thought of the clever and desperate Scheherazade, who told stories for a thousand and one nights to forestall her death, and I willed the story to be true, for Thomas and Ludwig to be spellbound. The violin might not have been my Stradivarius, but she was willing to help me...

Somehow, it worked. Ludwig froze halfway to the dresser—and the shotgun—and stared with a blank expression. Thomas stepped closer, eyes glazed.

*It worked.*

Ludwig had told me to bring the violin. Had he known? Part of me whispered, deep inside, *Of course he knew.*

I had no time to be surprised. I released Ludwig—I willed him to regain himself—and spoke to him and Solomon over the music. "Take my wife and baby and leave." I kept playing.

Solomon took the baby, and Ludwig picked up Destiny. They headed towards the door at vampiric speed.

I could hear Destiny in the hall. "But... but... Abraham! Put me down! We have to help him!"

"He can't stop," Ludwig said. "We'll send help."

"Go," I said, and could spare no more thoughts for anything but Thomas. If we were still here in the morning, I would lead him into the sun like the Pied Piper and fiddle while he burned—and we'd see which of us went up in flames first. How many men and women had he murdered with fire? Aside from my wife and children, of course. Burning had been the preferred execution method for the Inquisition, and my people had been the preferred victims. They were executed by the hundreds, sometimes the entire adult population of a community. How many Jews and witches had he killed?

My wife and children. *My wife and children.*

*Flora.*

The elevator doors opened and closed, but I didn't have a clear line of sight out the open door to see the elevator across the hall anymore. I assumed it was my wife, my baby, and my friends, and I kept playing. I played *Scheherazade*, followed by all twenty-four caprices for solo violin by Paganini. I played solos by Bach, Mozart, and Vivaldi. I performed Henryk Wieniawski's *L'ecole Moderne*, followed by Bartók. And then I looped back to *Scheherazade*.

I played, and I played, and after I don't know how long I heard the elevator ding, and two NYPD officers entered the room. *Fuck.*

"Sir?" the heavier of the two officers said. "We have reports of a disturbance in this room."

"This is the man who had the white supremacist rally in Atlantic Highlands and he kidnapped my wife and daughter," I called over the violin. "Those are his accomplices. You can call it in."

The police glanced at each other. I kept playing.

The other police officer shook Thomas. "Sir?" Thomas didn't respond. "Is he on drugs?"

The heavier officer turned to me. "I'm going to have to ask you to stop playing and take this interview seriously."

"I'm sorry," I said. "I can't. Please, he'll hurt you if I stop..."

He grabbed my arm and dragged me towards the door, causing a discordant scrape across the strings. Thomas blinked, then rotated his head to stare at us.

"Sir?" The officer who had shaken Thomas took ahold of his shoulder. "I need you to come down to the station."

Thomas ignored the police entirely. I suppose he thought they were unimportant. Instead, he smiled at me, a very unsettling type of slow smile that made my stomach clench. "I see Ludwig created something interesting, after all. I might have a use for you."

"I doubt it." I lifted the violin, and the heavier officer slapped it out of my hand. It landed on the floor next to the bed.

Thomas grabbed the first officer and snapped his neck with a loud cracking noise. The second officer pulled his gun and fired. Thomas lunged at him while I dove for the violin. There were more gunshots, and I saw red out of the corner of my eye and smelled the delicious scent of iron, but there was something off about it, almost like it was... old. Thomas.

I had almost arrived at the violin, but Thomas grabbed my foot, a gun falling to the floor at his feet. It was just out of reach. The officer was lying on the floor beside it, next to the unconscious thug.

I stretched my hand, fingers brushing the smooth, sensuous wood of the violin, but he dragged me away. So I seized a table as he hauled me past and smashed his arm with it, hoping to break his grip. The table broke instead. I wished the thing about wooden stakes were true, as I suddenly had a jagged surplus of them.

The violin was out of reach, but the shotgun wasn't, so I grabbed it and fired. He dodged, so it hit him in the shoulder rather than the heart. He roared in pain, and I racked it... empty. Fine. I used the muzzle to bludgeon him in the gunshot wound. He grabbed it out of my hands—I hadn't expected him to be so strong! I suppose I'd never fought another vampire before.

He swung it around and struck me in the head with it. I sailed into the wall, hitting it with a loud crash. I landed on the floor, seeing stars, and lunged for the violin. I *had* to win this fight so my wife and child could escape. Would he pursue them if I were dead?

Thomas stepped on my hand, causing a loud crunching noise. I cried out.

Thomas smiled, malicious, and stomped towards my other palm, but I pulled it away in time. I cradled my broken hand and glared at him.

"Don't be such a child." He curled his lip at me. "It'll heal in under an hour."

Outside, in the hallway, the elevator dinged and there was the sound of wheels rolling, one of which squeaked a little.

I lunged for the violin again. I could play through the pain...

Thomas reached out the door at vampiric speed and grabbed a terrified young woman in a maid's uniform and a sleek bun. "Drop it," he said.

I raised both hands and backed away from the violin.

"Please," she said. "I have a baby. I'm only seventeen!"

Thomas ignored her. "Put it in the case and hand it to her." He put one hand on her head and an arm across her shoulders, preparing to snap her neck. She was trembling, with tears running down her cheeks. She struggled against him, but he was too strong. He glanced at the two dead police officers on the floor. "Or she can join them."

I picked up the violin, slowly, and put her and the bow into the case and locked it. I walked over to hand it to the maid. "Don't hurt her."

Thomas smirked. "The violin, or the maid?"

"I meant the maid," I said, "but both?"

He laughed. "The violin is safe. I told you, I might have a use for you. The maid? That depends on you, and how cooperative you are." He jerked his head towards the door. "You first. We're going for a walk."

I headed over to the elevator and pressed the down button, and Thomas dragged the frightened woman with him. Her cart of sheets and toilet paper and cleaning supplies was outside the door.

"Please, I have a baby," she said.

"Silence," he said, giving her a shake.

The doors opened, and we rode down. I could see the maid in the mirrored walls, could see her tears. She was so young, so very young.

The elevator doors opened. "Go on," he said. "Out the front door."

As I left, I glanced over at Troy, the desk clerk with the wad of hundred-dollar bills in his sock, hoping Ludwig's bribe would buy me a little help.

Troy avoided my eyes.

*Oh.*

I didn't have time to be angry. I walked out the door, where a dirty white van was waiting. Some men with button-down shirts were sitting in the open cargo door. "We almost came in after you," one said.

"You probably should have," Thomas said, still serene, "but I managed, as you see. God is on my side."

Ugh. That was what *he* thought. Had my friends and family escaped? Surely Ludwig and Solomon could take these mortal thugs...

Thomas pushed the maid towards the van. She tried to run, to escape, but he had a firm grip on her arm that she couldn't break. The young men gathered around her. The street was empty, and they blocked the view of her being manhandled into the van.

Thomas looked me in the eye and said, "Get in."

———————⌒◇⌒———————

Destiny
New York
December 15, 2021

WE WERE HEADED the wrong way, the car speeding through the night. Morgan was driving us back into Manhattan, and Abraham was alone with the psychopath who murdered Abraham's wife and children back in the Victorian era. "Turn the car around!"

"We need to drop off your daughter, at the very least... and preferably you as well."

"Like hell you will!" There was a roaring in my ears that I realized sounded like fire, but I wasn't afraid. "That's my husband, and I'm not leaving him there with that... that..." After a moment of frustration, I finished, "...the sociopath who murdered his previous family!"

"We need to drop off the baby first," Ludwig said. "We can't allow Thomas to use her as a hostage against Abraham. Also..." He made a face. "Traditionally, vampire-human hybrids—dhampirs—were used as vampire hunters... assuming the folklore is true."

I blinked and stared at Miriam.

The conversation was too intense, and Miriam cried. I kissed her on the forehead and told her everything would be all right. Sometimes, it's a mother's job to protect a child from the truth.

"Is... will he be all right?" Bridget asked.

"It's all right," Ludwig said. "They're not moving, and when they are... I can guide you to where they go." He shivered, but his voice sounded determined.

The roaring in my ears intensified. I could see, in my mind's eye, the sweet faces of the children in the portrait Abraham had commissioned, and my heart broke for them. And poor Flora, she'd been in the position of my nightmare, the one I'd had even as a child. Some part of my brain could picture the children crying, feel the heat of the approaching flames. The little boy's face was covered with soot and streaked with tears, but he was stoically silent. The little girl screamed.

I wasn't afraid anymore. I should have been, but I wasn't. I wanted to see the one who took Abraham's previous family out of the world taken out of the world himself. Not very peaceful or vegetarian of me, I know, but fuck it. I'm an animal lover, not a sociopath lover.

I'd say I wanted to be the one to do it, but I thought it would change me in ways I didn't want to change. If it was a choice between Thomas and Abraham, though? I'd take it.

---

Ludwig
Manhattan, New York
December 15, 2021

I'D LEFT ABRAHAM with Thomas.

I was sitting in my penthouse waiting for Destiny to return, and my nerves...

I agreed with Abraham that denying Thomas hostages to use against him was the best course of action, but... I'd left Abraham alone with Thomas, and I didn't know what I'd do if he died. I'd focused my entire life around his safety for over a hundred years, but I'd been... *focused* on him since 1840. Did a life without him have meaning?

At least Abraham had spared me from shooting him. I'd only killed the innocent once in my life, and Thomas had forced me to, using his maker's abilities. I still prayed for the man's soul regularly.

If Abraham survived, would he think of me the same way after Thomas's accusations? I tried to remember if Abraham had ever expressed an opinion on homosexuality. I supposed he was a nineteenth century Jewish man and perhaps I needn't have asked what his opinion might be. He wouldn't be hateful like Thomas, but he could hardly approve.

I would simply explain that I wasn't... wasn't...

Was I?

If I'd needed to breathe, I would have been breathing into a paper bag at the very thought.

No. No, it was merely romantic friendship, as was popular in the nineteenth century. Anything else was too terrifying to consider. And whether it was true or false, Thomas had merely said it to throw me off balance and upset me.

———————⌒⌒———————

Abraham
Wreschen, Prussia
2 Nissan 5594 (April 11, 1834)

There are gates in heaven that cannot be opened except
by melody and song.
—Attributed to Rabbi Shneur Zalman

DRESSED FOR THE FIRST TIME in a prayer shawl, I stood in front of my entire congregation and led them in Shacharit, the morning prayers. My voice was changing, but it didn't crack once during the service, which I considered a minor miracle.

The synagogue was a lovely wooden building with black and white tile floors, red and gold wallpaper, wood columns and benches, and abstract windows. Sun shone in bright behind me, as the bimah—the altar—faced Jerusalem.

Jewish prayer is sung rather than spoken, and our cantor had a magnificent singing voice. I was only thirteen and didn't have his skill, but I did my best and my voice was clear. I pronounced all the words properly and hit the notes correctly. Some bar mitzvah boys were mumbling and tuneless, but not me. I glanced over at Rabbi Mendel at one point, and he beamed at me with pride.

When it came time for the Torah reading, I took a deep breath to calm my nerves, and went up to read from the gorgeous handwritten Torah scroll, our synagogue's most prized and beloved possession. Rabbi Mendel stood next to me, to the side, and followed along to prompt me if I got lost. There's a melody to reading the Torah aloud as well. I was very proud to not need any prompting and get the trop—the tune—correct and do it musically. My particular parsha—Torah portion—was continuing the purity laws and included mikveh use and leprosy. We can't all get the Ten Commandments for our bar mitzvah parsha. My thirteenth birthday fell on the Shabbat with Parshat Tazria, so that's what I got—leprosy—and I did my best with it.

(Okay, it's not technically leprosy. It's a spiritual affliction, often a punishment for being a "tale-bearer," or so say the sages of the Mishnah.)

My father was also called up to read. He beamed at me and had to be prompted twice to find the place because he was so busy being proud of me.

Each weekly Torah portion is paired with a thematically related reading from the Prophets, the Haftorah. It also has a melody. My Haftorah was about a prophet miraculously curing an Aramite general's leprosy. I sang it and the blessings, and then the congregation sang "Siman Tov u'Mazel Tov" to me.

It was in the haunting liturgical melodies of the synagogue that I first learned to love music. Jewish music has a scale in the minor mode that's uncommon in Western music. Western music theory calls it "Phrygian dominant," among other things, and it occurs in Arabic, Ottoman, Iranian, and Indian music as well. But when you hear music that sounds Jewish, it's because it's Freygish—the Yiddish term—or Phrygian dominant.

My mother wanted me to go to the yeshiva to be a rabbi, and Rabbi Mendel wanted me to study with the cantor, but I ended up going for a year of Talmud study, then studying violin and music theory at the academy in Berlin instead. The year of Talmud study was my mother's condition before allowing me to go to the Academy, so I wouldn't forget who I was.

I never forgot.

———————⸙———————

Abraham
Brooklyn, New York
December 15, 2021—December 16, 2021

THE VAN PULLED away from the curb and headed down the street.

It was icy and chilly, even though I didn't feel the cold like I used to. I listened to the crunch of snow under the tires, the soft sound of sleet hitting the windows, and the faint sniffles of the maid in the backseat. I glanced over my shoulder at her sleek black hair, her olive skin, and the tracks of tears. She was so young, and I felt a pang of pain for her trauma. I turned my head and stared out the window, watching the buildings move past.

My hand ached, but I could also feel bones knitting back together. Not a pleasant sensation—it alternately itched and twinged—but one that comforted me, nonetheless. The bastard was right. If I were mortal, I would have never played the violin again, but I wasn't, and it would heal in a trivial amount of time. I pushed my hair out of my eyes with my off hand and it came back bloody, but that wound, too, was healing. It would take decapitation, fire, or sunlight to be permanent. Anything else was merely a temporary nuisance. I stared out the window.

It had all been for nothing.

I'd stayed away from Ruth and Solomon, hoping to avoid gay scandal impacting their social lives, but also hoping they wouldn't notice that Ludwig and I weren't aging—and they knew all along what we were. How could they *not* know when they'd seen me rescue them from the Nazis? The masquerade had been for nothing. I could have tried to continue to be a part of their lives, if they'd have had me, and I'd squandered that chance for a futile attempt at providing them non-scandalous normalcy. For *nothing*.

I'd stayed away from my people, my community. First, because I was afraid that I might bite someone. Then because I feared my state prevented me from living as a Jew. Finally, out of the misguided thought that I was dead and therefore freed of all obligations. Jewish prayer is written in first person plural. On Rosh Hashanah, we ask God to remember *us* for a sweet year. On Yom Kippur, we confess that *we* have sinned—whether or not we, personally, have sinned. We list a litany of things that *we*, as a community, might have done and ask for God's forgiveness. The person standing next to you might have sinned, and not only should that person not have to confess alone, we are a community. I needed to be a *we* as well as an *I*.

I'd left my performing career for nothing. I'd believed that the public eye and Flora's winking insistence that we were vampires were what caused her death, but it was Thomas all along. Forgive me, Flora, my love, I have sinned against you. I loved playing, loved stepping out into a sunny, warm pool of light and offering beauty in bright, clear, sweet tones, and the response of the audience saying yes. Yes, we hear it, see it, feel it, too.

The van turned into a darker and more disreputable looking area. We were headed toward that abandoned warehouse Ludwig and the thug had mentioned. There were few other cars on the road, and no one spoke.

I'd let the shadow of Destiny's mortality hang over our lives together when I should have just enjoyed being with her. I was ruining my life—both our lives—with my refusal to accept that death was the mortal state of things. Even my kind could die, as beloved Flora's death proved.

And now, Solomon. He had extensive roots in his community, a family, grandchildren. What would he tell them? Would he have to fake his own death? Would he have to watch their accomplishments from afar, as I had with him?

I glanced behind me again. The maid was clutching the violin like a frightened child holding a teddy bear. I doubt she realized she was doing it. Next to her,

Thomas saw my gaze land on the violin and smirked at me. We pulled up to a loading dock at that point, and Thomas said, "Get out slowly and wait."

"What happens if I don't?"

"I kill the maid. Then I'll burn you at the stake, like we did in the Inquisition. I won't even give you a chance to convert first." He smiled, and the expression had a malicious edge. "Although I might give you some much-needed... correction... first. But no religious instruction. No conversion."

As if *that* were something I'd do. "I won't convert."

I stepped out of the van, snow crunching under my sneakers. Thomas pulled the maid across vinyl seats repaired with duct tape and stood in front of me, gripping her upper arm. She edged away as far as she could but couldn't pull free.

"Good." He smiled, and his voice was calm. "I should want to save your soul, but you've been such a long-term problem for me that I'd really rather you didn't." He stepped closer, dragging the maid with him.

"I'm glad we're agreed," I said. "I'll always be a Jew, just like Jesus."

Thomas slapped me with his free hand. Good. I'd been trying to provoke him. Moron.

"By the way," I said, in an intentionally false casual tone, "did you rape Ludwig when you bit him? Do you enjoy molesting pious young men?"

Thomas smiled at me in a way that was more a baring of teeth. "Hardly." He rolled his eyes and sneered. "Rape is simply another tool, crude but effective, and it wasn't required in Ludwig's case." He smirked. "Ludwig had other, more efficient handles."

Was that supposed to frighten me? It infuriated me instead. I thought of the poor inmates at the prisons where he had been a warden and silently vowed to them that if I managed my revenge for Flora, John, and Eliza, I would avenge them as well.

The maid whimpered, tears leaking out of her eyes at an increased rate. "Please, I have a baby and a sick mother. I'm only seventeen! Please!"

"Don't be ridiculous," Thomas said to her, giving her a little shake. "You're just a tool to harm *him*. You'd better hope he behaves and gets up on the stake like a good boy."

That was perhaps destined—no pun intended—to be my fate, unless I wanted to obey his orders to... what, neutralize the police with my playing? hypnotize others into joining his cause? That wouldn't happen.

If I were going to be killed for being a Jew, did that make me a martyr? There were stories of martyrs singing Aleinu on the way to their deaths at the stake in twelfth-century France. According to the martyrology that recorded the story, people wondered from afar at the melodious strains.

Aleinu is the closing prayer of the morning, afternoon, and evening services. The opening line is "It is our duty to praise the Master of all, to acclaim the greatness of the One who forms all creation." The traditional belief is that the prophet Joshua wrote it on the eve of the battle at Jericho, but some believe it was written by Rav in the third century.

I closed my eyes and breathed in the cool scent of fresh snow as Thomas and the maid walked away from the van. He grabbed her by the shoulders and said, "Let's go inside. Lead the way."

So I did, but I led the way singing Aleinu.

Aleinu might be the most controversial Jewish prayer. There's a line about other nations "bowing to vanity and emptiness and praying to a god who cannot save" that was outlawed by our Christian neighbors because they believed it was a reference to Jesus. The line was illegal even as late as 1750 in my native Prussia. In some places, the authorities went as far as sending observers into synagogues to make certain we hadn't included it. Obviously, if Joshua were the author, he was referring to the Canaanites and the prayer would pre-date Jesus. If it was written by Rav in the third century, it referred to the Greeks or Romans. We frequently omit this line nowadays, and I skipped it now out of respect for my friends of other faiths—including my wife, who might side with the pagans.

Okay, I admit Aleinu was a rebellious choice. I didn't consider Thomas' God to be the same God as Ludwig's God. Thomas' God was hate, and—although I eliminated the line—vanity and emptiness.

I'm not as good a singer as I am a violinist—I'm adequate—but the notes were clear, and I visualized the Hebrew text in my mind. I concentrated on my love for my people, this prayer, and its melody and tried to sing it as beautifully as possible, and I felt a sort of softening around the consciousness of those near me. I glanced around. They were following me, but Thomas's previously purposeful stride had become a shuffle. Their eyes were unfocused and their jaws slack.

Perhaps I *wouldn't* die a martyr, at least not today.

I stopped, turned, and inched over to the maid, being careful not to make any sudden moves that might startle someone out of their reverie. I had to move slowly, practically in slow motion, to avoid reaction. I gently took the violin case from her, still singing. No one reacted, although their eyes remained... more vague than fully glazed. I laid the case on a tall lip intended for truck unloading and pulled out the violin, but I finished the verse of Aleinu before playing. *Ein od*—there is no other.

And then I played. Thomas and his thugs, I had spellbound, and as for the maid... "Take the keys and go."

She blinked and glanced around, as if awakening from a nap. Thomas and his two thugs were staring at me, their eyes glazed. She edged over to the man who'd driven the van and snatched the keys out of his hand. He didn't react as she hurried back out of his reach. She gazed deep into my eyes. "Thank you." I didn't know whether she whispered or mouthed the words, because I couldn't hear them.

I nodded to her and kept playing.

She ran to the van, started it, and drove away. I began with the repertoire I'd played for Ludwig's company's party, then did *Scheherazade* and the twenty-four caprices for solo violin by Paganini.

The sky was lightening. I backed away, towards the human-sized door at the far end of the building.

I would have to stop playing to open it.

Ludwig
Manhattan, New York
December 16, 2021

THOMAS AND Abraham were on the move.

Destiny handed Miriam to Bridget. "You're on babysitting duty." She kissed Miriam's tiny cheek.

"My doorman can obtain diapers and infant formula for you," I told Bridget. "He and I have a fiscal arrangement." He provided me with a monthly snack, and I paid his college tuition.

Bridget nodded, and we headed to the parking garage together. Destiny was carrying a small pharmacy bag. "You should stay," I told her.

Destiny's eyebrows raised and her chin jutted out defiantly. "I'm fighting for my husband."

I wasn't certain what she could do—perhaps something in the bag? I didn't ask. That said, she was unaffected by sunlight, and modern women had their own minds and did as they wished. I wondered what my mother would have done with such freedom and was suddenly wistful. Mother had never offered an opinion on what she would have preferred to be doing. I supposed she'd enjoyed singing. I'd inherited her voice and had been a boy soprano a million years ago, but then my voice changed and became ordinary.

I climbed into the front seat of the Subaru. "Just head back towards the hotel for now, and when we get closer, I'll direct you."

Morgan started the car, and I closed my eyes and ignored the gentle rocking and swaying of the car. I focused on the shining golden dot and the angry dark red flame next to it, Abraham and Thomas. We drove on in grim silence, and I focused harder, deeper. I had the impression that they were in a van but couldn't tell what color it was. But Abraham was my north star, and I would always find him. He could board a plane to Thailand and I would find him there.

Not that Abraham would fly anywhere, given the choice. He suffered terribly from airsickness.

I smiled and concentrated again on the golden dot. I had a vivid sense memory of the two of us in the candlelight, with him playing, his hair falling over his eyes, his soft lips, and the sound as lush as velvet, brushing over me like fingers. The scent of wine, the taste of honey. It was almost carnal.

Was this romantic friendship, or was I in love?

The two dots stopped moving. "Turn left when you get a chance."

---

Destiny
New York
December 16, 2021

THE SUN WAS rising.

Ludwig sat in the front seat, gesturing and calling out directions and generally irritating Morgan. Me? I had a bottle of veterinary tranquilizer and a syringe. It would take the entire bottle to knock out Thomas, but I was willing to give it a try. I hadn't even showered, and I'd promised myself that the second I got away from the thugs with the shotgun, I would shower.

We'd left Miriam with Bridget as soon as I returned from the twenty-four-hour pharmacy to get a prescription filled "for my anxious dog." I felt guilty about misusing my vet credentials to get drugs, but it was for an excellent cause. I only hoped I had a chance to inject Thomas with it.

Under any other circumstances, I would have found Ludwig's directions hilarious. But the sun was rising, and I didn't know if my husband had shelter or not.

I was also... when this was over, I'd be more amenable to my husband's suggestions of picking up and moving. Okay, no. I loved our house. I loved being near my moms, but it would take a while before I felt safe again. They'd invaded my mothers' home, the place where I grew up. They'd pointed a gun at me and my baby. I'd have a new nightmare to replace the fire.

The fire was still worse.

---

Abraham
Brooklyn, New York
December 16, 2021—December 17, 2021

I KEPT PLAYING. We were on the west side of the building, at least, so we would be in shadow for longer than we would have been on the other side. I backed up some stairs and stood next to the door under an overhang that wouldn't be much help to me. The sky was turning gray behind me.

A car approached up the road, one that looked a lot like Morgan's Subaru at a distance. I hoped Ludwig was in the front seat, pointing and demanding that Morgan turn. I didn't have time to worry about it, as I needed to concentrate on my playing, but as the car came closer...

It pulled into the parking lot, a green Subaru Outback containing many people. As it came to a stop, Ludwig jumped out and ran over. He raced up the stairs and pulled on the door.

It was locked.

I stepped aside and kept playing. More Paganini, and Morgan and Destiny got out of the car, as did the pets. The cats jumped onto Freddy's back, and he trotted over towards the warehouse.

Ludwig pulled and pulled and then glanced around. He ran down the stairs and returned with a piece of scrap metal and wedged it into the door frame to lever the door open. It flew wide with a bang.

Followed by gunshots.

Ludwig evaded, faster than mortal eyes could see, and Freddy leaped over him with both cats still on his back. I glanced inside. The cats used Freddy as a battle platform to launch themselves at the gunman, and Freddy went for his throat. He screamed, and the gun clattered to the floor.

I looked around, still playing. Morgan and Destiny appeared to have ducked at the sound of gunfire. I hoped they had, at least.

Ludwig stepped inside, cautious, and gestured. "This way." I entered the warehouse and willed Thomas and his thugs to follow me.

Inside the warehouse, there was an area where the paneled roof had collapsed, leaving a large area open to the sky. In this area, someone had set up a wooden stake—a burning stake, as is pictured in history books—set on a low pyre of wooden pallets and similar scrap. Next to this, there was a supply of rope and chains, all covered with a light layer of snow. To the side of this, under the roof, there were also pokers, chains, a fire pit, a gallows, a sturdy table with what appeared to be chains and a butcher knife placed on it, a chair with a strange metal pyramid on the seat and handcuffs on the sides...

I felt my bile rise at the sight, and I heard Thomas gag before I looked away and concentrated again on the music. I led Thomas into the courtyard and stood in the shadows, playing. He ended up stepping right up to the stake. The thugs also remained under the open sky, but the sun wouldn't harm them. At least, I was reasonably certain they weren't my kind.

Ludwig took some of the rope and tied Thomas to the stake and secured him with the chains. His eyes were dark, cold. Then he frowned and said, "I'll see what's keeping Solomon."

I played *Scheherazade* again.

Ludwig returned, followed by Solomon, Destiny, and Morgan. Destiny opened her plastic bag and pulled out a syringe and a glass bottle. She pulled out a large dose of whatever was in the bottle and injected Thomas with it. His eyelids drooped.

"What was that?" I asked.

"Acepromazine," she said. "I considered xylazine, but city vets don't really have horse sedatives—"

There was a gunshot, the scent of iron with a faint floral scent, and Destiny collapsed. Blood pooled at her side, and her shirt turned crimson. Behind her, one thug smirked and pointed the gun at me. I hadn't been aware of him; he'd been hiding behind a crate.

"Destiny!" I started towards her.

Thomas roared with rage and pulled drowsily against his bonds, and the two thugs rushed forward to help him.

Ludwig shouted, "Keep playing!"

So I kept playing, although it was hard to keep Thomas and the thugs spellbound with my mind on what was happening behind me. I consciously shut it out of my thoughts and focused entirely on my music, half hypnotized myself.

I was so enthralled by my music that I missed the initial bits of smoke coming off Thomas. The sunlight hit the top of his head first, then angled downwards.

Thomas didn't appear to notice, either. He never reacted to bursting into flame. There was the horrible bright orange blaze, the blackening and withering flesh, and the smell of burning hair and cooking meat as he contracted into the pugilist stance. I willed myself to shut it out and played. I was vaguely aware of Ludwig beside me, watching Thomas burn with icy eyes.

When Thomas died, I knew it. His attention left me. I stopped playing and stared in horror at the flames spreading over and down his body. I heard regurgitation and glanced over at the thugs. One thug fainted into a puddle of his own vomit. The other screamed and charged at me, raising the gun. Freddy lunged at his throat, knocking him over. His teeth drew blood, red spraying up towards the ceiling. Freddy's... vampire? dog? both? ...instincts took over, and he savaged the man's throat, drinking. I didn't stop him, even though I should have. Inanna trotted over to lap at a forming pond of blood. Ivan watched on, radiating feline smug approval.

I turned. Destiny was lying on the ground in a pool of her own blood, wincing. Solomon pressed his jacket against her hip, trying unsuccessfully to staunch the flow.

I rushed over and took her hand, still clutching the loaner violin in my other hand along with the bow. Was she dying? What should I do? Was being a vampire better than death? Was I the one to make that decision?

I knew, deep down, that she would leave me for good if I did this without her permission, but... I wasn't considering doing this for me. Destiny was a mother. Would she rather die than watch her daughter grow up into a woman? I genuinely didn't know and didn't know how to ask in a way that didn't feel manipulative.

So much blood!

"Doesn't your saliva have healing properties?" Morgan asked.

Solomon blinked at Morgan. "Does it really?" He glanced over at Ludwig, who shrugged elegantly.

I stared at Morgan, and then I stared at Solomon. "Would that be bad? Do we need to remove the bullet first?"

Destiny reached over and squeezed my bow hand. "It's okay," she said, her voice soft and distant.

Okay? *Okay*, that she was dying? No! It was *not* okay!

My cheeks were wet, and I backed away from her. My hands were doing some kind of... like they were about to tear at my hair. Part of me was afraid that I would turn her if I lost control. "If you want me to..."

A shadow fell over us both. Ludwig stood over Destiny, eyebrow raised. "The time for prevarication is over."

"'Prevarication'?" The outrage in her voice was such that I was certain that if she had been healthy enough to do so, she would have stood with her hands on her hips. "I don't want to be a vampire! I've always said I don't want to be a vampire!" She made a disgusted noise. "'Prevarication'!"

Ludwig crossed his arms and stared at her, stern. "Understand, my dear, that I cannot permit you to die, especially not at Thomas's hands. It would destroy your husband. I won't have that. Not again."

"Ludwig, no!" I scooted forward. If that was what Destiny wanted, she knew she could ask for it.

Ludwig made the gesture at me and said, "Silence."

I froze, still clutching the violin and the bow. I tried to protest but found I couldn't. I struggled to lift the violin but was unable. He was trying to help; I was certain of that, but... my wife had made her wishes known. I didn't want her to die, and if she did, part of me would resent her not choosing to become a vampire instead, but that was *her* choice to make, not mine or Ludwig's. I wanted Destiny to be who and what she wanted to be, and I was grateful for however much time I had with her.

"It's unnecessary," Solomon said. "It's only a scratch. We need to stop the bleeding and maybe get her some blood. I'll bet you have some at home."

"She needs the emergency room," Morgan said.

"We can't," Ludwig said. "We'd have to explain why Thomas was after us, and what happened to him. And then the psych unit would come, as they wouldn't believe us—if they didn't arrest us for his murder." He shook his head. "Better to burn the building down, as you suggested."

I stood, but still couldn't raise the violin or speak.

"We have a doctor, we have a nurse, I'm a vet, and I'll bet you have blood at home." Destiny tried to sit up.

Ludwig frowned. "I have a nosy doorman as well."

Solomon rolled his eyes. "One who was told to feed the pets raw chicken liver puree fresh from the blender if we returned late." I couldn't have phrased it better myself. I supposed vampires were one thing but gunshot wounds were another?

"Touché."

I reached out and laid my hand on Ludwig's shoulder. He turned his head to look at me, and I shook my head.

He sighed and turned back to Destiny. "Very well, as long as you do nothing gauche, like try to die, we'll do it your way."

Destiny sighed in relief. I was surprised to realize that I was also relieved. I still wanted her to live forever, but it was more important to me now that she live the life she wanted to live on her own terms.

"Morgan," I said, realizing that I could speak, "can you pull the car closer?"

"We brought those foil space blankets," Destiny said. "To keep the sun off."

Morgan left, clutching her keys.

Ludwig made a face and muttered, "So much drama to avoid the precious gift of immortality!" We ignored him.

Morgan rushed back in, carrying the foil blankets, which we all tossed over ourselves, and rushed to the car.

We rode back to Ludwig's place with Destiny in my lap, her head on my shoulder. When we arrived, I carried her upstairs. Solomon cleaned and bandaged her wound, and Morgan gave her a pint of Ludwig's finest O negative. And then she slept, and I went into the other room, where Bridget had Miriam.

"Dadadadada!" she said, weepy. She wrapped her tiny arms around my neck.

"It's all right." I kissed her soft little cheek. "I won't let anything happen to you."

I had my family back. It was everything I wanted. Well. Almost everything I wanted. It might have been time to have a career again.

My immediate instinct was to change all our names and move, of course. I'd discuss it with everyone in the morning, including my accountant Dave, to see if they agreed. I suspected that the story "We were going to burn a Jew at the stake, but he hypnotized us with his violin and burned our leader instead and his dog killed my friend" wouldn't hold up in court, but it might not bode well for Freddy. Perhaps Ludwig could fix that, if it came to that.

We'd see.

———————— ⌒∞⌒ ————————

Destiny
Manhattan, New York
December 16, 2021

GETTING SHOT SUCKS, by the way. If that was "a scratch" I'd hate to get the full effect. But I would live, I could have my second baby, and I didn't have to drink blood and hide from the sun and quit the vet clinic and Furkids.

I lay in Ludwig's fancy-schmancy bed getting O-negative blood and holding Bridget's hand, with Miriam next to me. I'd had a moment where my life had passed before my eyes and a thought had popped into my head. *Don't worry, Abraham. I'll find you. After all, I did it before. I will always find you.* At the moment when I thought I might die, I *knew* I was Flora. My childhood nightmares were her traumatic memories.

I wondered if I should tell Abraham. I didn't think he believed in reincarnation, and he might find the remark hurtful if he didn't, so I'd keep it to myself for the time being. Maybe I'd share my suspicions later.

Even Ludwig's attempt to be helpful—ugh—hadn't frightened me like it would have before I'd had my odd vampire dreams. But the mortal life is best. I'd take the mortal, finite length and limits if it meant that I could keep the mortal meaning.

Birth, death, rebirth. The circle is open but unbroken. As the song says, *We all come from the Goddess, and to Her we shall return like a drop of rain flowing to the ocean.*

We were going to be all right.

Abraham
Manhattan, New York
December 16, 2021

DESTINY SLEPT IN Ludwig's guest room, with Miriam curled up next to her. I kissed Destiny on the cheek and Miriam on the forehead and tucked them both in. Then I left the guest room.

The penthouse was silent. Freddy was sitting outside the guest room, as if he was guarding it, and Inanna and Ivan had curled up on either side of him. They watched me leave with preternaturally intelligent eyes.

I sidled over to Ludwig. He was staring out his giant windows over the night city with a glass of wine in his hand. The UV shades had all been raised, but he'd left the lamps off. There were glittering lights spread out as far as the eye could see, except for a gigantic square of dark with curved lights across it that was Central Park.

I glanced over at him. "Are you all right?"

Ludwig started. "I... of course, why do you...?"

Please. I patted his shoulder and made deliberate eye contact.

Ludwig averted his eyes. "I don't know why he said the things he did. I mean, I don't... you know..."

"He said them to be hurtful," I said.

"But I don't... I mean, I'm not... I don't want you to think that I..."

I pulled him into a hug. He relaxed in my arms, letting out a deep sigh. We stood like that for a moment. Then I pulled back enough to look him in the eye.

"You're the best friend I've ever had. I know you well enough that I can say with some confidence that nothing would make me think less of you." Every word was true, and every word was essential for him to hear.

He closed his eyes and took a deep breath, then opened them again. He nodded silently and hugged me again. I patted his back and squeezed him closer. We stood like that for a while, with him slowly relaxing into the hug and placing his chin on my shoulder.

I wondered if I should mention that I, myself, was... not entirely straight. Would that be helpful? Perhaps I shouldn't make this moment about me.

After a few minutes at least, he finally pulled away. "I'm all right," he said. "Would you like a glass of wine?"

I smiled and held up a hand to decline. We stood like that for a while, side by side, staring out over the city together.

Then I asked, "How did I do that?"

"Do what?"

I rolled my eyes. "The thing with the violin."

He tilted his head at me. "It's your gift. You did it to me under the bridge, don't you remember?"

What? I shook my head.

Ludwig sighed, looking chagrined. "Clearly, I am Sire of the Year."

I stifled a laugh at his expression.

"It's your gift. You've dedicated your life to the violin, and that passion... The change enhanced your gift. We all have gifts based on our passions in our mortal lives." He frowned. "You really didn't know? I'd assumed Flora had told you our lore."

"I think she assumed you told me." I stared out over the city. "I usually deferred to her in vampire matters."

"Right." He took a sip of alcohol. "I'll tell you everything I've told Solomon, then." He glanced at his glass of wine. "After a few more of these." He sighed.

"If you ever want to tell me what he did to you, I'm willing to listen."

Ludwig gave me a sharp look. Appraising. Then he relaxed and said, "Not at this time."

I wondered about Ludwig's gifts. I considered his ability to track other vampires, and to pass himself and others off as someone else, and his clever, intricate, *perfect* forged documents, and his unerring ability to find the most valuable object in the room.

Then I wondered about what he'd done in his mortal life to earn such gifts.

———————⌒∞⌒———————

Ludwig
Manhattan, New York
December 16, 2021

I...

Abraham's declaration...

It was as close as he could get to saying that whether I was what moderns call "gay" or not, he wouldn't think less of me and would continue to be my friend. I know it's a cliché to say it *lifted the weight of the world from my shoulders*, but I felt notably lighter for his saying it.

I was still uncertain whether I wished to apply modern labels to my feelings, and what labels I would use if I did, but I wouldn't lose Abraham over it. I was also uncertain what purpose it would serve. Abraham was married. I still didn't want sex, but I wanted all the other things that came with marriage: commitment, sharing a life, cuddles... Was I, as the moderns phrased it, repressed?

I had killed again, but I had avenged the poor priest that Thomas forced me to kill in 1762. I would continue to pray for his soul, nevertheless.

———◇———

Abraham
Manhattan, New York
December 17, 2021

LUDWIG'S KITCHEN WAS unsurprisingly empty. The enormous stainless steel refrigerator contained some blood bags, some containers of bloody chicken livers for the pets, a carafe of blood—pig? cow? aardvark?—and that was all. I sent out for groceries.

When Destiny awakened, I made coffee and eggs and toast for three—he had no toaster, so I had to use the oven. He owned a coffee maker, but I had to rinse dust out of the carafe before using it. Ludwig had no high chair, but I put Miriam on my lap and we sat with a bowl so she could eat dry Cheerios with her fingers—or at least play with them. She'd nursed earlier; the Cheerios were more so she would feel included. The mortals ate silently, and I wondered if I was the first person to cook on his stove.

When they finished eating, I asked, "So, how do you feel about changing our names and moving?"

Bridget raised an eyebrow.

"I like my name," Destiny said. "I have a life here."

I nodded. I'd expected that. "Well," I said, "I might want to perform again, so we might end up needing to move to the city for that, if it's all right with you. We'll see how I handle the commute."

Destiny beamed and squeezed my hand. Ludwig looked as if he might dance a jig.

"We'll figure it out," she said.

———— ⌘ ————

Abraham
Manhattan, New York
December 17, 2021

THE NEWS TALKED ABOUT a "bizarre cult murder," but once they identified the victim as the man who'd led the hate march, they assumed it was an inside job by extremist elements—even more extremist elements?—in his own organization. Either way, they weren't looking for vampires or vampire pets.

The maid was named Maria Lopez. I called Dave as soon as I saw her on the television. "How much money can I give someone before they have to pay taxes on it?"

"Fifteen thousand dollars," he replied, with a promptness that spoke of his familiarity with tax law.

"Okay," I said. "I'd like to send Maria Lopez—the one on television right now—fifteen thousand dollars."

There was a pause. "Do I want to ask?"

"I hear she has a baby and a sick mother."

After another moment, Dave said, "Okay."

On the television, Maria said, "When they were distracted by the man, I took the van and escaped. I hope he's all right."

We would be fine.

# Coda

Abraham
Atlantic Highlands, New Jersey
December 18, 2022

I held the lit candle in Miriam's hand and made the blessings for her. *"Barukh atah Adonai, Eloheinu Melech ha'olam, asher kid'shanu b'mitzvotav v'tzivanu l'hadlik ner shel Hanukkah."* Blessed are you, Adonai our God, Ruler of the Universe, who makes us holy with your commandments, commanding us to light the Hanukah lights. *"Barukh atah Adonai, Eloheinu Melech ha'olam, she'asah nisim la-avoteinu v'imoteinu bayamim haheim bazman hazeh."* Blessed are You, Adonai our God, Ruler of the universe, who performed wondrous deeds for our ancestors in those ancient days at this season.

I helped her light the first candles in the hanukkiah—most people call them the "Hanukkah Menorah," but menorah is either the seven-branched candelabra from the ancient Temple or the modern Hebrew word for "lamp." Then I lit my own hanukkiah. We admired the lights, and I put my hanukkiah on the front porch. Hanukkah, Chanukah, the festival of at least eight different English spellings!

I went into the kitchen and fried up an enormous platter of latkes—potato pancakes—despite the fact that half the guests couldn't eat them. I fed them to Destiny, Miriam, Morgan, and Bridget with a dish of sour cream—and, after Dave insisted, applesauce. Ludwig, Solomon, and I had wine.

"Would I not be able to eat latkes if I... you know?" Dave moaned, sniffing the plate. He piled up his plate with latkes and applesauce. "Would just one latke kill me if...?"

"No," Ludwig said, "but it wouldn't be worth it."

Dave frowned and dipped a latke in applesauce.

I also made a huge salad and taught the non-Jews to play dreidel for Hanukkah gelt, which in our house was chocolate "coins" in little gold foil wrappers. I won spectacularly, but I distributed my candy winnings between the four human adults because I couldn't eat it, and because one really shouldn't give a toddler that much sugar.

I also gave Miriam actual money, $250, much to the shock of Morgan and Bridget. Well, she wasn't two yet. "Sweetie, this money... some of it is to give to charity, and some of it is to keep, and you need to decide how much."

She tilted her head at me. "What's charity?"

"That's where you give money away because someone else needs it. Like people who are hungry who need food, or homeless kitties and doggies, or little kids who have no toys."

She reacted with visible sadness at all three options and pushed the money back at me. "All."

"All the money?" I asked.

She nodded, solemn and sweet.

"Okay, which one?"

"All."

"Okay," I said. I put the money into a tzedakah (charity) box on the table and made a note on my phone that one-third of it should each go to a soup kitchen, pet rescue, and something that gave children toys. "Thank you."

I kissed her on the cheek. She beamed at me.

I pulled out a wrapped present. She tore off the wrapping and squealed as a soft toy kitty was revealed, white with long fur. She hugged it. "Kitty!"

Ivan appeared relieved that she was squeezing the toy instead of him. He was very patient with Miriam, but he didn't relish being manhandled. Inanna, of course, would have none of it, but at least she knew not to scratch the toddler. Freddy, on the other hand, adored being manhandled, and followed Miriam around the house as a combination playmate and protector.

I put Miriam to bed with her new toy kitty and kissed Destiny on the cheek.

Abraham
Eatontown, New Jersey
December 21, 2022

WE'D GATHERED AT Morgan and Bridget's, and it looked a lot like Christmas... but wasn't. There was a decorated pine tree and mistletoe—all the better to kiss under—and candles everywhere. They'd made hot spiced cider and Tofurkey, since half the celebrants were vegetarian. Morgan, Bridget, and Destiny made beautiful wreaths out of pine boughs and ribbons together and burned a beautifully decorated log. Destiny's friend and coworker Lucy was there, too; apparently, she was Wicca-curious.

There were presents, mostly of the handmade variety. Morgan gave Destiny a handmade—by her—quilted bedspread and gave Miriam a knitted sweater. Destiny gave her mothers a family portrait we'd had made for the occasion and a set of lovely colored and scented candles. Bridget gave Destiny some exotic teas and gave Miriam a handmade rag doll with long, red yarn hair. And they gave Lucy a deck of tarot cards, and Bridget read her tea leaves.

I put Miriam to bed in her grandmothers' bed and sat up with a book—a biography of Louis Lewandowski—while the three Wiccans downstairs watched the longest night of the year.

In the morning, I made pancakes, and then we went home, and Destiny went to bed.

Abraham
Manhattan, New York
December 25, 2022

IT LOOKED A LOT like Christmas—and was. Ludwig had gone all out decorating, with a gigantic tree and an enormous pile of presents. He'd also catered a ridiculously extravagant feast considering that half the guests couldn't eat, with Tofurkey, mashed potatoes, stuffing, gravy, root vegetables, green bean casserole, and a huge Christmas pudding soaked in brandy that was set on fire at the end. He'd even invited Morgan and Bridget so as to have more people to eat the food. Handel's *Messiah* played quietly in the background, followed by Bach's *Christmas Oratorio*, Tchaikovsky's *Nutcracker*, and Rimsky-Korsakov's *Christmas Eve Suite.*

Ludwig gave Destiny a pair of sparkly earrings in a Tiffany box, Miriam a child-sized violin, and me a new violin case and a watch that also came in a Tiffany box. I don't have Ludwig's eye for this sort of thing, but suspected that he had spent far too much. He gave Solomon a wildly expensive medical treatise and Dave a new laptop.

I gave Ludwig the only thing I knew he wanted: a promise of a free concert.

And then he ducked out for a midnight candlelight Mass.

Morgan and Bridget went home. Destiny and Miriam slept in his guest room. I gathered up leftovers and put them away in the refrigerator. Not that I knew what Ludwig planned to do with them.

In the morning, he sent the leftovers home with us.

Abraham
New York, New York
May 2, 2025

I CLOSED MY eyes, took a deep breath, and walked onstage. The auditorium was all cream, red seats, carved wood, carefully placed lighting, and curved balconies. I was behind a black screen, as was typical for auditions nowadays. They'd made me fill out a résumé as well, which was vaguely hilarious. The philharmonic had declined to let me audition because of the thinness of my résumé, which... obviously, I cannot list concerts at the Royal Albert Hall in 1899. Ludwig had offered to forge me a résumé, but I felt that was cheating. I'd wanted to play Paganini, but they asked me to prepare one movement of an unaccompanied Bach sonata, a first movement of a Mozart concerto, and one movement of a Romantic violin concerto—either Brahms or Tchaikovsky.

Someone on the other side of the screen said, "Please, proceed when ready."

So I did. I've been playing for about a hundred and eighty years, have supernatural speed and strength in my fingers and heightened senses, and can hypnotize people with my playing. Right then, I simply wanted to mesmerize people into passing my audition, which—all modesty aside—wasn't necessary.

The last clear, sweet notes floated away, and there was silence. I waited for someone to say something.

After a few awkward moments, I launched into Paganini's Caprice No. 5.

There was another brief silence, and the voice on the other side of the screen said, "You're in. What's your name?"

I stepped around the screen and bowed. "Abraham Levy." I don't need to point out that wasn't the name they gave me at birth, do I? The name they gave me at birth didn't include a surname; I was Avrahom ben Moshe (Abraham, son of Moses—one could add a "from Wreschen" for disambiguation if needed). But my father was a ben Levi, which made me a ben Levi, so I've always been partial to variants of that as a name. The ancient Israelites charged the Levites with singing and playing music in the Temple, after all.

They stepped forward to shake my hand, and I put my violin away in its case. The nearest person asked, in a tone of awe, "Is that a Stradivarius?"

I nodded and smiled.

"Why haven't we heard of you before?" another person, a woman, asked.

I lowered my eyes and told the truth—well, most of it. "I stopped performing publicly for a time after a traumatic death in the family."

"I'm sorry for your loss," she said. She handed me a packet of paperwork. "Our rehearsals are on Thursday nights, seven to ten p.m."

"Thank you." I took the papers. "I'll see you then." I was certain Ludwig would let me stay at his place on Thursday nights so I could take the ferry and thereby avoid driving in during rush hour in daylight. I'd ask.

I walked up the aisle and opened the doors. Destiny was waiting for me, holding Miriam's hand. Her other hand rested on her pregnant belly, under a vet uniform. She now worked for Furkids' new low cost/charity/rescue clinic. I gave her a cocky smirk.

Miriam had inherited her mother's beautiful red hair, which we styled in what modern Americans call "pigtails." In her other hand, she held the rag doll her grandmother Bridget had given her. She would start preschool in the fall. Morgan and Bridget had moved into in our mother-in-law suite. She also had a doting uncle who stayed with us every weekend and holiday, although Ludwig had thrown an elaborate hissy fit when a cat—forgive me, a "vile animal"—had coughed up a hairball on his overcoat. I feared he might not survive the world of infant regurgitation.

Solomon, well. If I was his onkel, did that make Miriam his cousin? We had her call him Zayde—"grandfather." She also had an Uncle Dave who stayed with us frequently.

Destiny let go of Miriam's hand and stepped out to hail a taxi.

Miriam played with her doll, wiggling her at me and creating dialogue for her. "Hi, my name is Anna. How are you?"

"Hello, Anna, nice to meet you." I shook the doll's soft, floppy hand.

Miriam giggled, and I pulled on my sun gear.

Destiny waved, and Miriam and I headed towards the door. A tiny black kitten with faint black-on-black stripes was waiting patiently by the door. I wondered if she was someone's pet, but she was dirty and toddled towards me, so I scooped her up in one hand and took Miriam's hand in the other. I have a sense for animals—what they're feeling, whether they need help—and they inherently trust me. This kitten wanted to come home with me, so she was someone's pet now. She reminded me of Victoria, of blessed memory, so much.

As we walked past a stairwell, Miriam dropped her doll. Almost faster than the eye could see, she was at the bottom of the stairs, picking up her doll. Then she was back at my side.

No, she'd never done that before.

We walked out into the sun, me rushing to get into the car. Miriam showed no reaction to sunlight at all.

Miriam climbed into the taxi next to me, and Destiny got in last. We gave the driver the address.

I apparently had something to tell Destiny when we got home.

# Acknowledgments

T hank you to the following people who helped with this book:

Alpha reader: Joy McQueen

Critique Partners: Elisabeth Allen, Susanne Allen, Joseph Cosentino, Timothy R. O'Neill, Matthew W. Quinn, Chris Riker, Dave Schroeder

Developmental Editor: Hannah Vanvels Ausbury

Structural Critique: Lyda Morehouse

Beta Readers: A. S. Akkalon, Cynthia Villyard, Deborah Ludlam

Sensitivity Readers: Juno Baker, Ennis Rook Bashe

Copy Editor: Aja Pollack

Proofreader: D. Joan Leib

Chapter Headings: Nathan Hansen

Map: Travis Hasenour
Book Cover: Damonza

Would you like to see Abraham and Ludwig hunt Nazi war criminals in South America? Check out the newsletter-exclusive "The Hunting Trip"!

# Author's notes:

Hi! Thank you for reading!

First of all, Abraham is not Louis Lewandowski, but he shares some biographical notes with Lewandowski, including his hometown, his birthday (moved a day), and his desire to study at the Berlin academy. Lewandowski wrote a lot of Jewish liturgical music and is generally awesome. If you like classical choral music, you should check him out.

Second, my amazing sensitivity reader, Juno Baker, says that the thing about the human brain not being finished developing until the age of twenty-five was debunked in 2022. The scene where they discuss this takes place in 2021, so I don't think Solomon would know that, so I left it, but I'm sharing that information with you.

Third, Abraham would almost certainly use Ashkenazi pronunciations, but I use Sephardi pronunciations and the Siddur Lev Shalem siddur. Sticking with Conservative liturgy also allowed me to refer my audiobook reader to sidduraudio.com for a pronunciation guide. If this level of inaccuracy offends you, please accept my sincerest apologies. My personal opinion—for what it's worth—is that the proper spelling is neither Beis Din nor Beit Din, but instead rendered in the Hebrew alphabet.

Fourth, one of my readers was dismayed that I had 19th century British Jews speaking Yiddish and serving cholent. This is historically accurate! Eastern European Jews, fleeing pogroms in the Pale of Settlement, fled to both the US and the UK. The ones who settled in the UK largely lived in the Whitechapel neighborhood of London. There are photos of 19th century Whitechapel businesses with Yiddish signs, newspapers from the area in Yiddish, etc. The UK Jewish population exploded, and the Jews that preceded them—largely Sephardi—were allegedly embarrassed by their poor cousins from Russia and Poland. So the people Ludwig found to pray with Abraham were, indeed, Eastern European Jews from the same general part of the world Abraham was from. There's a blog post about it on my website.

My undying gratitude and sincere apologies to my amazing copy editor, Aja Pollack. Thank you for finding all the weird time shifts introduced during the edit process, and I am so sorry that I stetted all of your patient corrections of "antisemitism" to "anti-

Semitism." I fear that I am one of the "no hyphen" people who thinks that the hyphen in "anti-Semitism" implies that "Semitism" is a thing that exists and can be opposed. Dictionary spelling be damned! https://www.jewishvirtuallibrary.org/anti-semitism-or-antisemitism

And finally, blessings and gratitude to my fabulous proofreader, D. Joan Leib, who found all the new typos I introduced while making Aja's changes. THANK YOU.

www.ingramcontent.com/pod-product-compliance
Ingram Content Group UK Ltd.
Pitfield, Milton Keynes, MK11 3LW, UK
UKHW041921060225
454797UK00011B/92/J